Legacy of the Heirs

Book Two in the Lost Kingdom Saga

Laura Carter

Legacy of the Heirs – 1st Edition

Copyright © 2024 Laura Carter

All rights reserved.

No portion of this book may be reproduced in any form or by any electronic or mechanical means including information storage and retrieval systems – except in the case of brief quotations embodied in critical articles ad reviews- without permission from the author.

The characters and events portrayed in this book are fictious and a creation of the author. Any similarity to real persons, living or dead, or other works, is coincidental and not intended by the author.

Paperback ISBN: 978-1-7394045-5-0

Ebook ISBN: 978-1-7394045-7-4

Edited by Eden Northover

Cover Design by Aly Scasares, Owner of Sincerely Theirs Ltd

Map by Cartographybird Maps

Chapter Heading Emblems by Aly Scasares, Owner of Sincerely Theirs Ltd

Formatted by Laura Carter via Atticus

Additional Information

Trigger Warnings:

Your mental health and experience whilst reading this book matters to me. This book contains death, violence, explicit sexual content, references to child abuse, references to sexual assault, references to the deaths of characters you may have liked in book one. If these are topics you find difficult to read, please approach with caution and at your own discretion. If you read Legacy of the Heirs and feel there are other trigger warnings missing, please notify me via my social channels so I can amend this page.

Due to the presence of more sexually explicit scenes than the first book in the series, this book is classified as 18+

Glossary and Pronunciation Guide:

If you wish to check the pronunciation of character and place names as you read them, you can find a pronunciation glossary at the end of the book.

Playlist:

I do some of my best writing after listening to music and as a result have created a very large overall series playlist. I have taken the songs relevant to certain chapters and placed them in a Legacy of the Heirs Playlist. You can find the playlist linked in my socials or by searching 'Legacy of the Heirs' on spotify and clicking 'playlists'. At the rear of the book, you will also find a guide for which songs relate to which chapters in the book. I recommend only listening after you have finished the book or finished the relevant chapter, otherwise the lyrics of some songs may act as a spoiler.

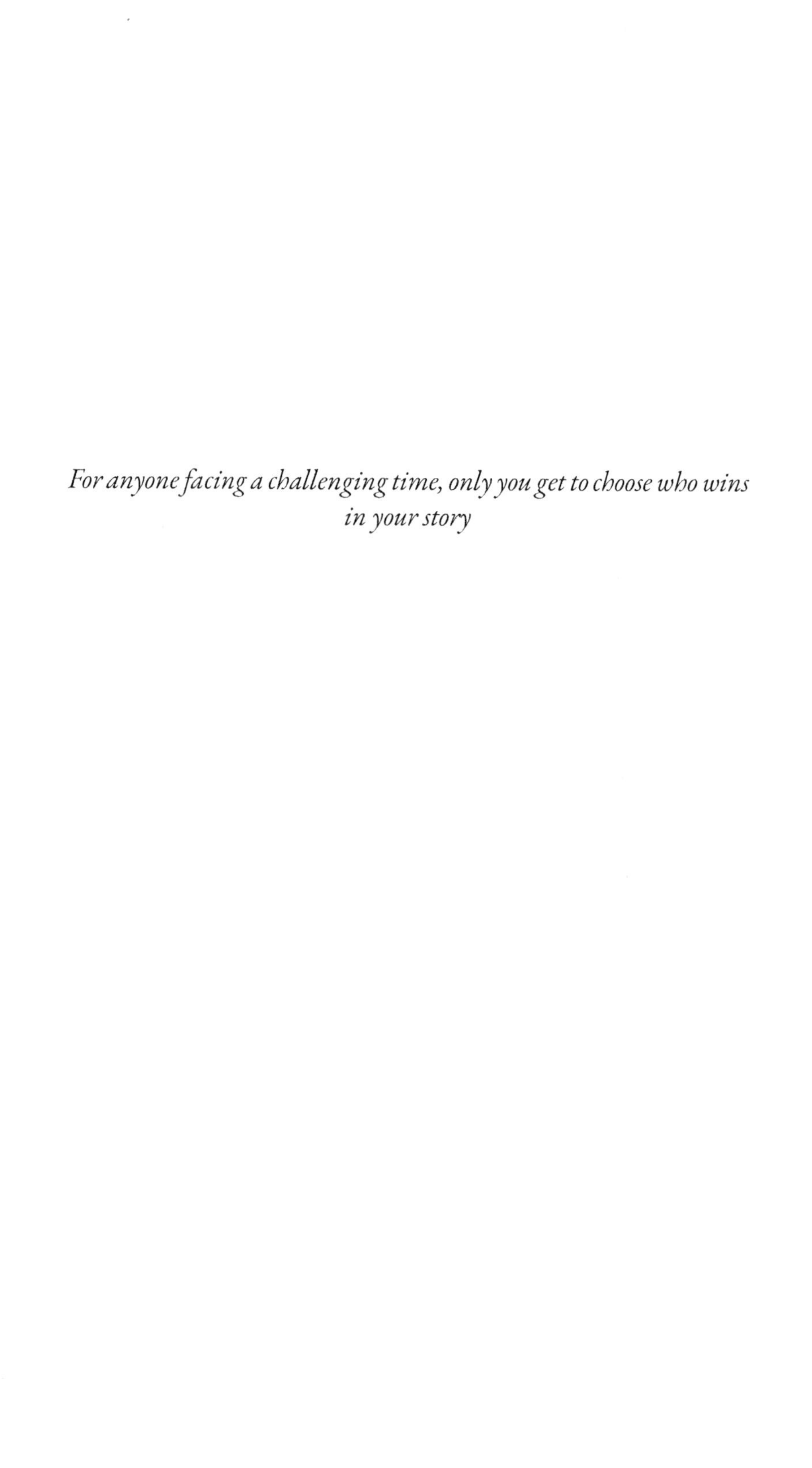

For anyone facing a challenging time, only you get to choose who wins in your story

ISLE
THE KINGDOM OF
NOVISIA
ELVERA
AZURIA
THE FROZEN FOREST
TISOVA
ZIVOI MOUNTAINS
MARNOVO
VOJTA
VALA
THE VELLIUS SEA
THE NEUTRAL CITY
AMORO
NERIDA
THE BAY
MERA
TROSSO
TO NOVISIAN SEA BORDER

NOTABLE SETTLEMENTS
CAPITAL CITIES
CITY STATES
MYARA
ABIS FORGE
KERES
TABHERI
THE ASHUN DESERT
NEFERE VALLEY
KHAMI
HYBROOKE FOREST
SELEY
STEDON
ANTOR
HYSTONE FOREST
DOLTAS ISLAND
GARRIDON
ALBYN
ASDALE

Contents

Prologue

Soren

The Day of the Explosion

The smoke rose thick and fast above the tree line in the distance: the Hybrook Forest of Garridon. Soren's eyes travelled from the smoke and over the peaks of the trees carefully acting as a barrier to block her view from Doltas Island to the City of Antor—the seat of the Garridon Royal Family. It was one of the first things King Jorah built upon seizing the throne. He erected a forest so tall it spanned the entire coastline of Garridon. He killed her grandfather, the rightful King Errard, but in Jorah's haste and greed, he missed the careful escape of Errard's wife, and Soren's grandmother. Lyra.

Soren was raised on Doltas Island and forever heard the tale of Lyra's escape. Jorah was power hungry and foolish, and failed to view the Queen as a threat, despite being the true Garridon Heir, and the family Errard married into. Lyra's father, however, descended from the Wiccan of Ithyion, and so she had inherited gifts from that family line, too. Her expertise lay in prophecies and predictions. Lyra had foreseen the death of her husband and was gifted with a prophecy.

Jorah only became King because Eddard allowed it, having sacrificed himself for the sake of the prophecy and the future his beloved had foreseen. His death created a distraction for Lyra's escape, and the only place she knew to hide was Doltas Island. While many married for politics, Lyra and Eddard had married for love, and Lyra wished to raise her unborn daughter and fulfil the prophecy once the day came.

That day had indeed now come.

This was it. The moment the prophecy predicted would arise, and now it was time for Soren to reclaim what was rightfully hers. She smiled as she calmly watched the waves crash against the high rocks of her island home before returning her gaze to the mainland.

Spiralling plumes gathered, a swirl of charcoal tendrils choking the bright, early afternoon sky. A blanket of darkness trailed in its wake, and all eyes that turned to it would wonder the cause, speculating what disruption had permeated the peace of the Neutral City while unaware of the chaos soon to ensue.

Those close enough would have felt the explosion and heard the rising panic as inhabitants of the city scattered. Others would have suffered, buried under the flying rubble of crumbling buildings, while those too close burned within the flames of destruction, their screams forever ingrained in the minds of their loved ones.

Word would soon spread across the realms as destruction unravelled in the city. Soren closed her eyes, wishing she could smell the smoke and feel the burn. Forcing her eyes back open, she watched with excitement, and desperately wished she were there to reclaim what was rightfully hers.

Turning her back on the realm she would soon set foot on, and guiding the winding tree roots from her path, she walked further inland. More trees appeared until she was fully engulfed by the tall evergreens expertly nurtured by her younger sister.

Soren's mother, Ellowyn, had decided to take a page from Jorah's book. If the royal family were going to hide Garridon from them, then they would hide all that Doltas Island had become, and what a prosperous island it was.

They set contingencies in place for hiding Doltas for the day the new King of Garridon arrived on their shores, who would be met with ruins coated in overgrown ivy and foliage, and a small collection of people coated in dirt and patchwork clothes.

When King Jorah had learned of their family fleeing to Doltas

Island, he had not questioned it, understanding it to be an abandoned island where they would likely struggle to forage for food until slowly dying out. The reality was far different.

When the original royal families settled on Novisia, they sailed the high-profile prisoners to Doltas and abandoned them there, unknowingly creating an army, who possessed a burning hatred for the royals. The rulers had unwittingly provided the land for those from all realms to build their own world within Novisia, which is exactly what they did. When Lyra and her unborn child fled from Garridon, the people did not hate or recognise the fallen queen as a descendant of someone who had imprisoned them, but a Wiccan who saw all Doltas Island could—and *would*—become.

Over the years, the few people from Nerida who wielded water, as distant relatives to the royals, ventured into Novisia, hidden as they journeyed to Keres. From there, they spread. Infiltrating the realms had been easy; the difficulty came in solidifying roots while also providing means to transport goods back to Doltas Island. It soon became apparent the nobles were ignorant to those of lower ranks, so they hid in plain sight as servants in the homes or as the homeless: a hidden collective, gathering information to provide for their Island.

The people under Ellowyn and her husband Arryn began to prosper, but it only excelled when Soren came of age at sixteen and formed alliances of her own. Her parents were rightfully King and Queen of Doltas Island, but Soren was the fallen princess that would one day reclaim Garridon. She would need all the inside help she could get.

Over the past ten years, she had formed alliances in all four realms ranging from sailors in Nerida to healers in Vala, the common people of Garridon, and the Red Stones of Keres. It was in Keres that Soren had found friendship while learning the skills in battle she now possessed. She wondered whether the Queen of the Red Stones had discovered Soren's infiltration into the Courtesans, where she planted the prophecy in the mind of the King.

Soren smelled the gifts of Keres in the air as she reached the town in Doltas, the many spices floating on the wind as the people prepared for the feast to be held that night. She motioned with her hand, untwisting the branches from the stone wall to reveal an archway, and through it, her sister who nurtured the flowerbeds. Gently, Sadira held her palm to the buds, easily flourishing the flowers from within.

Sadira was Soren's equal, but her opposite. Where Soren was powerful with battle, Sadira was powerful with words. Where Soren could lead armies, Sadira could lead nobles. Where Soren's power could destroy, Sadira's aimed to grow. It was those reasons, and many more, which made Sadira the obvious choice to marry the new King of Garridon. Jorah's grandchildren were not the true heirs; therefore, they were all hopeful the plans had worked, and Caellum was the last to remain. Her target.

Soren crossed through the courtyard towards the modest stone castle adorned with every flower imaginable climbing alongside it. She nodded at her soldiers as she passed their training grounds, the Keres steel a welcome sound to her ears. Pushing the wooden doors to the castle wide, she dominated the entryway. Kicking the door closed, Soren ascended the flagstone staircase until reaching the sitting room, where she expected her mother and grandmother to be. The room was her grandmother's favourite, the view from the window across the distant seas reminding her of all the stories her parents told of Ithyion. During her travels to Keres, Soren heard snippets of tales about Ithyion, learning what she could about the original settlers of Novisia.

Soren reached the archway to the sitting room, and sure enough, her mother and grandmother sat by the window, while her father stood before the roaring fire, staring mindlessly at the flames. The three of them turned when she entered.

"Well?" asked her father. Soren nodded, and her grandmother turned back to look out the window.

"They will all be dead," her grandmother confirmed. "And now we know what must be done."

"I will inform Sadira," Soren spun on her heel, and left the room, unable to continue the discussion. The plans were formulated many years ago; there was no need for further discourse.

The window on the second floor offered Soren a view of Sadira, blissfully calm and unaware. Part of Soren's day was to hike to the top of Doltas, checking for signs of disruption on the mainland, while Sadira's daily tasks involved tending to the gardens and foraging for ingredients for potions and poisons. Not only blessed with the gifts of Garridon, Sadira also possessed power from the Wiccan blood running through their veins.

Soren focused on the small sapling in Sadira's palm and halted the growth of the flower. The princess frowned until realisation dawned and she glanced in Soren's direction. Sadira calmly placed the sapling back in its bed and brushed her palms against the cloth apron tied around her waist. She murmured instructions to the fellow gardener before heading to the castle to join Soren in preparations.

***

Soren hated many things about today, but this was the top contender. She glared at her reflection as Sadira tamed the blonde mess on her head.

"Soren, there are endless matts in your hair. Do you ever brush it?" Her sister scolded, pulling unnecessarily hard with the brush. Soren did not bother to respond; only a minute apart in age, they read each other with ease. Folding her arms in the mirror, her eyes narrowed at the dress hanging in the reflection. It was breathtaking—undeniably so—but Soren was destined to destroy beauty, not behold it. The dress was a partner to the one expertly clinging to Sadira's figure, the dark greens bringing out the golden hue to her blonde curls. While it smoothed and complemented Sadira's complexion, Soren was certain it would dull her pale skin, the dress highlighting her muscles rather than feminine curves. She favoured her leathers and armours.

"How are you feeling?" Sadira asked, pulling Soren from her thoughts. A spark flickered in her sister's green eyes.

"How should one feel when they are to become a Queen?"

Sadira gave a soft smile.

"No one would judge you for saying something about this, sister."

"Do you have something to say about it?" Soren bit back, their eyes meeting in the mirror.

"I know the part I am to play, Soren, but I am allowed thoughts on the matter." She placed the final clip in Soren's hair and flattened the stray pieces before exiting the room without another word. Soren rebuked her inability to control her tongue. Over the next month, and perhaps longer, Sadira was to be her closest ally—a sister, not another soldier to command.

Soren's discomfort was evident as she tugged at the fabric suffocating her abdomen, quick to correct herself as the doors to the castle opened. She and Sadira followed their parents and grandmother out into the courtyard until reaching the opening at the east of the island. Branches expertly weaved along the forest floor to create a pathway, while vines formed lanterns with a black petunia atop it: a symbol of mourning. More flowers appeared until the entire opening of the forest was surrounded by them, creating a ring around the oldest tree on the island.

Sadira wavered upon noticing the flowers as the fallen family reached the tree and turned to their people. Groups of men set the tables down, while others began to fill them with foods. Tension lingered. No one knew how to feel—sorrow for what was to happen, or joy at the prospect of reclaiming Garridon? Silently, Soren and her family stood, and watched the procession filter into the clearing before they all took a seat. Eyes locked on her grandmother.

"You all arrived on this island from different realms, and yet you pledged your allegiance to the fallen family of Garridon. You recognised our honour and our pride in equality for all—the very reason the usurper wished us to be removed." Lyra paused, gazing at the people she held so dear. "Now, you pledge your allegiance to my granddaughter, Soren. Your future Queen, and her sister, Sadira. The Princess of Garridon."

Soren and Sadira bowed their heads.

"With the deaths of the royal families, there are four heirs. Heirs with generations of power in their veins. I have seen the prophecy; I have seen who will lead you and Garridon into the darkness to come, and who will ensure its end. Yet for that to happen, your Queen and Princess' power needs to match that of the other heirs."

The people rose in respect as her grandmother knelt, alongside Soren's father and mother. Reaching for the knife at her hip, Sadira sliced her palm and coated the blade in blood before passing it to Soren. With a steady hand, Soren grasped the handle and stepped behind her grandmother.

"Do you willingly give your power to your chosen heirs, Soren and Sadira Mordane of Garridon and Doltas Island?" Soren asked her grandmother, who stared straight ahead.

"I do, child." And with those final words, Queen Lyra closed her eyes: the only surviving founder of Novisia. Soren grasped the hair on her head and sliced the blade across her neck. She had not known what to expect when sacrificing her grandmother to their God, but she did not expect to feel nothing—numb—her body's way of protecting her from the onslaught of agony likely to ensue in coming days. Warm liquid pooled in her hand as she laid her grandmother down on her back and proceeded to her parents. It was as if Garridon himself had possessed her, as if he knew of the prophecy and aided Soren in the swiftness of the kills.

The final slice tore through the air, and she laid her mother down. Soren squeezed her own hand around the dagger, adding her own blood to the mix until the blade was coated with the blood of five. Five from the Garridon lineage. Dipping her finger in the blood, she painted a symbol on the trunk of the tree—a wreath of branches—an emblem that glowed in the firelight behind. When she turned, the bodies had been moved, and in their place stood a wooden throne. Sadira's face was blank, seeming to refuse Soren's eye as she gestured her sister to the throne, who trod through the blood-sodden grass to reach it. As she sat, Sadira gripped an emerald-encrusted crown and stepped behind her.

"All hail Soren: The Fallen Queen, Queen of Garridon, and Doltas Island." Sadira called, lowering the crown onto Soren's head, who closed her eyes as the people recited her name. It was then the sisters felt the power, the essence of Garridon singing in their veins.

It had worked.

They had never doubted their grandmother's Wiccan heritage, who promised the blood magic and sacrifice would transfer their powers equally. As the true heirs to the Garridon throne, Soren and Sadira both required power to seize it: Sadira to protect herself in King Caellum's web, and Soren to usurp the throne from the sidelines.

"The time has come to reclaim what is ours," Soren exclaimed to her people. The power hummed in her veins as she watched every black petunia turn white under Sadira's gaze: an effortless display of her power. "Tonight, we feast. And tomorrow, we begin. You know your orders. At sunrise, you travel to Garridon and begin planting doubt around King Caellum's claim." All cheered and raised their glasses to Soren, who smiled as she leaned back on her throne. It would not be long until the King succumbed to the demands of the Garridon people and sailed to her shores in request of a bride.

Chapter One

Larelle

The revelations weighed heavily on Larelle's mind, as deep and dark as the waves holding her below the surface. She arched her back, allowing the inkiness to cocoon her, keeping her mind grounded. Opening her luminous, deep blue eyes, she breathed in; despite how at one she was with water, it always took Larelle a moment to adjust to the feeling of breathing in the sea.

Upon bidding the Historian farewell outside Mera castle, Larelle immediately sought the comfort of the ocean, her feet guiding her to the spot where she was crowned. Perhaps she needed a reminder that she was indeed the Queen of Nerida and being queen entailed carrying the weight of secrets that could forever alter the path of her people.

Larelle floated effortlessly beneath the waves, maneuvering the water to hug her body and keep her in place as she gazed into its depths and saw only darkness. It served as a reminder of what the Historian had said. *Watch for the dark one that will bring suffering to all: the rise of old power, the Kingdom will fall.* The Historian had simply told Larelle to do with the information as she wished before requesting she escort him out. But the passing time had done little to advance her muddled thoughts.

She imagined Kazaar floating opposite and furrowed her brow, struggling to summon a clear image. Larelle had never been concerned enough to pay significant attention to the details of Vala's commander, but she would have noticed if there was a darkness about him. Surly, yes. The scowl on his face and the clench of his jaw were commonplace. Powerful, of course. Flames licked up his inked arms as she pictured him. But dark? Capable of causing a Kingdom to fall? She did not know. Larelle wondered what Elisara's judgement would be, who had spent much time with her new commander. When Larelle had last seen them before the pair left for Keres, they were on good terms, even friends. She could not imagine the Queen of Vala was someone who would allow darkness to seep into her mind and sway her thinking.

Something brushed Larelle's hand, tugging her from her thoughts. A blur of faint light washed away Kazaar's image. She glanced at her extended fingertips but saw nothing. When she turned back, only darkness remained.

Sighing, Larelle released the water's hold on her body and kicked her feet until breaking the surface, the air cool as it kissed her skin. Blinking the water from her now grey eyes, the setting sun greeted her as light danced across the rippling ocean. It appeared she had been below the surface for several hours, confirmed by the rough texture of her fingertips. Larelle leaned back, her hair splaying around her.

Dusty-pink tendrils of clouds floated across her vision as she sensed another presence approach the stone steps behind her. If it had been anyone else, Larelle would have immediately shielded herself with the water before addressing the visitor. Instead, a wave of calm washed over her.

"Either the meeting has just finished, and you are coming to drag me to say farewell, or it finished hours ago, and you have been kind enough to give me some peace." Larelle smiled at the deep chuckle following her words.

"Would you like to bet on which?"

"If it is the latter, I assume I must deal with the Lords, who are outraged by the rudeness of my absence." Dragging her hands through the ocean, Larelle propelled herself backward toward the steps and tilted her head back to meet Lord Alvan's warm hazel eyes. The corner of his mouth lifted.

"Would you rather them believe you are rude or bid them

farewell in water-soaked undergarments?"

A blush crept across her face, and Larelle sunk her body further below the surface before she turned to find a silk Neridian-blue robe open for her, hiding the view of her discarded gown inches from Alvan's feet. While his playful smile remained, he respectfully looked away as Larelle pushed aside her embarrassment and rose from the waters. She trusted his gaze remained on the Garridon horizon as she turned her back to him and slipped her arms into the sleeves.

Larelle froze as his calloused hands briefly caught her shoulders, gently wrapping the fabric around her body as she turned. Although he stood a mere step above her, she suddenly felt twice as small beneath his gaze. Noticing her discomfort, Alvan stepped aside to allow Larelle to climb the steps, who collected her gown as she passed and tucked it beneath her arm.

"I thought you could use some time," Alvan said as he followed her up the steps and into the castle hallways. She did not answer; instead, she wrung the water from her curls and waved it over the sandstone balconies overlooking the Novisian sea. "You did not return after leaving." He appeared to hesitate when she did not immediately answer. "Was everything okay?" An odd feeling washed over Larelle at someone other than Olden or Zarya expressing concern for her. Although Larelle had befriended Lillian and Alvan upon returning to royal life, the friendships felt unusual, as though her cracked heart could not accept others trying to mend the pieces.

Larelle nodded silently with a smile, uncertain whether she should tell anyone what the Historian relayed to her. She had not even told those closest to her what she and the other rulers had learned—nothing of the creatures that threatened them or their lack of plans to protect the kingdom. Alvan's thick brows pinched together; clearly, he did not believe her feigned attempts at reassurance.

"Mumma!" a tiny voice shouted as Alvan opened the door to

Larelle's chambers. Zarya bounded off her stool and knocked the table with her elbow, sending books thudding to the floor as she collided with her mother's legs. Larelle's hands twisted in Zarya's dark curls, her worries melting away as Zarya peered up at her with a grin, oblivious to the world's worries.

"Oh, please, Alvan. Do not worry," Larelle called, inclining her head toward the Lord as he crouched to pick up the books from where they lay scattered across the rug in front of the unlit fireplace. Larelle patted Zarya's back, who spun and skipped to Alvan, pulling some books close to her chest just as Lillian entered from the adjoining room. Her blonde hair was scraped back into a bun, several pieces beginning to fall free after the long day. Her eyes widened at the sight of the Lord tidying the mess.

"Please, allow me. It is not your job," Lillian extended her hand for the books, but Alvan shook his head as he rose, placing them on the table.

"You have been caring for Zarya all day, Lillian. It is your turn to rest now." Larelle reached for her friend's hand as Lillian crossed the room and squeezed it with gratitude.

"I would be happy to look after both Zarya and your son, Zion, for a day so you may have a break." Larelle smiled at Alvan's kind offer, though she wondered if he knew how much of a handful a five and six-year-old would be.

"I–" A knock at the door interrupted Lillian's reply, signalling the arrival of dinner. Zarya frowned; she did not yet understand the need to eat and sleep earlier than her mother. As the servants entered, Larelle's stomach rumbled at the smell of fresh pasta. Alvan chuckled.

"Mr Alvaaan..." Zarya dragged out his name in a way Larelle knew meant a request was coming.

"Princess Zaryaaa," mimicked the Lord, crouching to her level as she dangled her legs off the stool.

"Will you read me a story?" she asked, still clutching a book. Alvan's eyes widened as he drew back to glance at Larelle, whose raised eyebrows mirrored his surprise. Bedtime stories were the one request Zarya reserved only for Larelle, especially when returning home late. Yet her surprise was squashed at the hopeful look in Zarya's eyes as she played with the frayed leather corner of the book, waiting for an answer. Larelle nodded, offering Alvan a genuine smile.

"I would be honoured to." Alvan placed a hand on his heart, and Zarya squealed, sprinting for Larelle's bed.

"You have to help me up; I'm too small!" she demanded, and Larelle covered her mouth as Alvan stared at her, unsure what to do. "Quickly, or we won't get through the story!" Zarya said, attempting to climb onto the bed. It seemed Alvan would soon be as wrapped around Zarya's finger as Larelle was. He wasted no time striding to the bed and paused before lifting her under her arms and tucking a blanket over her. He glanced around several times before finally deciding to sit on the edge of the bed. He inclined his head towards the terrace, signalling Larelle to eat. She paused, conscious of the lost time with her daughter, but witnessing the grin on Zarya's face when she opened her book, Larelle knew she was unfazed.

Knowing the dinner would comprise her usual company, she did not bother to change from her silk robe. Olden rose from his chair on the terrace and closed his book with one hand, smiling at Larelle. The terrace had become Olden's favourite place since moving into the castle. All three of their rooms—Larelle's, Zarya's, and Olden's—had access to it, a reminder that one thing had remained amid the chaos of royal life. She still had her family.

"How was your day?" Olden asked. The scent of trailing clematis drifted to her on the evening breeze as he leaned in to kiss her cheek before returning to his chair.

"Fine." She smiled and reached to gather olives and bread onto her plate. Lillian filled her goblet with wine, tilting her head at the shortness of Larelle's answer. Larelle avoided her gaze and began pulling the bread apart in her hands.

"Well," Alvan began, gently clicking the glass doors of the terrace shut as he joined the group. "It is safe to say she was tired; we barely got through three pages." His chair scraped against the stone as he sat beside Larelle, who winced at the sound. The exhaustion of the day grated on her mind, and the group fell silent, except for their clinking cutlery against china plates and goblets hitting the table. Larelle awkwardly cleared her throat.

"Are we going to address the fact that something is wrong?" Lillian glanced around the table as Olden sat back in his chair, catching Larelle's eye. He raised his eyebrow.

"What do you mean?" she asked, flicking the curls from her vision and pouring herself more wine. Alvan matched Olden's look, a playfulness sparkling in his almond-shaped eyes. Larelle was uncertain if she could cope in the presence of two men who knew her mind so well. She compiled a mental list of everything that could go wrong by telling her confidants all she had learned since her reign began.

If the lords found out Larelle told them first, it could cause an uprising and risked the rulers losing faith in her just when they needed to trust one another. Endless thoughts and possibilities crossed her mind, branching from reasonable to outrageous, yet one stood out from the rest. She could put her family at risk. Larelle glanced at their concerned expressions, all attention to their usual evening meal discarded. Larelle sighed and picked at the skin around her nails.

"What I say cannot go any further." She looked intently around the table. "Because there is a risk that darkness could befall us all."

Chapter Two

Nyzaia

The flames in the great hall flickered with the same uncertainty haunting Nyzaia's mind. Guests danced and drank in honour of Elisara's visit to Keres, and tomorrow, the women would search Tabheri Palace to uncover their parents' secrets. Sipping from her goblet of wine, Nyzaia locked eyes with Tajana across the hall. The playfulness between the pair was clear despite their recent hostilities. In fact, she did not know how Tajana remained by her side, given her recent behaviour. Nyzaia was not trying to hurt her, but Lord Israar's threats plagued her mind and steered her actions. She found herself constantly creating distance between them and avoided being together in public.

Nyzaia trusted and loved Tajana endlessly, so why had the words of one man forced her to question a future that had always been so certain? For the hundredth time since her reign began, she mourned her former life, yet the Keres Queen was still no closer to understanding who had set the explosion that killed Novisia's ruling families. All she had was Isha's confession and the odd note sent from Isha to her father.

Ready to burn.

The prophecy had only created more questions. *From fire and ice, the King and Queen must hide; secrets of the past, the heirs must find.*

Nyzaia suspected Soren was involved. The fallen Queen of Doltas Island—and the true heir to the Garridon throne, as she so proudly claimed—had made targeted comments about Isha, leaving Nyzaia with more questions than answers. Had Soren ordered

Isha to come to Keres? Had Soren orchestrated the explosions to retake the Garridon throne somehow, with the deaths of the other families as mere collateral?

A visit to Myara may help. Keres' port settlement was the destination for all small boats coming from Doltas Island. Nyzaia had not informed the other rulers, but Soren and Sadira were not the first people Nyzaia had encountered from Doltas Island. The Red Stones had been providing the exiles with resources for several years in exchange for a hiding place in case they ever needed one. Perhaps visiting the port could offer Nyzaia the answers she needed.

Nyzaia scanned the mosaic floor, where a flurry of colours moved to the music. She was so encompassed by her thoughts she had not realised Kazaar and Elisara had finished dancing and left the room. She smiled. They deserved happiness. She hoped they had given into the tension that clearly fizzled between them and found one of the many quiet alcoves.

She glanced back at Tajana, but her love's brow was furrowed, frowning at the sconces along the wall. Flashes of white light punctuated the orange flames, raining light sparks onto the tiles below before fading. Nyzaia stepped forward, eyebrows raised. She had seen nothing like it before. Flames in Keres only ever burned orange.

People backed away upon noticing the unusual sight. Nyzaia waved her hand, trying to tame the anomaly, but the flames did not obey. She flourished her hand again. Nothing.

A chill rushed through the hall, and the music stopped, the revellers' murmurs swallowing the silence. Nyzaia moved to the nearest window, expecting a splattering of pink and orange as dusk neared. Instead, the deep, ominous night loomed in greeting, scattered by stars that peered intently at whatever was unravelling upon the realm. The glow of the white flames was the only light in the room, flaring brighter with every passing minute. The revellers pulled closer until they huddled in the hall's centre, as far from the flames as possible, as sparks burst across the room.

"Evil!" someone shouted. "There is evil power here!"

Another screamed.

Nyzaia remained rooted in place as her queen's guard moved into action. Across the room, Tajana scanned their surroundings while Farid moved to stand beside his queen. Isaam and Jabir circled the hall as Rafik approached the screaming woman—a Keres native, who clutched her bare arm. Tentatively, Rafik removed her hand. Gasps rang out from those closest at the glowing mark across the woman's brown skin.

Nyzaia stepped forward to investigate but halted before the sconces. It was not the flames that intrigued her; it was what gathered below every flame along the wall. Shadows. Shadows from the sconces, tables, and guards moved, swallowing all light and casting darkness in its wake. At first, Nyzaia thought she imagined it, but as the shadows crawled along the floor, she looked to Farid for confirmation he saw them, too. His bright blue eyes shone back at her before he stared again at the shadows and narrowed his gaze.

The movement of the shadows increased as if eager to meet their maker. Nyzaia flourished a hand one last time to see if she could dim the flames, but still, nothing happened. The shadows no longer flooded the floor, they crept up to engulf the walls instead. Nyzaia stepped back, and Farid gripped her arm.

"Who is doing this?" a female citizen shouted.

The shadows lifted slowly from the walls, and tendrils twisted into ropes of darkness, encompassing the bright flame. It was as though a puppet master controlled and pulled at the strings, suffocating all light.

Nyzaia had never witnessed such a thing. Light bathed the room once more before she could comprehend anything further, and the sconces returned to their natural orange hue. Nyzaia immediately sought Tajana and her syndicate. Issam, Jabir, and Rafik calmed the crowd. Farid stood rigid beside her, his hand poised on the pommel of his sword. Tajana was deep in conversation with two guards by the archway leading to the hallway near Nyzaia's father's office. She assessed Tajana's movements as she leaned forward and spoke intently to the two men—the furrow of her brow and the crossing of her arms. One spoke rapidly while the other stood pale by his side. The second the guard stopped speaking, Tajana whirled and ran to Nyzaia.

"It's Kazaar; he needs help!"

Nyzaia hastily followed Tajana down the corridor and up the winding staircase, unsure where they were headed. She was reminded of what she had told Tajana while awaiting Elisara and Kazaar's arrival—her concerns about Elisara's power and experiences in Keres. Had something happened? Had Elisara accidentally harmed Kazaar?

Nyzaia realised where they were going when Tajana turned down the hallway on the top floor. They headed to a room where Nyzaia had spent most of her childhood: Kazaar's chambers, her true brother. His chambers sat at the opposite end of the wing to her brothers, and while it was the most modest room, it had the best view of Keres, or so Kazaar said. Tajana did not knock as they approached but shoved the door open with a hurried force. Farid quickly sidestepped Nyzaia and surveyed the room before allowing her through. Nothing had prepared her for this.

On the large, low bed smothered in crimson silk sheets, matching the colour of her dress, lay Queen Elisara of Vala. Her dark locks appeared perfectly positioned past her shoulders; one hand rested on her stomach, while Kazaar gripped the other. He did not look up when they walked in, focusing only on Elisara's pale complexion and fluttering eyelids as though she was dreaming intensely. Hunched over on the small wooden chair, Kazaar wore a look of defeat as he traced small circles with his thumb across her hand. Moonlight streamed in through the balcony, painting the pair in a picture of silver against the darkness.

"What did the guards say?" Nyzaia spoke in a hushed tone, leaning into Tajana.

"That Kazaar was frantic and approached them while cradling the queen. He ordered them to find you and have you brought to his chambers." Tajana glanced at the pair bathed in light. "And that he would personally kill them if you weren't here in five minutes."

Nyzaia rolled her eyes at the dramatics yet pondered over the fact there were very few people Kazaar would kill for. Standing beside her brother, Nyzaia placed a comforting hand on his shoulder. He did not move.

"Kazaar," she whispered.

His shoulders slowly rose and fell as she maneuvered around the bed and knelt before him on the opposite side; her heart twinged as his gaze flickered to hers. He clenched his jaw as tears stained his face. The man who has been known as the breaker of men was broken.

"Leave us, please," Nyzaia said, her eyes locked on Kazaar as Farid's footsteps reluctantly left the room. Her heart ached for her brother. "You too, Tajana." She glanced at her love by the door, who opened her mouth to protest. "*Now*. Please."

Tajana closed her mouth and swiftly left the room.

When the door closed, Kazaar's shoulders collapsed, and a strangled sound escaped him. He released one hand from Elisara's and wiped his face while Nyzaia scanned his body for any bruising or cuts—any sign that showed Elisara and Kazaar had fought. Nothing. *Perhaps they had fought with their powers instead?* She trailed her eyes across Elisara's dress for any sign it had blackened beneath Kazaar's flames but found nothing. Had Nyzaia detected any of those things, she would have scolded Kazaar for fighting with a queen. But her stomach twisted at the weight of the unknown. "What happened?"

"I don't know, we were arguing, and..." Kazaar moved to stroke Elisara's hair with a tenderness Nyzaia had never witnessed. The pair had been on better terms as of late—and the sexual tension between the two was undeniable—but the emotion pouring from the man before her was far more than that. Something else had happened for him to be so distraught.

"I cannot help you unless I know everything," Nyzaia whispered, resting her clasped hands on the silk sheets.

"I cannot tell you everything—"

"Kazaar—"

"It's not because I don't want to, Nyzaia, but because not all of it is mine to tell. There are things Elisara must know first." He stared at his queen and gently stroked her collarbone. Whatever had happened somehow involved both of them.

"Tell me enough so I can help," Nyzaia said. He sighed.

"I betrayed her," he said, earning a frown from Nyzaia. "There is a secret I have kept from everyone, and I will tell you... soon." His eyes pleaded with Nyzaia not to ask more, and she nodded. "It hurt Elisara. She's been betrayed so much recently that this broke her. We fought with our powers, and something happened. They *merged* somehow." Kazaar appeared pained, recalling the fight. "The force of our powers colliding threw us back, and when I awoke, Elisara was like this."

Nyzaia did not want to push for more information but could not gather much from what little he had revealed. She had never heard of powers merging.

"It is odd for fire and air to merge," she said. But was it? After all, fire required air to survive.

"It wasn't fire and air." Kazaar looked up at Nyzaia, and for a moment, she thought his eyes changed—a flicker of shadow and light. "It was white, like the essence of our power."

The essence. Nyzaia first heard the term from the Historian when he explained that Sonos and Sitara created their children from the essence of their power. Nyzaia furrowed her brow, unsure of the connection.

"What do you need me to do?" she asked.

"I just—" Kazaar choked. "I want her to wake up, Nyzaia." A loose strand of his dark hair fell from his leather band. "I *need* her to wake up."

Nyzaia thought through her options. During her time in the Red Stones, she had seen plenty of individuals like Elisara unconscious and knocked out by drugs. She could send Tajana to the Red Stones for an alchemist—someone to gather the salts used to wake the Dealers from their drug-filled slumbers.

Essence. Sonos and Sitara had merged their essence to create the four gods. Yet if the combining of their power was similar to Sonos and Sitara's, perhaps it was not as simple as using salts to wake Elisara. The word 'essence' replayed in her mind; whatever kept Elisara locked in slumber was perhaps not something of this kingdom but of Ithyion. But Nyzaia knew little of Ithyion, other than what the Historian had told her and the stories passed down from the elders. But how could she decipher any of that if they had simply been myths?

Myths and Lies of Ithyion. Nyzaia recalled the name of the dustless book she had found in her father's study when searching with Tajana.

"I know where I need to look first," Nyzaia said. "But neither of us is any help to Elisara right now." She walked back toward Kazaar and squeezed his shoulder. He did not look up, staring only at his queen. "You need to rest, Kazaar; I will search for information in the morning." He tensed beneath her hands, desperate to start immediately. Still, as Nyzaia spotted the mark of a moon on Elisara's collarbone—directly where Kazaar had stroked her skin—she knew there was more to this than anyone realised.

Chapter Three

Sadira

Jasmine vines twisted around Sadira's wrists as she absent-mindedly re-arranged the flowers while her thoughts ran away from her just as wildly. Humming, she replaced the white roses with petunias. She missed her garden. Not the endless castle gardens, with their manicured lawns and rows of pristine flower bushes, but her real garden, where the plants reached for her touch, where no bare patch of soil or rock existed. A garden that was free to explore and grow of its own accord. The garden that lived and breathed with the freedom she had lost.

Once Sadira's name was no longer Mordane but Balfour, and this garden became hers, she would make Antor's manicured lawns and stone flowerbeds her own. She pictured scattering wildflower seeds throughout the lawns and turning the stone walls into a mosaic path weaving amongst the paradise, with the plants twisting in any direction they pleased. Sadira hoped then she might feel at home and accepted by these lands.

She turned the opulent vase and analysed every inch of the bouquet to ensure it was devoid of imperfection, readjusting the leaves with dainty fingers. Clouds floated in the early morning sky as sunlight streamed through the large, greenhouse-styled wing of Antor Castle. As Sadira straightened from her analysing stance, a single white butterfly drifted through the sunlit dust, dancing in the rays of light. She extended her hand to the creature and grinned when it eagerly landed on her finger. Sadira was enamoured by the creatures her nature called to.

Sitting on the worn sage chaise by the glass wall, Sadira sighed and imagined the butterfly did, too.

"Do you think my grandmother knows I am here?" she asked the butterfly. It fluttered its wings. "She told me about this wing. This is where she and my grandfather hosted their balls." Sadira glanced around the large glass hall, which would soon be the venue of her engagement ball later that week. She pictured her grandparents dancing beneath the sun. Caellum had not questioned Sadira when she asked to see it upon returning from Nerida. He had also not questioned the tears stinging her eyes when she asked to be wed there, too. "Do you think they are proud of me?" Sadira fidgeted with her hands in her lap and smoothed down the fabric of her dress. As if in agreement, the butterfly fluttered from her finger and onto the shoulder of her pearl-threaded dress. She chuckled. "If you say so."

No longer wishing to think of home, Sadira resorted to her usual method of distraction: growing. Beneath a banquet chair, a small green shoot appeared in the minuscule crack between the two flagstones until vines twisted around the wooden legs and coated the back of the chair; tiny white flowers dotted among it. With a flourish of her hand, the same artistry blossomed on every banquet chair until the hall was a field of beauty and light perfume. It wasn't long before a flight of multicoloured butterflies breezed in through the open doors, and she beamed as the white butterfly on her shoulder remained in place.

"You cannot stay with me forever, little creature." Sadira moved her finger, lifting the butterfly as green vines formed beneath her feet. "Beautiful things near me tend to decay," she murmured, placing the creature on the nearest stem. As if the gods wished to prove her statement correct, the plant wilted and browned, drying until it crumpled to the floor. Sadira closed her eyes and sighed as the butterflies in her vicinity fled. Soren entered through the large archway on the opposite side of the hall.

The scowl on her sister's face deepened as her deep green eyes glowed and scanned Sadira's creations. Soren's silver breastplate clinked against the metal cuffs on her forearms as she cracked her knuckles, both sounds echoing throughout the glass room. She proudly wore the Garridon sigil—three trees and a soaring hawk—on her chest. She had worn the same thing upon their return from Nerida, though that was unsurprising. After all, the attire was an obvious declaration of Soren's rightful place as heir.

"Please don't do it to all of them, Soren." Sadira tried to remain civil and glanced briefly at the crumpled plant at her feet with a wince. Sadira did not know why she even bothered. Soren's heavy footfall sounded on the flagstone as she circled the room, trailing her finger along the vines and flowers as a crisp brown tinge appeared in her wake.

"What is the point of doing all of this now?" asked Soren, rounding the head table until reaching Sadira. "There is still a week until your engagement ball."

Sadira had wished to start on the florals as soon as possible to ensure they were nurtured and fragrant for the ball.

"There is no harm in being prepared." Sadira flashed a tight smile, and her sister scoffed before whistling low. Her wolves prowled into the hall. "Must you take them everywhere with you?" Sadira glanced sideways at the large creatures stalking the room, searching for any smaller creature that may have ventured in to admire Sadira's work. Sadira wondered what the citizens of Garridon would think about the beasts prowling so freely around the castle. The public had only seen them once upon arriving in Garridon, yet they had been surprisingly tame. Sadira imagined that would change as Soren ventured deeper into the realm, using her wolves as a sign of power and a connection to nature's creatures—an ability Caellum did not possess.

"They assert dominance." Soren pulled one of the banquet chairs from the table and turned it to face Sadira, snapping vines as she did. Perching on the chair, she widened her legs and leaned onto her arms, glaring at her sister. Sadira shrank away at Soren's all-consuming presence and adjusted the weeds that formed in the cracks by her feet.

"I do not wish to argue again," said Sadira, remembering Soren's foul words upon returning from Nerida. Soren had cornered her in the gardens, where Sadira had planted a rose for Rodik, the love she had abandoned on Doltas Island. Soren had implied harm would come to him should Sadira continue to disobey her.

"Then I suppose you should have considered your words before belittling me in front of the rulers," Soren spat, glancing over her shoulder at the guard stationed by the archway, far enough away not to hear their conversation. "They need to know that I am the rightful heir to the throne, so there are no protests when I take it."

Sadira instantly looked up at her. Soren had never announced her plan outright. Their parents had instructed both girls to return to Garridon and offer hope to the people, nurturing their lands and inviting prosperity. Though Sadira guessed there were ulterior motives, she had yet to be filled in. How naïve she had been.

"And how do you intend to do that?" asked Sadira, calming herself with the growth of the small plant in her palms. "When Caellum and I marry, the crown will default to me if anything were to ever happen to him." Her heart skipped, fearing for a man she barely knew yet deserved better.

"Do not worry. Killing the king is the last option." Sadira lowered her head at Soren's words, wishing to hide the shock in her eyes that murdering Caellum was an option at all. "The aim is to cast doubt about his reign and create an uprising, forcing him to relinquish the crown to the true Garridon heir. Me."

Soren picked dead leaves from the vines on her chair while Sadira kept her mouth shut. While she had never wanted to be Queen, it was presumptuous of her sister to assume the people and lords would choose Soren over the king's wife, who also had Garridon blood running through her veins.

"Need I remind you again that I can easily have someone visit Rodik?" Soren sneered. Sadira whipped around to face her sister with fury and pain in her gaze. Soren smirked and ripped the plant from Sadira's hand. "This is taking too long, sister. We should have been able to take the throne immediately." Soren's tirade of hatred against Caellum and relentless desire to take the crown was tiring for a woman who simply wished for a simple life with her plants.

"Perhaps it was presumptuous of you to assume everyone would kiss the ground you walk on simply because of the blood in your veins," Sadira said, her bright green eyes locking with her sister's. Sadira did not anticipate her sister's reaction, who swung her hand and slapped her across the face. The sound echoed throughout the glass chamber. Neither said anything as Sadira clutched her cheek, blinking back tears.

"Look what you made me do," Soren snarled. "Now everyone will wonder who hit you!" She leaned back in her chair, a triumphant smirk forming as she smoothed her hands over her braids. The guard stationed by the archway with his back to them turned and surveyed the hallway. *He must have heard*. "How unfortunate," Soren drawled with hardly concealed sarcasm. Sadira could barely comprehend what had happened. "Now everyone will wonder if Caellum is just like his father, hitting you for disobeying him." Soren looked like a giddy child, and disgust filled Sadira as she realised Soren had planned the hit all along to further her twisted narrative.

"I am *not* telling people my betrothed hit me," said Sadira firmly, and Soren leaned in.

"I'm sorry, but that sounds as if you are disobeying me?" Before Sadira could retort, Soren's gaze caught on something behind her. With a false smile, she stood, straightened the clothing under her armour and called her wolves to heel. Yet Varna, the largest of the pack who reached Soren's waist, stepped toward Sadira, assessing her with its pale blue eyes. It lingered there until her sister was a comfortable distance away.

"I don't want to have this conversation again," Soren shouted over her shoulder. She did not look back as she left through the archway. Finally, Varna turned with a low growl and padded after her master. The guard by the door flinched as the white wolf loitered past. He stepped into the hallway and watched the wolf join Soren and the others. Only when they were gone did he return to his station and clear his throat with his back to Sadira.

"Are you okay, your Highness?" he called.

She opened and closed her mouth, unsure about what to say or how much he had heard. She sprang from her seat, struggling for words. He had protected the hall and kept Sadira company over the last few days while she worked on the room's décor. *Taryn*, Sadira remembered. Taryn had insisted on carrying every chair for her; this hall was his stationed post and, thus, his responsibility.

"I'm—" The guard turned, concern replacing his warm smile. His hazel eyes widened as he assessed Sadira, who instinctively moved her head, trying to shield the redness of her cheek with her long blonde curls.

"I'm fine." She examined the brown tinge, scarring her delicate white flowers. The guard cleared his throat, peering through the glass. Sadira turned to see if what had caught the guard's attention was the same thing that prompted Soren's exit.

Through the clear glass in the distance was the entrance to the walled garden, where Caellum, the King of Garridon, stood—her betrothed. Sadira's heartbeat spiked, and sweat formed on her palms as she twisted them in the skirts of her dress.

She wondered if Soren had left to avoid or confront him. But when her brash sister did not approach Caellum, who now strode alongside the wall with Sir Cain, her rush of anxiety mellowed.

Caellum was different from Rodik—opposites, even. Whereas Rodik was broad and dense, Caellum was muscular and lean. Rodik often wore his hair in the staple braids of the island, while Caellum's faded brown was short yet occasionally long enough to hide his eyeline. They had one similarity, though: the gentle way they cared for Sadira.

She did not know if she was foolish to assume Caellum cared for her, but she hoped his words were true. Hugging herself as she watched him through the glass, Sadira calmed her quiet sobs, conflicted by the feelings of homesickness and the calmness only Caellum brought her. He laughed at something Sir Cain said, and Sadira smiled at how his face came to life. She often watched him when he thought no one paid attention, noticing the pain only she could recognise—grief, heartbreak, loss, and the agony of deeming yourself so worthless it leaves you wondering if anyone believes in you.

Chapter Four

Caellum

Ethereal was the only way Caellum could describe Sadira as a rainbow danced off her complexion through the glass in the hall. She had not yet noticed he was watching her. A strange pull had turned his head in her direction the second he was within the eyeline of the castle wing, revealing his betrothed—the woman he was forcing into a loveless marriage. Even so, she made no complaints and disagreed with no suggestions. In fact, she actively encouraged preparations for their engagement ball. Caellum was in awe of her, wondering how she presented herself as so calm and collected when all he wished to do was scream at the gods for the hand they had dealt her.

While Caellum accepted his cards of fate, he wished there was something he could do to turn the tides of Sadira's. Tied to someone so undeserving of love was no easy feat, yet Sadira endured it with grace. *Elisara loved you,* prodded a voice in his head, though whether to remind him he could be loved or that he hurt those he loved, he did not know. He winced as the image of Elisara's heartbreak flashed in his mind. His parting words to Vala's queen followed him everywhere— lies conjured in the hope she would hate him. It was the only way to guarantee he would not crawl back to her begging, the only way they could rule their realms.

"You are selfish! You lack control, and you are emotionless when we are together. Why would I want to spend my life tied to someone so incredibly draining to be with?"

Caellum frowned as the image of Elisara's heartbreak morphed into wide eyes and a grin as she peered up at her commander.

Caellum had hoped someone would pick up the pieces of her heart but did not expect it to be someone so accustomed to breaking her into pieces. How could she feel anything other than hatred toward the man who played a part in her torturous training? The man who was the catalyst that nearly killed Caellum during his brief time in Keres?

The memory dissipated upon remembering Sadira's consolations in Nerida and how she had listened so intently as he explained all that transpired and all he had done. She had a way of balancing her thoughts with words of reassurance and uplifting his mood with merely a laugh. Yet there was no laughter now as he neared the hall.

Something was wrong. Wrapped in her embrace, Sadira cocooned herself as if desperate to disappear; her golden hair hung before her face, no longer pulled back in her usual silk ribbons, and her chest rose and fell with disjointed breaths. A tightness spread over Caellum.

"Did you hear anything I just said?" Sir Cain's words pulled his attention, and Caellum forced his gaze from Sadira to meet his commander's, noting the wry smile on the older man's freckled face.

"Sorry, I was"—Caellum glanced back at Sadira, and their eyes locked—"thinking." Sadira's eyes widened, and she turned her back to him, her movements frantic. Sir Cain followed his eyeline, and his frown matched Caellum's as they increased their pace, nearly jogging towards the open glass doors. Sadira cut them off moments before they entered, pulling the doors closed and stepping toward them with a wide smile that did not quite reach her eyes. The red mark on her cheek was stark against her snowdrop complexion.

"Good morning—"

"Who did this to you?" Caellum murmured. He reached for her but stopped himself, remembering his place. He hoped his expression conveyed his wish to help, but not overstep. Sadira's smile faltered, but when she nodded so imperceptibly he could have imagined it, Caellum stepped into her presence, casting a shadow across her face. Her bright eyes darkened, though not from the shadow but from a look in her eyes that felt all too familiar. A look of pain caused by those who are supposed to love you. Caellum slowly raised his hand, grazing his thumb across her cheek to inspect the forming bruise.

When she winced, Caellum's heart cracked, reminded of every memory where he flinched beneath Aurelia's touch whenever she tended to the consequences of their father's anger.

"Sir Cain, could you please retrieve some ice and cloth?" murmured Caellum, never taking his eyes from Sadira. Shared pain ebbed between them as he connected the puzzle pieces. Only one person would hurt Sadira, that she would try to protect. Caellum's nostrils flared, and his jaw clenched, failing to hide his thoughts about the fallen queen. No matter how he felt toward Soren, she was Sadira's sister.

"Tell me where you want to go?" he whispered, moving his hand from her cheek to her hair. He stroked it softly as her scent enveloped him—rose, sugar, and morning dew. Sadira blinked, but Caellum did not rush her thoughts.

"The walled garden," she whispered. Caellum stepped back and offered his arm. She silently took it, the pearl-lined sleeves of her dress catching on the golden thread of his emerald jacket, tying them together.

Caellum did not press Sadira further as they strode alongside the worn stone wall toward the garden in synchronised steps. He did not know enough about her relationship with Soren to pass judgement on the matter, not without hearing the truth from her lips.

As they approached the archway to the walled garden, Caellum reached to brush the tangled wisteria aside but halted as Sadira waved her hand. The branches and vines uncoiled, twisting and changing until they framed the archway and trailed along the walls in perfect formation. He smiled at Sadira, who blushed. As they entered the gardens, laughter halted their footsteps as they spotted a group of servants whispering in excited tones beneath the willow trees, skipping whatever duties they should attend to. Sadira's hand tightened around his arm. She wished to be alone. Caellum's heartbeat quickened as he glanced at the locked wooden door, the door that had remained locked since the day he broke his own heart. It was their only option of privacy. Catching the gardener's eye, Caellum inclined his head to the door that stood alone amongst empty flowerbeds once filled with sweet peas.

"No, Caellum—"

"Please. I want you to be comfortable," he reassured Sadira, whose eyes brimmed with concern.

"But not at the sacrifice of your own pain," she said. Caellum clasped her hand and squeezed it gently before steering her toward the door. The gardener unlocked it, unknowingly freeing the pain of Caellum's heart to allow entry for another's.

The scent of endless sweet peas suffocated him as he crossed the threshold. Behind the locked door of the walled garden, where he had only ever taken Elisara, sat a large glistening turquoise pond, surrounded by thousands of sweet peas in every colour imaginable: an oasis of colour shaded by a large willow tree at the pond's edge. Tears pricked his eyes, and he blinked them back, clearing his throat as he guided Sadira through and closed the door behind them, trapping the pair within a shrine to his heartbreak.

"Caellum." Sadira's voice broke, yet when he peered down at her, her pain was for him. She gazed at the scene before them while he guided Sadira to the spot beneath the tree. They sat on the small patch of grass devoid of flowers, worn from the times he had sat there with another. Caellum remained quiet, allowing Sadira to process her thoughts as she took in the scenery. She pulled her knees to her chin and wrapped her arms around her legs.

"I did not consider that Sir Cain would not find us here," said Caellum, voicing his mistake. Sadira tilted her head to rest her uninjured cheek on her knee and smiled softly. Where she traced her fingertips over the ground between them, several plants grew. She reached for a dark plant with rigid leaves and cracked one in half, releasing clear liquid. She placed it beside a flower with a large, yellow centre and a dark moss-like plant. Caellum did not recognise such specimens and wondered how many Sadira had catalogued in her mind. Her shoulders relaxed as her fingers trailed over each.

"If you can grind the yellow pollen of this plant"—she gestured to it— "The liquid in the leaves of this one and the sponge-like parts of these." She plucked at the mossy plant as she spoke. "They will turn into a paste that, when rubbed into the skin, provides a cooling effect." Sadira turned to gaze at the pond, surrendering to silence again. Caellum quietly set to work; he pulled bark from the tree and ground the gatherings until forming a pale green mixture.

"May I?" he asked hesitantly. Sadira turned her head back to him and nodded, closing her eyes. He gently brushed away a small tear trailing her cheek while her lips quivered. Remembering the times he cared for his sisters, Caellum gently rubbed the mixture into Sadira's skin, which felt so delicate under his rough fingertips. She did not wince this time but leaned into his touch.

"It has never happened before," she murmured, her eyes still closed. "It won't happen again." The slight rise of her tone gave away her uncertainty as Caellum finished rubbing the mixture into her cheek, her skin having cooled already.

"I once said the same." Caellum swallowed. Sadira opened her eyes then, the vulnerability in her gaze matching his as they watched one another. "It was not the only time," and with that, she fell apart. Her face crumpled, and sobs escaped her. She buried her head in the fabric of her dress, and Caellum instinctively reached for her, pulling her close beneath his arm and allowing her to cry into the dip of his shoulder. Locked in their embrace, he focused on the ragged rise and fall of her chest instead of Soren's face. He shoved away thoughts about punishing the fallen queen and exiling her from these lands.

Only when the afternoon was long past did Sadira finally lift her head. Caellum kept his arms around her, and she did not protest.

"Do you know what sweet peas symbolise?" she asked.

He swallowed hard. "I have never thought about it." But as he considered it, he supposed the flowers had always symbolised the innocence of his love for Elisara and the first moments they had truly fallen for one another. Sadira plucked one from the ground and twirled it in her hand.

"Flowers symbolise many things, depending on who you ask or what you read. Sweet peas can represent blissful pleasure and friendship." She glanced sideways at him. "They can also symbolise betrayal and goodbyes." *Accurate,* he thought as he stared across the field of flowers. It was all he saw then: a reminder of his betrayal and a goodbye to his first and only love.

"I think I would like to say farewell to this flower," he murmured before facing Sadira. "What is a flower that represents new beginnings?"

Joy returned to her bright green gaze, which glowed as her power bloomed. Shifting from his hold, she shook her hair behind her and placed her palms amongst the stems. A smile broke free as a ripple effect ensued. The sweet peas slowly withered, and in their place grew new flowers—thousands of white petals filling the space. He reached for one and plucked it from the ground, examining the delicate three petals. She shuffled back and sat opposite him, crossing her legs.

"Irises," she said, running her fingers through her creation. "They symbolise hope and new beginnings but can also represent a new outlook on life—" When she paused, Caellum drew his eyes from the flower to the princess before him. "—or a change of heart." Sadira peered up at him, and he could have sworn she blushed.

"Some might say you have had the newest beginnings of them all." Caellum plucked an iris and tucked it behind her ear. "Perhaps now is a chance to make new friends and find others to lean on."

Sadira sniffed. "Who would wish to befriend a princess absent from her homelands for so long? Nobody knows me."

Caellum frowned in thought. "Perhaps Queen Larelle?" he suggested. "She is kind and understanding and has experienced life far from what she now knows. She will likely understand your troubles better than I." He hoped Sadira would consider it. She nodded.

"Although I am in a new place, my situation remains mostly the same," she sighed.

"Soren?" he asked, and Sadira nodded.

"Do you remember what I said to you on the steps outside of the castle when I arrived?" Caellum frowned, recalling the moment.

"You said I made a mistake by allowing her into my home and that I would likely learn the price to pay as a result." Sadira was keeping something from him. He wished to probe and discover if his suspicions were true—that Soren would stop at nothing until she had the throne.

"She is still my sister," said Sadira. "But be careful, Caellum. I do not wish to see you hurt, nor do I wish to witness what would become of this realm with her as ruler." Caellum read between the lines of her words, and while he sat in a field of hope and new beginnings, the same reminders he was undeserving of the throne remained rooted within him.

Chapter Five

Elisara

Water and blood trailed down the wet brick walls of the hallway. Elisara rubbed the back of her head to ease the throbbing and narrowed her eyes, adjusting her vision in the darkness. With no clue as to her whereabouts, she trailed her fingers along the wet stone, yet felt no liquid on her hands. She felt nothing. Dripping echoed from where a puddle formed at her feet, mirroring her reflection. Elisara's black locks draped against the golden chains that supported her silk red dress.

Red.

Something tugged at her memory as Elisara stumbled forward, her bare feet splashing through the puddle and distorting her image. While she appeared mostly the same, there was no mistaking her glowing white eyes that cast a faint light in the darkness.

Elisara stumbled backward into metal bars, yet the expectant sting of cold metal did not follow. She blinked hard and rubbed her eyes. Moonlight filtered through a small hole at the top of the wall, illuminating the dark, damp hallway. There was something oddly familiar about her surroundings. Cautiously, she leaned forward to peer into the moonlit puddle, where her white eyes still glowed. Footsteps sounded in the distance.

Elisara slid with her back along the bars, feeling her way to the dark corner below the hole in the wall. The footsteps were heavy yet slow, as though the owner did not wish to alert anyone to their arrival. She pressed against the brick wall, concealed by the shadows. Metal bars glinted to her right, yet she remained focused on the dark hallway, holding her breath while waiting for whoever might emerge.

The boot stomped through the puddle, creating a ripple-effect beneath the light. Elisara's eyes followed the broad legs of the person who now turned to the bars, oblivious to her presence. She tensed when her eyes landed on the person's face and attempted to back further into the wall, desperate for it to swallow her whole. Elisara would do anything to avoid confronting this moment again.

Izaiah Hakim, Kazaar's second-in-command, stood before the bars, his expression hungry and demanding. His hunched back forced his head down at an angle that made him appear like a predator towering above his prey. Elisara's heart thundered and breath quickened as she wrapped her arms around herself, shrinking before his presence. Izaiah pulled a set of keys from his pocket, twisting one slowly in the doors to what she now remembered as her cell.

The suffocating, damp room neighboured many empty cells in the dungeons below the palace boundary wall. Its underground location only added to the chill, which became more apparent in the absence of the Keres sun. Panic chilled Elisara's bones, who trembled at the thought of returning here. She now remembered why she recognised the hole in the wall; it was her only glimpse of the outside world during the nights of her military training. She forced her feet to move as the cell creaked open, frantically looking at the past version of herself that Izaiah approached.

"Get up!" Elisara screamed at her sleeping form. "Get up!" She tried to make her way around Izaiah, but his broad build filled the doorway. He tossed the keys aside and fiddled with the buckle holding up his dagger-filled belt, which rattled as he approached. Elisara screamed at the young woman who lay on the low camp bed in the cell's corner, sleeping. When she woke, Izaiah's hand muffled her scream as he climbed atop her. Elisara froze at the sound of footsteps in the distance, having never considered what was happening outside of the barred walls. Young Elisara bit hard on Izaiah's thumb, and he cursed, clambering off her.

"You bitch!" he spat. Elisara knew what came next. She pressed her hands against the wet floor, the concrete turning to ice as she recklessly guided it towards Israar's boots. He sneered at her. "You think you can stop me?" Laughing, he took a step forward and his boot froze midair. He tried to shift his ankle, but the ice climbed until it encased his calves. Running footsteps sounded in the distance, and a shout rang out that Elisara had never recalled at that moment.

"Elisara!" a voice shouted.

Kazaar. An image flashed before Elisara of Kazaar facing her in a different room. She was with him before waking here, she realised. Elisara's heart tugged in different directions—toward the man coming to save this past version of herself, and the other who betrayed Elisara during her final moments of lucidity.

Before Kazaar made it to the cell, ice crawled up the body of the man who had haunted Elisara in every waking moment since then. Upon reaching his neck, Izaiah sputtered, no doubt trying to conjure another expletive. Yet when her saviour rounded into the cell, Elisara screamed, and Izaiah Hakim shattered. Blood and ice scattered, and the bloodied parts of him were indiscernible. Elisara instinctually raised her arm, and although she acknowledged this was a nightmare, it felt real. The smell of iron filled her nose while she stood in Izaiah's bloodied remains.

Sobs sounded from the corner of the cell. Elisara pulled her arm away to find Kazaar stepping tentatively towards her past self. He reached for her, and she sobbed again as his hand found her shoulder. When she didn't recoil, he pulled her into him.

"It's okay," he murmured into her hair, frowning at the shards of his second-in-command across the floor. Elisara stepped slowly from the cell's shadows, watching with intrigue. Ever since the night in question, she had tried to erase every reminder from memory. She had forgotten how quickly Kazaar arrived and his clear concern. He presented himself so differently compared to his demeanour throughout training.

"It's okay," he said again.

"No!" she shouted, shoving at his chest. "It's not okay! None of this is okay!" Elisara watched herself crawl backward on the bed, fortifying the icy walls in her mind as she shielded her face from him. Pain flitted across Kazaar's face.

"You go home tomorrow," he whispered. "It will all be over."

Elisara frowned at her past self, who cowered in the corner. *You go home tomorrow*. It had sounded different back then, like Kazaar was exhausted, tired of dealing with Elisara, desperate for her to leave.

Kazaar rose. His eyes glowed as he melted Izaiah's remains and backed out of the cell. "You won't have to see me again," he said.

Shadows crept into Elisara's vision and crawled along the floor toward him. Elisara stepped forward, feeling oddly drawn to the darkness as they surrounded Kazaar. She peered into the floor's wet reflection, where the same white eyes appeared—except now, tendrils of black streaked through them. She stumbled forward, and the darkness engulfed her once again.

***

Elisara blinked rapidly at the sudden change in light, confronted by the beating sun of Keres. She clambered back when she realised. She stood at the edge of the canyon rock, kicking up red dust as she did. She coughed and shielded her eyes, and after finally steadying herself, she assessed her surroundings. Twenty recruits stood lined up along the canyon rock above the Abis forge; half were dressed in emerald-green, while the others wore red. Elisara's heart quickened, recognising the next nightmare to unfold.

Elisara watched her past-self furiously summon gusts of air until a plume of red dust soared above her. She swung her arm, directing it toward Kazaar, who stood several steps away from the edge. He stood rigid with his legs braced wide and his arms crossed as Elisara strode forward, spreading her fingers apart and summoning her power as fury contorted her features. Elisara moved toward herself; she would do anything to prevent watching another nightmare unfold. Before the harsh wind reached Kazaar, Caellum stepped in front of the commander, about to confront him.

"Caellum!" a young Elisara screamed as the wind hurtled toward him, knocking him over the edge of the forge. Elisara ran alongside herself, peering over the precipice to the lava-filled river created by the deadly waterfall on the opposite side of the ravine. The clash and clatter of metal workers echoed as the young Elisara flattened herself on the dusty ground and extended her hand to Caellum, who hung from a tree jutting out from the side of the cliff top. Elisara frowned. The oddness of the standalone tree in an area so desolate had never crossed her mind before.

She remembered how this scene played out. Elisara would help Caellum up before Kazaar dismissed them for the day. So, instead of watching herself, she turned to watch Kazaar. He stood with the broad stance as before, except his arms were no longer crossed but hung loosely by his sides. She clocked the slight twitch of his fingers and frowned, glancing back over the edge. The tree branch moved so subtly she almost missed it, curving upwards as Caellum reached for Elisara, who pulled him back over the edge. Kazaar's hand flourished once more before he turned away, and the tree nestled back into the crack of the canyon. Elisara ignored the rest of the vision, staring at the spot where the tree had been.

Before now, she had always thought herself lucky that a tree had been there to save Caellum. But Kazaar had saved him, using his abilities to extend the tree and catch Caellum's fall.

"You are a flight risk, princess. You have no control, and that will end up killing someone you love," Kazaar said, tight-lipped. "You and the prince are dismissed."

Another image flashed through Elisara's mind of Kazaar standing opposite her in a small room as vines crawled closer before bursting into flames. She blinked and turned back to him, assessing the sudden softness in his eyes as a young Elisara stormed away. His familiar scent of smoke and embers drifted toward her, yet something was absent from his skin as if a layer of his scent was missing. Kazaar turned suddenly, and she faced her reflection in his dark gaze. Shadows reached out and overtook the white glow in her eyes, engulfing her yet again.

***

"You have completed your training," Kazaar's deep voice carried across the Ashun Desert, patrolling the lines of recruits. Elisara raised her hand to peer out across the bright sands, shadowing her face while looking for herself amongst them. When Kazaar patrolled the lines of soldiers, she spotted herself immediately. Young Elisara stood out in her ivory leather corset, a stark contrast to the burnt orange of Keres. The night before this was that of the attack. She had not slept after Kazaar left her cell. When sunlight replaced the moonlight streaming in through the hole in the wall, guards arrived with her uniform. She almost did not recognise it after two years.

Elisara walked down the dune toward herself and the other recruits. Overheated and sleep-deprived, she watched herself sway beneath the sun.

"You return to your homes." Kazaar glanced at the young princess, who scowled at the hatred she could have sworn was in his eyes. But as Elisara relived the moment from a distance, she questioned whether it was hatred after all. "You return to your realm, qualified to defend it should you ever be called to arms." Elisara glanced at her feet as she continued down the sand dune, pausing as shadows seeped into her vision. When she looked up, tendrils of darkness snaked across the once bright sands of Ashun Desert and blanketed the ground until not a speck of orange remained. The memory continued as normal despite the invasion of darkness. She tuned out Kazaar's last words as Vlad approached with her horse.

He would escort her to the Vala border, where her mother and father waited. Elisara hoped to experience that memory next. She would give anything for another moment with her parents, and to be on the receiving end of her father's smile.

"Princess, a word?" Kazaar's voice invaded her again, and Elisara watched as she ignored him and mounted her horse. A hollowness existed in the young girl's eyes, with dark circles etched below them. Her hands trembled as she picked up the reins and turned to Kazaar, her eyes darkening as she looked him up and down. Elisara felt a twinge of guilt; she could hardly imagine looking at him in such a way now. Her past-self opened her mouth as if to speak, and as Elisara watched the moment again, she noted the hopeful look in Kazaar's eyes, unlike the resentment she remembered. But the young, wounded version of herself saw only a reminder of the pain she had endured over the past two years. When she looked at him, she saw the man who trusted Izaiah.

The shadows below Kazaar's feet moved again, reaching for Elisara atop the horse. The sky changed. The sun dwindled until the sky reflected the shadows on the sand. Elisara looked up to avoid reliving her farewell with Kazaar. The stars had always mesmerised her, perhaps because she watched them every evening growing up from the open balcony of her chambers. She looked for the constellation her father often showed her but was drawn to a shooting star, and then another, and another. Stars began to fall like rain then—a shower of light drowning the darkness. She glanced back at herself and Kazaar, overcome by a cooling sensation as flecks of stardust landed on her skin. The shadows moved again and twisted around Kazaar as he reached for Elisara on her horse. Before he could touch her, Elisara turned and rode for Vala.

"Elisara!" Kazaar shouted as the darkness enveloped her again. "Elisara, please."

Chapter Six

Kazaar

"Elisara, please," Kazaar pleaded. "Please wake up."

The late morning sun filtered through the open balcony, and Kazaar refrained from yawning after staying up all night. He hoped Nyzaia would arrive soon with a plan. He squeezed Elisara's hand, but she remained still and unmoving. He loosened his grip reluctantly and trailed his fingers to her wrist, checking again for a pulse. The steady beat of her heart was the only thing that soothed him, one of the few sounds in his chambers. Nothing had changed about the rooms since he departed for Vala and handed his soul to the queen before him. When Kazaar departed for the air realm to serve the woman who had haunted his mind for years, he knew he would be ruined for another.

He brushed her collarbone with his thumb, where the raised moon scar had appeared after their fallout in King Razik's office. He did not need to see his reflection to know a matching sun-shaped scar lived on his right collarbone. Different marks had appeared on his skin from the moment he began using his powers—not his Keres-born powers, but the powers from all four realms. He had told no one about his ability to wield all the elements except for Elisara. He glanced briefly at his hands, where a scattering of raised, inked whirls twisted into vines and wrapped around his forearms and biceps. It was a symbol of the abomination he had become, markings which climbed until forming flames that burned across his chest and waves that attempted to calm him, matching those beneath the sails inked into the crook of his elbow. Other markings scattered across the once empty spaces of his arm, some of which—until he visited the Unsanctioned Isle with Elisara—he had never seen. Yet the inkings were now a reminder of their experience together, and his desire to crush his lips to hers as he pinned her within his flames, or the gentle way in which he wished to care for her after she was injured. He had immediately recognised the patterns on the throne room floor yet was not sure if he was disappointed or relieved Elisara had not noticed the markings on him were the same. She had never felt drawn to him as he was to her.

Elisara was a perpetual presence in his soul, consoling the darkness inundating his mind—a presence that made itself known the moment emotions consumed her. He recalled when he first felt the piercing of Elisara's hatred that shot through his chest after her first week of training. He had stood before her with crossed arms, admiring her determination while she wished for his downfall. It pained him to look upon her soot-covered face, where sweat streaked her skin after hours of standing at the edge of the lava rivers within the Abis Forge. He had immediately gone to his father, King Razik, and demanded they reallocate her to Garridon.

"It has already been decided," he had said before shunning him from his office without a second glance. Kazaar could never understand why an heir of Vala would be forced to train in Keres, yet he knew if he treated her any differently, word would reach his father, and the risk of revisiting his previous way of life was too great. At least as commander, he was shown more respect than he received as a child.

Ignoring Elisara was the only thing that worked. He delegated his second-in-command to oversee most of her training, unable to watch or feel the waves of Elisara's pain crash over him. He spent many a sleepless night wondering if he had been stronger or more resilient around her, whether Izaiah would have attempted what he did. On some nights, her scream still echoed in his mind as she reached for him, begging for someone to save her.

Sighing, Kazaar watched the steady rise and fall of her chest, the red silk thin against her skin. He clenched his jaw. Elisara's pain and hatred were not the only emotions he had felt from her. Eventually, they changed: the curiosity that originated on the Isle, the familiar warmth of friendship as he aided her through heartbreak, and the burning desire as he pressed her against the alcove wall. It was then that he had almost broken his vow of never succumbing to the pull he felt toward her. But the second he felt the reciprocated desire, he stopped himself. If Elisara felt even a fraction of what he felt for her, there would be no going back. If he were to have her and then lose her, the darkness he felt within himself would overtake.

Kazaar hung his head as he recalled the events in Razik's office. He wished for no part of his power to connect to Elisara, whether that was the elements or the unexplainable that squirmed beneath his skin. But with a fearful certainty, he knew something had happened to them. When the raw essence of their power interacted on the Unsanctioned Isle, it was chaotic, as if their abilities fought for control. The second time was different once Kazaar had revealed the truth. It was as though their powers were magnetised, trying to instil order before diving into the unknown.

When light meets dark in the rarest of times. The sudden emergence of the sun and moon scars was no coincidence. It was the symbol of Sonos and Sitara, the God of Dawn, and Goddess of Dusk. He pondered its meaning and questioned how the marks connected the two of them. Somehow, it was symbolic of their connection, like a mirroring of one another: Elisara's light carved into him while his darkness threatened to consume her. He hoped he was wrong.

He stroked her arm with his free hand and shivered at the cool morning breeze floating through the balcony. Goosebumps rippled along Elisara's arm, and Kazaar swallowed, reassuring himself that using his power would be fine. Nothing would go wrong. He turned his hand and willed flames to dance across his palm. He blinked and slammed his fist shut. Slowly, he unfurled his fingers.

Bright white flames lit up the room, aiding the sunlight trickling in through the windows. Kazaar frowned and leaned closer to inspect the flames, trying to understand if the difference in colour was some trick of the light. Rotating his hand, the flames twisted around him and flickered toward Elisara. He flinched the moment her fingers moved.

"Elisara," he said hopefully, but she remained still. Opening his hand again, Kazaar summoned the flames, and Elisara's eyelids fluttered, her fingers curling around his. Still, she did not wake. He let the fire burn. Perhaps this was her power's influence, her subconscious mind connecting and reaching for Kazaar's essence, even while asleep. Kazaar angled his head to glance at the sun, gauging how long he had sat with her like this. Last night, he had first instructed the guards to find Nyzaia. Their second instruction was to send a scrawled note to Helena, Vigor, and Talia, urging them to journey to Keres immediately. Vigor was the only physician he trusted to be near Elisara, and that was only because she trusted him. Aside from Nyzaia, Helena, Vigor, and Talia were her only friends, and when Elisara finally awoke, he wanted familiar faces to greet her. Yet something scratched at the back of his mind—a feeling that he was forgetting something. The door behind him slammed open.

"What did you do to her?" a voice demanded. Kazaar closed his eyes.

Vlad. He had forgotten Vlad.

The captain of Elisara's Queen's guard rushed into the room, his eyes fixed on his queen. A defensiveness overtook Kazaar, and though it pained him to part from her, he jumped to his feet and blocked Vlad's path. His pale hair shone beneath the light of the morning sun, and he narrowed his ice-blue eyes.

"Are you seriously keeping me from her?" Vlad hissed. Kazaar stepped forward, towering over him.

"You did not even know where she was. Why should I allow you near her now?" Before Kazaar left the hall with Elisara, Vlad was preoccupied, busy flirting with a Keresian maid.

"I knew she was with you, and I assumed the *commander* of an entire realm could keep his Queen safe." Vlad made to step around Kazaar, who quickly raised a hand to his chest to stop him. Vlad did not push again. He glanced at Kazaar's hand before meeting his eyes. Something changed in Vlad's expression before he stepped back.

"If you want to help her, head to the courtyard and await Helena, Vigor, and Talia's arrival," Kazaar said calmly, eager to once again be alone with his queen. Vlad raised his eyebrows but remained rooted in place.

"Not until I know what happened."

Kazaar sighed. "We do not know for certain. She expended a lot of power, and now she won't wake. Nyzaia and Tajana are looking into it, but that is why we need Vigor," Kazaar said. A battle played behind Vlad's eyes as he surveyed his queen with a frown. He glanced between her and Kazaar, attempting to piece together what had transpired. "I do not want to command you, Vlad," Kazaar added.

Vlad pursed his lips at the cold reminder of his station. While Vlad's sole responsibility was the queen, Kazaar acted for the entire realm, and this was a concern far greater than just their queen's safety.

"You send for me the second she wakes," Vlad relented. Kazaar nodded in confirmation before Vlad turned to leave without another word.

Kazaar was quick to return to his spot at Elisara's side. Pulling rank was a last resort. While plenty of stories circulated about Kazaar and his teachings under Razik's command, he was making a difference with Vala's guards and soldiers. They did not view him the way the stories painted him to be, and it was all because of her. When Elisara scolded him about implementing Keres' methods in Vala, he took a step back to consider their differences before changing his practices and commanding his soldiers how he always wished. What would Razik say if he saw how soft Kazaar had become under the influence of a woman?

Leaning over Elisara, he brushed her hair aside and took in the details of her face. He planted a soft kiss on her forehead before leaning his own against hers.

"Please, Elisara," Kazaar murmured. "I never wished for this to happen." Darkness flashed in his mind—an image of them on the Isle. He lifted a hand to cup her cheek, his forehead still against hers. While the image was a memory of the two of them on the Isle before their powers met, the surroundings were different. Shadows replaced the onyx and marble, and the surrounding walls were non-existent, fallen to reveal only the starry night encompassing all. Wisps of darkness became tendrils with a mind of their own, twisting until forming a blanket of shadows that Kazaar could not control. He pulled back to peer longingly at the closed eyes before him, begging them to open.

His darkness had truly invaded her.

Chapter Seven

Nyzaia

Upon opening the door of her chambers, Nyzaia stumbled and collided with Tajana, who reached out to keep her from tripping over the skirts of her lehenga.

"When you guard a room, I don't expect you to be standing quite so close to the door," grumbled Nyzaia, straightening.

"I told her it was too close," Farid said. He stood on the opposite side of the door, his back pressed against the wall. Tajana glared at him.

"Seeing as there is an unconscious queen in the room upstairs, and we have no idea what happened"—Tajana stroked Nyzaia's arm— "I thought it important to stay close while you sleep, in case anything went wrong." Nyzaia refrained from repeating their argument the night prior when Nyzaia had left Kazaar's rooms. Tajana had insisted on spending the night with her, as she did on most occasions when she was off duty, but Nyzaia wished to be alone, desperate for some time to think. Tajana had not taken it well.

"I feel like you're pushing me away."

Nyzaia ignored the pang of guilt and focused on the task ahead. She had already wasted time after sleeping longer than intended.

"You cannot honestly believe Kazaar did something to Elisara." Tajana kept pace on her left, and Farid positioned himself to her right, constantly scanning their surroundings.

"I don't want to believe he would, but..." Tajana hesitated, glancing cautiously at Farid, who remained expressionless.

"Farid is a member of the Queen's Guard as much as you or the others, Tajana. You can speak in front of him." Nyzaia continued toward her father's office, shivering again at the coldness haunting the corridor as she approached the dark doors. Nyzaia understood Tajana's apprehension; after all, Farid was simply a guard who won his position; he was not a part of the syndicate or even a Red Stone, yet they could not keep everything from him if he was to remain a part of her closest guards. Tajana would have to adjust to his presence like Jabir, Issam, and Rafik had.

"*Anything*?" Tajana emphasised. Nyzaia considered the implications. Something terrible had happened to one of Novisia's rulers; perhaps divulging her knowledge to her closest companions could be beneficial and keep them on alert. Farid had proved himself loyal so far.

"Anything," Nyzaia decided, opening the doors to her father's office. Tajana huffed and halted behind Nyzaia, who stopped in her tracks, her eyes immediately falling on the open door at the other end of the room. It had never been there before. Tajana made to walk toward it with Farid on her heels.

"No," Nyzaia commanded. Farid stopped instantly, but Tajana hesitated. While Nyzaia was clueless about what lay within that room, Kazaar was a brother to her. She needed to protect him, too, regardless of what he had hidden. Farid backed away, resting a hand on the pommel of his sword while his eyes roamed over the clear view of the Vala mountains in the distance. Tajana stepped forward.

"You don't know what could be in there, love," she said. Nyzaia blinked, and flames crawled up her arms.

"I am sure I can handle it."

Farid failed to hide his smirk as Nyzaia strode into the room and pulled the door behind her, leaving it slightly ajar. She slipped and gripped the wall for purchase, shivering as her body adjusted to the plummeting temperature; it was colder here than in the office itself. *Why did her father have a hidden room? And what within it caused trouble between Kazaar and Elisara*?

Finding her footing, Nyzaia carefully stepped forward and slowly turned to take in the glistening room of ice. Elisara's power had escalated, but why? With a wave of her hand, Nyzaia's flames made quick work of melting the ice-encased room, yet she cursed when glancing down at the pool of water surrounding her feet. A piece of parchment lay within it, the ink darkening. She grabbed it, squinting at the blurred lines. Only one was clear.

"The Gods may whisper and help them on," Nyzaia read aloud. The prophecy. *Why would my father have the prophecy?*

Nyzaia knelt, the hem of her skirts darkening in the water as she examined the statues on the table. Were they the Gods? Waves rushed at the feet of one, while flames, vines, and mountains marked the others. Her eye paused at the base of the pair in the centre, embracing in a way that spoke of desperation. A sun and a moon. Nyzaia's mind returned to the raised moon faintly etched on Elisara's collarbone. Was whatever happened in this room linked to those on the table before her?

The parchment in her hand peeled into pieces, the water having won the war. Nyzaia placed it carefully on the table before more pieces crumbled away, and she let her flames dry the parchment and the floor. Nyzaia's sodden skirts dragged behind her as she circled the room, trailing her hands along the cool glass of the gold-framed mirror propped against the wall in the corner. The engravings marking the glass felt harsh under her fingertips, as though someone had hastily etched the words. She did not recognise the symbols, but the mirror's words were forever ingrained in her mind. She read them again.

'The door to the soul bears all to hear,
Multiple generations is the rule of the seer.
With those of white and those of black,
The spirit of the first makes their way back.
When the darkness returns, sacrifice is made,
In the wake of disaster, the return of the blade.
When light meets dark in the rarest of times,

When all that is left is the last of the lines.
The power to awaken that of old lore,
Lies in the soul of those with all four.
From fire and ice, the King and Queen must hide,
Secrets from the past, the heirs must find.
Only together can they defeat and restore,
Only together can they gain so much more.
The Gods may whisper and help them on,
Only if all possess that from Ithyion.'

Nyzaia cursed. That was why Kazaar and Elisara had been in her father's office. They were searching for her father's secrets. Flames roared up Nyzaia's arms, her fury punctuated by the pain in her chest. Perhaps Kazaar was now more loyal to his new queen than her, his *sister*. Nyzaia would not have questioned him if he had requested to search the rooms alone. They were here as *her* guests to investigate what Nyzaia's father and Vespera had kept hidden. *They had no right to do this without me.*

"Everything okay, love?" Tajana called from the other side of the door. Nyzaia rolled her eyes.

"Hmmm," Nyzaia said through pursed lips. When she reached the desk, she frowned and glanced around the room. It was the only other piece of furniture present. Instinctively, she reached for the small, framed portrait lying on its surface. The woman staring back at her reflected many of Elisara's traits: thick brows and dark hair framing her face. Nyzaia had only met Vespera on a few occasions.

"You did not respond," called Tajana; the door creaked as she pushed it open. In an annoyed fury, Nyzaia summoned a tower of flames to block the opening, an evident signal to leave her be. Farid mumbled something to Tajana, likely along the lines of *I told you so*. Soon, the mumbling turned to shouts. Nyzaia sighed, dropped the portrait, and exited the room. She slammed the door behind her, blowing strands of hair across her face as she glared at her captain and guard. Tajana pointed a knife at Farid, who stood unfazed in the same place Nyzaia had left him.

"How am I to get anything done if I must constantly monitor you two bickering?" Nyzaia snapped. Farid had the sense to avert his eyes while Tajana opened her mouth to protest, stopping at Nyzaia's pointed look. Finally relenting, Tajana sheathed her knife and leaned against the worn blue armchair, flicking her dark braid over her shoulder.

Nyzaia glided toward the bookshelf where Farid stood and scanned the titles on the hundreds of dust-covered, leather-bound books, searching for the one she had seen before—one without a speck of dust.

Farid broke the silence as Nyzaia scoured the shelves on the left. "This room is odd. The King always struck me as someone incredibly proud of his realm, who would want to survey his city, not the mountains of another realm."

Nyzaia wondered what had suddenly made Farid so chatty.

"Well, the canyons house the Abis Forge, which is arguably the biggest source of funding for the realm." Nyzaia explained, stretching her back as she straightened. She did not miss the darkening of Farid's expression at the mention of the forge. She peered over her shoulder at the unobstructed view of the canyon and mountains. She had not thought about the oddness plaguing this room, but having been in the secret room beside it, she knew there was more to it. Nyzaia narrowed her eyes as she surveyed the room's contents again: the pale blue, the two wine glasses, the stark snow on the distant Vala mountains, and Vespera's portrait in the adjoining room.

"They were together," she breathed. Tajana tilted her head. "My father and Vespera were lovers."

"Could that be the secret that the..." Tajana paused and glanced at Farid.

"That the prophecy refers to," Nyzaia continued. "Perhaps." Farid barely batted an eye at the mention of a prophecy, his stark blue eyes still fixed on the view of the canyon and mountains.

She shared a look with Tajana, both seemingly confused by his behaviour.

"Should I look for more evidence that links them together?" asked Tajana, pushing herself off the armchair. Nyzaia shook her head and turned back to face the bookshelves, her jewellery clinking with her movements.

"We need to look for something to help Kazaar wake Elisara," she said. Farid finally moved then and turned to scan the bookshelf. He reached and gathered the volumes on the highest shelves while Nyzaia scanned for the book stuck in her mind—*Myths and Lies of Ithyion.* It was the only book she expected had answers and might reference the essence of one's power. Farid dropped a heavy pile onto the table between the two armchairs, the wine glasses vibrating from the impact. She cocked her head, glancing between him and the books.

"These are all the books not covered in dust," he said in his matter-of-fact way. "I assumed we wanted anything read frequently." He held his hands behind his back, standing tall and rigid.

"That's an odd assumption." Tajana narrowed her eyes.

"Is it?" he asked. "You referenced a prophecy concerning the King of Keres; it seems a fair assumption that we are here to find any secrets *he* could have hidden." He faced Nyzaia then. "Though I am uncertain how that relates to the Queen of Vala and her commander."

The queen scanned her guard. While he was a quiet man—mysterious, some would say—he had done nothing but prove his dedication to Nyzaia and his position. From his pristine uniform to his immaculately trimmed beard and hair, he struck her as someone who did not break from order and procedure.

"*Trust only the other heirs.*" Nyzaia was reminded of Isha's final words before taking her own life, so dedicated to keeping whatever secrets she had been privy to within Keres or those from Doltas Island as Soren had suggested. At her side, Tajana shook her head, but Nyzaia followed her gut.

"The prophecy states many things, but one line struck me when I was in the room with Kazaar: '*When light meets dark in the rarest of times.*'" Clasping her hands, she glanced at the patterns painted on the back of them. "Last night, there was a raised mark of a moon on Elisara's collarbone." Both members of her Queen's Guard furrowed their brows. "Kazaar said something happened between them, so I'm working on the assumption there is a sun marked on him."

"Light and dark, sun and moon," Tajana summarised. Farid crouched before the stacks before him and pulled out a large black leather tome. When he turned the cover, Nyzaia faltered, ensuring her eyes did not deceive her. *Myths and Lies of Ithyion.* Below the title was a silver marking of an overlapping sun and moon. She reached Farid in seconds and snatched the book from his hands before sinking into one of the armchairs. She trailed her rough fingers along the embossed author's name at the bottom.

Caligh Servusian.

Nyzaia did not recognise the name, but given how old the book appeared, that did not surprise her. Many people had passed long before her ancestors fled the siege in Ithyion. She opened the book and coughed at the dust floating into her vision. The crinkling stiff parchment confirmed her suspicions. The book was far too old to have been written by someone in this Kingdom. Tajana pulled a book from the remaining pile and took it to the desk, glancing between Nyzaia and Farid as she did.

Farid listed the other titles on the pile, yet Nyzaia remained too transfixed on the book to pay any notice. The first few pages had faded with age, and the cursive font was difficult to decipher, nearly illegible. She turned each page with care, conscious she possibly held one of the few items from Ithyion, aside from the talismans and Sword of Sonos.

Nyzaia had never been one for books. When her father sent her to spy on Elisara all those years ago, she had sat restlessly on the balcony, waiting until Elisara finally finished reading. She had never understood how Elisara was so immersed. Yet as Nyzaia sat with centuries of potential history before her, she wondered if she was not one for fiction or tales of love and romance but the mysteries of those who lived real lives. If only she could sit in her chambers and do nothing but read over the coming days. Instead, she scanned the pages for key information and analysed the words and drawings. She continued flipping the pages, searching for a picture of a moon, sun, or both, but found only passing drawings of creatures she did not recognise. She paused on an illustration of a giant winged beast in water; scales covered every inch of its body, from its head and an unusually long neck all the way to its four-taloned feet. Could it somehow be related to the creatures that had taken Ithyion, the beasts Elisara and Kazaar had killed? Nyzaia just about construed the smudged cursive below the sketch, marked 'River Drake.' On the opposite page was a similar creature poised atop a mountain. Flames erupted from its nostrils, yet no matter how much Nyzaia squinted, she could not read the name scrawled below it. Other than the titles of the creatures, none of the paragraphs were comprehensible, all written in a language that was not her own. She flicked the page again and paused. A plain page with a simple title stared back at her.

Celestial Ties, it read, and below was a sketch of the sun and moon, followed by four markings, all curved in some manner or another: some with multiple curls and flicks, others barer. Nyzaia frowned. *Four*. She glanced at the door of the hidden room. Similar markings etched the mirror frame but were less detailed, as though drawn from memory. Nyzaia turned the page, her eyes mesmerised by the drawing. Etched in charcoal, two hands reached for one another with twisting threads surrounding them. Despite the flat page, Nyzaia imagined they sparkled.

The celestial tie is thought to be bestowed upon two individuals who share a destiny. It is a bond presented by the Celestial Gods and anointed when two beings finally acknowledge their connection and allow their essences to merge. Some claim that, upon doing so, the pair are marked by the Gods. Such a mark grants them access to one another's powers, memories, and minds. Few known cases of such a bond exist. For many years, the bond was frowned upon as stories emerged, suggesting those bestowed with such a mark could become too powerful. It is, therefore, unclear if more celestial ties exist yet are hidden for fear the individuals may be forced to separate and kept from one another.

Nyzaia slammed the book shut. Overcome by thoughts, she rose from her chair and decided to finish the rest later. Farid moved with her as she handed the book to Tajana.

"Take this to my chambers," she commanded. Tajana began to speak but halted at Nyzaia's raised hand. "Farid, you are with me." Ignoring Tajana's scowl, Nyzaia picked up the skirts of her lehenga to free her feet. She exited the office and ran through the hallways while one sentence repeated in her mind: 'Granting them access to one another's powers, memories, and *minds*.'

Kazaar was the only one who could wake Elisara.

Chapter Eight

Kazaar

Kazaar continued watching Elisara, hoping the image of the throne room had not been a fluke and that, somehow, he could reach her. A bombardment of emotions hammered at his mind, trying to break through the walls compartmentalising the different parts of his life: fear, betrayal, longing. The emotions were not his own, yet he recognised their invasion in his body. He always knew when they were hers.

When he averted his gaze from Elisara's face, magic swarmed them. He froze, his hand still gripping hers as the magic twisted around them. It began at their conjoined hands. Kazaar's burning white flame sparked, sending beautiful pearls of light to land on his brown skin. He jumped at its coolness, expecting it to burn.

Dark wisps lingered in their wake—small at first until the sparks and wisps bounced off one another, growing more curious. The lingering wisps lengthened and twisted around Elisara and Kazaar's hands. The sparks responded like a kindred spirit, growing until silver threads of light intertwined with the darkness that appeared to tie Kazaar to Elisara. The threads coiled and danced, trailing up their arms until caressing the newly graced marks on their collarbones. Kazaar did not move, uncertain about what this power might do to her. He could not cause any further pain.

He closed his eyes as dark and light threads licked his skin, and behind his eyelids, a flash of the throne room appeared again. He opened his eyes, and Elisara's eyelids fluttered. His mind was trying to tell him something, but what? He closed them again and trusted his intuition. The image held for longer, long enough to envisage

Elisara yelling at him from across the ice tomb, where the Sword of Sonos had been encased.

A memory, he realized, yet something was different about it. The walls were missing; instead, the night sky surrounded the pair. He had seen the memory depicted this way when he last tried reaching out to Elisara.

"Is this what you are thinking about?" Kazaar murmured. He stroked her forehead with his free hand, careful not to disrupt the encircling threads of magic. They ebbed and flowed until shadow and light encased the pair. While he had no idea how he must look to an outsider, Elisara was easy to describe. The gathering of shadows resembled a dress scattered with specks of light as if she was made of the night sky itself. Tendrils flooded behind her like wings, wishing to carry her away on the night breeze. Kazaar squeezed Elisara's hand, and her eyelids fluttered until the glowing white threads formed above her head, reminding him of a drawing he had seen as a child.

An angel. She reminded him of an angel. He smiled despite his worry. It was apt that she should resemble such a serene and calm myth, given how she made him feel when he lowered his walls. If she looked like an angel, he only wondered what dark creature he resembled should anyone walk in. He sensed the shadows' caress, enveloping him like they did her, yet he was too blinded by the brightness that was Elisara to see if it touched him.

A door slammed shut behind him, and the power between them dissipated. An uncomfortable absence remained.

"What was *that*?" Nyzaia exclaimed. It seemed the unearthly power had not dispersed quickly enough. Kazaar turned his head, and Nyzaia stepped back, colliding with the door. He frowned.

"Your eyes," she whispered, taking slow steps towards Kazaar. He looked for a mirror before glancing at his hand intertwined with Elisara's, unwilling to part from her. He heard the soft padding of Nyzaia's feet as she approached and held a mirror out to him. His reaction resembled Nyzaia's. Kazaar jerked his head back and gaped. He had only ever seen eyes like this once before when he had stared into Elisara's in the moments of her rising power before she fell unconscious. Where Elisara's had glowed white with wisps of shadow, his own were now ebbed with darkness, dispersed with specks of white that changed each time he blinked. He blinked and dropped his hand from Elisara's, his eyes returning to their usual glow of amber before fading to brown.

He looked up at Nyzaia, whose eyes scanned his. Uncertainty crossed her features.

"Please tell me you found something," Kazaar choked, tossing the mirror onto the bed and reaching again for Elisara's hand. Nyzaia grasped the collar of his shirt, and he flinched.

"I need to see something to be certain." Nyzaia pushed his head to the side, and his hair tumbled with it.

"Careful," Kazaar exclaimed as she yanked at his shirt. He flinched the moment she touched the sun that marked him. *Wrong*. It felt wrong for anyone but the woman lying before him to touch it. Nyzaia took a sharp breath, circling the bed and kneeling before him. She glanced at Elisara, settling her gaze on the moon-shaped scar on her collarbone.

"On Ithyion—"

"I do not want to hear of a forgotten kingdom, Nyzaia. I want to know how to wake my queen," he snapped. She narrowed her eyes at him, like she had so many times as bickering children.

"On *Ithyion*, there is a myth of celestial ties," she continued. "A book in father's office explains a link of sorts between two people that marks them." She looked pointedly at the sun on his chest. "Such markings are a blessing by the gods. It means your destinies are tied to one another."

Kazaar frowned. "What does a baseless myth have to do with waking up Elisara?"

"I would hardly call it baseless, given you both now carry a shared marking." Nyzaia tapped her fingers against her knees. "The text explains that once you are tied together by the merging of your essences, you share not only your powers but also your memories and minds."

Kazaar recalled all that had happened with his queen: the threads tying them together, the change in his powers, the flashes of altered memories in his mind. *Had they been hers?*

"So, let's assume this celestial tie is real. Did it say how to wake her should something like this happen?" It was the only answer Kazaar cared about. Yet when Nyzaia cast her eyes downward, he sighed and scrunched his eyes shut.

"It said the tie could grant you access to one another's minds," she whispered while Kazaar tapped his foot, blinking back frustrated tears. "Kazaar, look at me!" He blinked and met Nyzaia's eyes. "You need to try to reach her."

He analysed Elisara's face again, and her eyelids fluttered.

"How?" He rose from the small wooden chair and knelt beside Elisara. Reluctantly, he let go of her hand to stroke her hair, running his fingers through it like silk.

"Have you ever felt any connection to her before?" Nyzaia asked. Kazaar did not answer. If he were to finally speak those words aloud, only Elisara would hear them. "What were you thinking about when I entered earlier? When those strange powers floated around you both?"

He did not recall doing anything out of the ordinary except simply holding her hand and thinking only of her. *But then the memory appeared.*

"I do not know if I can do this with you in here, Nyzaia," Kazaar murmured. His fingers paved a trail down Elisara's face and paused inches from her collarbone.

"What if something goes wrong?"

"You will hear from the other side of the door." His eyes did not leave Elisara. If he looked up, he would see the conflict whirring in Nyzaia's gaze. Instead, he waited for her to accept his request and held his breath as she strode to the door. Only when the door clicked shut did he release it all in a shaky, panicked sigh. "Please,

Elisara," he whispered, resting his forehead against hers, finding her warming skin a comfort. He traced the raised moon on her collarbone, wishing for something—*anything*—to happen before grasping her hand once more.

"Please." At his whimper, the same memory flashed in his mind again. *The Unsanctioned Isle.* Kazaar focused, searching for something to tether himself to in the memory. Elisara's face was all he needed—she was all he needed. The familiar draw to Elisara yanked him forward until he tumbled headfirst into her soul.

"KAZAAR!" Elisara screamed. Kazaar watched from the sidelines as Elisara screamed at the past version of himself, hurling the Sword of Sonos in his direction. His past-self reached for it and pierced the blade through the creature's skull.

He knew what happened next, so instead of watching himself defeat the creature, he turned to Elisara, who used the steel sword as a crutch, hobbling to the other side of the throne room. Shadows forced his eyes to the opposite side of the room, where another Elisara watched. They were both there, watching their past selves interact. Why had this moment prevailed in her mind?

The shadows concealing Elisara pulled further away, revealing her red silk dress that would be forever engrained in his mind. Her eyes flickered from the memory to meet his. One moment, he watched the scene of them, and the next, he glanced back at Elisara, who was no longer there. When Kazaar glanced down again, Elisara watched him; they were both fully immersed in the present while their past selves faded into nothing.

Kazaar pulled Elisara to him and grasped her face.

"You need to wake up," he said, transfixed on her eyes as the bright blue glow faded to brown, and when Elisara frowned, her eyes changed again, a blazing white. It was as if the shadows threatened to ensnare and punish the man who had caused the invading darkness.

"Get out," she hissed, shoving him backward.

"Elisara!"

"I don't want you here!" she spat.

"You know," he pleaded. "You know I did not intend to hurt you." He reached for her again. "I have been waiting by your side for every passing second, desperate for you to wake."

Elisara's glare faltered at his words. "It is your fault I am here."

"Which is why I am here now." He stepped forward again until the pair were toe to toe. "I wanted to tell you. But this"—Kazaar gestured between them— "This is what I feared. You still hated me when I arrived in Vala. If I told you the truth then you would hate me even more." Kazaar reached for her face, but she slapped his hand away. "I am not going back without you," he choked. "I cannot go back without you."

"I said I do not want you here!" Elisara bit back. Kazaar scanned her eyes, sensing the lies beneath her words. He did not know how to lower her defences. Elisara spun and walked away, but Kazaar reached her in seconds, grasping her wrist and turning her toward him. Colliding with his chest, she faltered, offering Kazaar a brief opening to keep her there—to say anything to keep her with him.

"Really?" Kazaar towered over Elisara and tilted her chin, forcing her to meet his eyes. She swallowed, and as he leaned in, he felt the rush of Elisara's conflicting emotions and heard her racing heart.

"Then, why were you thinking about me?" Restraint hit him in the gut—Elisara's restraint. She was holding back, but holding back what? Her anger? Her feelings? Or simply her words? Betrayal overshadowed Elisara's restraint as she summoned air, readying to use it. He guessed her intentions and braced against the force of her wind, sliding a few feet instead of the entire throne room. He corrected his balance with his own air and flourished a hand to push her back. Using the powers he had hidden for so long felt right, as he used them only for her.

Kazaar knew she was hiding from the truth instead of confronting it. If she did not wish to relent, he could easily do the same instead of hiding his truth behind teasing. Elisara made a disgruntled noise, and Kazaar refrained from laughing. She took heavy, determined steps toward him while the sky behind her brightened. The walls remained lost, yet the night sky was awash with falling stars that cascaded behind her as she stormed toward him. The shadows and light surrounding them earlier returned. A halo effect formed around Elisara and blinded him with her beauty.

"I expect more from you, my queen," he said. Her expression wavered at his change in tone as if suspecting his tactics had changed. She narrowed her eyes and jabbed a finger into his chest. He tried not to react to her touch.

"Do not call me that," she snarled, curls of hair half falling before her face. "I am not *yours*."

Kazaar inhaled Elisara's intoxicating scent of lavender and fresh snow. Her eyes darkened, but not with the shadows haunting her gaze—no, he sensed the desire buried beneath her fury.

"Are you not?" He reached for her collarbone, where the moon marked her skin. "Are you not mine?" The power within them sparked as his nose brushed hers, and she reached for his chest. This is what he wanted but had tried so hard to prevent himself from having.

"You hurt me." Elisara's voice cracked. "How am I meant to trust you?" Stars fell around them and washed away the memory, and when Kazaar opened his eyes, he was beside Elisara again in his chambers. He sighed in relief as she blinked, staring up at him.

"I'll spend my life proving myself to you, angel."

Chapter Nine

Larelle

"Are you always going to beat me when we race?" Alvan called, finally catching up to Larelle. She glanced back at him and laughed, slowing her horse. She recalled their first race to The Bay before they discovered the truth about Riyas' death. Yet instead of sand beneath the horses' hooves now, they rode across pale grass, darkening into emerald and swaying in the light breeze as they reached Garridon's border. After crossing the bridge over the last river in Nerida, they would now follow its path until hitting the point at which the river's curve ran adjacent to Seley in the distance. The river's pull to her right felt odd with the dark forest treetops in the distance.

"Mumma is just better than you!" Zarya giggled. Larelle kissed the back of her daughter's head, who sat before her, clutching the horse's mane. Zarya refused to sit in the carriage and instead insisted on riding with her mother. Larelle did not mind. She tried to spend as much of her spare time with her daughter as possible, especially as she would see little of her once they reached Garridon's capital.

Larelle was surprised when she received a letter from Princess Sadira the previous night. While they intended to journey to Garridon for the engagement ball, she had not anticipated the future queen's wish for company in the days prior. *I understand if you have other duties,* the letter had read. *There is surely plenty more a queen must attend to than providing conversation to a princess new to her realm.*

Larelle read between the lines. The princess was lonely, and

Larelle knew all too well how it felt to be an outcast in society. She imagined adjusting to royal life was just as difficult, perhaps more so, for someone who knew the crown was their birthright yet had been kept from it.

Larelle opted to be cautious, given the attitude of Sadira's sister, Soren, towards the other rulers. Nevertheless, Larelle couldn't escape an innate sense that Sadira was different. The Neridian queen trusted her intuition when it came to people and their intentions. Perhaps that was why Larelle trusted her small circle of friends and why a weight lifted from her shoulders the moment she revealed the prophecy to Lillian, Alvan, and Olden.

The three were calm as she spoke, their expressions neutral. It was a far easier experience than when the Historian had revealed Novisia's history to Larelle and the other rulers or when they learned of the prophecy from Elisara and Kazaar. Of course, the group had many questions surrounding what they should do for their people. Alvan questioned Keres' capability to build more weapons; Lillian asked if Vala could harvest more healing water from their stalactites, while Olden remained quiet throughout the entirety of their discussions, gazing glassy-eyed across the dark ocean, the sun having set behind the clouds. When Alvan asked for his thoughts, Olden's answer would forever be engrained in Larelle's memory. The man she had come to know as a father turned to face her, his eyes bloodshot.

"He's really dead?"

Lillian had silently risen, with Alvan following; he departed with a comforting squeeze on Larelle's shoulder. For the rest of the evening, Larelle and Olden spoke of Riyas, sharing stories interspersed with tears and laughter. They spoke of Riyas regularly over the years, but there was a sense of closure in that moment after finally discovering the truth behind what they had always questioned.

Larelle felt the effects of the late evening as she yawned and tightened her hold on Zarya. Alvan smiled and increased his pace until they rode side by side. She wished Olden were here. He insisted the journey would be too much for him, yet perhaps he merely wished for time alone after the revelations about his son.

With their talk of Riyas, Larelle had not shared the Historian's warning, which lingered heavily on her mind. Chewing her lip, she turned the words over until a gentle, fleeting touch on her knee turned her head. Alvan furrowed his brow, his hazel eyes intent. She shook her head and glanced pointedly at a sleeping Zarya. Not even the sound of the guards galloping on either side of them on horseback disturbed her daughter's slumber.

Alvan was quick to suggest they stop overnight at his settlement in Seley to ensure neither Zarya nor Larelle were too exhausted from the journey. Larelle was happy to oblige, having little memory of the place bordering both Nerida and Garridon. Given its historical tendency to change hands over the years, Larelle had rarely visited as a child and never since becoming an adult.

She was intrigued to see the place where Alvan had grown up and learn more about the person she had become so close with.

"Can you remember the last time you visited?" he asked.

"Honestly? No." She blushed, and he chuckled.

"I am not offended," he reassured her. "If I, too, am being honest, I hated living in Seley for some time. Perhaps that is why I was so quick to take Riyas up on his offer to train on the ships with him." Alvan's features glowed beneath the sun, and Larelle focused on the subtle downturn of his lips and the rise and fall of his chest. He glanced away upon catching her staring and cleared his throat. She knew little of the events that took his parents, only that a fire had burned his home to cinders, taking them with it.

"Do you miss being here?" she asked. "You have spent so much time in Mera with me."

He instantly shook his head.

"No," he said. "Seley is small, and its people are self-sufficient. I do not have a relationship with them like the other lords in our realm. They do not need me to govern them unless a problem arises, which is rarely the case."

"What problems do you come across?"

"Occasional disputes arise about the price of wood, but I can do little about that. Garridon has always set the trading prices," he explained. "Other than that, the issues are trivial, like bickering between children." He laughed.

"There are other children?" Zarya mumbled, still half asleep. Larelle stroked her daughter's hair, careful to avoid the tiara. Zarya rarely wore it, but as this was their first visit since the coronation, Larelle thought it sensible.

"I'm sure all the children will want to play with you, Zarya," Alvan said, yet the princess said nothing else, having fallen asleep again.

"She will be up all evening now, no doubt," said Larelle.

"I'm sure the evening festivities will tire her enough."

"Festivities?"

"Surely you did not think I would host you in my home without a proper welcome and celebration?" Alvan raised a hand to his chest, feigning hurt. Larelle rolled her eyes.

"You know I do not need such things."

"You may not *need* them," he said as the small, stately home appeared in the distance, "but you deserve them." Larelle glanced away, rubbing her arm with a frown at the sudden flickering in her chest at Alvan's words. She switched her focus to the approaching home.

Alvan was right: Seley was a humble, quaint town, which, at a distance, reminded Larelle of the small villages sketched in Zarya's storybooks. It was a comforting place, offering slower days than the hustle and bustle in Mera or The Bay. As they drew closer, the stamps of the two realms were evident. While some homes were crafted with Nerida's pale bricks, others were built from wooden beams with thatched roofs, a typical feature of Garridon. She did not know which she preferred, and despite their stark differences, it worked. The stately home was equally mismatched like a brick castle and wooden lodge melded together. Pain bloomed in Larelle's chest as they drew closer. She realised its odd architecture was not purposeful but a result of its reconstruction after the fire.

While the ash had been washed from the stone building, the remainders of the tragedy remained where the bricks joined the newer, wooden stature of the home. It was unique, though, and there was beauty in uniqueness.

***

Everything in Alvan's home was unique, including the hall in which they now sat as they enjoyed the music and laughed alongside the people of Seley. The hall was like nowhere she had dined before. The wing was closest to the edge of Garridon's Hystone Forest, a canopy of trees shielding the revellers in place of a wooden rooftop. She wondered if they dined here during the colder months or if perhaps they knew of a distant relative to the Nerida royal line who could control the rain and keep it from falling.

Instead of lines and rows of tables, the carved wooden slabs formed a circular shape around a fountain in the centre of the hall. If one peered into the room from the branches of the trees above, it would appear like the ageing rings in a tree stump. Sitting this way created a feeling of togetherness, one Larelle wished to emulate back in Mera.

Alvan's grin was wide as he introduced Larelle to his friends, who embraced him upon his return. She met Mari and Zedon, a couple he had grown up with as children, Riordan, who owned the tavern on Garridon's side of Seley, and Nathaniel, who led the few guards on the estate. Each recited many entertaining stories of their late nights at the tavern together. As the laughter ebbed, with many turning in for the evening, Larelle kissed her daughter goodnight as Lillian took her to her chambers.

After bidding farewell to his friends, Alvan leaned down from where he stood behind Larelle and offered his arm. "I have somewhere to show you."

She froze. She did not expect her sudden hesitation. After all, it was normal for a lord to escort their queen. Larelle broke their gaze yet looped her arm through his, the silk of her ivory gown catching against the deep blue velvet of his jacket.

"Do you require our attendance, Your Majesty?" asked one of her guards as they reached the hall doors. Larelle shook her head politely.

"I will be okay with Lord Alvan. Please stand by the princess's room in the meantime." The guard bowed before exiting ahead of Larelle and Alvan. An unusual silence lingered between the pair as he escorted her from the hall.

They did not journey far. They turned down a short stone corridor housing immense open doors to the library on one side and large windows offering a view into the hall on the other. Turning the final corner, they reached a dead end, where only a locked door resided. Alvan loosened his arm from her grip to pull a set of keys from his inside pocket. *This is a secret place,* Larelle realised, *somewhere just for him.*

"I hope you do not mind all the stairs." Alvan smiled. It was nearly pitch black, except for the occasional lantern. The chill night air brushed against Larelle as they rounded the final steps. She could not help but gasp as she gazed at the view before them. The turret took them to a platform amongst the top of the canopies, placing the pair above the tree line. If it had been sunrise, she expected the rooftops of her castle would be clear across the horizon. She did not care for that now, though, enamoured instead by the view of Hystone Forest. It was not pitch-black like she expected. Thousands of yellow lights floated among the leaves and stretched across the horizon, a blanket of golden stars reflecting the night sky.

"Fireflies," Alvan murmured, leaning onto the wooden railing inches from Larelle's side.

"It is breathtaking," she breathed.

"Indeed." Larelle turned her head to find him watching her with a soft smile on his lips, the light of the nearby fireflies illuminating the sparkle in his eyes. Larelle blushed and looked back at the view. She wriggled her fingers as one of the small creatures landed on her skin.

"I sensed there was more you wished to discuss after last night," Alvan prompted, and Larelle lowered her head, her curls falling to mask her expression. Her heart skipped as he reached out, tucking the hair behind her ear.

"You can tell me," he said.

Larelle looked up then, her face inches from his. He dropped his hand, brushing it against the silk of her sleeves as he stepped back and cleared his throat.

"Y-yes," she stammered, facing the view once more. She straightened. "There was something else—something the Historian told me." She searched for any doubt—any reason not to tell him—but felt only unwavering trust for the man beside her. "He visited me; that is why I left the meeting."

"He came to the castle?" Alvan asked. "He never leaves the Neutral City." Larelle hummed her agreement.

"He had a fear he wished to get off his chest." Larelle picked at the skin around her fingers, and Alvan reached for her again.

"Larelle," he said softly. "Please, unburden yourself." She glanced sideways at him, spurred on by the softness of his expression.

"He told me we cannot trust Kazaar," she said, and Alvan frowned.

"Queen Elisara's commander?"

Larelle nodded. "He informed me of something he read in a history book once. At first, he recited the final lines of the prophecy, but then he added two new lines. *Watch for the dark one that will bring suffering to all. The rise of old power, the Kingdom will fall.*" She studied Alvan's reaction but saw only confusion as he leaned against the railing.

"What does that have to do with Kazaar?"

"The Historian said he sensed his dark power when we were last at the temple."

Alvan stared out across the treetops, and Larelle waited while he processed this new information. "It is just one man's word with no proof. We cannot take it as fact."

"It would be an odd thing to lie about, though," Larelle countered. Alvan made a noise of agreement.

"Will you tell him or the other rulers?" he asked. Larelle embraced herself against the chill. "That's what you are so uncertain about." He sighed and reached for Larelle's waist, turning her to face him. "Larelle, you are wise; you have a natural instinct for things." Larelle avoided his gaze, uneasy at the compliment until Alvan moved her head to look at him with a gentle touch. "It is difficult being queen. I imagine it has been even more difficult bearing this secret, and I am honoured you trust me enough to share it. I trust you will make the decision you deem best. If you decide to keep this to yourself, I am here as your lord. If you decide to tell the other rulers, I am here as your confidant, and if you decide to wait and gather more information, I am here as your friend." Alvan stepped closer, brushing his hand against hers. Larelle did not move, holding her breath.

"Whatever it is," he said, his breath tickling her face. "I am always here."

Chapter Ten

Elisara

Elisara stared into the eyes of the man she had trusted, a man she could no longer deny her feelings for. How could she when he inundated every thought in her mind? He was everywhere. He was everything. Yet a part of her did not want him near, reminded by betrayal—not only his but the betrayal of her parents, particularly her mother, who not only had an affair with the king of Keres but conspired with him to set the explosion. The revelations bombarded Elisara, as did her warped memories. Yet one constant remained. *Him.*

"I'll spend my life proving myself to you, *angel*." His voice softened. *Angel.* Elisara did not react to him comparing her to the creatures of beauty foretold in children's stories, nor did she ask why he called her that, nor accept his declaration. She did not melt at his feet like he probably expected. Instead, a rush of emotions overwhelmed her, yet she focused on only one. Rage. Rage at her mother, the late King Razik, the gods and their damned prophecy, and Kazaar for looking at her with such longing as if he would offer her the world on a platter. Lightning struck outside the chambers. She did not recognise her whereabouts, but from the colours of the sheets and the mosaic on the floor, she assumed they were still in Keres, no longer trapped in the confines of her mind. Elisara stared at her reflection in the darkness of his eyes, the white light ebbing within her own.

"Your power does not scare me, angel." He raised his hand to stroke his thumb along her jaw, a flame flickering in response to the lightning she conjured. She tried not to react to the flame's white glow, retaining a neutral expression despite the comfort of the flame and the stirring within her at his new nickname.

"Do not fucking call me that," she hissed.

Neither made any attempt to move from their position. Elisara remained on the bed, and from its scent, she knew it once belonged to him. And there he knelt, Kazaar Elharar, the man who bowed to no one yet was on his knees before her, stroking her jaw.

"What would you rather I call you?" He hummed. "Angel?" He trailed his hand down her neck. "Elisara?" His fingers danced through her hair until skimming her collarbone. "My undoing?" he breathed, his thumb brushing against a spot that made her shiver. "Because that is what you are, Elisara. Knowing I hurt you, seeing the emotion in your eyes when we fought, and the agonising wait while I watched your chest rise and fall, fearing it may stop at any second... You strip away all my pretences. My mind is coming undone at your hand, and I have never feared for someone else before you. How am I to command at your side and lead armies if everything that makes me feared by others can be undone with just one look from you? What do I call you when you make me feel all that?" Elisara pulled herself together, burying the tears welling at the tenderness and raw honesty in his words.

"How about my queen?" she sneered, pushing him away as she stood. She stomped past him until pausing at the archway overlooking the Ashun Desert. Her legs wavered as she gripped the stone railing, unprepared for her weakness upon waking. Narrowing her eyes, she admired her power as lightning struck the sands. For once, she cared only about wielding it. Sensing his presence behind her, she felt the whisper of his scent floating to her on the Keres breeze. She peered up at the stars and prayed to Vala—or any god—to instil her with the strength to either forgive or forget this man.

"I thought you were not mine to have?" he whispered in the shell of her ear, his hand hesitantly reaching towards her. Elisara swallowed and leaned back against him; her body betrayed her.

Kazaar snaked his arm around her waist. It seemed the gods did not care for her wishes.

"I am not," she whispered. Elisara felt her heart beating in tandem with his as Kazaar stroked her abdomen in silent reassurance.

"*You don't sound certain.*"

Elisara pulled away instantly, flattening her back against the pillar of the archway. Kazaar's eyes were wide and mirrored hers, a confirmation she had not imagined his voice in her head.

"Was that in your—"

"*Mind.*" His voice rang through her head.

"Get out of my head!" she screamed. Kazaar stepped back, raking his hands through his dishevelled hair.

"Elisara, I have as little understanding as you do of what in the gods name is happening here." He locked his hands behind his head and paced the room.

"What did you do to me?" she demanded, flinching as pain pierced her chest, reflecting the pain in his expression. "The last thing I remember is—"

"*The essence of our power merging.*" The silkiness of his voice caressed her mind.

"Stop doing that!" she shouted again. Lightning flashed behind her, and ice crawled from her feet.

"I cannot stop *thinking*, Elisara!" Kazaar snapped and stopped his pacing.

She narrowed her eyes at him, channelling the thought as a shout. "*Try!*"

He returned her glare. "*Do you wish for a screaming match in our heads?*"

Elisara stormed towards him, yet with what intent she did not know. She halted after glimpsing his collarbone beneath his shirt. She only now noticed that it was undone, revealing his muscular chest and abdomen.

"What is that?" She grabbed his collar and pulled him to her for a closer examination of the raised mark on his collarbone. She felt drawn to it, tracing the raised sun gently with her fingers. Kazaar shivered and clenched his mouth shut as he looked down at her. She recalled her earlier reaction to his touch and stepped back immediately, turning to the tall mirror propped in the corner of the room.

Elisara analysed her skin while trailing the moon's outline on her chest. Draping the gold chains of her dress to one side, she flipped her hair to the other, too mesmerised by the mark to acknowledge Kazaar's presence behind her. His hands delicately moved to hold the chain, allowing her to inspect the mark more closely. She glanced up at him, noting the sun on his skin and its stark difference from the dark inkings covering the rest of his body.

"*What is happening to us?*" Elisara asked silently, blinking rapidly as she glanced between the two marks. She balled her fists into her skirts to dampen her rising panic and quickening breaths.

"I do not know, angel."

Elisara closed her eyes momentarily and jumped as Kazaar's hand returned to her waist, holding her still against him. She tried not to think about the melding of their bodies as tendrils of shadow and silvery white pooled at their feet and kissed her bare legs. At his touch, power hummed under her skin, reminding Elisara of their moment in the alcove.

"*They did not hurt you last time.*" While unusual in her mind, she found comfort in the closeness of Kazaar's voice. Elisara watched his eyes in the mirror, trained on the shadows. She believed him. Nothing felt dangerous about the tendrils twisting around her body. In fact, it felt as though they called to her.

"Last time?"

"While you were sleeping."

The tendrils tickled at her elbow, and she lifted her hand from where it had gravitated to Kazaar's. Twisting her arm before her, wisps of light and dark twisted until encircling her arm like an intricately woven piece of fabric, warming her.

"What does it mean?" she asked aloud this time.

"Nyzaia read something," he said cautiously. "About celestial ties."

Elisara frowned and gripped his wrist as the tendrils climbed higher around them while he traced soothing circles on her waist. "Apparently, these markings signify a shared destiny between us, tying us together."

Elisara scoffed. "And why should we believe that?"

Kazaar locked eyes with her in the mirror, pursing his lips.

"*It also said it allowed the two people access into one another's mind.*"

"*Tied?*"

"*Together,*" Kazaar confirmed.

How can I possibly live while tied to a man who has lied to me from the moment we met? Elisara stepped forward, breaking contact with him. The shadows and light ebbed, replaced with a sudden coldness.

"How many times must I apologise until you forgive me?" Kazaar asked as Elisara began pacing, creating further distance between them. Now and then, she glanced at him and changed direction. Kazaar lied to Elisara about the truth of his powers, despite knowing the pain she experienced from previous betrayals. Elisara covered her eyes, rubbed her face, and switched direction, the tiles cold beneath her feet. His only justification was not wishing to hurt her. Elisara swallowed the frustrated scream rising in her throat. She was in two minds, wanting to hurt him for the secrets he had kept while also wishing to collapse into his arms and believe all the sweet things he said.

"I did not lie to you, angel. I just did not tell you."

"That is the same thing," Elisara snapped, spinning to face him. With a wave of her hand, icicles formed midair and launched in Kazaar's direction. He flourished his own hand, and they parted around him, shattering against the wall.

"And what would you have done if I had told you the truth the moment I arrived in Vala?" he asked, stepping towards her. His shirt blew open further in the breeze. "Would you have trusted me then?" Elisara made a disgruntled noise as he continued towards her. "Tell me, my queen, when would have been the correct time to tell you? When would you have reacted in a more positive manner than this?" His voice adopted a taunting lilt, prompting Elisara to cross her arms. "Exactly, you do not know! I wanted to tell you, angel, but I was waiting until we were—"

"Were what?" she asked, scanning his gaze.

"Friends." He gritted his teeth.

"That's what you wish to be?" she asked. Something inside Elisara flickered with disappointment as he took a final step and tilted her chin to look at him. "Friends?"

"I will be whatever you wish," he murmured. "As long as I am something."

"You are something," she said, her eyes watering. A realisation hit her then. She could not forget this man, that she would be forced to forgive him. Slowly, he pulled her to him, offering an opportunity for Elisara to pull back. A contented sigh sounded from his lips when she did not. As his arms wrapped around her, Elisara nestled her head against his shoulder.

"I meant what I said. I will spend my entire life proving myself to you, angel." He brushed her hair behind her ear. "I will do whatever you ask—whatever you wish or need from me."

"Why do you keep calling me that?" she asked.

"Because that is how you looked when you laid there with this celestial tie binding us together. You looked like an angel: serene, beautiful, powerful." He smiled, and the memory flashed in her mind.

"Then what does that make you?" She instinctively reached for his arm to trail her fingers along his inkings.

"Perhaps your demon."

"That sounds like you would taint me," she said, as images of herself in the alcove flashed through her mind—*Kazaar's* memories.

"I could certainly taint you for any other," he whispered, gliding his hands up her bare back.

The door to the chambers slammed open, and Vlad rushed in with Nyzaia, Helena, Vigor, and Talia in tow.

"She's awake then," said Nyzaia, glancing between Elisara and Kazaar with a straight face. The pair quickly parted.

"Eli!" Vlad rushed forward, laughing, and pulled Elisara into an embrace. When the temperature in the room plummeted, Vlad pulled back. "Are you okay?"

Elisara gave a tight nod and glanced in Kazaar's direction. She had not been the one to lower the temperature.

I might have to pull rank if he touches you again. Elisara ignored the protective edge to his voice and the shiver his words traced up her spine. She turned her back on him.

"I'm fine," she said to Vlad, though he clearly did not believe her. She cocooned her arms around herself. For a moment, nobody spoke.

"They all wonder what happened."

"I know." She glared at Kazaar, and Nyzaia narrowed her eyes, glancing between them. Elisara avoided her gaze.

"Stay out of my head," she warned him.

"Worried about what I might see?" Elisara blushed as every memory of them together invaded her senses. Could he really see those? The darkening of his eyes answered her question.

Nyzaia cleared her throat. "I assume I was right," she said.

"Right about what?" Helena stepped around Nyzaia, her white-blonde hair a stark opposite to the Keres queen. Vigor rolled up the sleeves of his shirt and laid a leather case on the table, opening it to reveal rows of vials. That was why Kazaar had summoned them, in case she did not wake. Talia leaned against the wall behind Nyzaia. Unlike Helena, the pair were rather similar in looks. Talia picked her leg up and rested one of her feet on the wall behind her, giving Kazaar a once-over. Elisara refrained from rolling her eyes. She was always so distrustful.

"It's a long story." Elisara embraced Helena, and over her shoulder, she watched Talia approach.

"Your guard dog could have given us more details. We were worried," Talia said, giving Elisara a briefer hug before Vigor took over.

"What happened?" He guided Elisara back to Kazaar's bed while her mind wondered about how many other women had laid there.

"*None.*"

She glanced sideways at Kazaar and then faced the room with a sigh.

"Where should I begin?" she said.

Chapter Eleven

Nyzaia

Kazaar and Elisara were keeping secrets. They retold the events of yesterday evening to Nyzaia and Elisara's friends: the essence of their powers merging, the marks on their skin, the memories they shared. Nyzaia revealed what she had learned about the celestial tie, too, and though neither confirmed if they could hear each other's thoughts, she suspected they did. The only missing piece of information was what disagreement had caused the pair to turn on one another.

"What happened in the lead-up to this?" asked Nyzaia, straight to the point. When Elisara and Kazaar shared a look, she rolled her eyes. Would this happen from here on out, with the pair consulting in their minds before sharing anything with the others? Kazaar never used to keep secrets from her.

"I trust Helena, Vigor, and Talia with what we"—Elisara nodded to Nyzaia and Kazaar—"*know*, but are you happy for them to be told?"

Nyzaia understood what Elisara was implying.

"I have already told Farid and Tajana," she said plainly, and though Elisara's brow furrowed, she said no more.

"We know who set the explosion," said Kazaar, and a chorus of "who?" sounded across the room.

Elisara fiddled with the hem of her gown as she sat cross-legged on Kazaar's bed with him perched on a chair beside her. She looked directly at Nyzaia when she said, "My mother and your father—"

"They were lovers," Nyzaia finished.

"How did you know?" asked Kazaar.

"I saw the hidden room in his office while searching for the book to wake Elisara."

"It is not just that, Nyzaia." Elisara glanced at Kazaar, who nodded gently. "They also set the explosion."

Nobody spoke then. What was anyone to say upon discovering two rulers of different realms had killed not only themselves but all the ruling families and their children, too? Nyzaia digested the information yet was unsurprised her father was the cause of her suffering. She was only crowned queen because of that explosion. She cared little about discovering he had a lover or even that it was the late Queen Vespera; Nyzaia cared only that, even in death, he had ruined her life, stripped away her freedom and taken the one good thing in her life. The Red Stones. He had stripped it all from Nyzaia despite forcing that life on her to begin with.

"Why?" asked Talia.

"There was a letter. We can retrieve it," said Elisara. "They were trying to trigger the prophecy, but we do not know why."

Nyzaia scoffed and rose abruptly, the bangles clinking against her wrists. "So, yet again, there are more secrets and mysteries to solve."

"Nyzaia." Kazaar rose to meet her.

"Don't," she snapped. "I am tired of knowing nothing of this life despite my sacrifices."

"We have all lost someone or something, Nyzaia," Elisara countered. A flash of power burned in Elisara's eyes like it often did when she was angry. Nyzaia said nothing.

"I could retrieve the letter. Maybe fresh eyes would help?" Talia suggested.

"I can go with her," offered Helena.

Nyzaia sighed but nodded.

"My guard, Farid, can escort you. He is outside." Nyzaia opened the door for them and collided with Tajana for the second time that day.

"There you are," Tajana said cheerfully, flicking her braid over one shoulder. "I've put the books in your chambers." Tajana's smile wavered as she peered into the room and at the people inside it.

"Where is Farid?" Nyzaia asked.

"Here," called the deep voice of her guard, walking down the corridor. "There were reports of issues between Lord Israar and some servants." Nyzaia groaned at the thought of running into the lord. "Tajana asked me to intervene," he added, glancing oddly at the captain of the Guard.

"Now that you are here, could you escort Talia and Helena to my father's office?" asked Nyzaia, stepping aside to allow the two women through. Tajana offered an awkward smile. She was never good with new people.

"You can stay with us," Nyzaia began.

"It is okay, my love. I need to complete my usual inspection of the general guards' quarters." Tajana leaned in to kiss Nyzaia's cheek, who accepted it, knowing Lord Israar was likely still in the courtyard if Farid had been with him moments ago. Nyzaia watched Tajana walk away.

"I would quite like to be alone," called Elisara. "Would you mind guiding me back to my chambers and finding somewhere for Vigor?" she asked.

Nyzaia glanced back and nodded, noting the intent stare between Elisara and Kazaar before the Vala queen rose and left the room, taking Nyzaia's hand.

***

Elisara said little to Nyzaia, who guided her back through Tabheri palace until reaching the guest chambers. She wanted to ask more about the celestial tie and what had unfolded between Elisara and Kazaar. Nyzaia was certain something else had happened, as the pair were terrible at hiding the tension between them. It reminded

Nyzaia of when she and Tajana had first begun seeing one another, and their failed attempts to hide their relationship from the syndicate. The men had all bet on when they would finally confess to it.

Nyzaia could not remember the last time she and Tajana shared such heated tension or even the last time they were intimate; the moment after Nyzaia's coronation barely counted. With all the recent revelations, Nyzaia craved a constant—someone to always rely on. Why should she care what the lords thought? Would the people really dissent if they knew she was with Tajana? Nyzaia tried to calculate how many people might know Tajana was from the Red Stones as she strode to the guards' quarters to find her. She would suggest they spend the day together.

The palm trees swayed in the morning sun. Nyzaia had lost many hours of sleep, and though it had only been two days since Elisara and Kazaar had arrived, it felt like weeks.

Descending the tile steps of the palace entrance, Nyzaia crossed the courtyard to where the guards' quarters were located, and the horse and carriage remained tied up. Intricate gold markings and ornamental pieces blinded against the deep burgundy of the coach. Lord Israar was still here.

The guards' quarters were quiet when she approached. It should be loud on an inspection day, given over a hundred guards were stationed at the palace. Nyzaia slowed her steps. There was nobody here apart from the two men guarding the doors.

"Have you seen the captain?" she asked. The pair straightened.

"No, my queen," one responded.

"She said she was inspecting the guards' quarters; does that happen later? Am I early?" The two guards shared a look before one began to stammer.

"The quarters' inspections are only once a week, my queen."

"It was yesterday, my queen," said the other. Nyzaia maintained composure and suppressed the urge to clench her fists.

"I must have misheard her, thank you." Nyzaia turned and hurried back up the steps of the courtyard. She had not misheard, and as she rounded another corridor, she groaned.

"Queen Nyzaia," called Lord Israar.

Plastering a fake smile on her face, she greeted him through gritted teeth. "Lord Israar."

"Can I accompany you?" he asked.

"I am only returning to my chambers."

"Then please." He offered his arm with a forced smile, a flash of gold teeth glinting at the edges. No matter how gentlemanly Lord Israar appeared to others, the tainted calculation in his eyes was clear. He looked her up and down. "Lead the way."

Nyzaia sighed and took his arm. Wisely, she led him away from her actual quarters and towards her mother's old rooms.

"Have you thought any more about my proposal?" he asked, wasting no more time with formalities.

"Honestly, Lord Israar." Nyzaia paused, trying to place her words carefully. "I do not see a threat to my rule if I were to have Tajana as my legal consort."

The lord hummed and stroked his oily beard, pulling her to a stop by a balcony overlooking the oasis at the back of the palace before meeting the canyons. Nyzaia clenched her jaw and tugged her arm free of his hand.

"So, you have no concerns for your image but also none about her?"

"Should I?" Nyzaia countered. Lord Israar met her eyes with a smirk before placing his arms on either side of Nyzaia to grip the balcony, penning her in. Nyzaia jerked back until her hair dangled over the balcony.

"You tell me," he whispered in her ear before striding off. Nyzaia watched him leave, overcome by confusion. When she was certain he was gone, she turned back to look over the balcony and tapped a rhythm on the burnt-orange stone. She paused upon spotting Tajana. She crossed through the oasis towards the canyons, glancing behind her as she did. Other than the Red Stones' den, little resided in the canyons, except for the occasional runaway felon or orphans attempting to cross into a new realm. She seemed nervous. Nyzaia narrowed her eyes, a gut feeling stirring within.

Tajana was hiding something.

***

Stupid clothes, Nyzaia thought, trying to untangle herself from the skirts of her lehenga. Once she was naked, she secured her dark locks upon her head with a blood-red ribbon. She was exhausted and looked it. Nyzaia prodded the dark shadows below her eyes before striding for the hot bath in the open morning air outside her chambers. She groaned, sinking into its depths.

"There's a sound I like to hear." With her solace interrupted, she watched Tajana enter the chambers and strip off her clothes. Nyzaia followed her naked form as she confidently strode to the bath, descending the mosaic-tiled steps into the water. If Nyzaia was not so angry about Tajana's lie, she would admire her curves and the smoothness of her skin. Instead, she pursed her lips and stared ahead.

"What's wrong?" asked Tajana. Nyzaia lifted her foot and placed it between Tajana's breasts to keep her from wading closer. Tajana smirked. "Are we playing a game?"

Nyzaia's eyes glowed, and the flames in the sconces rose behind her.

"I'll take that as a no then," said Tajana, beginning to massage Nyzaia's foot. "Tell me what I have done."

"You lied to me."

Tajana's head jerked up to meet Nyzaia's eyes, though Nyzaia could not read her expression. "When?" Nyzaia was no fool; she was accustomed to dissecting words. Tajana did not deny it.

"You said you were visiting the guards' quarters, yet you were not there." Nyzaia tried to pull her foot away, but Tajana held it firmly in place. "Then, Lord Israar and I watched you skulking back to the palace from the canyons." Tajana narrowed her eyes.

"Lord Israar?" she asked, a sharp tone in her voice. "He is around here often." Nyzaia glanced away, and Tajana dropped her foot. "What is going on with you?"

"What is going on with *you*?" Nyzaia snapped. Steam now rose between the pair, dampening their faces and hair. Tajana's face softened.

"I did not want to worry you, but there are stirrings amongst the Red Stones," she confessed, reaching for the soap. She raised Nyzaia's leg and began washing. "They need a leader, Nyzaia, and sadly, you can no longer fill that role." Nyzaia pulled away in protest. "They need someone permanent, so I have been helping them to narrow down candidates for trial."

"Trial?"

"Yes, it is how you were chosen, and Arjun Qadir before you."

Nyzaia scoffed. "He did not exactly abide by the rules."

"No, he never did, and look where it landed him." Tajana took Nyzaia's next leg and slid the soap along it. Nyzaia ignored the rising sensations stirred from her touch.

"So, you are mediating. Is that all?"

"That is all," Tajana confirmed. "Now, you and Israar..." Tajana looked at Nyzaia with a suggestive look in her eyes.

"God no!" Nyzaia spluttered. The thought of his oily hands touching her made her feel nauseous.

"Then what is it if he does not wish to bed you?"

Nyzaia sighed as Tajana glided the soap up the remainder of her thigh. Hooking Nyzaia's knee over her shoulder, Tajana discarded the soap and stroked water over her skin to wash away the suds.

"He does not think I should be with you," she relented, gasping as Tajana's nails pinched her skin as she pulled Nyzaia closer, pressing her against the cold wall of the bath. Tajana leaned in.

"And why is that?" Tajana whispered. Nyzaia stifled a groan, and Tajana smiled against her ear. "Why, Nyzaia?" she repeated, gripping Nyzaia's thigh in one hand while the other trailed her abdomen below the surface until reaching the peak of her nipples. She pinched, and Nyzaia failed to keep quiet. "Why?"

"He knows you're a part of the Red Stones," she relented, tilting her head back as Tajana's mouth moved from her ear to her breast, taking her nipple in her mouth. She squirmed and reached for Tajana's hips. Tajana raised her head and brushed her thigh between Nyzaia's legs, pushing against her and gripping her hands.

"And does he know what I would do to him if anyone tried to take you from me?" Tajana asked. Nyzaia swallowed hard as Tajana's hand moved from her wrist to the apex of her thigh. She circled a finger between her legs, never quite meeting the spot Nyzaia so desperately craved. Tajana's other hand moved, tugging at Nyzaia's hair tied in the ribbon.

"Does he think that anyone else could make you feel the things I do?" asked Tajana. She whimpered and reached for Tajana's breasts while Tajana tugged at Nyzaia's ribbon, freeing her hair, which cascaded down her back. Roughly, Tajana grabbed Nyzaia's hands, pulling them above her head and licking the column of her neck in the process. She looked intently into Nyzaia's eyes as she tied the ribbon around her wrists. "Can anyone else make you feel this way, my love?" asked Tajana, her fingers returning to the spot between Nyzaia's thighs.

"No," Nyzaia whimpered. Tajana chuckled against Nyzaia's neck and lifted her until she sat on the edge of the bath, spreading her legs wide.

"And will you tell him that?" Tajana asked. Nyzaia leaned back until she lay flat against the tiles, her wrists tied above her head. Tajana kissed the insides of her thighs while two fingers teased her entrance, waiting for an answer.

"Yes." Nyzaia arched off the wet tiles as Tajana pushed her fingers inside her.

"Good," Tajana said, and Nyzaia closed her eyes, relishing in the sensation of Tajana's hands and tongue. How could she ever doubt

Tajana and the love between them?

Chapter Twelve

Elisara

"You are his star." Under the heat of the Ashun Desert sun, Elisara replayed one of the final things her mother said to her. All along, she knew she would die at her own hand and send the other rulers to their deaths. Had her father known? Or was he, too, betrayed and sent to his death alongside Elisara's sisters? Fury bubbled in Elisara's blood as she pictured her mother and the tormenting sound of her voice. Turning the words over, she stared at the back of Kazaar's head. With the oddity of their relationship—the sun, the moon, *celestial*—she wondered if a double meaning had existed in her mother's words that day.

Had she known of this ancient tie binding her and Kazaar? Elisara had believed the only mystery was discovering who plotted the deaths of the royal families in Novisia. Now, however, she found that mysteries seemed never-ending. Perhaps the mystery of mysteries was their infinite nature.

Elisara rode at the back of the group, having been the last to arrive in the palace courtyard before leaving Tabheri, in a bid to avoid alone time with Kazaar. Her fear had kept her from succumbing to his gentle caresses when she had awoken and from following the tie in their minds down dark corridors to find him during the night.

Despite being so far from Kazaar, she felt him. Neither Nyzaia nor her syndicate, Vlad, Helena, Vigor, or Talia, could create enough distance from him. She was foolish to hope distance would somehow erase his all-consuming presence in her mind, as though he was the ocean drowning her beneath his waves, never allowing her time to breathe.

Last night, Elisara needed space, the ability to breathe and gain clarity despite the invisible string tugging her back to Kazaar with every step she took towards her chambers. She had not uttered a word to Nyzaia, not because she couldn't think of anything to say after the evening's revelations but because all she could think about was him. His memories of her were entangled with her own, and with every light that flickered as she walked, a new memory emerged: Elisara on her throne, driving a dagger into the table as Kazaar arrived; Elisara sleeping on the Unsanctioned Isle with her back to him, her expression as he handed over his Keres sigil ring. Elisara could not escape him, though she found she did not want to.

Eventually, when Elisara lay on the silk sheets of her chambers, staring up at the canopy, her vision switched to his bed—his chambers. She tried to shake his presence, but Kazaar forced her to acknowledge his recollection of events. So, she did. Still in her red dress from the ball, she watched the moment they first met, his thoughts after saving Caellum, and his emotions as he found her that evening after Izaiah attacked. She felt it all. Tears rolled down her cheeks as he exposed his pain hidden behind the locked doors of his mind. Elisara did not know much about Kazaar's upbringing, though she assumed he was not ready to share it.

The next memory he shared was their quiet moment on the balcony in Nerida. She recognised it immediately, but seeing and feeling it from his point of view was different. Elisara heard Kazaar's thoughts after he declared to spend his life proving himself as her commander; a war raged in his mind, and experiencing it was like standing in the centre of a brewing storm. The desire to tell Elisara he wielded all four elements was overwhelmed by another emotion—fear.

Elisara hated her longing to forgive him despite the hurt infiltrating her very being. Perhaps she was destined for betrayal. After all, they were never-ending: when her parents sent her to Keres, the royals' secrets about the truth of Ithyion and the creatures,

Caellum kissing another woman before spewing his hateful words. It felt like every new day brought a new secret or betrayal, keeping her from returning to the way things were.

Those memories played at the forefront of her mind as they travelled to Garridon for her former lover's engagement ball. She hoped she could conceal her frustration at having to attend. But through it all was Kazaar and his promise: *"I'll spend my life proving myself to you, angel."*

"I meant it." His voice rang through Elisara's mind, returning her focus to the journey ahead. She narrowed her eyes at the back of his dark locks from where he rode several horses ahead.

"I do not care." She thought, and she could have sworn a smirk appeared in her mind. She ignored how he could likely see right through her pretences.

"If you do not care, why are all your thoughts of us?"

"I'm trying to determine a way to wipe them from my memory." A laugh rumbled through her mind then, rich and deep. She shifted in her saddle as the laugh trickled down her spine.

"You might need to try harder." An image of them in the alcove flashed in her mind: his feather-light strokes against her golden garter and the brush of his lips against her ear. Elisara blushed and shifted in her saddle again, ignoring the rising emotion as she recalled his lips inches from hers when he claimed she would be his undoing.

"Perhaps I am only overwhelmed by you because of this gods damned tie," she thought.

"I would not damn the gods who bestowed the tie if I were you." A playful lilt sounded in his voice as though he believed her hatred to be a game.

"I will 'damn' whoever I like if it means escaping you."

"I would damn whoever dared take you from me." Elisara gulped at the gravelly tone of his voice and watched the muscles flex in his back as he rolled his shoulders. He turned to catch her eye with a glint in his own, and she looked away, staring at Helena's smirk

instead.

"What?" Elisara said with an exasperated sigh. Helena looked pointedly to the commander ahead and then back at Elisara.

"You know what." Helena swept her white, blond hair back, dusted with red sand. "I knew he cared the moment he asked about you after the incident in the springs." Elisara nudged her as the two rode side-by-side on horseback.

"You did not," Elisara muttered.

"Nyzaia mentioned something about you two being able to hear one another's thoughts. Is that true?" Elisara glanced away, and Helena laughed. "I will take that as a yes." Elisara wondered if the other rulers should know of this development between her and Kazaar, though she trusted her friends would say nothing of it until she decided what to do. Yet she trusted many people once.

"*It is your decision*," said Kazaar.

"Stop eavesdropping!"

"Stop projecting your thoughts so loudly, then."

"Are you doing it right now?" Helena asked. "What is he saying?"

"Nothing important," Elisara grumbled.

"That doesn't surprise me. Most men think of nothing except swords, drink, and their cocks," Talia called over her shoulder from where she rode behind Kazaar.

"Talia!" Helena scolded. "You should not eavesdrop nor generalise in such a vulgar manner."

"She's not wrong," laughed Vlad, dropping back to join the group.

"I would like to remove myself from such a generalisation," requested Vigor, and Helena flashed him a sweet smile as he reached over to squeeze her thigh. Elisara smiled. She could not recall the last time they had all been together, particularly as Vlad was absent during the incident at the springs.

Elisara was struck by the difference in her life since then. Ruling Vala and deciphering the prophecy encompassed all else. These were the people who had shaped Elisara when she returned from Keres, and yet, she continued to neglect them.

"They do not see it that way," Kazaar reassured her.

"How do you know?"

"Because they came when I called."

Elisara glanced down at the reins in her hands and turned over his words. She relished in their laughter, smiling as she half-listened to their words. The other half of her focused on their surroundings, watching the Ashun Desert sands rising in the breeze, reminiscent of the black, sparkling sands of the Unsanctioned Isle. She wondered if she would ever return and pondered the two thrones that bore the markings of the sun and moon. She rubbed her collarbone, the loose white shirt thin against the raised mark.

Darkness darted on her left, and Elisara whipped her head to face it. She could have sworn a shadow trailed into her vision yet found nothing, only the distant rocks forming Nefere Valley. She faced the front again to where the palm trees lining Khami approached. The precession slowed.

Elisara had never visited Khami. Long ago, she would have preferred to ride late into the night until reaching Antor. She was unsure whether her preference to remain in Keres was to do with avoiding her—until recently—betrothed or because the wrongness she once felt clouding her in the fire realm had dissipated. Now she felt indifferent to it.

The sun sunk in the horizon, casting an orange glow over the pale estate and Nyzaia and Kazaar who rode ahead. Why could Kazaar so easily hear her thoughts, but she struggled to detect his? She watched the two converse back and forth and frowned as Kazaar tensed. Elisara closed her eyes and thought only of him.

"I cannot tell you," was all she heard him say to Nyzaia. She wondered what secrets he kept from his closest friend and if it was also something he had not shared with Elisara. Nyzaia redirected her horse.

"Will you dine with me tonight?" she asked Elisara, who raised her eyebrows. "I expected neither of us had the energy to entertain, and I would much rather keep away from the public eye. It is the first time I have visited Khami as queen, and I know it will be a spectacle if I host—"

"Of course," Elisara said.

"I feel we have been distant since—"

"That is my fault," Elisara reassured her. "I have been… adjusting."

Nyzaia smiled.

"Then allow me to help you adjust. We can have an evening with laughter and drinks and forget about our other halves for a while." Nyzaia reached for Elisara and squeezed her shoulder. *Other half.* She was not sure she and Kazaar were two halves in the same way Nyzaia and Tajana were, but she did not wish to speak more of him right now. Elisara glanced at Tajana, who from up ahead had turned to find Nyzaia.

"That would be lovely," Elisara said. Perhaps for the first time since the gods had tainted her with this tie, Elisara would be able to forget about him. Kazaar caught her eye, the two nearly side-by-side as they approached the archway marking the entrance to Khami. She did not need to hear his thoughts; they were clear from the look in his eyes. She would never be without him.

Chapter Thirteen

Nyzaia

Nyzaia felt oddly sentimental as they arrived in Khami, though only Farid appeared to notice; her syndicate did not. She could not deny the hurt that neither Tajana nor the rest of her syndicate had referenced their time here together, yet the Red Stones rarely shared their feelings. Since leaving that way of life behind, Nyzaia realised how much of a front one had to wear, like the one she wore now of an unburdened queen, not a queen who fretted about the correct way of behaving in the public eye.

Khami was where the syndicate's first mission unfolded after they completed the trials and gained full membership with the Red Stones. It had also been the place of her first kiss with Tajana, yet Tajana barely batted an eyelid as they passed under the palm tree where their initials remained carved. Farid had seemed to notice Nyzaia's lingering look as they entered the city and simply inclined his head, his way of checking in.

Nyzaia spent a lot of time in Khami when she first joined the Red Stones, having been first appointed to the Spies, one of the six pillars. It was the most common camp for the Spies, given it was the only settlement with a close border to another realm. While the Abis Forge neighboured Vala's Zivoi Mountains, there was little activity there. Some places in Khami offered visibility of the Garridon soldiers in their watchtowers, as well as a view of the Neutral City, allowing spies to keep watch of those who entered and departed. It also offered the spies insight into stray wanderers roaming Hybrooke Forest or the Ashun Desert.

After becoming queen of the Red Stones, she had spent little time there and had not visited at all since becoming queen of Keres. It was different from Tabheri: less crowded, shorter buildings, and paler walls to stand out against. She felt too exposed.

Farid nodded at Nyzaia as they arrived at the large wooden doors marking the entrance to Lord Arnav's home on the edge of Khami. Farid was ready. He had asked no questions, having immediately agreed to tail Tajana that evening. Something still felt wrong. After they were intimate, Nyzaia expected their relationship to return to normal, yet something remained amiss. It was unlike Tajana to find any opportunity to disappear; she had always been protective of Nyzaia, yet lately, it felt like Farid was the captain of her Queen's Guard. The wooden gates opened.

"My queen!" Lord Arnav boomed. He stood on the tiled steps leading to his home, his yellow sherwani and turban matching the bright flowers lining the walkway. His eyes were young—playful, even. He flashed a smile, revealed by his closely shaved beard that was a pleasant contrast to the thicker facial hair favoured by the other Lords. Nyzaia raised her eyebrows. The home was much changed from when Arnav had taken over from his deceased father. The walls around the home distinguished it from the rest of Khami, as though an artist had started their work here and left the remainder of the city a blank canvas. There was not a single tile, piece of brick, or flowerbed without colour. The pillars the lord waited in-between were tiled in the brightest fuchsias, standing tall on a mosaic of a rising sun above the desert. The procession dismounted from their horses in the courtyard and immediately led them to the fountain in the centre to relinquish their thirst.

Nyzaia stepped towards the lord and brushed the desert sand from her clothing. It made little difference.

"Lord Arnav, it is lovely to see you again. You left so soon after our ball for Queen Elisara." Nyzaia gestured to her friend, who approached with Kazaar by her side.

"Ah yes, Queen Elisara," said the lord. With a glint in his eye, he glanced between Elisara and her commander. "A pleasure to see you again." He bowed and kissed the back of her hand. Nyzaia practically felt the testosterone rise as Kazaar stepped forward, introducing himself to remove the lord's lips from her hand. "I hear I missed quite the show. I left long before the dancing was over," Lord Arnav said, addressing Nyzaia again.

"A show?" she asked, confused. The Lord cocked his head to one side and straightened his sherwani.

"Yes. I hear you had some sort of magical display—a fancy talent involving the smoke from your fire, perhaps?"

Nyzaia realised he referred to the shadows that appeared right before she was called to find Kazaar. She was grateful her lords' minds were too small to ponder bigger threats. Razik, Issam, and Jabir had quickly handled the concerned crowds, explaining that the show was an intended display of magic.

As though sensing her thoughts, Farid said, "My queen, we should really retire to your chambers so you can rest," interrupted Farid. "You do not wish to dine with us?" asked Lord Arnav.

"I would love to, but next time, Lord Arnav. We must rise early tomorrow to reach Antor for the engagement ball. A quiet evening would be best," she explained, while Farid asked a guard for directions to her chambers.

"I was disappointed not to receive an invitation," said the lord. Nyzaia would determine whether to pre-warn Caellum about offending Keres' lords, depending on how he acted upon her arrival tomorrow.

"It is a small affair. The future bride and groom do not know each other well. I am sure you will be invited to the wedding along with the other lords," Elisara said beside her with a tight smile. Lord Arnav did not push the matter further and allowed his guards to guide the group to their rooms. Farid discreetly tapped the side of Nyzaia's elbow and stepped away from the others.

"I shall knock three times upon my return," said Farid in a hushed tone. She nodded as he backed away and feigned a position at the door with the rest of her Queen's Guard. Tajana peered back at Farid as she moved gracefully towards Nyzaia in her leathers.

"What did Farid want?" Tajana reached towards Nyzaia's arm. She angled herself away and Tajana sighed. "This? Again?"

"He's going to guard tonight along with Elisara's Queen's Guard. We are spending the evening together." Nyzaia smiled sweetly. "You and the syndicate can have the night off." Tajana did not respond. Reaching for her hand, Nyzaia gave it a gentle squeeze and watched as Tajana's shoulders relaxed. "You've been doing so much for me with your role as captain and mediating with the Red Stones. You deserve a break." Tajana tucked a strand of hair behind Nyzaia's ear, who allowed it, hoping she would accept the offer without a fight.

"Thank you, love. I appreciate that. Would you like me to pick you up some of the pistachio dessert you like from the evening market?" A pang of guilt flooded Nyzaia then, yet why had Tajana so easily accepted an evening away? It made little sense. Nyzaia prayed the person who had once calmed her fire was not about to burn her.

***

Elisara's disappointment caught Nyzaia off guard when she said she was sick and could no longer dine together. She had never intended to; Elisara was an alibi to allow Tajana the evening off, while Nyzaia sat alone and read until Farid returned with updates. She had never been one for reading, but the book weighed on her mind all day, burning a hole in her back.

Nyzaia bathed long enough to wash off the sand and dirt from the journey before rushing to pull on her robe and dive under the bedsheets that matched the vibrancy of the rest of the home. The interiors were similar to the exterior of Lord Arnav's residence, with Nyzaia's room a vibrant shade of teal. She ignited a flame in the lantern beside her bed and dragged the *Myths and Lies of*

Ithyion tome onto her lap. The bed was all-consuming as she sank further into the mattress and tucked her knees up to prop the leather book against her thighs.

She scanned the faded contents for something legible, but when she discerned nothing, she flicked to the book's centre where she had first read about the celestial ties. She read over it again, but the passage was so short she would have labelled it a lie if not for watching it manifest between Kazaar and Elisara. Flipping to the next page, she read the beginning of what she assumed were chapters or volumes, and when she opened the book wider, she found a tear down its middle. She pulled the book closer. A page was missing, but after flipping through it, it was clear someone had torn out several pages. What information did her father wish to keep secret? Or had someone else from long ago pulled the pages? It made sense why the passage on celestial ties was so short; the rest was simply missing. Nyzaia turned back to that page. The next page was labelled *Q'Ohar.*

She flicked through the pages and scanned the titles, searching for anything related to the prophecy. She paused on a page of sketches etched in worn charcoal. There were three odd symbols, and below each was a different drawing that she could barely make out. She sighed at the book's poor condition, wishing the previous owners had taken better care of it.

Nyzaia squinted and tucked her hair behind her ear. She was uncertain about one illustration in particular, which was either a person shrouded in smoke or simply where the charcoal had smudged. The second drawing depicted a sword of some form, yet she could barely make out the third. Flames appeared to gather behind an indiscernible figure. When a knock sounded, Nyzaia slammed the book closed. By the second knock it was under the bed, by the third knock, she breathed a sigh of relief, recognising the owner.

"Come in," she called, pulling her robe tighter and crossing her legs beneath the sheets. Farid waited for several seconds before entering, and she smiled at his caution. "That was quick," she said. Farid lingered at the door and pressed his ear against it. She frowned, but he brought a finger to his lips.

Trusting his judgement, Nyzaia remained silent and tried to gauge where he had been. His uniform was pristine; he favoured the red uniform of Keres over the black leathers worn by her syndicate. Mud lined his shoes, and a sheen of sweat glinted on his forehead. After a few minutes, Farid drew away from the door and took two steps forward, resuming his usual rigid stance by Nyzaia's side. He tucked his hands behind his back. Nyzaia was an excellent judge of character; as queen of the Assassins, she had to be, but she could not read the many emotions swimming in Farid's pale blue eyes.

She patted the spot on the bed beside her, and conflict plagued his glance at the break in protocol. She patted the bed again with dramatic flair.

"Do not worry. I will not let the syndicate know you dared to break professionalism." Nyzaia rolled her eyes, attempting to lighten the situation. Farid's feet were slow as he crossed the room, and she stifled a laugh as he awkwardly sat on the edge, placing his palms face down on each thigh.

"You seem uncomfortable, Farid," she said. He turned his head to look at her.

"It is not normal for me to be alone in another person's chambers, let alone my queen's," he said, and Nyzaia grinned.

"You have not had many partners?" She regretted the question when Farid winced and looked away. Nyzaia had hoped Farid would continue to lower his walls with her and become a friend, but he appeared to control his approach to others. She changed the subject, relieving him of any awkwardness.

"So, give me your full report," she said, leaning in. His face lit up at the request and he turned to face her, lifting his leg onto the bed to mirror Nyzaia. She smiled.

"Apologies, my queen. I should in no way be joyful about

what I discovered." He returned to his usual stoicism, and Nyzaia straightened, surprised he had found something. She urged him to continue. "I followed Tajana like you requested. First, she went directly to the market and picked up the pistachio dessert you like, though I am uncertain if this one is as good as the one you get in Tabheri."

"It's better," she said.

"Noted." Nyzaia was surprised he noticed what foods she ate. "I expected her to journey to the tavern to join the others, but she left the city. I followed her as far as Garridon's border, and she checked no one was following before she ran into Hybrooke Forest. I apologise, my queen, for not following her further. I didn't wish to risk a Garridon soldier finding a member of the Keres Queen's Guard entering without decree."

"No, Farid, do not apologise. That was wise," Nyzaia folded and unfolded the top of the sheet. "How long was she there?"

"Not long. Thirty minutes, perhaps. But when she exited, she was further down the border, closer to the sea. I had to run back to avoid us crossing paths." Nyzaia nodded, uncertain of what to say. "It may be nothing to worry about, my queen." He lifted his hand as though to comfort her but appeared to decide against it, awkwardly lowering his hand to pat the bed. Nyzaia laughed.

"Perhaps not," she said. "She has been mediating for the Red Stones. It is plausible she was undergoing some business for them, though that in itself is a problem. I cannot have an active member of the Red Stones as captain of my Queen's Guard. It creates too many blurred lines." Farid was silent and stared off into the distance.

"Farid," Nyzaia said, but he did not move. "Farid," she said again, more gently this time. He blinked yet was unresponsive. She touched his arm, and he snapped his hand around her wrist. Gasping, Nyzaia snatched it back.

"Gods, Nyzaia, I—" Farid stumbled over his words. "My queen, I apologise. I did not mean to lay a hand on you." He stood abruptly and walked to the door, his hands shaking. Nyzaia rose and tracked his movements as questions raced through her mind. Did he possess power? After all, he never spoke of his past; perhaps he was an illegitimate son of a lord. Nyzaia winced as a tingling pain bloomed along her wrist.

"Farid, it is fine. Please, do not worry." She did not wish to admit he had hurt her.

"It is my past. I—" Farid rushed to the door before Nyzaia could request he stay. "Is that all for the evening, my queen?" he asked, straightening and avoiding her eye.

"Yes, Farid. Thank you." He abruptly left, and Nyzaia frowned, uncertain what could torment him enough to make him lose control. She moved her hand to extinguish the flame by her bedside, but in the light, she caught sight of the markings on her wrist.

A burn in the shape of a male handprint.

Chapter Fourteen

Sadira

Choices were like flowers; some flourished easily with little required to grow, while others took time and consideration. Sadira wished she was deciding between flowers right now. She let out an exasperated sigh and threw what must have been the twentieth dress from her armoire. Indecision always plagued Sadira, who feared how each choice affected another's perception of her, and the implications of her actions. What if she inadvertently caused harm to another?

She imagined her mother would laugh if she were alive, telling her it was simply a dress, while her grandmother would say, *"An outfit speaks volumes when one is a princess."* It was the latter that stuck in her mind. Sadira had formally met the people of Garridon twice now: once upon her arrival and once when visiting Antor, but something about an official engagement ball felt different. Perhaps it was the thought of all the attention or the anticipation of being in a room with all the rulers and Soren for a second time.

Sadira stared at her reflection and brushed her cheek, unsure of how to act. Soren had been clear about her feelings after the way Sadira spoke to her in front of the other royals in Nerida. Yet to instil trust in the Garridon people, they would need to perceive Sadira as the future queen, which involved garnering the attention of a room. But would Sadira be the future queen? She was not so certain, based on Soren's words.

Tears pricked her eyes as vines of doubt twisted around her lungs. She scraped back her hair and secured it with a ribbon before padding to the windows of her chambers, gazing out across the greenery that kept her calm. Somehow, Caellum had chosen the perfect rooms for Sadira before ever meeting her.

Tugging the silk robe tighter around her waist, Sadira embraced herself and admired the view. The wall of her room was crafted of paned glass, allowing an unrestricted vision of the gardens below and the forest surrounding the castle. With a deep breath, she closed her eyes. *You can do this*, she thought. She frowned when she opened them again. She did not recognise the simple carriage entering the estate, though that was unsurprising given she knew so few people in the kingdom.

A gentle knock sounded at the door, and she called for them to enter, expecting Roslyn, her lady-in-waiting. Sadira sighed again. No matter how many questions she asked Roslyn, the older woman participated little in their conversations. The sun lowered behind the tree line, casting a silhouette of the carriage as it drew closer.

"I take it you are an indecisive person," called a gentle voice. Sadira whirled, blushing as she realised the owner of the gentle knock was not Roslyn after all.

"Queen Larelle!" Sadira said, flustered. "I do apologise." She scooped the dresses from the emerald chaise beside her before remembering herself, dropping the pile to the ground. She dropped into a curtsey, avoiding stumbling over the dresses.

"No, no!" Larelle said quickly, stepping over the dresses to reach her. "Do not apologise. I was the exact same the morning I met my lords for the first time." She reached for the dresses in Sadira's hands and carefully draped them on the chaise.

"I must apologise," said Sadira. "I am not respectfully dressed to greet a queen." She hid her face between her hands and turned back to face the windows. Sensing Larelle's approach, a gentle hand touched her shoulder.

"Sadira, please. You are to be a queen soon; we are of the same station. Even if we were not, it would not affect my judgement of you." Sadira removed her hands from her face and glanced at the queen. After Caellum's recommendation to reach out to Larelle, Sadira had paced back and forth with the letter for hours until requesting the staff take it to the aviary. Caellum was right again. Larelle was likely the person Sadira could connect and relate to the most.

"I should be the one to apologise," Larelle said. "It seems my response to your letter did not meet you in time, and if my unexpected arrival has added stress to your preparations, I will not be offended if you prefer I leave." Though it was not Sadira's wish, she believed the queen, who always had a way of speaking that flowed with sincerity.

"No, please," Sadira said. "I welcome the company. Perhaps you can help me decide on what dress to wear." She gestured at the many gowns, but her eye caught again on the carriage finally arriving in the courtyard. Sadira stepped closer to the glass, her breath fogging the panes. She did not recognise the hunched man exiting the carriage in parchment-coloured robes.

"Do you know who that is?" Sadira asked Larelle. The queen furrowed her brow as the old man shuffled from view.

"That is the Historian," Larelle murmured. "I did not know he was invited."

Sadira frowned.

"I handwrote all the invitations myself; I do not recall addressing that name."

"How odd," Larelle murmured. "He resides in the Neutral City. Growing up, we all attended his lessons." Larelle turned from the window and began filtering through the dresses.

"What kind of lessons?"

"Mainly history of the realm, lineages, and what little information remained on Ithyion." Sadira perched on the chaise while Larelle separated the dresses into piles. The Neridian queen paused and fiddled with the beading on a lavender gown; she opened and closed her mouth before pursing her lips. She wished to say something more, but Sadira remained silent, allowing her time.

"Could I ask you something that I hope is not insensitive?" Larelle finally said. She perched on the bed opposite Sadira.

"Of course. Anything!" Sadira responded eagerly.

"When we last met, you mentioned that some parts of your family descend from Wiccan." Sadira nodded. "What do you know about the abilities of Wiccan?"

Sadira frowned. "Abilities?"

"Are there certain things Wiccan can do that, let's say, *I* could not? Or someone else from Garridon could not?"

Since Sadira's arrival, nobody had asked about her heritage except to learn of her claim to the royal line. It did not surprise Sadira, as she expected; most people assumed the Wiccan were extinct. Caellum's grandfather, King Jorah, had all Wiccan killed after he usurped the throne. Sadira's heart bled for those connections. Given the Wiccan had an affinity for earth power, Jorah believed they posed a risk to the throne, and their connection to the earth could prove their greater entitlement to the throne. Some had managed to flee to Doltas, while the other Wiccans were born there—descendants of the prisoners abandoned on the island by Novisia's original settlers. Her mind wondered to Rodik.

"I only know of a few, but they are rare from what I am told," began Sadira. "I have an affinity for healing. While the growth of plants comes from my connection to the royal line, my innate knowledge of what can heal different ailments comes from my Wiccan heritage." Larelle nodded in encouragement. "My grandmother had a subtle gift of foresight, though it rarely came to her. The last time she foresaw something was the death of her husband, my grandfather." She appreciated Larelle's solemn look at the mention of losing a family member, regardless of whether or not Sadira had met him. "In seeing it, the gods also gifted her knowledge of the prophecy." Larelle pulled out the chair at Sadira's dressing table, and Sadira sat. She smiled as Larelle undid the ribbon holding her curls and began rearranging them.

"Are those the only two abilities you know of?" asked Larelle, and Sadira nodded. "And the prophecy your grandmother was gifted—what was shared in Nerida—is that the entire prophecy?" Sadira frowned. Of course it had been. Did the other rulers trust her that little?

"Yes, of course. Why do you ask?" Sadira locked eyes with Larelle in the mirror.

"Just something someone said to me keeps playing on my mind." She continued moving Sadira's hair and reached for pins on the table as she did. Sadira relished the moment of having someone other than Caellum or Soren to speak with, and to converse with so effortlessly. Sadira had no female friends on Doltas Island. She had kept to herself. Everyone saw her as the princess who would one day return to Garridon, placing her on a pedestal. Except Rodik. She lowered her gaze.

"I imagine you left a lot behind in Doltas," Larelle said, and Sadira nodded solemnly. "Did you leave *someone* behind?"

Sadira blushed at how easily Larelle could read her thoughts.

"I had a partner. Rodik," Sadira answered.

"How long were you together?"

"Five years." Larelle nodded slowly as she fluffed out the remaining curls falling down Sadira's back.

"You gave him up for your realm. That must have been difficult."

"It was, but it was foolish. I was raised knowing I would one day return to Garridon. I suppose a part of me always pretended like it would never happen." Sadira admired her hair in the mirror. Larelle had softly pinned overlapping pieces from the front of her face and pulled back her curls. Sadira waved her hand, and delicate white flowers grew from the pot before them. Sadira jokingly questioned whether Larelle had a gift of foresight, too, as she instinctively picked the flowers and placed them in Sadira's hair.

"It is easy to live in delusion when love is at play," said Larelle. Sadira examined Larelle's expression in the mirror, one of faraway longing and grief.

"I hope you do not mind me asking, but how did you do it?" Sadira queried. Larelle tilted her head. "Move on from him?"

Soren had connections across Novisia; it had not taken long for news of Larelle's banishment and lost partner to reach them. Larelle offered a sad smile.

"You never move on. They are always there in your heart and in the back of your mind. But with each passing day, it becomes a little easier to accept happiness, even though they are not here." Larelle stepped back to admire her work.

"Do you think there will ever be another for you?" asked Sadira. Larelle cleared her throat and turned away, reaching for a dress. "Or is there already someone?" Larelle sighed before sitting beside Sadira.

"Honestly, I do not know. If you had asked me a week ago, I would have answered no, but then..." Sadira turned to face her with giddy excitement. She had never talked to a woman about personal matters; her family had only ever cared for the prophecy.

"Did something happen?" Sadira probed.

"I'm overthinking it," Larelle said. "What about you? How are things with the king?" Sadira noticed the obvious deflection, so obliged.

"I think he will be a good friend," Sadira said, standing to admire the dress Larelle had picked. It was the dress she kept gravitating towards, but she had been unsure if the statement it made was too bold.

"And do you think that is all he will ever be?" Larelle asked, pulling the dress off the hanger. The kindness on Caellum's face as he gently held her in the walled garden came to mind then. Sadira could not keep a small smile from tugging at her lips as she relived the moment.

"I think we are both recovering from heartbreak, but there is an understanding there. Regardless of what happens, he will be a good husband."

"Well, I look forward to seeing the two of you presented at the ball this evening. I will leave you to change." Larelle strode to the door, her gown trailing behind her.

"Larelle," Sadira called, and the queen paused, resting her hand on the doorknob. She turned back with a smile and a gentle gaze. "Thank you for this. I will see if I can find out any more about the Wiccan for you." Larelle thanked her, and for the first time since arriving in Garridon, Sadira felt like she belonged.

Chapter Fifteen

Larelle

"Queen Larelle and Princess Zarya of Nerida," announced the man to Larelle's right. She reached for her daughter's hand and helped her slowly descend the steps into the hall. Four of Larelle's guards followed, though their presence was hardly necessary given the number of Garridon guards lining the glass and stone walls. The ten long tables began to fill with at least twenty seats placed at each. Those who had not yet taken their seat greeted one another on the ballroom floor.

"Mumma! Look!" Zarya said in an excited, not-so-quiet whisper. Larelle followed Zarya's pointed finger to watch snow-white butterflies sail through the air and occasionally land on the twisted vines and flowers gracing the backs of chairs planted in rows along the long tables to one end of the hall. Larelle gripped Zarya's hand tighter, who stumbled over the hem of her dress when they stepped onto the stone floor.

Zarya immediately let go to chase after a butterfly, and Larelle hurried to keep pace with her, slowed by her sheer blue cape trailing along the floor. She grinned as she followed her daughter, who laughed in acknowledgement to those who greeted her. They all smiled at the young girl frolicking through the hall, but Larelle noticed the moment people realised who she was and whispered gossip among one another behind feigned smiles. Zarya gave up chasing the butterfly once they reached the last row of tables before it met the dance floor marked by a half moon display of candles in varying heights. Zarya curtseyed to an approaching couple while Larelle reached for a goblet of red wine from a passing servant.

Sipping it, she admired her daughter, who twirled to show off her gown.

Larelle had allowed Zarya to pick her dress from a collection of childhood gowns Lillian found in a dusty chest. After trying on every single one, Zarya eventually settled on a seaweed-green dress and claimed it would make Princess Sadira happy because it was green, like Garridon's sigil. Larelle did not know where Zarya got her sense of intuition but suspected she was right. She already acted like a queen.

"You should be very proud." Larelle jumped, not having realised Lillian had arrived. She kissed her cheek in greeting.

"As should you. You have spent as much time raising her as of late," said Larelle, squeezing Lillian's hand before folding it back around her own waist and sipping her wine with the other.

"The early years are the ones that matter," said Lillian, "and that was all you."

All her. Larelle looked into her goblet. Riyas would be proud of her—of both of them.

"Are you happy to spend some time with her? It will only be brief while I greet the others." Lillian nodded, and as if on cue, the herald announced, "Nyzaia, Queen of Keres!"

Larelle turned to watch Nyzaia descend the steps. The candles lining the bannisters glowed brighter as she passed. Her dark hair hung in waves, pinned back by jewels and her golden crown. A chain linking the gold hoop in her nose to her ear glinted beneath the candlelight. She held her clasped hands against her stomach and watched her steps as the skirts of her lehenga pooled around her feet. The Keres queen appeared more confident than her last royal outing. Her Queen's Guard filtered in from the side doors, all but one dressed in black leathers. It was the man from before with the curious pale-blue eyes. Something permeated his presence as though a deep trauma inhibited and tainted his aura. Larelle watched the woman whom she had previously seen interact with Nyzaia—Tajana, Larelle believed she was called, except this time when she offered her hand to Nyzaia, the queen did not take it. Something had happened since Larelle last saw them. The two conversed quietly in the corner of the room.

"Lady Soren of Doltas Island," the male voice boomed. This time, every head in the room turned to face the staircase. However, Soren did not descend. She remained at the top in her brown leathers and the silver breastplate of the Garridon Army. She glared at the herald. The poor man said nothing but stared back, his face paling as low growls sounded from the hallway. Seconds later, wolves entered the room and flanked their owner. Several guests stepped back, muttering to each other. Larelle glanced for Zarya and found her sitting close by, swinging her feet, and gaping at the wolves.

The pack bared their teeth at the herald, who gulped.

"Queen Soren of Doltas Island, and—" he stammered, "—heir to the Garridon throne." The mutterings only increased as a wry smile graced Soren's face. Her thin braids swung behind her as she descended and dismissed her wolves, who began stalking the hall. Larelle's attention flitted back to Nyzaia, who spoke to Tajana yet fixed her eyes on Soren. Nyzaia's captain nodded before making her way over to the Doltas queen. Nyzaia had been quick to accuse Soren of setting the explosion; it made sense to instruct Tajana to gather information.

"Queen Elisara of Vala." When Elisara arrived, the whispers quickly morphed into gasps and gawping faces. Her entrance was punctuated by a gush of wind that nearly extinguished the flames.

"I can't believe she came," whispered one woman to her friend.

"You would not catch me dead at the engagement ball of a man I should have married," giggled another. Yet those not gossiping about the queen of Vala watched open-mouthed, and it was clear why. Larelle was used to seeing Elisara in white and pale blue, perhaps the occasional lavender, and while the style of her dress was like the ones Larelle had seen before—billowing sleeves cuffed at the wrists, a cinched waist, and loose fabrics cascading into a waterfall at her feet—silk replaced the usual chiffon, and the pastel blues typical of Vala were exchanged with a blood-red. The cut of her dress was deep, revealing delicate golden chain jewellery that cupped her breasts and chest; her silver crown seemed out of place amid the golds and reds.

Larelle almost approached Elisara but stopped when Commander Kazaar entered the room from a side door at the bottom of the staircase, his eyes trained on his queen. Larelle noted how his gaze roamed Elisara's body and how he strode instantly for her. The last time she saw the pair was in Nerida when they appeared to have set aside their differences. Elisara narrowed her eyes at her commander when he approached, though her body betrayed her true intentions; she shifted to mirror his every movement as though strings tied their limbs together.

Larelle could see nothing dark about the commander, and his gaze held no malice when he beheld his queen. In fact, Larelle saw something else—devotion, protection, and something more.

"Can you sense it?" spoke a quiet voice. Larelle turned to find the Historian withdrawing a chair to sit beside her. Noticing his unsteadiness, she offered her hand and helped him lower into the seat. Larelle glanced around, wondering if he had a caretaker or someone to look after him. If Olden was this frail, Larelle would want someone to support him.

"I did not expect to see you here, sir." Larelle sipped from her wine again, avoiding his question. After speaking with Alvan, she decided she needed more evidence before drawing conclusions about the Historian's warnings.

"I received no invitation," he said. Larelle could not tell if a note of disdain tinged his voice. "But it is tradition. I have attended all rulers' engagements and weddings, so I made my own way here." His hand shook lightly as he drank from the water before him. "I had to speak to you again to hear your latest thoughts. Can you sense it? The darkness?" He inclined his head towards Kazaar and Elisara, who now stood side by side, peering out of the glass walls into the castle's gardens.

"Honestly, sir, I cannot say I do," she said. "Are you quite certain you felt something dark about him?" The old man nodded, the wisps from his hair falling from the tie at the nape of his neck.

"It is odd, is it not?" The Historian took a sip from his goblet. "That he was found at the steps of Tabheri palace as a baby and grew into as much power as any of you, despite not being a royal by birth." Larelle contemplated his words. She had heard stories about the commander over the years but had never questioned it, assuming he was either the illegitimate son of the king or a lord with connections to the royal line. Larelle had no reason to listen to rumours suggesting otherwise; she had been subject to enough gossip to know it usually held no factual basis. But given the rise of the prophecy, perhaps there was more to it. She supposed someone with such a level of power and a reputation for causing pain could have an added darkness. But something gnawed at Larelle; she was not yet convinced.

"Will you tell the others?" asked the Historian. Larelle contemplated her response, having thought about it on many occasions since informing Alvan.

"Not until I am certain of my opinion," she responded, draining the last of her wine. The Historian hummed.

"Then let us hope you come to your opinion before it is too late."

Larelle spun her head to the Historian and opened her mouth to scold him.

"Lord Alvan of Seley," the herald called.

Larelle's attention flitted to Alvan, an element of pride warming her heart to see him dressed in Nerida's deep blue—a statement of his loyalty to her, not Garridon. The velvet was fitted, highlighting the size of his arms; one swung at his side while he tucked the other under the breast of his jacket. His hair was freshly trimmed to his scalp, and as he drew closer, she could make out the inkings beneath his hair.

"Look, Mumma! Mr Alvan!" Zarya said gleefully, her eyes shining as she ran over to her mother with Lillian in tow. Alvan scanned the room, and when his gaze found Larelle, he beamed.

He weaved amongst the throngs of people, who now headed to their tables for the celebratory dinner.

"Hello," she breathed. *Hello? Is that all you can manage*?

"You look beautiful," he said, bowing to kiss her hand. His fingers lingered, reminding Larelle of his touch during their visit to Seley. She cleared her throat.

"Thank you; you look very—" But words escaped her.

"Nice!" Zarya shouted from her seat. "Mumma means to say you look nice!" Alvan laughed, and Larelle grinned. "You should ask her to dance, Mr Alvan."

"Zarya, there is no one else dancing right now. We are about to eat," Larelle said, and Alvan crouched to Zarya's level, balancing on the balls of his feet.

"We need to wait until the guests of honour arrive first," Alvan explained, taking her hand and twirling her daughter.

"The ones who are getting married?" asked Zarya. Alvan nodded enthusiastically and continued to spin her. "Mumma and Pappa are married," she said. Alvan's hand faltered, and Larelle knelt beside him to intervene, grasping Zarya's waist to halt her spinning.

"Zarya, sweetie. Mumma and Pappa were never married," she explained. Zarya fiddled with the petals on the back of a chair.

"Yes, you are." Larelle blushed at Zarya's boldness. "I saw it in my dream; you and a man were standing together where they put the crowns on our heads, and this lady tied something around your hands, and then you kissed." She picked the leaves off the chair, and Larelle hung her head, laughing.

"Like in the story I read you last night?" she asked, stroking her daughter's hair. Zarya stopped pulling at the leaves and frowned. "Perhaps it was someone else in your dream."

"Like Mr Alvan?" She looked at the pair with curiosity.

"Maybe you saw me and Mumma dancing because you knew we would dance tonight!" Alvan said, reaching for Zarya's hands. "But I think I want to dance with *you* first!" He pulled up a giggling Zarya by the hands and swung her. Larelle grinned. In the last few weeks, Zarya had become particularly fond of capturing Alvan's attention. Still, perhaps Alvan was spending too much time with them if Zarya was becoming so attached that she dreamed about him.

"King Caellum and Princess Sadira will arrive shortly. Please take your seats," boomed the voice from the top of the stairs. Larelle smiled as Alvan offered his hand to Larelle and balanced Zarya on his hip, who was flushed from spinning. Larelle accepted and allowed him to guide her to their places, side by side.

Chapter Sixteen

Caellum

Stupid. This is a stupid idea. Caellum paced outside the doors of Sadira's chambers, rotating the velvet ring box in his jacket pocket. She never asked for a ring. *She never wanted to get married.* Caellum sighed, faced the door again, and raised his fist to knock. Sadira swung the door open.

"I thought I would relieve you of further contemplation after you passed for the fifteenth time," Sadira sang. He looked foolish as he stood at the door with his mouth half open. The subtle light of the lanterns glowed behind her, framing her golden hair that fell down her back in curls. Her cheeks flushed in a naturally endearing manner and matched the pink hue of her lips. Her dress reminded Caellum of the day they first met; the palest of green chiffon cut into off-the-shoulder sleeves, effortlessly highlighting her lightly sun-kissed skin and the shimmer of her collarbones. He could not stop his eyes from trailing further, mesmerised by the spattering of tiny white flowers gathering in fields at the bottom of her skirts. He realised they were irises, the flowers now blooming in the walled garden. Had she made the dress herself? It would not surprise him; she was creative and skilled enough. Smiling, Caellum shook his head.

"Is it okay? Is it too much? After the other day, you were so nice to me, and I could not stop thinking about the flowers. I wanted a symbol of something that was just, well, *ours*." she rambled. He grasped Sadira's hands and guided her back into her rooms.

"It is perfect," he said softly.

Sadira cocked her head. "Then, why did you shake your head?"

She rubbed her arm as he released her hands.

"Because"—Caellum reached into his pocket and pulled out the green velvet box. Flicking the gold clasp, he opened it to face her—"I had the same thought." Sadira covered her gasp with her hands; her eyes watered, and nose twitched. "It is beautiful," she breathed.

"May I?" he asked, pulling the ring from the box. Sadira nodded. Her hands felt dainty in his as he slid the gold ring onto her finger. The opal stone matched the white flowers on her gown, and the three claws encasing the gem were shaped like irises as a reminder of their day in the garden. The place no longer reminded him of heartbreak but was a symbol of new beginnings, just as Sadira had explained.

"Why are you crying?" he whispered, brushing a tear from her face as she examined the ring.

"Because I do not deserve this," she said. Caellum frowned and stepped closer. He cupped Sadira's face, urging her to look at him. She clasped his wrists.

"Do not say that."

"But it is true. I wanted to believe I was sent here to ease the tensions in Garridon and that perhaps, at a stretch, you may wish to step down from your role if the people favoured Soren." Caellum waited patiently for her to finish while knowing there was no bone in Sadira's body capable of betrayal. "But I fear Soren will stop at nothing, Caellum." Sadira looked straight into his soul. "I fear she will try to kill you, and I cannot—" Sadira's face crumpled, and more tears fell. "I cannot lose someone else." Caellum pulled her closer, wrapping his arms around her.

"You will not lose me, Sadira." He breathed in the scent of her hair: morning dew, roses, and sugar. "We are in this together." When he pulled back, Sadira's green eyes glowed faintly in the dimmed light as flowers crept into his vision on the wall above the fireplace. "Until death do us part."

"It is the death that I fear."

"Then we must make it impossible for her to hurt us. We need to be perceived as the strongest rulers for Garridon, so she knows any move against the crown would lose the will of the people."

"I fear she does not care for the people."

"She will have to. The people will turn to their ruler should the creatures return." Caellum trailed his hand down Sadira's arm until intertwining his fingers in hers. "She is but one of the weeds surrounding us that I promised we would blossom amongst." Sadira smiled at the reminder of his words when they first visited the city together.

"If we are to help the people and defend ourselves not only against Soren, but external threats, there is something I would like to do." Sadira said.

"Anything. I will give you anything." The smell of the blooming flowers trickled closer as they began to carpet the floor.

"I wish to learn more about my heritage. The Wiccan," she said, and he nodded. "Perhaps there is something extra I can use against her, or maybe something exists in our history that might offer a different way to defeat the creatures. We must prepare for any threat."

"Where shall we start?" he asked. Her brow knitted together, while Caellum traced circles on her hand.

"I must speak to someone old in Garridon—a healer, perhaps."

"I will ask Sir Cain to gather some information. I will journey wherever we need to to get you answers," he said.

"Thank you," she whispered. The two stood before one another in a field of white flowers. Caellum did not wish to join the others. He yearned to stand like this with Sadira for hours. Yet, they had to leave if they were to show a united front against Soren.

"Are you ready?" he asked. Sadira took a deep breath and nodded.

***

"King Caellum of Garridon, and his betrothed, Princess Sadira of Doltas Island," called Orrick, the royal herald. His voice was deafening as Caellum guided Sadira from the corridor to the top of the stairs, descending into the hall. He gulped when he took in the number of people filling the room. Though this would be normal to most rulers, Caellum still felt uneasy in the spotlight. He thought back to the last time he was presented to his people, only to be escorted out with mud on his face. Elisara was always a natural at royal functions. Caellum hoped she did not feel out of place at this one, an event that was once destined to be theirs. The room sparkled. Hundreds of candles reflected off the glass walls and ceiling, adding to the stars aglow outside. The surrounding vines and flowers were symbolic of Sadira's grace and beauty, the room proving to be a true representation of her and all she was.

"Wow," he breathed, taking in the hall. "You did all this?" Sadira's grin struck him with warmth.

"With some help from the servants," she said modestly. Caellum lifted his hand, and together, they descended the stairs. Revellers gazed up at her with adoring smiles. Sadira truly glowed as he guided her around the rows of long tables until reaching the one at the head, raised on a dais. He acknowledged Nyzaia first, who returned a tight smile. Larelle helped her daughter to hold her cutlery correctly, yet grinned at Sadira as they approached. His betrothed returned the warm smile, and Caellum was grateful she had heeded his advice. He caught the eye of Vala's commander next, standing to the side of the table. He narrowed his eyes at Caellum, and the temperature in the room shifted before he refocused on his queen. Elisara was the last person whose eyes met his as he reached the table. He smiled through the awkwardness, but did not attempt to converse. Her returning smile was brief before she glanced back at her commander.

Caellum pulled out Sadira's chair beside Larelle before moving to take his own. However, he did not sit. He waited for the last guest of the honoured table to take her place. He cleared his throat awkwardly and remained standing until Soren sat. She did not acknowledge him. Caellum peered out over the tables and the joyous faces of everyone present. It was such a change to his last royal event. He raised his goblet, clinking a fork against it.

"First, I must ask you to applaud my betrothed for how breathtaking she looks this evening," he called to the crowds, glancing down to meet Sadira's eyes. A ripple of applause sounded through the room, echoing against the glass. "It has been a tumultuous time for us all"—he gestured to the room— "We have faced tragedy, not just within our realm, but throughout our entire kingdom. We have lost loved ones and faced change." He looked at Sadira again. "But in the face of change and uncertainty is the promise of friendship, hope, and new beginnings." Sadira reached up and squeezed his hand before he turned back to the room. "I wish for you to see that promise reflected in our marriage: a union that brings stability and peace to our realm." He glanced at Soren then, who played with a knife wedged into the table; she refused to meet anyone's eye. She sat at the end of the table alone, except for two of her wolves: a sable-coloured one curled at her feet and a large white beast who acted as a guard. It growled, forcing Soren to glance up. She did little more than glare between the pair before patting the wolf's head to settle her.

Sadira rose and looped her arm in his.

"It is our honour to rule this realm and stand beside our friends in Nerida, Keres, and Vala. Our marriage not only brings you unity, but it promises you a queen. As your king and queen, I promise we will protect you." While the people knew nothing about the threats they faced, all four rulers did. Sadira was cementing their place, not only among the people of Garridon, but their worth among the other royalty, ensuring that, together, they would offer their defence against any imposing threat.

Applause broke out again, and Larelle raised her glass.

"To the king and future queen of Garridon," she called, and the room echoed the sentiment.

Chapter Seventeen

Elisara

Elisara swilled the wine around her goblet. It was her third that evening after determining alcohol was the only way through this, a decision that merely served to heighten her emotions as she reflected on how this night could have been hers. Caellum twirled Sadira around the dancefloor and trailed his hands down her bare back, whispering in her ear; she blushed and giggled at his words. Watching their smiles, Elisara wondered if her smile would have been the same or if a small part of her had always known that life would never be enough: shipped to a different realm for marriage, a political tool to unite the realms. Elisara gulped the remnants of her wine and signalled for another goblet.

Elisara had thought she loved Caellum, though perhaps she merely loved the idea of being in love, especially as their relationship was all she had ever known. "*A love that lights your soul on fire*," Kazaar had said on the Unsanctioned Isle. She was uncertain what that looked like, yet felt the fire burn within her at every one of Kazaar's glances from where he leaned against the wall, pretending to survey the room.

A henna-covered hand appeared in her vision, and Nyzaia's gold bracelets rattled as she placed her goblet beside Elisara's. She scraped a chair back and sat beside her.

"I could do with something drastically stronger. Couldn't you?" Nyzaia asked. Elisara chuckled and leaned back, crossing her leg over the other. She picked up her glass.

"It's like you read my mind."

"To a complicated love life." Nyzaia clinked her goblet against

Elisara's before downing her wine.

"There is nothing complicated about my love life," Elisara scoffed. Nyzaia rested her head on her palm and angled her chin to face Elisara.

"Oh, is that so? Are we not at the engagement ball of your previously betrothed while your commander, who is definitely falling for you, stares at you from across the room? Nyzaia raised her eyebrow.

"Point taken," Elisara grumbled. Nevertheless, she did not believe Kazaar was falling for her; their bond was merely that of a shared destiny. "If we are cheering to our complicated love lives, what is wrong with you and Tajana?" Elisara put her goblet down and shook her head at a servant who moved to refill it. She did not trust her emotions should she have another. Elisara scanned the room for Tajana and found the captain leaning against the wall in a similar fashion to Kazaar, intently glancing between Soren and Sadira on the opposite sides of the hall. While Sadira danced joyfully in Caellum's embrace, in a way Elisara struggled to believe was a ruse, Soren sat at the far end of the royal table, glaring around the room. "Should Tajana not be watching you?" Elisara asked. Nyzaia shook her head and locked eyes on Tajana.

"I asked her to watch Soren and Sadira. I do not trust them, mostly Soren. When we met in Nerida, she said something that made me question if she had stepped foot in Keres before and perhaps had a hand in instigating the explosion. My father had to find out about the prophecy somehow."

"So, what is the complication?" Elisara asked. Nyzaia swirled the liquid in her goblet before glancing away.

"I had her followed," she said finally. Elisara uncrossed her legs and leaned forward.

"Nyzaia!" she hissed. "What on earth for?"

The Keres queen inclined forward until their heads almost touched.

"She was acting strange," Nyzaia whispered. "I cannot place it, but she keeps disappearing. Farid followed her yesterday in Khami, and she crossed into Garridon."

"Perhaps she was scouting ahead." Elisara reached forward to rest a hand on Nyzaia's arm, who recoiled as her sleeve rode upward. Elisara seized her wrist.

"Did she do this to you?" Elisara gasped, running her finger over the burn marks on her wrist. Nyzaia pushed back from Elisara.

"No, it was not her. It was an accident," she mumbled, and Elisara suppressed the urge to reach for her friend again.

"My queen, could I speak with you?"

Elisara turned to the deep voice behind her and peered up at one of Nyzaia's guards. Farid. Despite Elisara's protests, Nyzaia rose, and soon, the pair were in deep conversation. Elisara scanned the room again, looking for Soren and Sadira. Sadira now stood conversing with Larelle and Lord Alvan, though Soren was nowhere to be seen.

Elisara avoided Kazaar's eye yet sensed him watching. A smirk appeared in her mind. He knew she was avoiding him. Continuing to do so, Elisara focused on her friends and smiled as Helena and Vigor dragged Talia up from her chair, forcing her to dance to the high-tempo string melodies. Vlad caught Elisara's eye and nodded to her from the other side of the room. She raised her empty goblet to him.

"*You should join them.*"

Elisara rolled her eyes, and the music changed, replaced by a slower ballad. Vigor pulled Helena into the dance, and Talia left the floor to allow the couple a moment together.

"*And who would I dance with?*" she asked. Kazaar raised an eyebrow from across the hall, eliciting yet another eye-roll from Elisara.

"*You know, you could have any man in this room.*"

"*Perhaps I will have any man then.*" She smirked and pulled at her neckline to expose more chest. The gold admonishments glinted beneath the candlelight as the flames grew brighter. Elisara tossed her head back to loosen her curls, mesmerised by the stars through the glass and the silver glow of the moon that matched the mark on her collarbone. Kazaar's image obscured the sky as he came into view, peering down at her. His hands gripped the top of the chair as Elisara met his eyes, her head still tilted. As his finger grazed her back through the spindles of the chair, the light in his eyes changed to a glowing white, and the shadows returned.

Elisara pushed up from her chair and strode towards the dancing couples, knowing he followed close behind. She scanned the room for a partner, someone to distract from his presence.

"Are you looking for someone?" he whispered in her ear.

"So, he *does* know how to use his voice."

"I'll agree to use my voice more often if you agree to use yours," he said, his breath tickling her ear.

"I am using my voice now, am I not?" She ignored the pull to lean back into him.

"I like to imagine you using your voice to say other things." His fingers brushed the inside of her palm, and Elisara pulled away at the sparks lighting between them. She glanced around to check no one had seen.

"And what kind of things are those?" she asked, and he chuckled behind her.

"Look inside my mind and find out." Elisara cleared her throat, doing everything in her power not to seek his thoughts.

"You are preventing me from finding someone to dance with," she hissed.

"What kind of man are you looking for? Perhaps I can help. After all, I agreed to do anything to prove myself to you." Elisara scoffed and faced him, holding a finger up as she recounted a list of qualities.

"A talented dancer, tall, and handsome."

"I recall proving myself to be a good dancer."

"That's not what I—" Elisara squeaked as Kazaar grabbed her hand and spun her onto the ballroom floor. When she twirled back into him, he locked her in a dance hold.

"I do not recall accepting your hand to dance," she said.

"I do not see you declining, either." He smirked, and Elisara looked away, focusing on the steps and allowing the music to guide their movements. The slow melody steered them around the floor in soft patterns, and the pair swayed delicately in time with the string instruments.

"So, you do not think I am handsome?" he asked.

"Of course not," she said, tight-lipped. She focused on the candles as he guided her around the floor, ignoring the sensations of his hand against her back and her stomach against his abdomen.

"I could have sworn in Nerida you said I was the most handsome man in the room." He pushed again, and Elisara ground her teeth.

"I lied. Does your ego so desperately need stroking at my hand?

"Angel, lies sound so pretty on your lips." Kazaar spun Elisara again, and she saw a flash of Soren's blond braids return into the hall.

"I am not lying."

"Then, how do you explain our behaviour when you awoke in my chamber?" he asked. Elisara blushed, remembering the restraint she put in place to resist his pull.

"It is the tie. Nothing more."

"More pretty lies," Kazaar murmured, spinning her to the next dance partner. Elisara immediately went rigid in the next dancer's hold as her eye tugged on the single silver ring on his hand. Reluctantly, she glanced up at the eyes matching a similar shade of brown to her own. She glanced at the scar on his cheek from when they were children.

"Elisara," Caellum said.

"Caellum," she greeted just as awkwardly. It felt wrong in his grip, and her back felt cold beneath his hand.

"You look different."

Her eyes finally met his. "Different? After everything, is that all you have to say to me? You look *different*." Caellum opened and closed his mouth, but she ignored him and stared at her surroundings, waiting for the beat in which he would spin her back to Kazaar. Caellum tensed and sighed, focusing on someone behind her. When they spun, Elisara found Kazaar, his eyes on hers rather than his new partner's. The flames flashed white, and for a second, shadows seeped into her vision, but when she blinked, they were gone. Caellum spun Elisara again, and she collided with Kazaar's chest, an image flashing in her mind. A blur of black. She could not make it out. Her head shot up to look at Kazaar, who frowned.

"Did you see that?" he asked. Elisara nodded as they continued dancing, with Kazaar pulling her closer. The same image of black shadows flashed in her mind.

"What is happening?" she asked. Kazaar's hold tightened, offering comfort from the unknown. Another image appeared, but this one was of the night skies: an expanse of darkness littered with clouds blocking the stars. The music's pace increased, and Elisara struggled to keep up as images invaded their minds—transparent glass, a glow, blurred movements—it was so quick, she could not make out its significance. As the song drew to an end, Elisara panted, standing in the hall's centre with Kazaar. Couples separated, laughing between themselves, with some more intoxicated than others. Elisara looked around the room. Vlad stood by the entryway and frowned at her expression before attempting to navigate towards them. Larelle sat with Alvan and Zarya, eating dessert. Nyzaia appeared to be in a heated discussion with Tajana on the stairs; Caellum swayed with Sadira in the candlelight, and Soren sat with her wolves at a table. Alone.

"Something is wrong; something feels off," she murmured to Kazaar.

"I feel it," he said, reaching for the pommel of his sword. The shadows appeared again, yet they did not disappear this time; they crawled across the floor from under Kazaar and Elisara's feet. Under the flurry of feet, no one seemed to notice, except for Larelle, who caught Elisara's eye as she stood and glanced at the Historian.

Black appeared in Elisara's mind again. The night sky. Glass. Black. The night sky. Glass. Trees. A glass room. Flowers. People.

Elisara and Kazaar looked up as he pulled a sword from his back.

"Everyone take cover!" he shouted, yanking Elisara with him as the glass ceiling shattered and rained down on them all.

Chapter Eighteen

Nyzaia

Blood oozed from Nyzaia's hand as she tried to rise from the floor. She clenched her fist and winced at the shards of glass slicing her skin and shredding them further. Ringing sounded in her ears as she rose onto all fours. Yet, through the sensation, she heard growls and wondered if Soren's wolves were nearby. Carefully, Nyzaia crawled to the wall at the base of the steps. She did not remember walking down them. The last thing she remembered was a disagreement with Tajana after questioning where she was headed as she tried to leave the hall.

"Why are you suddenly concerned about my movements?" Tajana had asked. Nyzaia was about to snap about Farid following Tajana in Khami before the glass ceiling shattered.

Nyzaia's ribs roared in pain. The force of whatever crashed through the rooftop must have sent her flying.

She turned and used the wall to prop herself up. That's when she saw them. The ringing eased, replaced with screams as creatures she had never seen descended on the citizens. If Elisara and Kazaar had not described these creatures before, she would have convinced herself this was a dream, but no description would have prepared Nyzaia for the horrid reality. The creatures bore torn black wings threaded with thick veins that knocked people to the floor with ease. Growling, they roamed the hall, alternating between murderous methods: wrapping their wings around their prey before snapping their bones or using their dagger-like teeth to tear heads from shoulders, splattering blood across their faces and into the empty pits where their eyes should be.

Double the height of a normal person, the creatures appeared like disfigured humans coated in black leather skin, except they switched between walking on hind legs to using their front claws to crouch and tear at the faces of those in the room. A flip inside Nyzaia switched. Her role as queen of Keres dropped like a mask, and adrenaline rushed through her blood. The queen of the Red Stones narrowed her eyes to survey the room.

Chaos filled the hall. No one appeared to know what was happening, and no one fought back. But who was left to fight? Garridon soldiers lay scattered along the walls where they were stationed, most of them ripped to shreds; many were unrecognisable as the creatures feasted on their remains before prowling again. Nyzaia paused on some bodies who did not fit that pattern, victims who lay with their eyes open and limbs still intact, except for a simple slash across their necks. A pale blue uniform passed Nyzaia and ascended the steps. She grabbed his ankle.

"You cannot abandon!" she shouted over the noise.

"I am not!" It was Vlad, the captain of Elisara's Queen's Guard. He reached for Nyzaia and pulled her up, steadying her against the wall. A dull throbbing ached in her side from where she had fallen, but besides that, and the glass pinching her skin, she was stable, her mind focused. She snatched a knife from Vlad's thigh and cut at the skirts of her lehenga, freeing her feet and legs. "Elisara and Kazaar need a sword. It is in her chambers," he explained. *The Sword of Sonos.*

"Go! Quickly!" she said. The only method of defeating these creatures was not even in the room. Foolish. They should have been prepared. They were naïve to not expect the creature to return for the sword, and it appeared it brought friends.

Nyzaia counted five creatures: four hunched over bodies, intent on feasting before moving to the next victim, but one prowled the room, disinterested in the bloodshed. It crawled on all fours, sniffing the air and scanning its surroundings. Nyzaia followed its eyeline to where it landed on the crowd that had gathered by the music. She glimpsed a dark braid and raised hands clutching knives. *Tajana*. Nyzaia's heart raced until she realised it was not her. Elisara's friend, Talia, battled her way through falling people, intent on reaching her queen. Nyzaia could not see Elisara as the imposing size of the creatures blocked her view, jumping between victims.

One raised its head and gave a high-pitched shriek, forcing everyone still standing to cover their ears. The screech could pierce eardrums and reverberated across the floor, flinging people back. Nyzaia summoned fire and aimed it at the creature's wings, though it did little but singe them before dissipating. The creature was at the edge of the dancefloor, clambering over broken tables when it turned its head to search for its attacker. Nyzaia stared at the dark sockets where its eyes once were, and it turned towards her while the other creatures spread throughout the room. It screamed as someone slid beneath its legs, slicing at its feet with two long blades. The signature red uniform came into view as Farid rose and ran towards her.

"Are you okay?" He passed her two long daggers and retrieved the two sickle blades from his back. Nodding, she discarded Vlad's dagger and positioned herself at Farid's side.

"The others?" she asked. While the other creatures feasted, the lone beast circled the hall. Nyzaia narrowed her eyes. Were the other four merely a distraction? She lost sight of it behind another set of large wings as a flurry of people tried to flee into the castle or out towards the gardens. Nyzaia searched for Caellum and Sadira; after all, it was their home. What if they were the targets? A flash of blonde hair slid past a creature, but it was Soren who rose, not her sister. The king and his betrothed were nowhere to be seen amongst the chaos, yet it was difficult to focus on anything for long enough before something—or someone—captured her attention.

"Somewhere over there," he said, gesturing to where her syndicate attacked two creatures. A dark braid flashed again, ducking under mighty wings. She hoped Tajana was okay. Issam cupped and lowered his hands as Rafik, the slightest of the men, ran towards him, wedging his foot in Isaam's palms, who threw him into the air to land on the creature. As Rafik plunged a dagger into the creature's back to offer a distraction, Jabir sliced its legs. Nyzaia gave a sigh of relief. They were okay. Knowing the three were skilled enough to deal with this alone, she switched her attention to the creature beside them.

The beast was distracted as blonde braids ran circles around it. Soren's furious screams attracted a third creature, the one Nyzaia had targeted. It took a step towards her and another.

"You take its legs, and I'll go for the wings," Nyzaia commanded Farid, who nodded. As they approached, Soren roared as a claw sliced her face, and the creature moved towards them.

"Protect the queen!" called a voice Nyzaia yearned for. Tajana was okay. She was calling for her syndicate to assist Nyzaia and Farid. As a Garridon soldier lunged at the creature before them, Nyzaia scanned for Tajana, preparing a formation in her mind. Her staple black leather and dark braid emerged from the chaos, and Nyzaia breathed a sigh of relief, one that left her winded with a blow of betrayal when Tajana screamed again. "Protect the queen!"

Instead of running to Nyzaia, Tajana rallied to Soren's aid and braced an arm around her shoulder. Nyzaia stumbled, and Farid caught her elbow. A second tanned-skinned beauty with matching dark hair assisted Tajana, defending her and Soren from the creature. She was not from her syndicate. When Nyzaia finally locked eyes with Elisara across the room, they wore matching expressions as they watched Talia fight for the fallen queen.

"Nice of you to join me, sister!" Tajana shouted to Talia, who grinned and sliced her sword through the creature's wing, buying the women time to reform before the stump grew back. The fighting in the room seemed to slow as Nyzaia stepped forward, watching the person she had shared everything with—her life, her love, her soul—check Soren's wounds before throwing themselves back into the fight. She did not even glance in Nyzaia's direction or bother to find her whereabouts. Anger consumed her, and flames flooded her arms as she strode forward. How dare she? How dare she betray Nyzaia after all they had gone through? Furious questions rushed through Nyzaia's mind as her flames burned, running rampant along her arms and igniting across the floor. She did not need to focus on it as it weaved amongst bodies towards Tajana. How long had Tajana known Soren? Was her story ever true? Had she ever been an orphan, or was Tajana from Doltas Island, too? Nyzaia blinked, watching as the flames reached Tajana, whose back was turned, checking Soren's wounds again while Talia shielded them. Did Nyzaia know Tajana at all?

A firm hand grabbed Nyzaia's wrist, extinguishing the flames on their warpath. She spun her head, and sparks ignited in her hair. Farid gripped Nyzaia's wrist, unflinching against her flames.

"Later," said Farid. "She is not the priority."

"I want to see her alight in flames," hissed Nyzaia, but Farid stepped closer, tightening his grip.

"And you will." Farid's gaze was intense as he stared into Nyzaia's eyes. "If there is anything left of Tajana once I get my hands on her." Farid's menacing promise was a testament to his loyalty, which burned in his pale blue eyes. She believed him. "What can we do right now to turn this battle?"

Nyzaia whirled to analyse, implementing the skills she had acquired as a Red Stone. She avoided looking in Tajana's direction but focused on the right instead. Garridon soldiers formed a line to shield Sadira, while Caellum drew his sword alongside them, protecting her from another prowling creature. In the centre of the room, Elisara and Kazaar stood back-to-back: Elisara with a dagger, and him with a sword, each facing a creature of their own. The rest of Nyzaia's syndicate approached the creatures from behind to distract them. Relief settled in her heart as she realised they had not followed Tajana's call but remained loyal to Nyzaia. Still, the fifth creature still stalked the edge of the room, batting off soldiers attempting to reach it.

Pale blue appeared in her vision again as Vlad ran down the steps, crunching on glass underfoot. He held two swords.

"Cover him!" Nyzaia pointed to Vlad. She and Farid took off in a run until they reached Vlad, standing on either side of him. He panted, sweat dripping from his forehead.

"There were two; I didn't know which," Vlad said between gulps for air.

"They need the gold one, but Elisara doesn't currently have a sword. Give her the dull one." When Nyzaia stepped forward, someone screamed. She stood on someone's hand, belonging to a mauled victim, who stared up at her, his features obscured by five claw marks so deep she glimpsed bone. His other hand reached for her ankle.

"Help me," he groaned, dark blood spewing from his lips. Someone lodged a dagger in his mouth. Farid removed the blade and wiped it clean against his leg.

"It was the only way to help," he said, and though Nyzaia agreed, Vlad turned green. She analysed the position of the creatures again; the safest route to Kazaar was along the left wall, which looped around the back. It meant going past Tajana, Talia, and Soren. Nyzaia narrowed her eyes.

"Ready?" Farid asked from Vlad's other side.

"Ready." Nyzaia nodded, and the three took off at a run along the wall, jumping over body parts and debris. Nyzaia ignored the fresh slices in her feet as glass crunched underfoot. She was fixated only on Tajana, who swung repeatedly at the creature, synchronising with Soren and Talia. The three women moved like extended parts of one another like they had known each other for years. Tajana spun low, slicing off the creature's foot, but paused upon spotting Nyzaia.

Tajana rose with wide eyes and stepped towards Nyzaia, opening her mouth to speak.

"Tajana!" called Talia. A flash of indecision crossed Tajana's features. *I'm sorry*, she mouthed before joining Talia. Nyzaia buried her pain beneath the flames burning within and continued her run, intent on reaching Elisara and Kazaar.

Chapter Nineteen

Larelle

"Shhh. It is okay," hummed Larelle, rocking Zarya beneath the table and muffling her cries against her chest. "It is okay." She did not know if she was reassuring her daughter or herself and flinched as a roar echoed throughout the hall.

When Kazaar shouted for everyone to take cover, Alvan had been quick to pull the tablecloth up and push Larelle and Zarya beneath it, cocooning the pair in his arms to protect them from whatever had crashed through the ceiling.

"Where is Lillian?" Zarya sniffed. Larelle exchanged a look with Alvan. Lillian was getting drinks when the attack happened. Alvan's eyes widened, and he clenched his jaw.

"I will look for her," Alvan said, stroking Zarya's hair as he shifted onto his knees. Larelle grabbed his arm as screams sounded from outside their table, followed by crunching that she did not think was simply the splintering of wooden tables.

"You cannot go out there," she pleaded. Alvan looked at Zarya and then Larelle.

"I cannot let her lose someone else," he said, and Larelle turned his face to meet hers

"And what would I tell her if we lost you?" Larelle argued, blinking back tears.

"I told you: I am here. I will always be here," he said before pushing himself out from under the table.

"Alvan!" She tried to call after him, but it was no use.

That felt like an eternity ago now. Something thudded above them, and Zarya cried into Larelle's shoulder as it shook the table.

"Where is Mr Alvan?" Zarya sobbed, trying to lift her head. Larelle kept her head down and stroked her hair with trembling fingers.

"He will be right back," Larelle murmured. "He will be right back."

Larelle could see blood dripping onto the floor through a short gap under the tablecloth. Screams filled the hall, and Larelle tried to cover Zarya's ears while intently assessing the gap. She refused to blink as she watched the stone, preparing to move should anything pass into her vision. The shadows that had crawled across the floor prior to the crash were gone, but she could not forget the display of darkness seeping from below Kazaar's feet as he and Elisara stood toe to toe. Larelle had sought the Historian immediately, who watched with a knowing look. How could she deny the darkness after witnessing it with her very own eyes? It appeared like a fog at first, trickling beneath their feet and floating across the stone before darkening around the pair. It did not reach the crowds or attempt to inflict harm; it simply sat, waiting, until Kazaar called to take cover. Yet Larelle could not discern if the darkness called the creatures or if it warned of their arrival. Nobody had gasped or pointed at the shadows buried under dancing feet. She felt as though she was the only one to notice.

With Alvan having acted so quickly, Larelle had not caught sight of the creatures until feet appeared beneath the gap in the tablecloth. Larelle pulled Zarya closer and held her breath. The creature crouched, its front two feet curled under like fists, almost as if they were once hands. It dragged its claws through the blood accumulating next to the table from whoever had been thrown above her, and a foul stench drifted under the table as the creature lowered to flick its tongue in the crimson puddle. She hoped the beast would not hear her daughter's muffled sobs. Larelle's heartbeat pounded in her ears as she held her breath, waiting and preparing. She glanced at the space beside her, readying to throw Zarya towards it and lunge at the creature should it reach for them, sacrificing herself. The creature's tongue paused before flicking back into its mouth and angling its head towards the table. It growled low, and Larelle felt its rumble in her chest as she removed one arm from Zarya and placed her hand on the floor. Fog rose from the creature's nostrils when it exhaled and hooked a claw beneath the tablecloth.

"Over here!" Alvan shouted. The creature raised its head from the ground and leapt over the table, allowing Larelle a moment to finally breathe. She jumped as the tablecloth flew open but sobbed to find Lillian crouching before them.

"Quick! While Alvan is distracting it, there is a clear route to the servants' entrance." Lillian reached for Zarya, who crawled out from the table, sobbing harder upon reaching Lillian's arms. Larelle followed closely behind, her stomach turning as she took in the blood and limbs scattered throughout the room, a river of red flooding the stone floor. Zarya lifted her head on Lillian's shoulder, but Larelle gripped her cheeks, forcing her eyes to hers. Her daughter's midnight blue eyes were rimmed red as she looked at her mother.

"You do *not* look. Do you understand?" Larelle told her. Zarya stared back, her lip quivering. "You keep your head down on Lillian's shoulder until Lillian tells you otherwise. Okay?" Zarya nodded and buried her face into Lillian's hair.

Larelle searched for something to protect them. All the creatures were distracted, including the two battling Elisara and Kazaar at the far end of the hall. When Larelle spun, she found what she needed. Summoning water from the outside fountain, she brought it towards them and created a barrier as they clambered over bodies and debris to reach the door.

The three reached it at the same time as Alvan, who scanned Zarya and Larelle. She nodded to answer his silent question before expanding her thin barrier of water to include him. A man huddled behind them.

"Are you okay, sir?" Larelle asked the Historian. He met her eye and nodded, his face pale. Larelle opened the door and hurried them all inside, where multiple citizens sat crowded on the steps, frozen in fear.

"Lillian," Larelle said, grasping her free hand and scanning her eyes intently. "Please look after her."

"You know I will," Lillian said with a squeeze. Larelle took one last look at her daughter before closing the door on them.

Peering through her shield of water, she assessed the chaos. Bodies lay strewn across the room in pieces, except for those whose necks were slashed. Surviving citizens crawled or scrambled for the stairs or tree line now the glass walls had fallen.

"Is that Tajana fighting with Soren?" Larelle asked with wide eyes. Alvan lowered his head.

"I heard Tajana call to protect the queen, but then she ran for Soren with that other woman." Alvan pointed to someone who looked very similar to Tajana. Nyzaia and one of her guards fought to their right, alongside the captain of Elisara's guard, who held two swords. Larelle looked ahead, following their path. Elisara and Kazaar stood back-to-back, facing two creatures. A scattering of Nyzaia's guards surrounded them, aiding the pair.

A large, leather-clad man stabbed at the back of a creature, who spun, outraged, before noticing the Sword of Sonos. Shrieking, the beast staggered for Nyzaia, who had not yet noticed. Larelle moved her water barrier to shield the Keres queen, and the creature stumbled back, momentarily confused. Yet it was not long before it stalked forward again. Nyzaia spotted the beast and ran as it swiped a claw through the wall with ease. Larelle swallowed. It could have easily caught Nyzaia's flesh had she still been there. Yet Larelle had stopped Nyzaia by forcing her to change direction and offering a clear route to Elisara and Kazaar, who now faced only one creature while the Keres guards cornered another.

"We need to reach them." Larelle grabbed Alvan's hand, placing it on the hem of her gown. "Rip it," she said.

Alvan was quick to do as his queen commanded, but she noticed the blush creep across his cheeks as his hands brushed her thighs and tore the fabric. Larelle reached for his hand and interlocked their fingers, holding him tightly as they ran into the chaos to defend their kingdom.

Together.

Chapter Twenty

Elisara

Elisara felt no fear this time as she stared into the creature's empty sockets. She was unsure if her confidence came from knowing how to kill them, the need to defend the people, or fighting with Kazaar by her side. His back stood firm against hers, a reassuring presence.

It only took a second to realise what was about to descend on the engagement ball the moment Kazaar reached for his sword. The images flashing through their minds had been unclear; that was until the scene of the ball appeared, showing the dancing revellers, the flickering candlelight on the dancefloor, and Elisara's red dress pressed against Kazaar. It was not his vision, but someone else's—*something* else's.

Elisara saw nothing when glass rained upon them, and the creatures descended. A wall of black shadow rushed up below her and Kazaar, shielding them, if only momentarily. It dropped the second the creature roared and flung the pair apart. Elisara used the air to brace herself and balance her fall; at least, she thought it was her own until the subtle spiced scent in the breeze hinted it belonged to someone else.

"Are you okay?" Kazaar's voice sounded in her mind. Elisara nodded, though she could not see him. A creature stood before her, the stench of its breath tossing back her hair as it bared its teeth. Elisara narrowed her eyes and clenched her fists; she needed a weapon.

"On your right," said Kazaar. A second later, a dagger soared through the air, and she caught it, slicing at the creature's throat.

It hunched at the sudden attack, allowing her time to survey the damage and count the creatures. "*Five,*" Kazaar confirmed, swinging at the creature, spraying black blood onto the floor as he connected with the creature's side. With the surrounding carnage, how could they possibly kill five creatures? *"I've sent Vlad to retrieve the Sword of Sonos."*

Elisara nodded as her eyes skipped over the falling bodies, searching for the others. She could not see Caellum or Sadira, but a line of emerald uniforms stood in rigid formation on the other side of the hall, and she assumed they were among them. While searching for Larelle and Nyzaia through the blurred movements of darkness, a scream sounded above the chaos.

"Protect the queen!" a voice she recognised as Tajana's called. Elisara whirled. *No—not Nyzaia*. She panicked until spotting her friend's golden lehenga on the opposite side of the room. Nyzaia was unharmed. Elisara frowned and ducked to avoid a claw as a brown-haired beauty slid across the floor. It was not Tajana, however. Talia ran to Soren's aid and joined Tajana's side. *No.* Elisara's heart sunk, a pit forming deep within her stomach.

"Nice of you to join me, sister," Tajana jested.

Sister. Elisara had always said Talia had always looked like she hailed from Keres.

"Elisara!" Kazaar shouted. Elisara spun just as a claw swung at her shoulder, its onyx nails grazing her skin. She fell to the floor, and pain flooded her arm as she pushed herself up with one hand. Her eyes met those of a dark-haired woman drenched in blood with both arms missing. Elisara swallowed, recalling the last time she had stared into such lifeless eyes, recalling her father on the temple floor. The memory almost cost her as large, padded feet stood on either side of her body, caging her in. She peered up at the creature's eyeless face, its lips dripping with drool. It tipped back its head and roared.

Elisara screamed as someone grabbed her ankles and pulled her across the floor beneath the creature's legs.

"Hello, angel." Relief flooded Elisara as Kazaar leaned over her with a smile, undeterred by the chaos. But then he cried out, crumpling beneath a creature's claw. It did not get another chance to swing again as a man Elisara recognised from Nyzaia's syndicate embedded his sword into the creature's stomach, shoving it backward. Kazaar grunted and held himself above Elisara, who pushed up against his weight as she tried to position them to kneeling. She touched his back, her fingers suddenly wet. Too much. He was losing too much blood. Her knuckles whitened as she gripped Kazaar's shoulder. He would not last long without a healer.

"We will get you help," Elisara murmured, her eyes wide as she scanned the gardens behind Kazaar in the hope of finding more soldiers or someone to carry him. She pulled her hand away and blinked to his blood was no longer crimson but shimmered silver. She did not know whether to be relieved at the lack of red blood.

Kazaar panted and wiped his thumb over Elisara's collarbone. She flinched when he brushed the spot caught by the creature, yet when he inspected his thumb, the same silver liquid marked it. Elisara's blood was silver, too. *Their* blood was silver. She grabbed his hand, their changed blood intertwining. They gasped as threads of shadow and light drifted from their hands and reached for their wounds. Awe-struck, Elisara gasped as the threads that tied them floated behind his back, the same threads knitting and binding the skin above her collarbone. Elisara glanced around to check if anyone had seen, or for reassurance she had not lost her mind, but they were all too encompassed by the chaos to notice.

Kazaar straightened with no hesitation in his movements as he examined her collarbone. Behind him, Vlad, Nyzaia, and Farid approached.

"What do we do with one sword?" asked Vlad. Elisara reached for the second in his hand: a dull grey sword she had nostalgically kept after leaving the Unsanctioned Isle with Kazaar. He reached for the Sword of Sonos. She looked to the others in case they wondered why it was he who wielded it, but their expressions were unchanged, with Nyzaia too focused on assessing Kazaar for injuries. Elisara was the only one to note the soft light emanating from Kazaar's hands when he gripped the sword seconds before shadows twisted from his grip to secure the weapon in place. When she looked at her own, nothing happened.

Elisara felt compelled to touch the Sword of Sonos to see if it responded to her the same way. She did not get the chance to try. A creature charged, the crook of its wings pinning her against the stone wall of the castle once connected to the glass exterior. Elisara's hair was slick against her face as she grunted, using her elbows to shove its wings off her. The creature did not budge. For a second, she thought this was it. This might truly be her end.

With a push of resolve, she struck the creature. Lodging her thumbs in its empty eye sockets, she shoved with all her might. It screamed and stumbled back as the silvery blood painting Elisara's fingers marred its face—a face that no longer moved. The creature froze, paralysed, before its head tumbled to the floor, spewing red blood as Kazaar sliced the Sword of Sonos through its neck. Elisara stumbled back, watching as the flesh where its eyes had been sizzled under their blood.

"Our blood... it paralysed it," she whispered. Kazaar nodded and called for Nyzaia, who instantly joined him. Grabbing her dagger, he sliced both his and Elisara's palms. She flinched as the glittering substance spilled from her skin, coating the dagger silver. Nyzaia only frowned when Kazaar returned the weapon.

"Trust me," he said before continuing to collect weapons from her syndicate, marring each one with a combination of their blood. Elisara watched as Nyzaia sliced the wings off a creature, but they did not grow back this time. In its confusion, Kazaar pierced its chest with the golden sword, the light glowing brighter with every defeat. *Two down. Three to go.*

A rush of water sounded near Elisara's ears, who turned to find Larelle behind her, summoning an aquatic barrier to pen two of the creatures in yet only slowing them. The third was too focused on breaking through the Garridon line. Elisara threw her blood-coated daggers, bypassing Larelle and Alvan and paralysing the legs of two creatures in one hit. Seeming to realise their plan, Soren fled towards the Garridon line to where the final creature loomed. Though Elisara did not like her, she trusted Soren would defend her sister.

Chapter Twenty-One

Caellum

Adrenaline coursed through Caellum's veins as he swung at the creature, targeting the line of his remaining soldiers. The soldiers were quick to arrange into formation, their movements succinct and focused as they protected their king. Caellum saw the fear in their widened eyes and felt uncomfortable at their speed to protect him, a clear show of their loyalty. When the creatures arrived, Caellum pulled Sadira to him and searched for Sir Cain, who ran out of the shattered glass wall for the training yards. Caellum assumed he was raising the alarm for the resting soldiers and guards. He hoped he was quick.

Channelling all his pent-up anger, Caellum fought with the added strength from his lineage, which aided every swing against the creature. Nevertheless, he could not help but feel inadequate upon realising there was little else he could do to protect his betrothed. Even if he had the powers gifted to those in the Garridon line, it was clear from the ease with which the creature broke through Sadira's vines that the power was of little use against them. They were not equipped for this; this attack could very well be the end. The line of soldiers pushed ahead of Caellum, allowing him a chance to breathe. They had worked in sync ever since the creatures landed, and this one creature in particular seemed intent on reaching him and Sadira. Caellum glanced at the surrounding devastation and instinctively reached for Sadira, finding her hand.

A calm washed over him as their fingers intertwined, the feel of her silver engagement ring cold against his skin. He grew more focused as he scanned the room. Only two creatures remained:

the one bombarding his soldiers and another targeted by Kazaar and Alvan. Caellum frowned at the absence of the other creatures, yet he finally understood when he glimpsed the glint of gold in Kazaar's hand.

A roar sounded from the creature before him, who swiped at Caellum's men, brushing them aside in one swoop. Caellum backed up, and Sadira stumbled behind him.

"Caellum," Sadira said urgently. He raised his sword. This was it: life or death. A moment to prove himself strong or weak—to be a saviour, or a man who needed saving. *Weak*. His father's voice flashed through his memories, but Caellum was not beaten by those words. When Sadira spoke his name again, Caellum wished to prove his father wrong and show his worth, if only for the woman behind him. He swung his sword, grazing the creature, who reached for him with its talons. Behind, Soren charged towards the beast, her wild braids flowing behind her while blood oozed from a slash across her face. Crimson dripped off her silver Garridon armour mixed with the creatures' black blood. Caellum could have sworn it sparkled as she moved beneath the candlelight. Snarling, Soren's deep green eyes glowed as she raised her sword. The creature had not yet seen her; it growled and lowered onto its front claws, which appeared more like knuckles that crunched beneath its weight when it lowered its head to their eye-level.

Caellum's eyes locked with the creature's, and instead of hollow crevices, it had eyes of dark black. The beast's movements were specific and composed compared to its counterparts, and it seemed intent on reaching them. Amber rings glowed in its irises, and Sadira gasped. Soren's approach slowed, though her sword remained raised as she advanced.

Caellum angled his head to check for Sadira, which was his mistake. In mere seconds, the creature rose and towered over them, its claws glistening as it knocked Caellum's sword from his hand, sending it skating across the room. Caellum shifted to shield Sadira, and hesitation crossed her sister's face.

Soren looked at the creature's raised claws and met Caellum's gaze. Her eyes flitted to Sadira behind him. Stepping back from the creature's reach, Soren lowered her sword and called her wolves to her side.

"Soren!" Caellum screamed as the creature swung. Soren disappeared as a wall of trees shot up before him, shattering the stone beneath his feet. The wood splintered as the creature swung again, offering Caellum a split second to grab Sadira and lunge from the path of death. Caellum fell atop her, peering into Sadira's bright green eyes that glowed. She had saved them. Him. *She* had saved him.

Caellum tried to catch his breath as he gazed down at Sadira beneath him and gulped at the flush in her cheeks. Relief filled her eyes as she reached for his face, but upon realising his position, Caellum cleared his throat and rose, offering her a hand. She clung to his chest while he searched for the creature, but it did not stand behind the pile of splintered wood. Soren did. Her expression was unreadable as she stared at Caellum and Sadira, who, still embracing, stared right back. This was war, and all three knew it. Soren had declared her intentions. Anger brewed in Caellum's chest as he thought of Soren's willingness to sacrifice her sister's life to secure the throne. Turning, he looked for Elisara but found Kazaar instead, piercing the Sword of Sonos through the beast's skull before him. Alvan rose from the ground beside Kazaar, coated in a mixture of blood: red, black, and a shimmering liquid Caellum could not comprehend.

Kazaar offered his hand to Alvan and patted his back as he rose. Alvan grinned. They were nearly there, and only one creature remained. Alvan's grin fell, and he shoved Kazaar aside.

"No!" Alvan screamed, the sound so raw it sent shivers up Caellum's spine, emulating the panic and pain only heard about in stories. Alvan made to run past Caellum and Sadira, but Kazaar grabbed him, locking his arm around his blood-spattered chest to keep him back. "No!" Alvan screamed again. With four of the five creatures defeated, the room fell silent. Sadira turned, the fabric of her gown catching against the shards of broken glass. Her face paled. Caellum looked behind him and grabbed Sadira, guiding her back towards the others. The creature had chosen a new target, redirected by Sadira's defence. It stood and faced them all. The creature panted heavily on its hind legs, and in the clutches of one clawed hand, poised perfectly around her neck, hanging mid-air and choking for breath, was Larelle.

"No," Sadira breathed.

Tears pooled in Larelle's gaze as the creature's hold tightened, yet behind her eyes was a look of resolve and determination—a queen who accepted her fate. Larelle's voice cracked as she spoke in forced breaths.

"I, Queen Larelle of Nerida..." Caellum pulled Sadira close as they edged towards the others who gathered before the creature in the centre of the room. Elisara gripped Nyzaia's arm, who frantically scanned their surroundings. Following her lead, Caellum searched for a distraction and checked the gardens outside, hoping for a miracle of more arriving soldiers, to no avail. There was no way out. "... declare, in witness of my fellow rulers." Larelle gasped, and Caellum looked at Kazaar, who held Alvan back with one hand while gripping the Sword of Sonos in the other. They needed to find a way for the creature to drop Larelle. He looked at Elisara, who also explored the room. Their eyes met as Larelle continued, "That upon my death—"

"No!" Alvan yelled again, struggling against Kazaar. "Larelle, you are not dying!" The creature shifted on its feet and jerked its head in different directions, narrowing its amber-ringed eyes on each of them. Larelle offered Alvan a sad smile, watching only him. She struggled to open her mouth again but managed to force the words.

"That upon my death, Lord Alvan shall rule the realm of Nerida until my daughter is of age." A tear fell down her cheek.

"Larelle, please!" Alvan whimpered. "PLEASE!" He screamed,

frantically looking at everyone else in the room. Slowly lowering into a crouch, Caellum's eyes remained locked on Elisara's as he reached for a sword in a dead soldier's hand and angled it in a way she would recognise. He jerked his head towards the creature and tapped his arm. Elisara nodded. Positioning the sword, Caellum prepared to throw it towards the creature's arm, knowing Elisara would use her power to guide it.

"Look after her," Larelle sobbed. Tears streamed down her face as her eyes stayed locked on Alvan. Sadira sobbed beside Caellum, her hand over her mouth. "She loves you as much as she would have loved her father."

Caellum raised his arm while the creature angled it's head at Alvan and threw the sword. He saw the moment Elisara caught it on the breeze, but the creature saw it too. With a shattering scream that matched Alvan's, shards of glass rattled on the floor as the creature launched through the remains of the shattered ceiling with Larelle still in its clutches, disappearing into the darkness of the night.

Chapter Twenty-Two

Sadira

"How dare you?" Alvan shrugged free from Kazaar's hold and rounded on him, shoving him back. Kazaar stood his ground, hardly budging against Alvan's fury as his tirade of hits continued. No one spoke, a solemn and shocked silence heavy in the air. "I promised her!" Alvan screamed as his shoves against Kazaar slowed. Tears rolled down his face. "I promised her I would always be with her.

Sadira swallowed tears as Alvan's emotions weighed heavily on them all. This was more than a man losing his queen. Sadira thought back to Larelle's reaction when she asked if there was a man in her life, and while Sadira knew little of the queen's feelings, Lord Alvan's were evident.

Alvan wiped his face and turned to the rest of the group. "We need to get her back."

"Alvan, we have no idea where it would have taken her," Elisara reasoned, and Nyzaia nodded beside her, though her gaze tugged toward Tajana who was tending to the victims of the attack.

"I do not care," Alvan snapped. "We. Need. To. Find. Her!"

Sadira's head turned as the servant's door at the far side of the hall squeaked open, and a woman's voice called out, "Larelle?"

"Caellum!" Sadira urged, signalling to the door. He ran over to it as a blonde woman appeared holding the young princess, who nuzzled into her neck. Caellum blocked their view as he approached, shielding them from further devastation.

"Vlad!" Elisara shouted to the captain of her guard, who assisted the flood of Garridon soldiers arriving to support the injured.

"Can you take Princess Zarya to her rooms? Make sure she is comfortable," Elisara said. Alvan's face crumpled again, and he turned his back on the princess. Sadira wiped the tear from her cheek, ignoring the ache in her chest upon knowing the child had now lost her father and mother.

Vlad jogged over to where Caellum shielded them, guiding them back through the servant's entrance. He stepped aside to allow someone entry. The Historian shuffled through and clasped Caellum's arm for stability. While Caellum guided him to where the group stood, shell-shocked, Sadira surveyed the situation. After all, she was the future queen of Garridon, and this happened in her realm. She handled what happened next. Soren leaned against what remained of the long table while the rest of it was mostly scattered in pieces across the hall; vines left from Sadira's decorations wilted behind her amongst the blood. Soren wore a sullen look as she surveyed the room, watching the Garridon Soldiers following Sir Cain's commands. Sadira lifted her chin, recalling the ease with which her own sister lowered her sword and refused to save them. She refused to allow her emotions to take over.

Elisara stood opposite Sadira on what had once been the ballroom floor, her arm braced around Nyzaia, whose face remained unreadable. A pale blue-eyed guard plucked the glass from her hand while the Keres queen stole glances at Tajana and the similar-looking woman beside her. Something had happened during the devastation. Nyzaia's syndicate were mixed among the Garridon guards, checking the pulses of those who lay scattered across the floor. So much loss and devastation. Sadira would visit the infirmary later to gauge the survivors.

Kazaar stood close to Elisara and held Alvan's shoulders, talking to him in hushed tones. When Kazaar clapped him on the back and headed to his queen, Alvan strode towards Sadira, and it took everything in her to keep the pity from her face.

"I need to do something," he said. "Anything: a distraction, a plan—anything to stop my mind from pondering every possible scenario of what could be happening to Larelle right now." He gulped, and Sadira nodded, glancing at the surrounding devastation.

"Help me clear the debris from this table," she said, turning to clear the scattered wood and broken flowers. As Alvan cleared the debris, Sadira got to work. She flourished her hands until vines grew and twisted, reforming and securing the tables and chairs, weaving the wood with flowers and plants until they formed a vague resemblance of what they once were: a mismatch of wood and greenery rather than their previous, finely carved, state.

"I've never seen the Garridon powers in action before," Alvan said, his face down-turned.

"That would be because there hasn't been a true Garridon heir on this land for so long." Soren's dull tone approached the table as she pulled back a chair and took a seat. Sadira clenched her jaw as she watched her sister, who was fortunately smart enough not to rot the vines this time for risk of falling through it. Alvan barely acknowledged the statement but helped Caellum lower the Historian into the chair beside her. The Historian studied the room as the other rulers approached and took a seat. Elisara and Nyzaia sat on one side of the long table, with Soren and the Historian on the other. Alvan took a seat at the end, staring teary-eyed into the distance, and Sadira waited until Caellum joined her. Together, they each took a seat at the head of the table.

Kazaar stood firm behind Elisara and Farid behind Nyzaia. The Keres queen's syndicate and Vlad formed a line to keep anyone from approaching the table, and when Tajana and the other woman approached, the steely gazes from Elisara and Nyzaia were clear. The women opted to stand beside Alvan and Soren, far enough to survey the room but close enough to hear the conversation. Elisara clasped Nyzaia's hand.

"Are we all comfortable with those present, given the sensitivity of this conversation?" asked Caellum, directing his question at Elisara and Nyzaia. Nyzaia opened her mouth as if to speak, but

Soren cut her off.

"Yes," she said simply. Sadira glanced between Soren and Nyzaia, who glared at one another, yet Nyzaia did not challenge her.

"We were not prepared for today," Caellum continued. "It is evident now—more than ever—that we must work together as a kingdom to protect our people." He led the conversation, and Sadira watched him with pride swelling in her chest.

Alvan was the first to challenge. "How do we do that when we barely even survived five creatures? The Sword of Sonos is not enough if an entire horde arrives at our shores."

"How do you know about the Sword of Sonos?" Elisara asked, frowning. Alvan hesitated.

"Larelle told me," he admitted. Sadira exchanged a glance with Caellum, wondering how many others had shared the information they had all agreed to keep to themselves. Yet when nobody challenged, her question was answered.

"Vlad knows," Elisara said.

"Olden, Larelle's father-in-law, and her lady-in-waiting, Lillian, know," said Alvan.

"Farid knows," Nyzaia echoed before glancing across the table. "As does Tajana." Tajana examined her feet.

"As does Talia," Soren continued. Sadira raised her eyebrows until realising that Soren referenced the woman standing beside Tajana. Was Sadira the only person clueless about the conflict between Soren and the queen of Keres? She did not wish to raise it and derail the conversation. Everyone's heads turned to Caellum and Sadira then. Caellum scoffed.

"It appears we are the only ones who have kept the promise to keep it amongst the rulers," said Caellum.

"I do not believe that for a second," Kazaar said, clenching his hands on the back of Elisara's chair. The queen of Vala reached up and squeezed it, silencing him.

"You cannot work together if secrets remain between you all," the Historian finally said, breathing heavily. "If you have found anything—*anything* that might prove useful—I suggest you speak now."

Sadira looked around the table. Perhaps she was the only one without secrets, although she trusted Caellum was honest, despite what the other rulers assumed. She caught Soren's eye. It was no secret among them that Soren wished Caellum dead. Alvan cleared his throat.

"Larelle's father had Riyas killed," he stated, allowing the statement to hang in the air.

"Would she want people to know that?" Elisara asked, raising her eyebrows. Alvan looked at the queen of Vala; his face morphed with pain.

"She cares about what is best for Nerida, her people, and the kingdom. She is selfless. If airing all our secrets allows us to piece together the prophecy or some sort of plan, then she would want it known." Sadira's heart warmed at his devotion.

"How did she know that, Alvan?" Sadira asked softly, and Alvan peered down at his hands, cracking his knuckles.

"Something never sat right about how Riyas left, so we went to the docks a few weeks ago. The records indicated he was sent on a scouting mission upon King Adrianus' request." He looked up at the Historian. "On the Royal Maiden."

The group lowered their eyes. The Royal Maiden was the vessel that was destroyed during its voyage to find the creatures.

"That is not all," Alvan continued. "A hidden room is connected to the battle room in the Castle of Mera. In it, there is a large map of Novisia, surrounded by the Novisian Sea Border, and an Outer Border covered in scattered Xs."

"What did they signify?" Kazaar asked from behind Elisara. Alvan shrugged and wiped his eyes again.

"We did not know, but the King kept other secrets. He had a portrait of each of the gods. Larelle could not understand why but deemed it unusual." Nyzaia's head whipped up.

"All four rulers?" she asked, and Alvan nodded. Hesitation

flickered on Nyzaia's face as she glanced at Tajana.

"It is safe to speak your mind, Nyzaia," Sadira reassured her, trying to mediate like Larelle always did. Caellum stroked circles on the back of her hand, sending reassuring waves through her skin. Nyzaia looked at Soren.

"Is it?" Nyzaia asked Soren, who smirked. "Is it safe?"

"It has to be if we are to get anywhere," Elisara said. "Why do you believe it is not?"

Nyzaia's eyes flickered to Tajana and then back at Soren. Leaning forward, she sneered, "Because *her* spy told me to only trust the other heirs."

Chapter Twenty-Three

Nyzaia

Hatred burned bright within Nyzaia without Tajana by her side, who so often kept it from consuming her. Nyzaia's eyes burned into her lover, who stared at the entrance, her eyes devoid of guilt as she stood by Soren's side, her true queen. She did not spare Nyzaia a glance. When Soren smirked, flames flickered at Nyzaia's fingertips and burned Elisara's hand. Still, Elisara did not flinch; she allowed Nyzaia to burn her instead of the fallen queen, who was to blame for her lover's betrayal. That was an easier pill to swallow than the truth of Tajana leading Nyzaia on for all these years and twisting the knife into her back.

"What do you mean, *spy*?" Kazaar asked from where he stood behind Elisara. Nyzaia recognised his tone; he spoke like the old commander of Keres, the man responsible for detecting spies like Isha and torturing people like Soren who dared to move against his realm. A part of Nyzaia warmed, knowing that despite his loyalties to Elisara, he had not forgotten where he came from.

"Isha," Nyzaia hissed. The others around the table exchanged glances. Feet shifted behind her at the mention of Isha's name. "When we last met in Garridon, Soren said she knew an Isha in Keres." Nyzaia tore her gaze from Soren's deep green eyes and peered at each person around the table in turn. "An Isha who was in secret communication with the king of Keres, whose last communication before he died said, '*Ready to burn.*' I do not believe it is a coincidence that shortly after, he and our parents died in an explosion. Isha told us to only trust the heirs." Soren smirked at the tension unfolding as the group looked at her. The

Historian leaned away and watched too. She swung on the back legs of her chair with her arms crossed. Although Tajana and Talia's eyes remained on the hall's entrance, Nyzaia noticed their hands shift as they touched the weapons at their sides.

"Well, do you see Sadira and I as true heirs? Or Caellum as an heir to a tainted throne? Because that will significantly change who you trust," said Soren, smirking. Nyzaia glanced between Caellum and the two sisters. *Who were they meant to trust?* "Are you also accusing me of having set the explosion, Nyzaia? And using Isha to do it?" When Nyzaia glanced at Elisara and Kazaar, Soren added, "No, you are not." She leaned forward, the front leg of her chair slamming against the stone, and pointed at Nyzaia. "Because you *know* who really set the explosion."

Nyzaia wanted to cut the smug look from her face and provide a matching scar to the one forming on her cheek.

"What does she mean?" asked Sadira.

"Do not act innocent, as though you are not on her side," spat Nyzaia. Sadira recoiled while Caellum leaned forward on the table, mirroring Soren's stance.

"She *is* innocent," he said sharply. "Trust me, Sadira has nothing to do with any information or plans Soren has."

"Trust you?" Kazaar scoffed, and Caellum clenched his hands against the table's edge.

"I do not know all her previous or present plans," said Sadira, bowing her head. "But I know she had spies across the realm."

"Can we cut the petty fighting?" snapped Alvan. "We need to be on the same page so we can plan to get Larelle back." Nyzaia flinched as she realised the pain Alvan was in, pain that stemmed from loss rather than betrayal. "Nyzaia, you looked as though you were going to say something when I mentioned the four portraits." Before Nyzaia could answer, Soren cut in.

"Are we simply ignoring that she knows who set the explosion? After you have all suspected me?" Soren raised her voice.

"Isha had drawings all around her rooms at the Red Stone Den.

Each wall was covered in sigils of all four realms, drawn in her blood." Nyzaia wavered at Soren's frown, which was the only indication of her confusion.

"All four?" Alvan asked, and Nyzaia nodded. Elisara took a deep breath. Nyzaia suspected she and Kazaar were mentally discussing how much to reveal to the others.

"On the Unsanctioned Isle, there was a room with all four statues of the gods, including Sonos and Sitara," Elisara began. The group fell silent until no other sound in the room remained. The soldiers had taken the remaining victims to the infirmary. "When we were at the Palace in Tabheri, we found a hidden room attached to King Razik's study." Alvan leaned forward at Elisara's words. "It had replicas of their statues, the full prophecy on a mirror, and—" Elisara paused and swallowed. "Letters between the King and my mother." Elisara looked at Kazaar, who nodded reassuringly, and Nyzaia squeezed her hand. "My mother and the king set the explosion."

Nyzaia expected chaos to erupt, yet Elisara's revelation was met with stoic looks, as though the news bore little impact compared to the death and destruction of the evening. It seemed no one was surprised by their parents' secrets.

"What if it was not just them?" Alvan asked, breaking the silence.

Nyzaia frowned. "What do you mean?"

"Well, the commonality in all of this is the four gods. There are four statues in your father's office and on the Isle, four sigils in Isha's room, and four portraits in King Adrianus'." Alvan looked at each ruler, notably ignoring Soren. "Larelle said the explosion was to trigger the prophecy, so what if all the rulers tried to trigger it? Could it relate to the gods?"

Nyzaia looked at the Historian to gauge his impression, but he sat silently with his hands in his lap, frowning.

"Why would they all want to trigger it, and why use references to the gods to do so?" Caellum asked, raising questions Nyzaia had no answer to.

"The prophecy," Sadira said suddenly, her eyes widening. "There is a line in the prophecy, '*only together can they defeat and restore; only together can they gain so much more. The Gods may whisper and help them on, only if all possess that from Ithyion.*'"

"They were trying to speak with the Gods," Elisara surmised. "In her letters to King Razik, my mother said they could not change the prophecy's course, so what if they tried to speak to the gods to stop the prophecy and prevent the return of d-darkness?" Nyzaia frowned as Elisara faltered.

"But then why would they set the explosion to trigger the prophecy? Why would they not leave it be in the hope it did not play out in our lifetime?" asked Caellum. The Historian cleared his throat.

"I believe there is likely more to this than we will ever learn, seeing as no one who set the explosion is present." Elisara flinched at Nyzaia's side. She and Caellum were the only ones among them who still grieved the loss of their families. "While this is the first I have heard of a prophecy, I recognise the last two lines of what Sadira recited in a history book from Ithyion." He coughed again, and Nyzaia noticed Alvan's stare as though waiting for him to elaborate. "The line about the gods was scrawled at the back of it." Nyzaia thought of the book hidden in her guest chambers. She wondered if she would discover more about the prophecy if she continued reading.

"If your parents were looking to commune with the gods, which is what this prophecy states, then I can only surmise that should be your next steps," said the Historian. Elisara shifted in her seat and adjusted the strap of her dress. Soren's eyes narrowed on the mark on Elisara's collarbone, the scar no longer pale but outlined in the same glittering silver where Kazaar's blood had been.

"Only if all possess that from Ithyion," Sadira repeated.

"We do not have anything from Ithyion," said Elisara. Nyzaia looked at Elisara's mark again, resting inches above her talisman.

She grabbed her own.

"The talismans!" Nyzaia exclaimed. "The talismans were created from parts of Ithyion."

"*All*," Sadira emphasised. "You need the other halves, too."

Nyzaia sighed, though she was relieved they were finally getting somewhere.

"You will all need to discover where in your realms the other halves are hidden," the Historian agreed. "Only with those can you then consider how to use them and connect to the gods."

"And ask them how to defeat these creatures and their darkness," Caellum replied. Everyone nodded, seemingly on the same page.

"You will need more than the talismans and a sword," said the Historian, dampening the mood. "If there is an entire horde on Ithyion like there was when your families fled, you will need more soldiers than your armies possess."

"Where do you suggest we find more bodies?" asked Kazaar, and the Historian sighed.

"We are but one kingdom; Ithyion was another. Who is to say there are no other lands out there—other beings able to send aid?" The Historian rose unsteadily from his seat. "I will leave; I will search for help," he concluded, though his trembling hands did little to reassure Nyzaia he was capable of such a thing, and it was a fool's hope to believe they would find other lands after all these years. Elisara said as much while Nyzaia grew distracted, watching Tajana whisper with Talia and noting their smiles and the family tie between them. How had she never realised?

"Ithyion was my home—*this* is my home." The Historian raised his voice. "I cannot fight here, but I can try to find others. I cannot stand by and lose another home." He choked, fighting his emotions.

"How can you be certain there are others?" Nyzaia asked.

"The creatures had to originate somewhere. When the beasts invaded Ithyion, where had they come from? It makes me suspect more lands exist," the Historian answered. "This land that is now Novisia was the first your ancestors found. Had they sailed further or in a different direction, they may have landed elsewhere." Nyzaia turned over his words. He was right. There could be much beyond the borders of their kingdom that had not yet been explored.

"You cannot do this alone," Elisara said softly. "You will need aid."

"My brother is a fine sailor. He is of station to have a ship." Alvan said and then clenched his jaw. "If I am to rule in Larelle's place, as she stated..." He glanced at his hands. "Then I can provide you with a ship and a crew." He nodded to the Historian, who gave him a pitiful smile. Tajana and Talia moved closer to where Alvan and Soren stood.

"You will need fighters," Kazaar added. "In case the lands you come across are hostile to visitors."

"Tajana will go," Nyzaia said bluntly. The room fell silent as Tajana looked at her, unspoken words flickering behind her eyes before facing Soren for approval. Flames ignited in Nyzaia's fingertips and licked up her arms. A hand brushed her shoulder, and Nyzaia angled her head up at Farid, attempting to calm her.

Soren nodded.

"I will go," Tajana said.

"Talia will join you," Elisara said, her coldness clear.

"Talia will join her," Soren agreed, smirking. Sadira's confusion was apparent as she watched their exchange beside Caellum, who squeezed her shoulder from where he stood.

"We shall all meet back in the Neutral City," Nyzaia said, eager to leave Tajana's presence. "It makes the most sense to try to connect with the gods from each realm."

"And Larelle?" Alvan asked, fighting back tears. "Where does saving Larelle fall into all these plans?"

"If we can speak to the gods, we can ask where we may find her." Nyzaia reassured him, but Alvan laughed without humour.

"How do you intend to speak to the gods when Larelle has half her talisman still around her neck?" He shouted.

"Shit," Kazaar swore. In the excitement of forming a plan, they had all selfishly forgotten their fellow ruler. Shame barraged Nyzaia's mind.

"It likely will not have travelled far," said the Historian. "They arrived as a pack; after such a battle, it is unlikely it could travel far carrying Larelle."

"The Trosso shores," Elisara said. "The first return of the creature was found on the shores of Trosso in a cavern. Perhaps that is where they kept hidden before their attack. What if that is where it has taken her in the meantime?"

Alvan nodded tightly, though his face was devoid of hope.

"I will send ships to patrol the Novisian border and with your permission, the shores across all four realms." He looked at Nyzaia, Caellum, and Elisara, who nodded in unison. "I will head to Trosso at first light." He said no more and left the room, his head lowered. Sadira hurried after him, with Caellum in quick pursuit.

"Vlad, could you escort the Historian to his Chambers?" Elisara called to her captain, having returned from aiding the Neridian princess. He did as asked until only Nyzaia, her syndicate, Soren, Tajana, and Talia remained. Soren rose from the table and clapped the backs of the two women standing to attention on either side of her.

"Talia, could you escort me to the infirmary?" Soren asked, gesturing at the wound on her face. Talia nodded, and they walked past Nyzaia, though not before a final taunt from Soren. "Tajana!" Soren barked. "Say your goodbyes," and then she left the room.

Nyzaia felt the presence of her syndicate behind her: Rafik, Issam, and Jabir. Farid moved to her side, drawing his sickle blade from his back. The clang of metal as the men withdrew their swords and daggers sounded next, and Nyzaia finally met Tajana's eyes. Every happy memory flashed through her mind then—every mission, kiss, and night together, the plans they made, and the life they dreamed of. It was all a lie.

"I loved you," Nyzaia choked, struggling to hold back the emotions she exposed to only *her.* Tajana said nothing, her face devoid of feeling. Nyzaia did not discern the emotions swimming in her green eyes: was it pity? Disappointment? Regret? Tajana opened her mouth to speak.

"Ny—"

"Do. *Not*. Speak. Her. Name." Farid stepped forward, and Tajana reached for the pommel of her sword. "You once said that to become captain of my Queen's Guard, I must best you." He took slow steps across the stone, but Tajana did not draw her weapon. The red of his traditional uniform was stark compared to her black leathers that once symbolised her dedication to the Red Stones. Tajana's eyes narrowed as she looked from Nyzaia to Farid. "I do not need to best you in swordplay when I have beaten you without ever needing to try."

Nyzaia stepped closer to Farid.

"What are you talking about?" Tajana sneered.

"I surpassed you the second you showed your true hand—the second you betrayed YOUR QUEEN." Nyzaia flinched, having never heard him raise his voice. "I bested you because I still have her trust." He glanced at Nyzaia as if seeking confirmation that she trusted him despite what happened in Khami. She nodded, and in one quick motion, Farid swung. Nyzaia gasped, taking a hesitant step forward, but Tajana still stood. The only mark was the torn leather on her chest.

"Pick it up," Farid growled. Tajana stood her ground and looked at Nyzaia, who ignored her. "I said, *pick* it up." Farid angled his blade at Tajana's cheek as she crouched and reached for the fabric on the ground. When she rose, she handed the Keres sigil to Farid—the mark of loyalty to the realm and Nyzaia, who she had betrayed.

Farid turned from Tajana, and Nyzaia almost missed a flash of flames in his eyes that were gone in seconds before returning to their otherworldly shade of blue. He handed Nyzaia the pin, and she crushed it with her fist.

"Nyzaia, please, you need to understand—" Tajana strode towards her but was met by a fiery wall, forming a shield around Nyzaia and her heart. When her lip quivered, Jabir reached for her, but she had already turned for the exit.

"I am fine," Nyzaia said. "I am always fine."

Chapter Twenty-Four

Soren

This was not part of the plan. At no point in the prophecy was Soren meant to nearly die at the hand of a creature before reclaiming her throne—a throne she had been seconds from taking, if not for her sister's intervention. The unpredictability of the evening sunk in as Soren thought of the events that had unfolded, ones *he* had told her nothing about. She could only assume it was his undoing and would confront such secrecy later that night. Soren despised being unprepared or thrown off by events outside her control, like when Nyzaia mentioned the state of Isha's rooms. Soren did not know why Isha would have a shrine to the four realms when she believed the woman was loyal to her alone. It bothered Soren, not knowing if she had been double-crossed. Yet Soren focused on the minor details to avoid bigger confrontations; it was why she had left Tajana to clean up her mess with Nyzaia.

Soren recalled the look in Sadira's eyes when Soren lowered her sword and stepped back, accepting the fate that would befall her sister. It was Sadira's fault; she had grown too attached to the usurper. She paused in the hallway, wondering if a touch of regret would seep into her blackened heart. Nothing.

"Is all going to plan?" asked Talia to her left, returning Soren's focus to her surroundings as they strode through the vaulted hallways of Antor Castle. Trails of blood marked the stone, highlighting a path to the infirmary.

"Of course it is not going to plan," Soren snapped. Talia clenched her jaw, and a pang of what she assumed was guilt pierced her, but only for a moment. "I apologise." Soren glanced around to ensure no one had heard her moment of weakness, and the pair continued walking, silent but for their footfall. "It is just—"

"Yes?" Talia asked eagerly.

"Your cover is blown," Soren sighed. "We have no more close spies remaining near Asteria Castle other than the few servants." She turned the corner and reached the infirmary. Talia put a hand out to stop her before they entered. From the many voices within, Soren knew it was overcrowded.

"I do not believe you have anything to worry about when it comes to the queen of Vala," Talia said, her tone hushed. She glanced at the Garridon soldiers, briefly filtering past them.

"How would you know when she has been spending all her time with her commander?" Soren hissed. Talia rolled her eyes.

"The last few months are nothing compared to having known her for years. She does not want power; she never has." Although Talia tried to reassure her, Soren was not so confident. She had seen how unchecked Elisara's power was and how easily the weather changed with her emotions. Soren would not put it past Elisara to lash out with her power should Soren do anything to anger her. "The commander is simply a distraction," Talia finished. "What are the next steps?"

Soren contemplated her answer, wondering how much of the long-term plan to reveal.

"I cannot tell you here," Soren said at last, nodding to those gathered behind Talia. "There are too many ears."

The Keres-born beauty spun her head and groaned at the sight of Helena, Vigor, and Vlad at the end of the hallway, marching straight for them.

"I will leave you to deal with *that* fallout." Soren laughed humourlessly. "Find me in the morning. You and Tajana need to debrief before you leave with the Historian." Soren spun before Talia could protest. Talia would not wish to be far from Soren, having only just reunited. Yet Soren could not gauge Tajana's intentions.

Soren had met Tajana and Talia when she was sixteen during her first visit to the mainland. At such a young age, the first step of her plan was to create a network of loyal spies. Perhaps she had been naïve to pick the first two girls she saw, or perhaps some Wiccan blood ran through her after all, and the gut reaction to the pair was a gift from her ancestors.

The girls huddled in an alleyway under a makeshift tent of scrapped fabrics. Talia had been close to death due to an infection spreading from a wound in her abdomen, inflicted after their final attempt at stealing food from the market. Part of Soren believed they would have signed their lives away to anyone who had offered them aid, yet the other part felt the odd tie of friendship between them all and knew they would not abandon her.

Soren had taken a vial of healing salve Sadira had made from the island. While it did not work as quickly as if Sadira had applied it, it worked all the same, and so Tajana promised their service for life—a deal she had signed willingly in blood, as was the old Wiccan way. A blood tie was said to kill the party who betrayed it. Nothing suggested it was true, but she thought neither woman dared risk it.

On more than one occasion, Soren questioned if Nyzaia would be Tajana's breaking point after her friend had lied on countless occasions. "*She is simply the target!*" she promised, but Soren saw how Tajana looked at her on the few occasions they had been in the same room. Tajana loved Nyzaia, but deciding whether she loved Soren or her life more was up to her.

Soren barely acknowledged the guards as she entered the crowded infirmary but scolded herself afterward. She was far from winning their favour, and without an army on her side, she was powerless. Scanning the room, Soren felt the stretch of dried blood on her cheek. The wound must not be deep if it was drying already, but it would likely scar, knowing her luck. Her eyes narrowed on the halo of blonde hair near the far window.

Soren watched Sadira for a moment—the gentle movements of her hands as she bandaged the guard on the cot, her genteel smile, and regal posture—she was a perfect fit for the queen of the people.

But Soren would be the queen of the realm. Sadira navigated the maze of cots, reassuring those who sobbed and begged within them. Soren froze. Over the sea of heads and bodies, she had not seen Caellum kneeling where Sadira stood. Soren had left him to the beast, knowing it would kill him. And yet, she had failed at the last hurdle, all because of her sister's emotions.

She could not comprehend what had caused Sadira to fall for the usurper, but she saw the look in her eyes, the same look once reserved for Rodik. There was something different, though—something raw in the way Caellum returned her gaze as he accepted her hand and rose to join her side. Anger flooded Soren, and she reached them quickly. Their calm expressions changed the second they noticed her. Caellum wrapped an arm around Sadira, and Soren noticed blood on the sleeves of her dress.

Soren hesitated. *When was she injured*?

"We have nothing to say to you right now, Soren," Sadira said, and Soren raised her eyebrows. After what happened, she expected the usurper to have plenty to say.

"You do not wish to make plans for the realm or the next steps to aid the people?" she asked, keeping her tone level. Caellum narrowed his eyes in disbelief. "Finding the other half of the talisman," Soren prompted, glancing to where Caellum's shirt fell open and exposed the wooden half of what was rightfully hers.

"We need some time, Soren. Allow us the evening," Sadira said, lowering her head.

"Why?"

"Because we lost a friend," Caellum snapped. "Because *you* got our friend taken!" Sadira placed a hand on his arm.

"And how do you surmise that?" she asked, raising her eyebrows.

"If you had attacked that creature instead of allowing it to approach us, it would not have detoured for Larelle! It would not have taken her."

"Caellum, please," Sadira said, *always the peacemaker.*

"You do not know the hands of fate," Soren sneered.

"But I *know* it could have changed the course," Sadira replied. "She was my only friend." Tears pooled in Sadira's eyes, and Soren frowned as a lingering emotion tugged in the back of her mind.

"Must everything be about you?" Soren snapped. "The lord is tasked with finding her." Soren was not one to store the names of those of no interest to her. "If he cares as much as he says he does, he will find her."

"As we said, we can talk in the morning," Caellum said, but he would not command Soren.

"The talisman is on Doltas Island," Soren said bluntly, forcing the topic of conversation.

"Sadira already told me," Caellum kept his arm protectively around her sister, and the two women locked eyes.

Sadira raised her chin. "As I said, we can talk in the morning."

"We will need to travel immediately," Soren continued.

"Soren!" Caellum shouted. The room fell silent as all eyes turned to their King. Soren stepped forward, reaching for the pommel of the sword. Two guards mirrored her actions from behind Caellum and Sadira, assessing her. "In the *morning*," he finished.

Soren narrowed her eyes. He was not usually so bold. Sadira removed herself from Caellum's grip and stepped towards her sister.

"Have your wound tended to, Soren, and we will speak in the morning." Soren heard the pleading in her voice, the same tone she would use when attempting to calm her on Doltas. Soren glanced around the room; she would not win this argument if she continued to resist. Stepping back, she watched her sister with the man she wished dead and turned to head for her rooms; she had no intention of having the wound seen to.

"And Soren?" Sadira called. Soren paused by the door. "I will be moving rooms for safety."

She read between the lines of her words. Sadira did not wish to change rooms in fear of the creatures or to move closer to Caellum.

This was decided after Soren left her to die. She did not respond, nor did she turn to see the betrayal in her sister's eyes. She simply left, as what was the loss of a sister compared to the gain of a throne?

***

She sensed the shadows before she saw them. They crawled at the corners of her mind, stroking and coaxing her to come out to play and listen to their wisdom. The same occurred every night she wished to speak to *him*—the man who had told her of the prophecy at the young age of twelve before her grandmother had. That was when she first realised he cared more for her than her family did. He informed her about what he foresaw, including Soren's part in everything and the realm she would win. The kingdom was hers if she wanted it.

The cloudiness of her vision in her dream state cleared, and the shadows receded to reveal the ruined castle that was her mind: crumbling stone with half-formed walls coated in a mesh of ivy and spiderwebs. Black smudges remained on the open gaps where the powerful shadows frequently climbed and left a stain in their wake. The castle felt like home, but Soren was unsure if it was. She stepped out of the darkness and into the streaming moonlight. Their usual place. She wondered how her body looked during her dreams and if the shadows seeping through her mind coated her body in the living world, too.

Usually, Soren welcomed them and let them lick her skin as he approached. Not tonight.

"You are angry," his silky voice called. Soren said nothing but narrowed her eyes as his outline appeared before the cell bars. She was forbidden to approach him. "Soren, Soren, Soren," he said as the shadows caressed her arms, coaxing her coldness to yield. "How many times must I tell you? Emotions are a weakness."

Shadows tickled her cheeks like tendrils mimicking his fingers, attached to arms hidden in the darkness that belonged to a man she trusted so deeply despite never having seen him. When she was younger, she would beg him to drop his shield and show his face. He had come close once—a glimpse of dark stubble, a flash of scarred arms—but never since. As a child, she named him the Lord of Night when he appeared in her dreams. The name had stuck after he refused to provide his proper title, even after all these years.

A shadow licked her wound, but when she batted it away, it wrapped around her wrist and held firm.

"Are you really that self-absorbed to care about a scar?" His voice drew nearer.

"I care that I was not informed of the plan," she snapped, turning her back on him. "I assume those creatures were your doing."

"Does it matter if they were my doing or that of my followers?" he asked, and she supposed not. But if the idea was his, she needed to know why he had kept it from her.

"If they are to one day be my followers, then I should know. *They* should know the creatures spilled my blood." Shadows tugged Soren back, forcing her to turn and face their owner. "Taking the queen of Nerida will slow things."

"That was not part of the plan," the Lord of Night sighed, and she pictured him tapping his foot impatiently.

"So, your followers do not listen to you?" Soren asked. "Or respect you?" She stepped closer, forcing him to step back towards the iron cell he guarded.

"The creatures can be *irrational* when backed into a corner," he concluded. He was careful with his words; he always was.

"Do you know where they have taken her?" she asked. The quicker Larelle was returned, the more reasonable Sadira would be. The lord said nothing, and his shadows paused as if they, too, were thinking. *He does not know.*

"We need to be quicker," he said, changing the topic. He withdrew from her while the shadows trailed back and forth. "I will not lose this kingdom, Soren."

He is pacing, she realised.

"Tell me why," she urged. "Why do you want this kingdom?"

"This again?" he hissed. "Again?" Soren refrained from pushing, having asked endless times before. "Why does it matter when I have promised you will keep your crown?"

Soren stepped forward, wishing to make amends before he left, but the Lord of Night backed away, the shadows completely hiding the cell bar behind him.

"You are disappointing me, Soren. It may be worth keeping my distance for a while, and perhaps when I choose to return, you will have better news." His voice became distant.

"No, please! Please do not leave."

"Just do as I ask Soren," his silken voice returned. "Take the throne, and I will reveal more."

Chapter Twenty-Five

Nyzaia

Everything reminded Nyzaia of Tajana. The twists of the awful shade of green ropes hanging from the drapes were her braid, the crackle of the fireplace mirrored Nyzaia's response to her touch, and her syndicate's leathers ignited memories of when they all sat at the table, playing cards.

Nyzaia sat in the middle of the canopy bed, which felt far too large and empty without her. Tucking her knees under her chin, blood seeped from her feet into the sheets, cut from the shards of glass while fighting. Elisara's friend, Vigor, had offered to tend to her, but she refused.

"My queen," Farid's voice sounded distant despite standing beside the bed. "My queen," he repeated, though she did not answer. She thought only of how he had defended her against the woman she loved. "Nyzaia." His voice was even quieter now, and she barely moved as his hand cautiously brushed her bare arm. Slowly, she looked down at his hand before looking up at him. Her eyes felt puffy as she met his, the pale blue of his gaze now reminding her of an icy fire that burned for her protection.

Farid offered his hand, and Nyzaia's eyes flickered down, taking a moment to analyse the strips of scars on his palm. She had not noticed them before.

"You need to bathe," he said in his usual matter-of-fact way.

"Are you saying I smell?" she asked. Farid's lip twitched before returning to its usual straight line.

"Yes."

Sighing, Nyzaia looked at his hand again and accepted it. He pulled her up and quickly stepped back, gesturing to the bathing room adjoined to the guest chambers in Antor castle. The wooden floor was cold, though the entire room was compared to Keres. It was dark, too, and the wood and deep greens were suffocating.

Nyzaia stepped into the room and stared at the steaming tub in the centre. She wished it was bigger, like the pool in her chambers at home.

"I will be right outside," Farid said.

"No, stay." She bit her lip to keep it from quivering. She did not wish to be alone with her thoughts. Farid did not falter as he closed the door behind him, though she suspected he looked elsewhere as she began peeling off what remained of her lehenga.

The colour of the water rapidly changed as she sunk below its surface, drawing the blood and grime from her skin and leaving only the stain of heartbreak behind. She raised the temperature, hoping the water would burn every one of Tajana's imprints on her flesh to ash.

"Was I blind?" Nyzaia asked numbly.

"No."

Nyzaia nodded, and then a silent sob escaped her.

The water splashed against the tub as Nyzaia quickly hid the sounds of her cries in her hand; finally, she released her pain. Farid shifted on his feet.

"I do not wish to assume I can approach you, but given I am not your type—and will not be looking at your body—may I?"

Nyzaia could not help but laugh in between her sobbing. She nodded silently as Farid quietly approached the tub and knelt beside it.

"None of us were to know," he said, looking only at her eyes.

"I should have known. I was trained to spot things like this," she mumbled.

"And she had the same training as you; she would have known what you would look for. You were beginning to question her; if this had not happened now, I am certain you would have discovered the truth." Nyzaia crossed her arms and sank further until the water reached her chin.

"You do not believe me," Farid said, and Nyzaia flicked her eyes towards him. Anyone else would feel inadequate beneath his intent stare, but Nyzaia saw only his dedication—and an emotion she feared everyone would have towards her.

"Do not pity me Farid," she grumbled, raising the temperature again. The water reached boiling point as dirt floated to the surface. Farid remained silent like he weighed each word for his queen before speaking again.

"My father would tell me to be pitied was to accept weakness and inferiority." Farid's words seemed familiar to Nyzaia, whose own father often told her such things. Nyzaia did not flinch as Farid reached into the scolding water and gently grasped her hand. "But my mother..." He looked down briefly at the stone floor before meeting Nyzaia's eyes again. "My mother told me to be pitied was not something to be ashamed of, for if someone feels or expresses that to you, they are acting in the most human way possible... with *care*." He squeezed her hand again before pulling his arm from the water. Nyzaia did not know whether to address the references to his family or the lack of burn marks on his arm. The water should have scolded him, yet his golden-brown skin appeared no different. She wanted to raise their encounter in Khami and question if his resistance to the water's temperature was because he wielded flames.

Nyzaia opened her mouth to speak until Farid winced, as if he had expected her next question. She remembered the many moments she had tried to include Farid and the walls he had rebuilt when she did. Instead, she said nothing but relished in the feeling that he trusted her enough with such a small insight into his life before service. Nyzaia's stomach rumbled and broke the silence. Farid's mouth twitched again. She wondered if she would ever see him smile.

"Stone fruits?" he asked, bracing the side of the tub to push himself up. He had clearly paid enough attention to know her favourite foods. Nyzaia nodded. "I will leave the door open," he said gently as Nyzaia pulled the towel from the stool beside her. Farid's footsteps faded, swallowed by the sound of the other men's laughter, who played cards in the next room. *You are not alone.*

When Farid returned, Nyzaia had returned to her spot, sitting cross-legged with her damp hair hanging to one side of her robe. Jabir sat perched on the bed beside her, his gangly body leaning over the large book laid out before them. On the table in the corner, the decks of cards had been replaced with a large map, and they used the empty goblets as paperweights. Issam hunched over it, his colossal frame covering most of Keres. Nyzaia could just discern Garridon's border from where she sat. Rafik furrowed his brow as he peered down at the map beside Issam; he pushed his dark curls from his eyes, smudging ink across his forehead from where he had marked spots on the map.

Nyzaia's syndicate did what they always did when she was troubled, though she had never experienced heartbreak like this. They were strategizing to give her mind something else to whirl away at. While she appreciated their efforts, it reminded her of when they usually schemed together like this, with Tajana often taking the lead and sparing glances at Nyzaia for approval.

Nyzaia thanked Farid as he passed her the bowl of stone fruits and a small dagger. She bit the slices straight from the blade and wiped the juice from her chin.

"You were never a polite eater," Jabir murmured. She feigned an offended gasp but nudged him with her elbow, earning a smile from him as he trailed his finger under the sentence he was reading. Nyzaia sensed Farid's awkwardness and glanced up to find him shuffling.

"Sit," she said, patting the spot on the bed opposite Jabir. Farid opened his mouth to protest. Nyzaia knew it was to insist he was fine. "*Sit*, Farid." she repeated. Farid's brow furrowed, and he kept his back rigid while perching on the bed with his hands on his thighs.

"Myths and Lies of Ithyion," Nyzaia told him in between bites.

"And are they? Myths and lies?" asked Farid.

"From what I've read so far, they seem like stories you would tell children," Jabir mumbled, carefully turning each page, worn with age. Nyzaia exchanged a look with Farid.

"One of them is true," Nyzaia said, wiping her hands on her robe. "About celestial ties." Jabir lifted his head from the book and raised his eyebrows. "That is why Kazaar and Elisara are so different lately."

Jabir laughed.

"I cannot imagine the commander is best pleased about being tied to her. Do you remember how frustrated he was after training her group of recruits?"

Farid tilted his head at Jabir's words.

"Sometimes frustration is used to cover true emotion and hide the truth of your greatest desires," Farid said plainly. Jabir looked at Nyzaia, who raised her eyebrows teasingly at him, and tilted her head with a smile.

"No!" Jabir gasped. "Kazaar and the queen?" he asked, beaming. "Have they..."

"Have they what?" asked Farid.

"Oh, come on, have you *seen* them both?" Jabir's attention was fully removed from the book now. "They are remarkably attractive. There is not a chance they have not slept together."

"Jabir!" Nyzaia chastised. "This is not gossip over tea with the Courtesans!" She glanced at the table, where Issam and Rafik listened intently. "But no, they have not."

"This sounds like a bet in the making." Humour laced Issam's voice.

"We are not betting on when a queen sleeps with her commander!" Nyzaia scolded.

"Three golds it is before we next see them," said Jabir eagerly.

"Five if it happens in this castle."

"Ten it does not happen at all," Farid said, and Nyzaia raised her eyebrows at him.

"I did not take you for a gambling man, Farid."

Farid raised his shoulders in a half-hearted shrug, and Nyzaia smiled. Perhaps those walls would slowly crumble, and he would truly become a part of the syndicate.

"If you are all finished with your childish bets, can we refocus on the plan?" Nyzaia pulled the book towards her and analysed the sketch of a sword.

"What is the plan?" Farid asked as Issam and Rafik approached the bed and rolled out the map again.

"We need to find the other half of the Keres talisman." Rafik's large hands pointed to the Xs across their realm. "These are the places we considered so far." He gestured to the oasis at the edge of Ashun Desert, the vaults of Tabheri Palace, the white rock face meeting Myara's ocean, and the thinnest walkway within Nefere Valley. None of them felt right.

"What was the purpose of hiding the other half?" Farid asked, scanning the map.

"Hiding it within the realm allegedly allows the power of Ithyion to flow through the land and provide other citizens with connection to the royal line's power," Issam confirmed, and Nyzaia nodded.

"It also had to have been hidden somewhere difficult to access to ensure no power-hungry royal accessed it alone and took it for themselves. We do not know what effect it might have on me once it is connected with the other half."

The men scanned the map again, deep in discussion. Farid was quiet at her side, rubbing his beard in thought. There was something in his eyes, something that indicated he had an idea. Nyzaia nodded in encouragement, and Farid leaned forward, pointing at the map.

"It's hidden in the rock face of the Abis Forge behind the lava flow." The other three all looked up at him, their confusion clear.

Jabir watched Farid intently, who shifted beneath his gaze. "How can you be so certain?"

"I spent a lot of time there growing up," Farid said plainly. "It is there." Everyone exchanged looks, and Jabir shifted in his seat, watching Farid closely. There was something else to Farid's story. Nyzaia recognised his usual discomfort.

"You are certain?" she asked, and he nodded. The other three men were clearly sceptical, analysing him and questioning what he knew.

"I trust him," Nyzaia stated. "We head to the Abis Forge at sunrise."

Chapter Twenty-Six

Sadira

Sadira's eyes were still rimmed-red as the cold wind lashed at her face as rain descended in the City of Antor. She forced her gaze downward and not at the approaching buildings. When she had awoken that morning and pulled back the drapes from her chamber windows, she was faced with not only the rising sun but the sight of Lord Alvan leading Princess Zarya around the gardens. He gently lifted the princess onto the wall above the flower beds and crouched before her, and Sadira could not suppress her tears as the princess fell into Alvan, her body shaking with tears of her own.

Other than Caellum, Larelle was the first ruler who made Sadira feel welcome. Sadira had pictured them becoming friends, yet now she did not know whether to grieve or act hopeful. Their last conversation played on her mind as Sadira dismounted her horse, and her guards came to a stop. Taryn reached for the reins. Now that the hall from their engagement required repairs, Sadira had sought a change in his position and requested he become one of her personal guards.

Larelle had asked Sadira about Wiccan and whether they had any other abilities besides what Sadira knew, like the gift of sight and an affinity for healing. Although Sadira was unsure, she decided to help Larelle in the hope she would speak to her again. The trip also allowed her to avoid Soren while searching for anything about Wiccan that may give Sadira an advantage against her sister.

A dull brass bell rang above Sadira's head as she pressed on the glass-paned door, the navy paint peeling away onto her fingers. She lowered the hood of her forest-coloured cloak in the hopes she could see better. She could not. Despite the early hour, little light streamed through the one window as though the weather itself mourned those lost during last night's attack. Her eyesight was no better by the lack of sconces or fireplace in the small shop. Only a few scattered collections of pillared candles burned on the worn, wooden worktops, with wax slowly dripping onto the books.

"Hello?" Sadira called into the small space.

"One moment," a quiet voice called from behind a door, propped open by a jar of dark liquid. Sadira waited and patiently folded her hands in front of her woollen dress. She took in the singular room that was Athena's Apothecary. A large wooden table was pushed against each of the open stone walls, leaving Sadira in the centre spotlight. Little of the wooden surfaces could be seen beneath the scattering of leather books, random jars, string-wrapped herbs, pestles, and mortars. Behind a taller counter were countless mismatched shelves nailed into the wall, each housing rows of different-sized jars, all labelled in scrawled ink.

"Sorry for the delay." A short elderly woman kicked away the jar by the door, wobbling the contents inside. She kept her head down and wiped her hands against what Sadira imagined had once been a pale linen apron yet was now covered in a spattering of colour. As she inspected her nails, grey hair tumbled over her face.

"It is not a problem," Sadira said. The woman finally looked up as she stepped onto a stool behind the counter, elevating her to Sadira's height. The woman raised her eyebrows, the gesture widening her hazel eyes and lifting the wrinkles on her forehead.

"The fallen princess wishes to grace my shop with her presence?"

Sadira winced. She hated that term.

"Sadira is just fine," she said as the elderly lady's eyes roamed Sadira's body with a tense jaw.

"You look like your grandmother," the woman said with a tilt of her head. Sadira could not hide her shock.

"You knew my grandmother?" she asked, and the elderly woman chuckled.

"I do not find it a surprise that it is my apothecary you walked into and not one of the finer ones in the square. She mentioned this place, didn't she?" The woman's eyes lit up as though recalling a positive memory. Sadira nodded.

"She mentioned it in passing, but not that she knew the owner." When Sadira asked Caellum about the healers or elderly in Antor, he had listed the apothecaries in the square the next morning, like the woman referenced. When Sadira mentioned this one, he claimed it was used by those wishing to keep their purchases a secret. But Sadira's grandmother often mourned the herbs she could gather in Antor and claimed Athena's apothecary was the only place for the most trusted resources.

"Ha!" The woman laughed. "That bitch." She shook her head as Sadira recoiled, taken aback. "Oh no, dear!" The woman raised her hand. "I mean no offence. Lyra was the closest thing I ever had to a sister; she always kept my secrets, though it was typical of her to take that promise so literally and not even confide in her granddaughter." The woman's laughter trailed as her smile faded. "I assume she is gone," she said softly. Sadira nodded. The woman blinked rapidly before looking back at Sadira. "Which one of you did it?"

Sadira shifted on her feet, opening and closing her mouth.

"Come now, dear. I know about her vision. Which of you did it?"

Hundreds of thoughts rushed through Sadira's mind. If she knew the vision, did she know the prophecy too? Had she told it to anyone else? What secrets had her grandmother kept for this woman? Sadira glanced at her hands, wondering why Lyra had never revealed the true extent of their relationship before.

"Soren," Sadira whispered, trying to push away the memory of her family's blood on her hands and their dead bodies lifeless at her feet. The woman hummed before offering her hand to Sadira.

"Athena," the woman said. "I am Athena." Sadira politely took her hand and shook it. The woman was elderly but did not appear as old as Sadira expected, given she had been friends with her grandmother. "What can I do for you?"

Sadira was grateful for the change in subject.

"I am travelling to Doltas Island in the morning. I require some supplies for the people, mostly herbs they struggle to grow without my presence, all dried: hibiscus, lavender, sage, and basil." Sadira handed her the small list, and Athena began pulling bunches from where they hung from the ceiling, the rustling of the dried plants and the outside wind filling the silence.

"You know, you could have just grown and dried these yourself with your abilities," said Athena, glancing at her from the corner of her eye. She stood on her tiptoes to reach for the dried hibiscus.

"I needed to get out of the castle." Sadira glanced away. "It was a last-minute decision to travel to Doltas." Athena hummed in question, so Sadira deflected.

"You said you knew about my grandmother's vision." She faced Athena again, who wrapped the order.

"Is there a question to follow that statement?"

"Why did she tell you?" Sadira asked. The woman pushed the paper bag of items across the counter towards Sadira.

"A secret for a secret," Athena said. When Sadira raised an eyebrow, she continued. "I told Lyra a secret, and she told me one in return. Go on. Ask." Athena prompted with an encouraging smile.

Sadira chewed her lip and glanced around the room. "What was your secret?"

"Are you going to offer me one in return?" Sadira pursed her lips, thinking of all the secrets she could not divulge. Athena chuckled. "Do not worry, child. I likely know all your secrets." Sadira frowned, feeling a twinge of irritation that this woman presumed to know her.

"Even the creatures?" Sadira asked, and Athena looked her dead in the eyes.

"Even the creatures," she said. "I saw their arrival in a vision."

Sadira tried to maintain her temper as she crossed her arms.

"You *knew* people would die?" she asked, but guilt immediately washed over Sadira at her hypocrisy. She now realised how the others had felt when Soren revealed they had known the ruling families would die yet did nothing about it.

"That is the misfortune of being a Wiccan gifted with sight," Athena said, stepping from her stool and heading back to the door from which she emerged. Sadira wished to ask Athena more questions—anything that could answer what Larelle had asked of her, yet *her questions may not matter if she is dead*. Sadira blinked rapidly, stopping her mind from roaming such a path.

"Do you know others? Where are they?" Sadira asked. Athena held the door open and paused.

"You will not find the answers you crave from me. Visit Albyn. There, you will find your answers."

Sadira had even more questions than before. Albyn sat at the edge of Garridon before the sea and was the closest to Doltas Island. "And take the King with you," Athena said, looking intently at Sadira, who read between the lines. While Athena could not reveal her visions, she could guide her. Sadira needed Caellum.

"Wait!" Sadira called as Athena turned to close the door. "Your secret to Lyra was that you were a Wiccan. You told her your secret because she told you that all those with a connection to the earth would be killed should Jorah usurp the throne. You wanted her to know that you would be included." Sadira concluded, realising this woman had hidden in plain sight beneath the nose of Caellum's father and grandfather before him. A coy smile spread across the woman's face.

"You owe me one secret, princess." With the ominous words and the weight of a debt on her shoulders, Sadira was left to take her ingredients and return to the castle.

Chapter Twenty-Seven

Elisara

Elisara thought of the last time she had seen Talia before awaking in Keres to find her there with Helena and Vigor. Had it really been that night at the springs after risking Helena's life? She had not even addressed those events with Talia as Helena advised. Everything had been a whirlwind since, one she could not escape. She wished she had not left Garridon so soon so she could spend more time with Helena and Vigor, who were the most hurt by Talia's betrayal. Given that Elisara and Vlad lived at the castle, the trio often spent the most time together. Although Elisara had offered for Helena and Vigor to journey back to Vala with her, the pair decided to stay and offer aid in Antor's infirmary.

How had she not anticipated Talia's betrayal? Elisara could hardly trust her own judgement. Sensing his presence in the periphery of her mind, she waited for Kazaar to speak. She had misjudged him, too.

"*Ouch.*" There he was. Elisara glanced at Kazaar atop his horse as the two rode side by side. The wall of the Neutral City rose high behind him, but they continued riding until light snow soon dusted the cobbled path. She tried to return his smile, but he was merely another reminder of the many secrets that had been kept from her. His face changed. He had heard that thought, too.

"Why can I not hear your thoughts as easily as you hear mine?" she asked aloud, and he shrugged.

"I have lived a harder life than you. Perhaps I protect myself without even realising." Although his tone was nonchalant, it made Elisara question what had been so hard about his life. He winced. She really needed to keep her thoughts to herself. "I see it as a wall in my mind," Kazaar continued. "A physical, iron-clad wall preventing anyone from entering. You should find something similar."

Elisara pondered that. She had fortified her emotional walls for years after training in Keres, so why was this any different? "*Because someone is chipping away at it.*"

She glanced at Kazaar again, her eyes scanning over him, instinctively checking the wound on his back to ensure it had not reopened. She thought back to the attack and how their blood and bodies responded to one another. They had endless questions to find the answers to without a spare second to do so, not with Larelle missing and their quest to find the talismans.

The weather shifted as they continued riding until exiting the ring around the Neutral City to be welcomed by Vala's icy air. It felt different. While Elisara still relished the cold, her body seemed less accustomed to it when it pierced her skin. It was likely due to her long absence from home, she thought, though she was pleased to be back. The snow-capped trees bordering Vala formed a clear line of defence but instead of riding towards Asteria, they took a left alongside Nerida's river, the snowy trees on their right.

Elisara and Kazaar had quickly deduced where the second half of the talisman was likely to be hidden. Immediately, their minds went to locations in Vala that were well-guarded and difficult to approach alone to prevent the monarch from pursuing the talisman to gain more power.

The Vellius sea soon appeared as they journeyed through the snow-capped trees, the opposite watchtowers on the outskirts of Marnovo offering a clear view of the small island surrounded by dark waters. The morning after the attack, Elisara sent Vlad ahead of them to alert Marnovo's guards to set up base at the edge of the lake to keep watch until their queen arrived. Elisara stayed in Garridon an extra night to attend the service held for all those lost during the attacks. A pang of sympathy had flitted through Elisara when she watched Caellum speak, who often paused to clear his throat and struggled to make eye contact with his people. She knew he had been trying not to cry at all the loss.

Vlad had made it in good time. As Elisara trotted through the trees, the late afternoon sun broke free across the lake, highlighting the pale blue tents set up meters from the water's edge. Vlad emerged from the one closest with two guards in tow. Elisara had requested a small, discrete group of guards to assist to minimise the risk of anyone discovering what they were looking for or why. It was also why Elisara and Kazaar journeyed from Garridon alone, because even though Kazaar's secrets hurt Elisara, she still trusted him with her safety.

"You made it in good time." Vlad reached for the reins of Elisara's horse as she dismounted and embraced him. When they pulled apart, Vlad offered Kazaar a curt yet respectful nod as he, too, dismounted and took Elisara's horse, guiding the steeds to the lake to drink.

Elisara tried to focus on Vlad as he spoke, but her eyes followed the movement of Kazaar's arms as he stabbed the ice at the edge of the lake to gather water for the horses, the muscles in his back and shoulders rippling with each thrust. Kazaar tilted his head towards her, and she blushed, turning her back on him. "*You could have just melted it.*"

"*And miss the opportunity of your eyes on me?*" His voice teased her mind, and she rolled her eyes, refocusing on Vlad.

"Did anyone ask about this mission?" she asked, but the captain shook his head, strands of golden hair falling before his face. It had not been cut for months, and his appearance was far different from his pristine portrayal when her parents were his employer.

"If you request something by order of the queen, people tend to do as you ask," he chuckled, his breath rising in plumes. "Although, the guards appeared wary. They say odd noises have been coming from the lake at night." Elisara frowned but brushed it off, assuming it was the wind whistling through the trees and over the ice.

"How do you think we should proceed?" she asked. Vlad crossed his arms, looking out over the Vellius Sea. Elisara turned with him. While the dark waters lapped in the distance on Nerida's side of the border, Vala's side was completely frozen, a glittering surface that welcomed adventure. Very few people, except those from Vojta and Marnovo, made the effort to visit the lake, too enticed by the hot springs in the capital. As a child, her father would tell her stories of children mysteriously disappearing when they visited alone. Now, though, Elisara knew it was likely a tale to keep her from foolishly trying to cross it, as they now planned to do.

"It is risky to walk across, and although the commander could melt it, we would then waste more time dragging the boats from Vojta." Vlad rubbed the stubble on his chin. "If we stay overnight and start first thing in the morning, it should be cold enough for the lake to further solidify, making it sturdier for us at dawn."

Elisara nodded. "I could probably reinforce it with my power, but I am uncertain how big of a surface area I could freeze." Her eyes tugged on Kazaar, who allowed the horses to roam as he approached the pair.

"I am sure you could probably freeze a fair amount of it, but Vlad's plan allows for added safety," Kazaar agreed. "If we begin at sunrise, it should be cold enough to attempt walking across the lake to the island."

Elisara rocked back and forth on her heels, her cloak scraping across the snow as she tried to ignore the tingling of her skin at the closeness of his presence.

"I will continue readying the tents and then get to work on some dinner." Vlad began to walk back towards the tents and the guards he brought with him before pausing and glancing back. "Oh, I forgot to mention," he said. "Marnovo only had two other tents to hand, so Elisara can have one and Kazaar, I'll bunk with you."

"No," Kazaar said quickly, and Vlad stopped. Elisara glanced between them both. "Given the recent attack, it is unsafe for our queen to sleep alone. I will stay in her tent." His voice left no room for negotiation. Elisara crossed her arms and narrowed her eyes at Kazaar, who raised his eyebrows in challenge. Vlad looked between them both, struggling to hide his smile.

"As you wish, Commander." Vlad bowed mockingly before walking off.

Elisara spun to face Kazaar, so they stood toe to toe. "And what if I do not wish to share a tent with you while I sleep?"

"You were asleep for nearly two days while I stayed beside you. You had no problem then," he countered. His breath mingled with hers, creating a fog in the breeze.

"That is different! I did not know you were there," she said, and Kazaar rolled his eyes, taking three steps back. He grinned.

"If you can best me in a fight, you will have it your way."

Not one to back down from a challenge, especially not from him, Elisara unsheathed the dull sword at her side. She recalled the last time they had fought with swords when he had invited her to Vala's training yards. She had kept up then, and she would now.

"Who said a fight with swords?" he asked, cocking his head. He turned on his heel and beckoned her to follow with his hand.

"*Obnoxious piece of—*"

"*I can hear you.*"

Elisara followed Kazaar's footprints in the snow until they were hidden behind the tree line from Vlad and his guards.

"Vlad will worry," she said.

"He saw us walking in this direction. He is fine." Kazaar undid the leathers across his chest, and Elisara followed suit. She removed her cloak, avoiding how bare Kazaar now seemed as he rolled his shirt sleeves. She swallowed and tossed the cloak aside, where it landed in a crumpled pile at the base of a tree.

"Are you not cold?" Elisara asked, placing her hands on her hips. The sleeves of her sheer white shirt billowed in the breeze, and the leather corset around her waist provided the only layer of warmth. She was grateful for the thick socks beneath her long, laced boots.

"Are you?" he asked, glancing at her attire. Elisara scoffed.

"Of course not. I was born with ice in my veins."

Kazaar smirked. Flicking his hand, he tossed an icicle from a tree branch in her direction, forcing her to duck.

"Kazaar!" she exclaimed.

"It appears, so was I," Kazaar said. Elisara narrowed her eyes, reminded of when he revealed his powers to her in Keres.

"You need to move past it, angel," he said, but Elisara waved her hand, sending snow from the tree above him to fall on his head.

"I told you, stop calling me that!" she hissed, and he dared to laugh. "I'm serious, Kazaar!"

"Why does it make you so mad?" Kazaar knelt and raised a palm over the snow until it melted beneath the flicker of his flames. A pool of water emerged at his feet. He rose, and as he did, the water plumed and rose with him.

"That is exactly why!" Elisara exclaimed, pointing towards the tendrils of water he now controlled. He raised an eyebrow. "You are acting as if nothing happened, as if I should simply be fine with what occurred and allow us to jest and act as if we are—"

"Are what?" he asked, hurtling the water at her. Elisara was quick to raise her hand, freezing it mid-air so it formed a long, smooth spear.

"As if we are friends!" She hurtled the spear towards him, but vines rose from the ground, catching it before it pierced his chest. "Now, stop using your powers against me!" Elisara exclaimed.

She glanced around to ensure no one was hiding or watching him master all four elements.

"Friends?" Kazaar asked. Vines crept towards her along the ground, and she froze them.

"You do not want to be my friend?"

"Damn it, Elisara! Try something other than your air powers." Kazaar sent more vines towards her, but these were coated in flames. Elisara's eyes widened.

"What on earth do you mean?" she asked, extinguishing them

with a gust of wind.

"You heard what Nyzaia said. This tie between us allows us to *share* powers," Kazaar explained. "That means you should be able to access mine: fire, water, earth—" *Darkness.* The word flickered in his mind, breaking through the edge of his iron-clad wall. Her mind flashed to Garridon where dark shadows surrounded them both. It did not scare her, though; it intrigued her.

"This is ridiculous!" Elisara retrieved her dull-coloured sword and stormed towards him, raising her arm to swing. He rolled out of the way, forcing her to spin to face him. He stood with the Sword of Sonos and swung back at Elisara, forcing her to duck and shift.

"And no, angel"—He swung at her again, forcing her to deflect— "I do not want to be your *friend.*" Kazaar must have felt the flicker of hurt that passed through her as he frowned, but she ignored him and swung again, pushing him further back. Sparks rose with every clash of their swords.

"Fine, we won't be friends," Elisara breathed. Sweat beaded on her forehead but froze just as fast. "You are my commander; perhaps we both need reminding of that." A rush of emotions burst through her, yet they were not her own. Kazaar twisted his sword at a different angle, and Elisara stumbled to meet it. He had the upper hand again and drove her back, the clash of their swords ringing with every hit. With every spark flashing from their weapons, Elisara noticed the growing twists of shadow and light climbing their arms. The rise and fall of their chests quickened.

"I do not want to be just your commander, angel." He stepped forward, forcing her back. "If I were merely your commander, I would have to stand by your side as countless suitors asked for the hand of my queen." He swung, and white light danced across their bare arms as their eyes locked. "If I were only your commander, I would have to punish myself for every thought I have of you." When she stumbled, the sword caught the fabric of her shirt and ripped open her collar, exposing her flushed chest. She gasped as her back hit the tree, yet she raised her sword, crossing it again with the Sword of Sonos. "For every moment I think about how you looked in red." She was reminded of the alcove and how closely their bodies pressed together. "For every memory of when you finally awoke and how all I wanted was to take you in my arms." Elisara's arms weakened, but Kazaar did not push further, allowing the swords to hover between them. "Do you know how scared I was? How many regrets I had? I regretted not telling you of my powers sooner or revealing how I truly felt and how all I want from this life is to be by your side." Elisara swallowed hard. His eyes darkened, speckled with shadow and light.

"So no, angel, I do not want to be *just* your commander. Because a commander would not look at his queen and feel like she is the other half of his soul."

Kazaar's chest quickly rose and fell. His hair, having fallen free, now framed his face. Elisara's breathing matched his as the raw truth of his words hit her. Desire tingled through her body, though she was unsure if it was hers or his. Her eyes trailed his features, searching for the truth in his eyes as her grip on her sword weakened. This man wanted to devour Elisara, hold her—he thought only of her.

She could no longer deny she reciprocated those feelings. Elisara dropped the sword, and Kazaar matched her actions as she pulled his face to hers. Their lips collided, the kiss one of urgency, desire, and untamed need. It was instinct—all of it. He reached around Elisara, and his warm hands caressed her back as he lifted her up against the tree. She wrapped her legs around his waist as his hands freely roamed her sides until settling on her face to hold it close to his. She never wanted him to let go.

Chapter Twenty-Eight

Elisara

Tendrils twisted up and around them both as if the gods who blessed them with this celestial tie ensured they stayed as one. Elisara knew if she looked down, she would see the spiralling shadow and light, but she wished to focus on nothing else but Kazaar's lips against hers or the taste of his tongue as it gently teased her. A twig snapped in the not-so far distance, and Kazaar moved his head from hers. She groaned at the sudden coldness on her lips, where his mouth should be.

"You lost; we share a tent," he whispered, in her ear as his hands gripped her waist and gently lowering her. He stepped back and retrieved his sword.

"Dinner is ready," Vlad called, appearing from behind the trees two seconds later. Elisara combed her hair with her fingers and picked up her sword, brushing Kazaar's shoulder as she walked past him, sending tingles up her spine. Vlad glanced between the two of them and then at Elisara's torn shirt. He lifted one eyebrow with a grin and opened his mouth to speak.

"Thank you, Vlad," Elisara called, her voice breaking as she wobbled with each step towards him.

"All okay?" he asked, and she nodded enthusiastically.

"Fine. We were sparring."

Vlad hummed. "Work up a sweat?" Elisara elbowed him in the ribs.

"She lost," Kazaar called from behind, forcing Elisara to walk through the trees towards the tents and blazing fire. The weight of those words weighed heavily on her; she had lost more than a mere spar. She had lost the protective shield fortified around her and the promise to keep her heart as one of ice. She did not want to get burned, yet here she was, with every part of her on fire as she thought of him.

***

Tension crackled around the campfire, though Elisara imagined she was the only one who thought so. The men, Kazaar included, jested amid discussions of training and military tactics, though Elisara was barely listening. Instead, she sat with a rigid back, conscious of the spark fluttering within her every time Kazaar's knee bumped against hers as he reached for more food or stoked the fire. Her mind kept rewinding their kiss, and each time, she focused on a different part: his lips, his hands, his hips as she wrapped her legs around him. If Vlad had not arrived, where would it have gone? Elisara did not think she had the strength to stop herself.

"Are you coming?" Kazaar's deep voice asked beside her.

"What?" she exclaimed. Her face flushed as she shifted on the tree trunk. Kazaar tilted his head and peered down at her with amusement in his eyes. Vlad leaned against the tent pole behind Kazaar, grinning.

"To the tent," he continued. "We are all turning in for the night." He offered his hand, waiting for her to accept it. Elisara placed her hand in his and felt incredibly small as he helped her rise, especially when she stumbled into him. She was never this clumsy. She cleared her throat and signalled for him to take the lead. Elisara glared at Vlad when she walked past.

"I hope you sleep so *very* well," Vlad said.

"I hope you don't get killed in your sleep," she said with a sickly sweet smile. Vlad laughed before retiring to his tent. Elisara stared up at the night sky, cursing silently to herself as if this was the first time she had ever kissed a man.

Kazaar held open the tent flap, the soft glow from the lanterns illuminating the side of his face. His expression held no traces of his former amusement, and his eyes focused intently on her as she brushed past him into the tent. The tent must have been from the Lord of Marnovo; it was as grand as any royal tent she had entered before. The space was as large as a guest room in the castle, with the same opulent blues woven into the fabric. While Elisara stood upright, Kazaar's head scraped the fabric above as he entered behind her and tied the tent shut.

The embers of a fire glowed in the centre, emitting warmth throughout the space. Lanterns rested atop a vanity, where to the right was a large bed roll propped atop the crates in a makeshift bed. The only bed, Elisara realised, as Vlad had originally planned for her to rest here alone. Elisara sat awkwardly on the edge of it and crossed one leg over the other. She reached below her knees to untie the bootlaces wrapping around her calves yet paused as the mixed aroma of spices and pine drifted towards her. Kazaar towered above Elisara, his legs touching hers.

"Allow me," he whispered, kneeling before her. Kazaar Elharar, the commander of Vala, knelt before his queen and, with a gentle touch, began unlacing her boots. Her mind recalled the soft pull of his fingers when he untied the back of her corset on the Isle. Had that been their turning point? Saving one another's lives? While being so close to him on the bed had felt awkward and uncomfortable then, being this close to Kazaar now felt right. He glanced up at Elisara, and her breathing faltered. He smiled, acknowledging the memory she had projected and slid the boot off her leg before undoing the other.

Elisara said nothing but watched Kazaar in silence. She expected it to feel awkward, but it felt comfortable—*right*. After sliding the second boot from her leg, he massaged her calves and trailed his hands higher until gently uncrossing her legs, his eyes questioning. She opened them wider, a shiver trailing up her spine as they locked eyes. In one quick movement, he tugged her to the edge of the bed and knelt between her, lingering his hands on her hips. She took a sharp breath as his chest pressed against hers, arching her back in response, desperate to keep him close. She was a moth to his flame, desperate to bathe in his warmth as his hands travelled up her sides to reach for her exposed flesh where his sword had sliced the fabric.

"Did I hurt you?" he asked, brushing the skin below her neck.

"No." Her breathing halted as his fingers slid beneath the tear, grazing the raised moon on her collarbone. When she sighed, Kazaar leaned closer, and Elisara parted her mouth for his lips. He shifted at the last minute and instead planted kisses along her neck. Elisara's head fell back, her hair tumbling behind to allow him better access. Her eyes fluttered closed as his lips kissed a path towards her chest, his warmth melting into her. In one tug, he ripped the tear in her shirt, which fell free, exposing her white brasserie and stomach. She expected to feel awkward at being displayed for him and having a man take full control, but she relaxed, falling into the touch of his hands as they gripped her waist, keeping her from lying back on the bed, completely at his mercy.

The flames in the lantern flickered, turning Kazaar's dark locks a burnt orange. He lowered his head to kiss down her body, and she reached for him, brushing her fingers through his hair to free it from the leather band. Kazaar looked up at her as his hands shifted, his thumb trailing the waistband of her leathers.

"*Yes.*" Elisara sent the word clearly to him, and the corner of his lips lifted as he unhooked the leathers. She leaned back and lifted her hips, allowing him to drag them off her body at a tantalising pace, revealing the white undergarments beneath. She shifted her elbows to prop herself back up, but Kazaar splayed his large palm against her stomach, holding her down.

"Stay still, angel," he murmured, his breath tickling the tops of her thighs. She leaned back and splayed her hands against the bedsheets. "Good girl," he breathed, kissing the skin meeting the apex of her thighs. Elisara shuddered at the gentleness of his touch as he glided his thumb over the thin fabric separating his hand from her.

"Tell me what you like, angel," he whispered against her skin, stroking tantalising circles on just the right spot. She moaned at his touch, which felt like lightning crackling across her skin, desperate for release. His fingers paused their movement. "Answer me." Caellum had never asked Elisara's preferences before; she was always in control.

"That," she whispered, hoping he understood as she thought of his hand again. He did. Her undergarments were rough against her thighs as he dragged them down her body while Elisara undid her brasserie. A sound close to a growl tore from Kazaar's mouth, and she glanced down at him to find his eyes on her chest before he refocused. She gasped as his fingers met her bare skin again, repeating the slow circles from before.

"You must learn to be quiet for tonight," he murmured, continuing his pattern. Elisara suddenly remembered where they were. "Next time, I want to hear every curse from those pretty lips."

Next time.

Kazaar glanced at her mouth.

"*You did not think I would have you once and then never again?*" His voice whispered. She was about to reply, yet all thoughts escaped her as his mouth replaced his fingers. Elisara could not contain the sound that escaped her mouth. She flexed her hands, and a breeze rushed through the room, carrying her sounds with it. Closing her eyes again, she focused on the coaxing of his fingers as his tongue circled the spot she needed most.

"You're so ready for me, angel," Kazaar murmured. She shifted onto her elbows to watch him. His lips were plump, and she glimpsed the strain in his leathers. Elisara wanted him—every part. "Not tonight." Elisara frowned, unable to disguise her disappointment. "The first time I have you completely, it will not be in a tent with your guards close by," he said, locking eyes with her as he continued stroking. "I want to take my time and hear your name on my lips when you beg for more." Elisara blushed, but not from embarrassment; it was from the thought of losing all control and pleading with him for more. His fingers entered her, and she fell back with a whimper.

"Kazaar," she breathed. The bed dipped as Kazaar moved, and she opened her eyes to find him leaning over her.

"What did I say about being quiet?" He trailed his left hand up her neck and squeezed gently; his right hand continued his movements, and he brushed his thumb against her with each thrust of his hand.

"What if I don't want to be quiet?" she breathed. His hand stopped, and she whimpered again.

"What did I say about you begging me?" he asked. "Do you want me to continue?" Elisara's stubbornness took over then as she wished to test his promises. Saying nothing, she narrowed her eyes, and he chuckled. "Do you really want to test this now, angel?" He removed his hand and replaced it with featherlight touches against her thighs. Elisara bit her lip.

"Answer me." He gripped her jaw and angled her head, forcing their eyes to meet. Desire burned within his gaze, yet there was no amber glow or speckles of black and white. There was no sign of power at all; they were his usual deep brown. Just Kazaar. Her Kazaar.

"Yes," she breathed, waiting for him to increase the pressure.

"Yes what?" he whispered.

"Please, Kazaar." She felt Kazaar's smile against her neck as he applied more pressure, quickening the circling pattern of his hands. His lips moved to hers, and she lost all focus, her mind switching between the taste of his lips and the feel of his hands. The pressure mounted. While she twisted one hand in the bedsheets, the other gripped his bicep, her nails leaving half-moons in his skin in the rise of her climax. His lips moved in tangent with his hand, and she groaned in release while his other hand supported her back as she arched into him. Kazaar pulled his lips away from hers to plant delicate kisses across her collarbone. He slowed his hand as she came down from her high and evened her breathing. His hand moved to gently stroke her thigh.

Kazaar pulled Elisara's legs around his waist and lifted her against him as he stood. Draping back the bedsheets, he placed her gently beneath them and stood to slowly undress. The raised sun on his collarbone was tinged the same silver as their blood, she realised as he climbed into bed beside her and leaned on his side. He propped his head up on his hand and smiled at her, tracing her arm with his hand.

Everything was different now. While Elisara could pretend she had given in to him, the reality was she had desired this for some time. Pieces of her heart had been handed to the commander over the past few months: when they saved one another on the Isle after he pledged himself to her during the Nerida ball, and when they stood in that alcove together. Slowly, Elisara handed pieces of herself to her commander, and she was unsure if any part of her remained that was not completely and utterly his.

Chapter Twenty-Nine

Caellum

The foliage-covered cliffs of Doltas Island rose before the ship as they docked, unchanged from when he first met Soren at its peak. Much had altered since he last stepped foot on the island: his engagement to a princess, battling the threat of deadly creatures all while trying to uncover a prophecy. The realisation struck him more when he offered Sadira his hand to help her exit the ship. She stepped onto the dock of the place she once called home, a term stripped from her when she was forced to become his betrothed. The sun glinted on her golden hair as she smiled at him reassuringly. His stomach was in knots, though he was unsure if it was from the uneasy journey or the princess standing by his side.

He intertwined his fingers with Sadira's as they walked down the narrow wooden dock, his footing uneasy. Caellum glanced behind him to ensure Sir Cain was close by. The commander of the Garridon army nodded firmly to him, and Caellum turned back, watching his footing as waves threatened to spill over the planks. The same surly men from his last visit greeted them yet their clothes appeared newer, their braids less frayed, and their skin less dirty. Sadira had forewarned him that the island would appear much different from last time and admitted that her family hid the reality of Doltas from any outsider who stepped foot upon it. Looking at Sadira now, with her straight posture and her head held high despite the weight of the Garridon crown, she looked different. She had offered to return the heirloom to him, but he insisted she kept it. It was as if the crown allowed her to present as someone else in her high-necked, thick velvet green dress, much different from her usual bright florals. Caellum could not imagine how odd it must feel for Sadira to return home.

He gripped her hand as the men bowed, though he quickly realised they bowed to Soren as she stepped around the pair and clapped the men on the back. They grinned and began climbing to the top of the island, deep in conversation. Sadira and Caellum exchanged a look. Silent communication had become common for them—an easy glance here or there, the squeeze of a hand, and the angling of a head. As traumatic as their engagement ball had been, it appeared to have brought them closer, as had Soren's antics, though she would hate to know such a thing. After Soren had confronted them in the infirmary, an unspoken agreement was forged between Caellum and Sadira, neither of whom trusted her.

Sadira tensed at Caellum's side as they reached the top of the Island.

"I can't say I'd like to do that climb regularly," Sir Cain huffed beside him, yet despite his commander's age, he was fitter than most men Caellum knew. Behind him, waves crashed against the rock face, like a permanent warning against those who visited. His stomach turned at the thought of peering lower at the narrow steps they had climbed. Instead, he focused on the towering trees looming over him on either side of the clearing. To his left was a man with a bow strapped to his back and furs acting as a shield from the wind. Rigid, the man looked out over the ocean. A guard, Caellum realised.

Many footprints marked the mud before him, a sign the watch post was constantly manned. He glanced at Sadira, whose eyes looked anywhere but ahead of them, where a single track led deep into the forest. On the track was a group of men and one woman standing in a row, deep in conversation, except for one man, who watched Sadira intently. His strong build exposed his biceps through the cuts in his sleeves as though any shirt would be too small for them. Caellum peeked at his own arms before looking at the man again. A slit carved his eyebrow, though Caellum was unsure if it was purposeful or inflicted. His hair was shaved at the sides, yet remained brown at the top, secured in a knot. It was not a hairstyle typical of Garridon; perhaps it came from his Wiccan culture.

"Is that him?" Caellum asked in a hushed voice, his lips barely moving. Sadira nodded. The pair had quickly realised their return to Doltas would involve Sadira crossing paths with her former lover, Rodik. Although Caellum knew Sadira loved Rodik, he was uncertain about her current emotions and whether she wished to reunite with him someday. Early in their betrothal, Caellum said he valued their friendship to make their marriage work, but he had not considered how either might feel if someone else was in the picture. Rodik stepped forward.

"Princess Sadira. King Caellum. Welcome back to Doltas Island." Rodik's voice was deep and matched his overall appearance. Caellum could not help but broaden his stance to match the welcoming, muscular man. Sadira remained rigid as she offered Rodik a polite smile. Behind them, Soren cleared her throat and stepped forward, peering intently at Rodik, who clenched his jaw, refusing Soren's eye. "Welcome, Queen Soren."

Soren smirked beside Caellum and pushed past the group. The three men from the dock followed suit, leaving Sadira and Caellum in Rodik's company while others lingered nearby. The men dressed similarly to Rodik in fitted trousers, boots, accompanied by leathers, and furs. Each had an axe strapped to their backs, along with bows and arrows. *Hunters or guards?* Caellum wondered. The woman, however, would not look out of place in Nerida, if not for her thick cloak. Underneath, Caellum spotted the sandals on her feet, and a thin dress tied with woven fabric, similar to those he had seen on Neridian women. She wore nothing else but a small dagger on her hip, yet she tugged the cloak tighter to hide it and crossed her arms. When Caellum met her eye, her gaze was wary.

"Princess Sadira, I would appreciate a moment with you," said Rodik, and Caellum held his tongue. He had expected Rodik to want time with her, though it was bold to make the request so quickly without meeting Caellum's eye. Caellum squeezed Sadira's hand in support of whatever decision she made.

"Very well," she responded, a nervous lilt in her voice.

"We will take you to the quarter." The woman in the Neridian dress raised her chin, her voice more certain than her previous expression implied when she addressed Caellum.

"Thank you, Eliza," Sadira said at Caellum's side. "I shall not be long, but I will meet you there. Please offer the king and his commander some food in my absence."

Eliza glanced at Sir Cain behind Caellum before gesturing them to follow her along the winding path that led to the crumbling wall he had visited once before. Caellum felt Rodik's eyes finally land on him. Caellum tugged gently on Sadira's hand and turned her to face him. The engagement ring glinted beneath the streams of light filtering through the trees when he brought her hand to his lips and placed a gentle kiss on her knuckles. Sadira blushed, and their eyes met. He stepped away to follow Eliza.

***

Sadira had been right to forewarn Caellum about how different Doltas Island would appear. When the group reached the crumbling wall, instead of stepping through the torn fabric he had peered through once before, they detoured to the right and circled round following the wall, which seemed in better repair with every step he took. Ivy continued to grow, but instead of tearing the wall apart, it seemed to entwine and nurture the bricks, as if it was at one with the wall, standing tall. The wall continued to grow, stretching higher until the group gathered at a large archway with wooden doors reinforced with iron. It looked like the entrance to any castle. Eliza knocked in a specific pattern, and the gates creaked open.

"Princess Sadira wasn't joking," Sir Cain murmured beside Caellum in his gruff accent. "This is far different from what you described." Caellum nodded and hummed his agreement. He paused as he was met by floods of noise and took in the sights before them. An entire town square led to a castle that stood as strong as Antor's. Different people crossed his path, all dressed in varied clothing; it was as though Caellum was in the Neutral City, where the influence of all four realms was felt. While some women dressed similarly to Eliza, others wore brightly coloured sarees and lehengas like Nyzaia often did. Many men wore clothing similar to Rodik, while others sported tailored jackets that matched Caellum's. He increased his pace to catch up to Eliza. The sound of clashing metal reminded him of the Abis Forge, as did the spices in the air drifting from several butcher stalls lining the wall of the quarter, where a line of people queued with plates. Laughing children ran past him, looking no different and no less healthy than Edlen and Eve had growing up.

He surveyed each stall. A woman knelt, pouring liquid on a child's knee, the clear gel reminiscent of the liquid in Vala's healing potions. A man cleaned bottles of Neridian wine before pouring new contents into them. Every stall reminded him of one of the realms. It hit him then. Soren must have an endless network of spies hidden on the mainland to have transported such copious amounts of goods back to her people.

"Are you fussy?" Eliza turned to Caellum, who raised his eyebrows. "About food? Are you fussy about what I get you to eat?" While he did not think he could eat just now, he did not wish to deny their hospitality. He shook his head.

"I would be happy with whatever you recommend," he said politely. Eliza seated him at a large outdoor table before fetching his food. She was pulled into many conversations along the way, so much so that he expected she would not return.

"The quarter might be big, but I can see you from all angles," Sir Cain said, resting a hand on the table as he leaned down to speak to

Caellum. "I'm going to patrol to see what I can overhear." Caellum never doubted the commander's intuition or plans; he nodded in dismissal.

He did not know how long he sat there, watching the surrounding community, but he regained focus when he sensed Sadira's presence. He turned his head to the gates where she appeared; she gathered her cloak around her and walked alongside Rodik, deep in conversation. Rodik's arms swung loosely at his sides, occasionally bumping Sadira's arm, though she kept her hands firmly clasped before her and her arms tight by her sides. For the first time in his life, Caellum wished for Elisara's powers so he could listen in as Rodik bent slightly to murmur into her ear. Sadira smiled, and Rodik chuckled. An uneasy feeling festered in Caellum's stomach as he twisted the ring around his finger while watching his betrothed. He wished he was next to her in that moment, and that it was him who she laughed with.

"They've been in love for a *very* long time."

Caellum stiffened. "Soren," he acknowledged as she sat down beside him. She huffed.

"You know, I would also feel somewhat insecure about my betrothed spending time alone with the man she loves," Soren goaded, though Caellum tried his best to ignore her and not fall into the trap she so obviously placed before him.

"Sadira and I were very clear on the grounds of our betrothal," he said, clenching his jaw. Soren rested her clasped hands on the table and angled her head towards him.

"Ah, I see. So, it was fine that another man took her to bed while you waited on the sidelines?"

The wooden table splintered beneath Caellum's grip, a crack stretching down the middle. The children at the other end of the table turned to him, wide-eyed.

"Sadira can do as she wishes, but I will *not* have my future wife spoken about in such a manner. Do you understand?" he snarled.

Soren laughed. "I wish I could take you seriously," she said, rising from her seat when Sadira approached. Rodik was no longer with her.

"I will leave you two to talk." Soren smirked. "Meet me at the gates in an hour to leave for the talisman."

Caellum glared at Soren's retreating back as she strode towards the entrance to the quarter, nodding to the people she passed, who smiled back at her. She did not acknowledge Sir Cain, who watched from beside a meat stall. After Soren passed, Sir Cain met Caellum's eye, and Caellum nodded for the commander to follow the fallen queen.

"I have news," Sadira whispered, resting her hand on Caellum's arm, her touch gentle. Caellum looked up at her, searching the emotions in her eyes to detect if anything had transpired between her and Rodik. Her eyes were wide and hopeful as the light caught them. "Come." She grasped his hand and led them into the castle. He was reassured when she did not let go of it.

"So, this is where you lived?" Caellum asked, taking in the grand stone hallway and the ivy crawling along the cracked wooden banisters of the staircase.

"Yes, but I can give you a tour after. This is more important." She grabbed his other hand and turned him to face her. Caellum scanned her expression.

"What did he ask you?"

"Rodik said that after I left, Soren had a guard post set up to monitor the Garridon shoreline."

"Oh? Is that all he said to you?" Caellum glanced away, fearing what her expression might reveal, but Sadira reached for his face and turned him to face her. She smiled.

"The guards saw a creature," she said, and Caellum's eyes locked on hers. "They only saw one; they did not see all five as it was too dark, but the view from the post looks past Garridon to the rocks rising off Nerida's shores. They saw a creature flying into one the morning after our engagement ball. It could be Larelle! It could be the one who took Larelle." Sadira's eyes were wide with excitement, her lips upturned in a grin. "She could be okay!" Lost in her elation, Caellum held her forearms, grinning back at her.

It took Larelle to the rocks. Caellum's smile wavered. Sadira had not mentioned the creature leaving the rock since, so what if it held her there as a captive? Or worse... dead.

"I do not wish for you to get your hopes up. It has been nearly three nights since she was taken," he said. Sadira gripped his hands.

"But it could be her, Caellum. We must tell Alvan. He needs to search them all." Caellum nodded, her hope infectious.

"We need to get a message to him. Quickly."

Chapter Thirty

Soren

Whoever said 'patience was a virtue' clearly never had a throne to take from a usurper. Soren leaned against the towering tree, tapping her food against the large, overgrown root. The thick Garridon armour shielded the wind intent on whipping her braids across her face. Soren did not wince, but Varna grew agitated. Perking her ears, she grumbled and paced along the trees. The two matching sable-coloured wolves, whom Soren liked to imagine were twin brothers, Baelyn and Tapesh, huddled by her shins. They had never liked the wind, though perhaps Soren would take them to Nerida one day to enjoy the warm breeze. While the two males remained huddled, Soren could not help but smile at their opposites, Octavia and Serene, who hurtled through the air in their attempts to catch leaves in their jowls. Octavia lunged from a tree trunk for a spinning leaf but was knocked down by a flash of deep grey fur. She growled low when Seiko batted the leaf with his paw. Soren's smallest wolf. Serene grumbled from Seiko's other side, and both black females prowled towards him.

"Let him join in," Soren commanded, and the two black wolves immediately turned their heads before stalking away from the smallest wolf. Seiko glanced at Soren with the leaf hanging from his mouth; his one pale blue eye stared back at her, seeking her approval. "Show me then," Soren urged, holding out her hand. Seiko padded over to rest his head in her hand but missed and stumbled into her. Soren gave him a sympathetic smile. He had always been half blind, with one eye pale blue and the other milky and glazed. "Do not let them bully you," she said. Seiko whined but it was barely audible over Varna's deep growl. All six wolves turned their heads in the direction of the tree line.

"Are you going to hide behind those trees for much longer, Sir Cain?" called Soren. She had sensed him following her the moment she left the quarter. The commander cleared his throat and stepped out from the tree; it was a miracle he had found one wide enough to hide his broad frame. He stroked his red beard as he approached, eyeing the wolves with caution.

"Just scouting ahead for the king and princess," Sir Cain said. Soren assessed him, taking in the armour that so closely matched her breastplate.

She turned her head at the sound of crunching leaves, where Caellum emerged, holding back branches for Sadira, who wrapped her cloak tightly around her. Caellum placed a hand on her lower back to steer her into him rather than her sister. Soren rolled her eyes.

"Why are we meeting here?" Sadira asked, assessing the dark space overcrowded with trees and wolves.

"Would you rather risk the more public path and answer questions about where we are going and why?" Soren asked, her voice monotone. Sadira pursed her lips, and the four stood in silence. Soren was testing them to see who would break first and acknowledge that they needed her guidance. She smirked when Caellum finally sighed and gestured ahead of them.

"After you," he said. Soren removed her foot from the raised root and stomped it on the ground before turning in the opposite direction to his hand. She flicked her wrist, unfurling the branches and roots to create a path before them. She tried to eavesdrop on Sadira and Caellum as she walked but could not hear their hushed tones over the wind other than Caellum instructing Sir Cain to wait where they had met. The Lord of Night's words flickered to the front of her mind. *Take the throne. We must be quicker.* She did not know what suddenly prompted the lord's rush; perhaps the creatures had failed their mission. Or maybe he was frustrated with Soren's failure. Fury propelled Soren's movements through the upward hike.

"How much farther?" Caellum called, though Soren did not bother to answer. They were close. Sadira would soon realise where they were headed. She glanced over her shoulder to where Caellum held her sister's hand to steady her footing. Soren rolled her eyes. Sadira needed no more help than she did. They had grown up among these trees.

Soren returned her hands to her sides; she no longer needed to control nature as the path widened into a small clearing at the top of the incline, so she rested her hand on the pommel of her sword. Would anyone really know if she were to kill Caellum here and toss his body over the cliff? *Sadira would.* Would she try to save him again, like she had at their engagement ball? Soren glanced between them and wondered if she could sacrifice her sister a second time. If she failed again, that would be two assassination attempts on the king and his betrothed. Was that risk enough to stop her?

"We are here!" Soren shouted; she marched over the incline and took in the clearing. The last time she journeyed here was the night she was crowned—the night her parents and grandmother died at her hand. Little remained of the white petunias Sadira had turned from black that night, nothing but a web of tangled roots. It was odd that nature had not reclaimed the space, almost as if it wished to remain desolate as a reminder of the historic event.

Soren strode through the path where the tables had been for the celebrations. So much had changed.

"Soren, wait!" Sadira called, but she ignored her. "Soren!" Soren shook off Sadira's arm as she reached her and stopped, spinning to face the pair. She rested her hands on her hips.

"What!"

"We need a plan; you cannot just storm ahead," Sadira exclaimed.

"The plan is: we approach the tree; you and I manoeuvre the roots, and then we reach in and take the talisman. What else is there to discuss?"

"*Caellum* reaches for the talisman. There is no *we* in this, Soren," Sadira stressed. Soren rolled her eyes and turned. She was done with conversing. She was unsure if she could wield the other half of the talisman on its own or if it had to be paired with its equal, which hung around Caellum's neck, secured by a leather rope.

The oak tree loomed above the three standing in its shadow. The vines twisting around the trunk were wider than the three of them combined, and so rooted in place, untouched, that it would not have been unusual to see a layer of dust on them. Soren analysed the worn bark. The painted wreath of blood had since faded. An odd feeling clutched Soren's heart as she recalled the night she killed her family. *Feelings make you weak*. That is what the Lord of Night always warned. She pushed away the memory, which was an easier task for Soren than her sister. Sadira watched the ground where the blood had been. *Too emotional. Too caring*, Soren thought, until her eyes tugged towards two hastily engraved names in childish handwriting.

Soren and Sadira. She did not remember when they had done that, though she did not care to recall. Memories swayed her mind from the plan—her path.

"This does not look like a difficult place to get into," Caellum said, acting as a buffer between the sisters. "I thought the talisman was somewhere difficult to reach." Soren looked up at the sky to keep from snapping.

"It likely was when it was in Garridon," Sadira interrupted gently. "Our grandmother took it when she fled, though I never knew where she hid it." Sadira looked at her sister, and a smile tugged on Soren's lips when she realised her family had kept certain truths from Sadira. *I was always meant to rule.*

"Shall we begin?" Sadira asked. She stepped towards the tree, caressing the green vines and ivy. "I will take the living and you take the dead?"

Seems fitting, Soren thought as she stepped forward and grasped the thicker, older vines, nearly matching the brown of the trunk. She locked eyes with Sadira as the two stood opposite one another, each with a hand on the tree. Her eyes glowed their usual bright green, and Soren knew hers shone in a similar vein, though darker than her sister's—always darker than Sadira's. Soren glanced to her right, where Caellum stood with his arms crossed, flitting his gaze between the sisters. She tossed him a patronising smile and wondered how inferior he must feel.

The vines retracted, twisting and unravelling until they dangled like ropes at their feet. Soren let go as Sadira manoeuvred the final green vines, revealing a small hole in the trunk's centre just wide enough to fit a hand. Soren instinctively stepped forward, her soul reaching for the talisman—her birthright. Sadira moved to block the opening, her face like stone as she looked down at her sister. Their eyes locked as Sadira reached for Caellum and pulled him towards her. Soren refused to look away, but Sadira turned and guided Caellum to the opening. Scowling, Soren tried to peer around them.

"Just reach in. You should be able to feel it; it will match the half around your neck," said Sadira reassuringly. Soren observed how vulnerable Caellum was, his back turned towards her. Soren's hand twitched at the pommel of her sword. It would take only an instant for the throne to be hers so she could get everything she wanted and finally please the Lord of Night. She glanced at Sadira. They were not yet married; Sadira had no claim should Caellum die. *I am the oldest; I am the heir. It could be mine before they even realise what has happened.* Soren stepped forward and began pulling the sword from its sheath.

"I have it!" Caellum called. *Too late.*

Soren tried to step around Sadira to look at what would one day be hers. The opening appeared designed for someone smaller as Caellum tugged the talisman from the tree, grazing his hand. He unfurled his fingers to reveal the other half of the talisman lay flat on his palm. The half-moon-shaped piece of wood was paler than most trees, likely carved from deep in the centre of Ithyion's oldest tree. Its edge was clean, showing that whoever chopped the talisman had done so with ease. Vaguely, Soren discerned the burnt engraving of a tree and half of another. She felt the tug towards it, like an invisible rope urging her forward. It belonged to her; it was her right. It should be in the hands of a Garridon heir, not this imposter. Soren wanted to inspect and feel it, channelling the connection to her god and ancestors.

When Soren looked up at the face of the hand who held it, his eyes narrowed as if he sensed her hunger to take it. Caellum clasped his hand tightly around the talisman and dropped it into a velvet pouch held open by Sadira. Soren had expected the talisman to repel Caellum's efforts, but as it dropped into the bag, a gust of wind whipped at Sadira's hair and cleared her face, exposing the glow in her eyes before the moment passed, and she tied the pouch. Caellum tucked it inside the right breast of his jacket and wrapped his cloak around him. The three of them stood in a triangle on the blood of Soren's family, glancing at each other.

"Well, that was..."

"Easy," Caellum finished Sadira's sentence. *Anticlimactic was more like it.*

"I wonder if the others will gain their halves as easily," Sadira pondered.

"Perhaps not, especially if they remain in their initial hiding place." Caellum replied, and silence returned. Soren felt like an odd piece as she watched the two gravitate towards one another, their arms always touching. They had built familiarity and trust. Soren looked away to where her wolves patrolled the open expanse. *Feelings are a weakness.* She had no time for relationships or friendships with a throne to take. Soren had felt out of place for as long as she could remember. Why should that change now?

"There are some things I wish to gather from my rooms before we leave," Sadira declared, leaning into Caellum. She looped her arm through his, and he looked down at her with an emotion

Soren had always yearned for from the Lord of Night. *Pride.*

"I will meet you at the dock before sunset," Soren confirmed. When the two passed her, there was no mistaking the caution in Sadira's eyes as she glanced back over her shoulder. Soren kept her expression blank until the two disappeared from sight. Whistling a command, her wolves returned from their patrol, with Seiko leading the group. He set a slow pace while Varna took the rear and scanned their surroundings.

Soren leaned against the tree and slid until hitting the cold dirt. She pulled a dagger from her side and hacked off a piece of wood from the nearest root before. Resting her forearms on her knees, she began carving at it. The wolves settled around Soren, who huffed as Baelyn and Tapesh curled either side of her like warm blankets against the wind.

"Is this for your benefit? Or mine?" she asked. Tapesh glanced sideways at her and sighed. Octavia and Serene huddled in front of her shins but were more intent on cuddling one another than Soren. Nevertheless, she appreciated the warmth the barrier of her wolves provided. Varna assumed her usual spot off to the side, sitting and watching as Seiko padded over and mirrored her stance. Soren smiled at the contrast; white and grey, largest and smallest.

She closed her eyes while her hands worked; she focused on the mess of shadows that made up the Lord of Night in the hope he would appear. He did not. He had meant it when he said she would not see him for a while. It was not uncommon. Many times over the years, he had announced his departure before reappearing weeks later, leaving Soren in a state of anticipation, awaiting his next visit. Soren had hoped this spot under the tree might prompt his appearance. She recalled the day the wolves had come to her—the same day *he* had first entered her mind. She had been thirteen and wild, dashing through the tangled maze of roots and hanging branches. Soren heard the collective howl of wolves, but instead of feeling scared, she was intrigued and changed her course to find the source. It was as though the wolves waited for her—a pack to take her in. All six stood in a row, watching and whining as they wished to step forward, but Varna kept them in check. Only when the leader approached and sniffed Soren did the other five bound over, fighting to lick her arms. The tree held those memories for her, of the times she fell asleep under the setting sun, only to awake in her dreams and find him. "Hello, little bird," were the lord's first words.

Soren's mouth twitched at the memory, but when she opened her eyes, she accepted defeat and inspected the carved bird in her hands. Seiko whined, turning his head to stare intently at her.

"You will never leave me, will you?" Soren asked. Seiko padded over, clambering over the other four until he could rest his head on her knee. Her mouth twitched again.

Everyone always leaves.

Chapter Thirty-One

Nyzaia

"Thirteen."

"Twenty."

"Two," Rafik chimed in.

"He's been with more than two women!" Issam exclaimed, his voice bouncing off the high sandstone walls as the group rode through the canyons in a line, with Nyzaia in the middle.

"Look at those eyes; there is no way only two women have fallen for his smoulder!" Jabir, who estimated twenty, shouted at Rafik.

"So, you think his eyes are *smouldering*?" Rafik called back, grinning.

"That's, uh—no. I—"

Nyzaia shook her head and glanced sideways at Farid, whose expression was unreadable as he stared straight ahead. *He is in her spot,* she realised, and her smile faltered.

"Come on, Farid! Put us out of our misery. Am I taking Rafik's gold for his poor bet of two?" Issam nudged Farid from atop his horse beside him, who jostled slightly and glanced at Nyzaia with widened eyes, pleading for help.

"None of you were right," he relented.

"Who was closest?" Jabir asked, dropping the horse's reins and opening his water pouch.

"Rafik," Farid said in a clipped tone.

"Ha! I knew it wouldn't be many. Farid oozes respect, you idiots," laughed Rafik.

"So how many?" Jabir asked before taking a swig of water. Nyzaia looked at Farid, unable to deny her intrigue, though she wished they would change the topic; poor Farid had been berated since leaving Nefere Valley. The other men appeared more interested in Farid and showed him more respect since he had defended Nyzaia from Tajana. Farid glanced at Jabir, who still guzzled water under the heat of the sun.

"One."

Jabir sputtered, spitting water as he choked. Issam slapped him on the back.

"Only one?" Issam exclaimed, and Farid nodded.

"Was she the love of your life?" Rafik asked. "Did you declare she was the only one for you?" Rafik continued with a dramatic gesture of his arm. Nyzaia rolled her eyes.

"No. It only took one woman to realise I prefer men," Farid said flatly. Silence followed. "So, does that mean I get all thirteen golds on offer?"

Laughter erupted among the men.

"I expect better of you all. How could you assume he was only interested in women?" Nyzaia asked. Issam emptied coins from his pouch and handed them to Farid, who tucked them in his pockets.

"He has this 'I'm tall, dark, and mysterious' air about him," Issam jested. "Women like that."

"Men like that too," Jabir said, having recovered from choking. A coy smile crossed Nyzaia's face as Farid's lip twitched.

A dark figure flitted high atop the rock edge. Nyzaia refrained from fully turning her head but did so enough to recognise the uniform of the Spies. She rolled her eyes. It was once standard to have a Red Stone trailing royalty, lords, and the wealthiest of Keres, but it was bold of them to continue such acts when she had become queen.

"I see him," Rafik confirmed beside her before veering into the shadows. He kicked his horse into a gallop beneath the cliff edge, where the spy likely crawled.

"A threat?" Farid asked at Nyzaia's side. She shook her head.

"Unlikely."

The group continued their journey through the canyons while awaiting Rafik's return. The mid-afternoon sun was sweltering, and although the forge would be hotter, the sun would have lowered by the time they arrived, offering a reprieve from the flow of lava as the metal workers finished their shifts.

A short scream echoed as the trail inclined, guiding the group to the top of the forge where endless recruits had trained over the years. Rafik would shortly be on his way with the spy in tow.

"A bet on how terrified the guy is?" Issam chuckled.

"No more bets! You are banned from betting for the rest of this trip, Issam!" Nyzaia scolded, and he rolled his eyes as they reached the summit to find Rafik waiting with his hands grasping the collar of a slight boy, barely eighteen. He was likely only two years into his training, which explained the ease with which Rafik had caught him.

"Do I want to know why you were spying on your queen?" Nyzaia asked. She dismounted her horse and passed Jabir the reins. The boy shifted on his feet, his toes scraping the red dust. Rafik raised him higher. The boy's wide eyes scanned the circling syndicate, sweat beading on his brow.

"For your safety," the boy gasped.

"Why would she need safety from you when she has us?" asked Farid, placing his hand on his blade. Nyzaia summoned a flame to dance across her palm, waiting for the boy's answer. He gulped. The former queen of the Red Stones advanced until her flames licked the hairs on his arms.

"Okay, okay. The committee asked me to!" *Too easy.*

"The committee?" Nyzaia repeated. She walked towards the cliff edge to find the workers slowly packing for the evening.

"When no one replaced you, the heads of each pillar formed a committee," said the boy.

"A democracy," Nyzaia scoffed. "The Red Stones have never been run in such a manner; they have always had a leader." Nyzaia recalled the time she had challenged Tajana's whereabouts, who revealed she had visited the Red Stones. They needed a leader, Tajana said, though it appeared her lover had lied again. The pillars had formed a committee. She turned against the setting sun to face her syndicate. Rafik and Issam wore matching frowns while Jabir focused on Nyzaia, waiting for further instruction.

"They said if you would not lead, then they would," the spy added.

"They are constantly bickering; that will not work," Nyzaia said firmly, and the boy stared at his feet.

"They said you abandoned them."

Nyzaia narrowed her eyes.

"Abandoned?" she sneered. "Do you think I had a choice in this?"

"They said Arjun would never have abandoned us," Nyzaia scoffed. She had once placed Arjun, their previous leader, on a pedestal, but that time had long passed.

"For the love of the gods! Stop digging yourself into a hole!" shouted Issam. Nyzaia took slow steps forward, elongating each movement as Rafik dropped the boy's cloak. He landed, eye to eye, with Nyzaia. Flames engulfed her arms. The spy tried to step back but quickly collided with Rafik's hardened stance.

"Arjun Qadir was greedy and power-hungry; he planned to leave you the second he had a chance. That is why he was killed at my hand." Nyzaia's voice was a deadly whisper. "You can tell your committee that I will pay them a visit, and they better be ready." The boy trembled, and Nyzaia felt his shaky breath on her cheek. "GO!" He took off at a run.

"If that had been a bet—"

"Shut it, Issam!" Nyzaia commanded.

"Was that really why Qadir was killed?" Farid asked as Nyzaia strode back to the edge of the cliff, waiting for her syndicate to join.

"We discovered he was funnelling funds from the wealthy and withholding earnings from nearly all the pillars," Jabir confirmed, crossing his arms to match Nyzaia's stance.

"He had bought a ship and was packing his things when we found him," Nyzaia continued.

"Why was he fleeing?" asked Farid, and Nyzaia shrugged.

"No idea. It does not matter. Abandonment is punishable by trial and then death." Nyzaia finished. Farid seemed contemplative beside her.

"A traitor is not worthy of their life," Farid said, and Isaam gave a bark of laughter.

"Careful, Farid. You're starting to sound like one of us." Nyzaia was uncertain if her syndicate was a bad influence or if Farid's experiences had shaped him into the defensive yet protective man he was.

"So, where do you think it will be?" Jabir asked Farid, gesturing to the forge. Nyzaia regarded the forge, trying to determine herself. The forge was a wise place to hide something so valuable. No one from the other realms could withstand the heat for long. Nyzaia was unsure if even those with a tie to Keres' power could wield the lava, herself included.

The forge split into parts. The main strip running through the canyon was a river of flowing lava, bubbling up from the large crack down the middle and gushing from the crevices in the rock where they stood. At regular intervals were stations housing metal ore and blacksmith tools to meld, hammer, and shape the metal into weapons. Watchtowers were stationed at each end of the river to survey the workers.

"Surely it is not beneath the lava?" asked Nyzaia, looking at Farid.

"It is below where we stand," he said. The other four shared a look before peering cautiously over the edge to where lava flowed roughly halfway down like a waterfall.

"You are lying," Jabir said with a nervous laugh, but Farid looked him dead in the eye.

"I do not lie."

Nyzaia cleared her throat and waited for Farid to untense his shoulders. He did so when he met her eye, his face softening.

"The lava hides multiple alcoves, with some small enough to hide items and others big enough to hide people," Farid continued. Nyzaia opened her mouth to question him, but Farid quickly steered the conversation. "Are you affected by lava?" he asked. Nyzaia recalled her earlier days of training with Kazaar and the Red Stones. She had never wielded lava, yet she had not tested it since becoming queen and inheriting all her power.

"I could never control it, but that does not mean it will harm me." Nyzaia's voice lacked confidence.

"If you can scale down until you're in line with the flow, you will see a wide gap where it falls away from the rock. It should offer enough space to reach under and check for cavities within the wall."

"Great, this sounds like fun," Nyzaia muttered. Rafik jogged to the horses and back, returning with thick rope.

"We need to be quick; the lava will offer some light, but the sun will soon be behind the Zivoi mountains," said Jabir, analysing the horizon where the sun began to fall, their path aglow in countless shades of orange and red.

"So, I will quickly scale the rock, stick my arm behind lava, and search for a talisman that we *hope* is there," Nyzaia mocked as Rafik tied the rope around her and secured it in place.

"I will follow; I know some spots," said Farid, tying the second rope around himself.

"How do you know all this?" Nyzaia asked. Jabir reached forward to tighten Farid's rope, who stepped away before he could.

"I worked here," Farid said, passing Jabir the end of the rope and backing towards the cliff edge. He stared back at their surprised faces, Nyzaia's included. "Are we beginning?"

"I guess so," Nyzaia said, matching Farid's stance. Jabir and Issam each held one rope and braced their legs as Nyzaia pushed off the edge with Farid in tow. In her twenty-five years of life, she never expected to scale the edge of the forge. Her footing felt secure as she lowered, the temperatures rising as they approached the starting point of the lava flow. She looked up at Farid, who waited for a nod of confirmation. When she returned the nod, they continued. The stream of lava was surprisingly loud from where it exploded from the rock face. The heat differed from the sensations she felt when controlling her flames, and she flinched as the stream spat and burned her skin. At least that answered her question about the lava. Nyzaia peered down at the lava stream to where it met the boiling river below, trying not to think about how it could kill her if she fell.

Farid was right. When Nyzaia lowered several more inches, the lava flowed out and away from the wall, likely from the pressure.

"You should be approaching two small openings now," Farid called. Nyzaia reached to the left, wincing at the heat emanating from the lava. It was hot, even for her. Her fingers found a small hole, no bigger than two of her hands, and the surface was rough and jagged when she reached in. Untouched. She shook her head at Farid, who pointed down.

"There should be a larger one next."

Nyzaia nodded and slowly descended once more, hearing the rubble fall below her.

"Three more steps," Farid called. One. Two. Nyzaia's foot slipped, and parts of the rock face suddenly began crumbling and falling away. She gasped as her feet slid below her, slamming her into the rock. Her hands burned as she held onto the rope and pulled herself up to reposition her feet.

"Are you okay!"

Nyzaia nodded, though her hands trembled. *This may put me off heights,* she thought while regulating her breathing. She turned her head to examine the wall and found a different opening. It was far bigger than the previous, large enough for Nyzaia and Farid if they squeezed in. She scanned the spot, using the lava as a torch as the sun began to fade. A glint of metal caught her eye on the far side of the opening. It was a streak of metal ore, as if someone had carved the rock and poured the metal inside it. In the centre was a small broken piece. *The talisman.*

"I think I see it!" she called to Farid, who began lowering himself towards her. She reached for the opening, trying to pull herself close enough to hook her leg over and climb in.

"I can't quite reach!" She shouted over the gushing lava crashing into the river below.

"Wait! I will be there in a moment!" Farid yelled. Nyzaia reached again, the temperature scorching as she attempted to slot her arm under the gap. Sweat dripped down her forehead as she pushed her body to its limits, her muscles burning as she attempted to hook her foot for purchase.

"I have an idea!" She lowered her leg and took a deep breath before pushing away at an angle, swinging sideways in the hope of creating enough momentum to make the distance.

"Nyzaia! Wait!" Farid shouted, but she pushed again with a forceful swing. It worked. "Nyzaia! Your rope!" Farid yelled, hurrying down the wall to reach her. She looked up at the rope as she tried to haul herself onto the ledge. Her eyes widened. A glow slowly blazed across the rope and worked its way down. Nyzaia waved her hand to distinguish the embers, but no fire was left to latch onto. The rope blackened and frayed before she could make the final push into the opening. Then it snapped.

"Nyzaia!" Farid cried as she plummeted with the flow of lava towards the scorching lake below.

Nyzaia screamed and tried not to flail her arms as her body rotated with the force of falling. A sea of orange blurred before her: the setting sun, the canyon rocks, the scorching lava. She focused on nothing as she fell through the air, the flow of lava seconds away. Nyzaia summoned all her strength and willed the lava to part—anything to avoid plunging into it headfirst—but nothing worked. Would she survive this? Was a connection to the God of Fire enough to keep her alive? Something hit her then, and Nyzaia screamed as flames engulfed her and a force sent her flying. But Nyzaia was not propelled into the lava river to be met by death; she was thrown into darkness.

Her body screamed in pain as she hit a hard surface. Fire blazed around her, though it was not her own. It retracted, pulling away, and when she opened her eyes, she faced a dark wall. She did not understand how she was alive. Her eyes adjusted to the cave-like space, lit by an all-encompassing glow. Nyzaia blinked, grasping a hand to her side as she slowly turned her body towards the source of the light. It was not her own flames lighting the way nor the lava flowing from the opening. It was Farid. He knelt in the opening, panting. His pale blue eyes glowed in the darkness, a sign of power. But it was not his eyes Nyzaia focused on; it was the glow emitting from the blazing, feathered wings protruding from his back.

"Please do not tell anyone."

Chapter Thirty-Two

Larelle

Darkness had become the new normal, weighing on Larelle's chest. She had tried to conserve her breaths for what she believed was three days now, provided her counting method was correct. A slither of light had broken through a crack in the piled rocks to her left three times: three moments of daylight from the world outside and three days without food. Her only source of water was what she drew from the rocks. They had left her there to die. The hard ground was moist and seeped through her dress; she had torn it several times on the first night and grazed her hands as she sought a way out of this makeshift prison. Her slow shuffles and stumbles around the small space confirmed her suspicions about where they kept her.

When the creature took Larelle, dragging her from her daughter, Alvan, her home, and all she had, Larelle was certain this was the end, which was why she named Alvan her successor. Forever a forward thinker, even under the notion of death and panic. Larelle also learned about her drastic fear of heights that night, scrunching her eyes shut as the creature soared from Garridon.

Larelle was unsurprised when she felt the familiar call of Nerida's waters, but their landing soon after came as a shock. Her body jostled in the creature's claws as it flung her against the slippery rocks. She had assumed it would drop her somewhere to die—or kill her itself—not land on one of the rocky islands protruding off the coast of Mera.

Larelle quickly understood the creature's intentions as it advanced with a growl and backed her into a small opening at the back of the cave. When she was inside, it pushed and gathered rocks to block her exit. Yet, in doing so, it showed the creatures to be smarter than they appeared—calculated. Such information would prove of use should she ever escape. How else would it know to trap Larelle? She was yet to understand its motives, but surely, they did not want her dead if they kept her here alive.

During the entire first night, she heard it. Its claws scraped outside the cave as it growled to itself, and when that first slither of light shone into her prison, it had sniffed once at the rocks separating them before she heard the flap of wings fading into the distance. It left and had not returned since.

She hoped to have found a means of escaping by now or a way to use her power. Instead, she was plagued with the look on Alvan's face when she was taken—the twisting of his features as though a dagger pierced his chest. His scream rang through her mind as he insisted she would not die. Screams of sheer agony. Then, her mind flitted to Zarya and the fear her daughter would grow up without a mother. *Alvan will look after her.*

Larelle stiffened as a thud sounded outside, followed by a growl—*two* growls. It had returned, but it was not alone. She pushed her hands against the floor, forcing her body to slide up the wet wall. Yet there was nowhere for Larelle to go should the creatures come for her. Her heart thundered, but she kept quiet and listened for anything that might help. The growling stopped.

"I swear to Makaria, are you a fucking fool?" hissed a deep voice in an accent she did not recognise. It came from the other side of the rocks. *Makaria?* Larelle heard a scuffle and then a thud against the wall outside. "What were you thinking by taking one of them?"

"What was I supposed to do?" barked a higher, younger voice. Larelle's eyes widened. People stood outside. "They waved that sword around, and I didn't want to turn out dead like the others, or worse, trapped—"

"Shhh!" snapped the deeper voice. "You do not know what she could hear."

"She might not even be alive!"

"What do you mean?"

"After I left her here, it took me two days to get back and find you, which is a reasonably long time without food and water." *Back to where? Had he been in Novisia? And then left?*

The deeper voice, likely belonging to the superior, sighed.

"Let me get this straight." His voice changed, a menacing undertone in his words. "You took a queen of their kingdom, hid her in her *own* realm, and then left her to starve?" Silence was his answer. "It is like you are asking to be a part of this war."

Larelle shuffled, straining to hear more. She did not recognise the voice.

"*Please*! We became a part of this war the second he called in the debt that was owed and had us hunt for that damned sword."

Endless questions whirled through Larelle's mind: the war, the sword, these people, and the debt they owed. Pushing closer to the rock, she turned over his words. *"I left her here,"* he had said, *but since when could the creatures speak?*

"Be careful how you speak to your superior officer." Larelle heard movement—the rustling of fabric, as though unwrapping something and then the sound of clinking metal.

"What are those?" asked the second man with a youthful lilt to his voice.

"You wanted my help, did you not? This is our way of talking to her without her escaping."

Larelle frowned, itching to see the creatures and figure out their plan. The goddess must have heard her wish, for it was granted almost instantly. The rocks shifted, and the blinding light from outside entered the cave, forcing Larelle to shield her eyes and stumble back.

She blinked rapidly and slowly withdrew her arm. She tried to discern the dark silhouette, who stood against the backdrop of the rising sun over the oceans.

"Queen Larelle. I must apologise for the length of time you

have been kept here in such ungodly conditions," said the deep voice. *He knows my name.* As her eyes adjusted, she took him in. Larelle had not known what to expect; she was unable to match his accent to a location or culture and could not decide if she was surprised or mesmerised by the man before her. He was taller than most men with a similar stature to Commander Kazaar; his long hair was sleek, as though woven of silk stolen from the night itself. Although it appeared as though he rarely saw the sun, there was an iridescence to his skin that made him seem far from sickly, and his eyes—unlike any she had seen before—scrutinised her in the same manner she watched him. She saw no malice in his gaze, which made her uncomfortable. Was this man truly a foe or indifferent to her plight?

His eyes narrowed on something behind her, and he tilted his head to his companion. Golden rings circled his dark irises, far darker than her own. She would have assumed them black if he had not been bathed in light.

In the same spotlight, she discerned a faint scar running from halfway down his cheek all the way along his neck and beneath the high collar of his black jacket. His clothes were embroidered with amber swirls that matched the flower pin on his jacket breast. Larelle did not recognise it. His clothes were similar to those a lord or king would wear in Novisia, but there was something different about it, though she could not place what.

"I realise you do not know who I am, Queen Larelle, but it is rude not to greet your hosts." Larelle refrained from dropping her jaw at the man's audacity. Instead, she pursed her lips and looked to his companion, the man—or rather, the boy—who brought her here.

He looked no older than sixteen; his deep umber skin reminded Larelle of her father, but in place of multiple braids was a close-cut style, the tight coils of his hair flat against his head. His height and features gave away his age; he was less chiselled and had gangly arms to grow into. She wondered how someone so young had kidnapped a queen.

"He is not as young as he seems," said the pale man. Larelle's head whirled to him. Was she so easy to read? The man smirked. Larelle became acutely aware of the silence in the cave and glanced around. The creatures she had initially assumed were talking had not returned, though she could have sworn she had heard them since being brought here. The pale man chuckled again.

"You do not strike me as someone who is easily confused, Your Majesty," he taunted.

His smirk twisted then. Long canines began to protrude from his lips as his face elongated and his stance broadened. Larelle stumbled as dark leather wings extended from his back. As they grew, the golden rings in his eyes glowed brighter. She could not tear her eyes away from his transformation as the man formed into the creature like that which had taken her.

"I think she understands, Osiris," the younger boy mumbled. In the blink of an eye, he returned to his previous state, yet his wings remained free.

"What—what are you?" Larelle stuttered, trying to regain the regal composure she possessed so easily.

"That is not a question I can answer, nor is it relevant to you," Osiris responded.

"How can it be irrelevant when your people murdered innocents in Garridon and Ithyion and destroyed our home?" Osiris' demeanour quickly changed, his arrogant smirk replaced with a tight jaw and clenched fists.

"Do not make assumptions based on myths and lies," he sneered, stepping towards her.

"Then speak to me in truths," Larelle countered, refusing to cower under his stare as he approached. Osiris towered several feet above her and tucked his wings behind him, though even retracted, they were large enough to cast a shadow over Larelle, shielding the light and her escape to freedom.

"I am not here to give you the information you seek, queen," he whispered, reaching for her hair. She batted his hand away, and the smirk returned as laughter rumbled through him and reverberated off the surrounding walls. "I am here to find out just how much you know, as requested."

"Requested by whom?" She turned her head as he leaned closer. The silky sweet scent on his breath reminded her of the over-perfumed flowers possessed by the wealthy in The Bay. The smell made her nauseous.

"Not important."

"Who do you owe a debt to?"

"Also, not important."

"What do you fear of the Sword of Sonos, if not death?" His eye twitched upon her mention of the sword.

"Do you always ask so many questions?" he asked, searching her eyes.

"Do you always avoid answering a queen?"

He laughed at her response.

"If I were to serve a queen, you are not the one I would choose." Before Larelle could ask her next question, something cold nipped at her wrists, followed by a firm click. She glanced down at two metal rings clasped around her wrists, binding them together. Osiris smirked again and stepped back. He had distracted her.

"It is not as if I planned to go anywhere with you two in the cave." Larelle feigned confidence, and Osiris turned his back to her, walking towards the cave's edge and peering out across the ocean. The sky slowly lost its pink hue as the sun rose higher.

"They are simply to stop you from using your power against us while we talk." He hummed and turned back, leaning sideways against the damp wall. Larelle reached for the ocean, but nothing happened. She reached for the water pooling in rocks, but again—nothing. She reached for the tears threatening to spill in her eyes at the emptiness blooming within her. Nothing.

"Now that you have confirmed you indeed have lost access to your power, let us discuss what you know." Osiris examined his fingernails. "I would hate to do this the hard way when we have only just met."

Chapter Thirty-Three

Elisara

"What about this one?" Elisara asked.

"When I was seventeen, I tried to steal liquor from Razik's personal stash. I summoned vines for the first time to lift it from the shelves." Kazaar lazily traced circles on Elisara's shoulder while she examined the vines inked on the inside of his left bicep.

"This one?" she asked, pointing to a sail in the crook of his elbow, hidden among small symbols. She frowned.

"Razik wanted me to commandeer a ship he believed was stealing gold from him. I accidentally sunk it instead of setting it on fire," he murmured, turning his head to face her. She smiled.

"And they just appeared?" He nodded while she grazed her finger over them, wishing she had all the time in the world to count them and inspect every inch of him. She could not begin to guess how many markings there were, which left her wondering about his many stories. The corner of her lips tugged upward as her finger trailed back to his collarbone. There was no inking yet on her favourite mark—their mark—but the feeling of it under her thumb felt the same as the other inkings and scars.

"Each time I used a new power or used it differently, the scarred marks would appear. I felt nothing when they appeared, but I inked over them so they would appear superficial." Elisara frowned as her pinkie grazed a familiar small symbol, a memory tugging in the back of her mind.

"Are these small ones the same as those on the floor of the throne room on the Unsanctioned Isle?"

"I was so worried you'd notice when we were there," Kazaar murmured.

"Did you ever figure out why they appeared?"

"I have no answer to that except for the celestial tie keeping your freezing body glued to mine." She smacked his chest, and he chuckled. Elisara had awakened to Kazaar, gently stroking her back to gently wake her. That had been an hour ago, but they would need to rise soon. Instead, she spent the hour examining the many inkings across his upper body as he held her close in the bed designed for one. The inkings were a welcome distraction from her insistent thoughts that coaxed her into a spiral of overthinking about everything that transpired the evening before. She wondered if he meant his words before she kissed her, or when he promised there would be a 'next time.' Elisara focused on each mark on his skin to distract from the feeling in her heart that was so intent on carving itself into her permanently.

"What about this one?" Elisara pointed to a flaming dagger hidden beneath the vines on his forearm. Kazaar pulled his arm out from under her and rose from the bed, inviting the breeze of the early morning air to rush under the blanket, which she pulled close to her body as she sat up, spilling her dark waves over her shoulder.

"What's wrong?" she asked as Kazaar hastily pulled on his leathers. She was very conscious then of her naked body underneath the blanket.

"We need to get moving. That talisman won't collect itself." His lip lifted, though it lacked the sincerity she expected. Elisara tried to push into his mind, but dark walls shot from the ground within and blocked her instantly. She narrowed her eyes.

"Do not," he said, his voice clipped. She wrapped the blanket around her and shifted to the edge of the bed, where he had undressed and done so much more to her last night. The memory must have flashed in his mind, too, exposed by the look in his eye.

"You are keeping something from me." She frowned, trying to keep the accusatory tone from her lips. Kazaar avoided her gaze as he buckled the straps on his leathers and adjusted the fit of the Sword of Sonos on his back. "You said I could trust you, Kazaar."

Sighing, he closed his eyes and crossed over to her, gently tilting her chin.

"You can trust me, angel, but there are some things I am not ready to face myself yet, let alone share with someone who has only just begun to look at me with such endearment." Elisara's heart softened, though the wish to know the meaning behind the inking remained. He traced his thumb over her lip, reminding her of where those hands had been.

"At least bathe before we leave." She rolled her eyes and made to stand, but he pushed her shoulder gently, forcing her to sit. Leaning down, Kazaar kissed her cheek before whispering, "I think I would rather have the reminder on my skin that you are *mine*."

***

"That's not eerie at all," Kazaar muttered to Vlad as Elisara approached the shore. A soft fog drifted in the frigid morning air as the sunrise peeked over the tree line, highlighting the distant watchtowers on both Vala and Nerida's borders. The black of Kazaar's leathers was stark against the frost, while the pale Vala blue of Vlad's uniform seemed at home amongst the frozen colours. Elisara smiled at her commander and her captain, appearing to share a friendly moment.

"Try it," Vlad said. Elisara's feet crunched on the frost before she jostled the pebbles that lined the shore. Kazaar's head tilted at the sound before he offered Vlad his hand. Vlad's pale, gloveless hands dropped a smooth, flat stone into his palm. "You need to get a low angle on it."

"I have skipped stones before," Kazaar grunted as he twisted his body. "Water does exist in Keres." As Kazaar turned, Elisara caught the glint in his eye as the sunrise bathed him: playful, relaxed, and comfortable.

"Yes, but Vlad has always been the *best* stone skipper," Elisara emphasised, laughing at their childish behaviour. Kazaar smirked, and she rolled her eyes, knowing this had quickly become some kind of competition between them. Crossing her arms, she inclined her head as he watched her from the corner of his eye, silently telling him to throw the stone. He leaned back and, in one fluid moment, propelled the flat stone across the sparkling ice that trapped the waters below on Vala's side of the Vellius sea.

An eerie, high-pitched frequency echoed across the surface, a sound that mesmerised Elisara. It was an unexplained spectacle to watch a stone skip across ice and hear the haunting echo that followed, as though it called out to someone—somewhere—waiting for an answer.

"I'm certain I sent that all the way to Nerida's border," Kazaar said, and Vlad scoffed. Halfway across the glistening lake, the ice thinned where it met Nerida's dark waters, forming its border. The high-pitched sound skated across the lake again as Vlad threw a stone towards it.

"Perhaps those are the odd sounds the guards in the towers have heard," said one of Vlad's men, leaving the tents. "Children from Vojta skipping stones." Elisara held in a laugh at the embarrassed look shared between Kazaar and Vlad.

"Perhaps." Kazaar crossed his arms and stared at the border with narrowed eyes. Elisara followed his eyeline to the water, appearing to ripple more than usual.

"Do you think the water senses their queen is missing?" Elisara whispered.

"Can nature sense such things?" Kazaar asked, and she shrugged.

"Larelle is always so calm and collected, like the water is an extension of her. I do not think it absurd that the element understands her in return." She smiled when Kazaar looked down at her, the warmth brightening in his eyes.

"We should get going," Vlad said. He took a step onto the ice to test it before allowing his queen to cross. Elisara nodded and waited until Vlad was several steps ahead. He paused and inspected the frozen lake below him before jumping.

"Vlad!" Elisara hissed, who flashed her a boyish grin.

"Just checking!" He motioned for them to follow.

Elisara sighed and followed Kazaar's lead. The lake groaned beneath his dark boots, but he continued slowly and intently forward. Elisara's breathing halted with her feet as she stood to listen, certain the lake could crack at any moment. When he was several steps ahead, Kazaar turned back.

"It is merely the sound of the water and ice shifting beneath the surface," he said, and Elisara nodded, convincing herself he was right. Yet she trained her eyes on the ice as she continued behind him, with the two guards following at the rear. Reaching for her power, she waved her hand, though she could barely see through the ice to discern whether she solidified it.

The glistening white surface changed to light blue the further they walked, growing shinier and more slippery with every step.

"Shit!" A guard swore, and Elisara spun to watch him fall on the ice with a thud. The lake appeared to vibrate below her feet, stretching out to Nerida's border. Everyone paused, listening for any sign the surface would crack. His partner helped the guard to stand.

"It was nothing!" he called, yet a chill settled in Elisara's bones, suddenly overcome by a sense of urgency to reach the island. Glancing up from her feet, she breathed a sigh of relief when Vlad reached it, his body small but safe on the distant snowy island. They would make it. In the distance, Kazaar waited midway between her and Vlad.

"You've got this, angel," he called in her mind. Her lips twitched at his nickname as she steadied her breathing.

Waving her hands, Elisara pulled on her power to fortify the frost against the surface for extra purchase, which worked, though only for a moment. But with every step on the frozen path, the ice melted away and left a sheen in its place. Elisara frowned but continued walking.

"Not much further," Kazaar said, but her focus was torn, distracted by the groan below the ice. Elisara swallowed and stopped as the frost she had formed slowly melted back to blackened ice, which was clearer now, offering a view of the lapping water beneath. The lake was thinning the closer they made it to the island and the talisman. Elisara made to move again but paused, holding her foot mid air as a dark shape shifted below the ice. A groan sounded below, clearer this time. Elisara's foot still dangled inches from the ice as she slowly lifted her eyes to meet Kazaar, who walked towards her.

"Do not move!" she called silently. He was meters from the island now and stopped at her command. She glanced back down at the shape shifting under the ice. *"There is something in the lake."*

"Are you certain it is not ice shifting or fish that can withstand the temperatures?" Elisara shook her head and checked for the dark shape again. It did not take long before it headed in Kazaar's direction. She squinted and studied its approach, assessing its size. Elisara could not compare it to any animal or fish she had seen before; it was far too large—even larger than the winged beasts that had descended on Garridon.

"I see it," Kazaar confirmed as it appeared to head back to Nerida's waters. When it cleared the last piece of ice, the briefest flash of a ridged back breached the surface. Elisara had only heard of fish in the lake, but that creature was far too large. She exhaled and resumed walking, training her eyes on the movement of the water on the other side of the lake. Occasionally, a ridged back glided above the surface, sending a stream of water rippling in its wake. Elisara increased her pace when it reached the furthest end of the lake and refrained from running. When the creature reached the furthest end of the lake, she turned to warn the guards to remain quiet.

The men nudged one another playfully and tossed something between their hands. Elisara's power emphasised every sound then as she summoned everything to her on the breeze: the sway of the surrounding trees slowed, the crunch of the guards' feet faded, and her own heartbeat paused, a final breath. Nothing but silence followed as Elisara opened her mouth to stop the guard from tossing the flat stone across the ice, but she was not quick enough. She could only listen as the high-pitched echo resounded across the lake.

All sounds rushed back to her as the shadow in the water spun and sped below the ice towards them.

"Run," Kazaar commanded.

Elisara did not wait. Propelling herself forward, she balanced her focus on the speed of her legs and the control of her power as she willed the slippery surface to freeze with each step. It was not enough, though, with her mind refusing to increase the pace for fear of slipping. A rush of air blasted either side of her, cocooning her in a breeze that urged her forward yet kept her balanced. The air was safe and sturdy, different from the delicate edge of her own abilities. She found Kazaar braced on the ice, and although she could not see his eyes from here, she knew he was protecting her.

An arrow flew overhead towards Nerida's border, and Elisara glanced at both of the watchtowers on either side of the lake. She was unsure if the arrow had come from Vala's soldiers or Nerida's. Taking comfort in the safety of Kazaar's power, Elisara slowed briefly and glanced at the water. She no longer saw the creature. She scanned the ice, and at the same moment, a warbled roar sounded below. The lake vibrated with a groan, and cracks rippled across the lake.

"Get to the island!" Elisara commanded though Kazaar did not listen. He took sure and steady strides towards her while scanning the ice.

"I am not abandoning my queen." Elisara slowed as the ice vibrated too close for comfort. She focused on Kazaar's words. *"I am*

not abandoning you." The softness of his voice cradled her mind. Kazaar paused and mirrored her stance, their shared minds sensing the threat creeping closer. They needed to be quiet and wait for it to swim away again. Elisara could not see it and focused only on the sound of her panting as she tried to keep calm. She watched the rise and fall of Kazaar's chest beneath his black leathers as they waited, readying for a fight.

Darkness swept beneath the ice, roaming between Elisara and Kazaar before turning back towards Nerida. Elisara eased her breathing and tried to relax her shoulders. Kazaar drew his sword while the men in their watchtowers shouted in the distance. Elisara waited for the ridged back to appear in Nerida's waters.

"I think it's gone—"

Elisara fell to her side as the lake shook. Cold pierced her cheek as she collided with the ice, where an elongated black shape rose fast towards the gap between her and Kazaar. Frantically, she tried to push herself up but instead was forced to shield her face as the lake splintered. The ice beneath tilted, and her body rolled with it. Using her gloved hands to find purchase, Elisara pushed to her knees, surveying the broken ice, her only path to the island—her only path to Kazaar. Large cracks fragmented the lake, creating pockets of floating platforms, one of which she knelt on now. Kazaar crouched, and green vines twisted from below him, gathering the floating pieces in a bid to reach her. She glanced behind at the two guards crawling towards Elisara. One attempted to pull the ice towards them so the other could reach her.

"Elisara!" Kazaar shouted. She whipped her head back round. "Brace yourself!" He turned his head, his gaze fixed on something. Elisara gripped the edges of the ice, tracking the movement in the slithers of water that now appeared amongst the broken ice. The creature glided in her direction before its ridged back disappeared, reappearing moments later as it rose fast towards the surface. Elisara gasped and clung tightly to the ice as a monstrous scaled tail broke through the surface and crashed against the ice. Elisara's eyes widened as the flash of deep blue scales disappeared beneath the water.

"What is it?" Elisara asked Kazaar.

"I have no idea, but I'd rather not wait to find out." Kazaar pushed himself up and tightened the vines around the floating platforms on his side.

"Plan?" Elisara asked, trying to control her breathing as she frantically searched for more movement.

"I can pull more vines between us to create a path, but you must run fast. If it comes back while you are on it, try to freeze some of the water in its path." Kazaar began filling the space between them with vines as the platforms of ice floated further away, spurred by the creature's movements. On the island, Vlad ran to the other side of the lake, far from their destination point.

"Over here!" Vlad screamed. His sword glistened as sunlight peeked through the trees on the island; he swung it repeatedly at a rock, creating as much noise as possible. "Over here!" he yelled again. Elisara pushed to her feet as Kazaar's vines twisted around the platform where she stood and formed a sturdy path between them. Another crash resounded as the creature flicked its tail through the water and swam towards Vlad on the island.

"*Go*!" Kazaar urged, and Elisara ran. She summoned a thin wall of ice to encircle the vines as a fail-safe should the creature change direction, but they snapped, with Kazaar's power faltering like her own. Kazaar's air kept Elisara steady as she ran towards him. Behind, the creature's tail appeared again and flailed, attempting to hit out towards Vlad. Her captain continued taunting it as Elisara leapt from the breaking vines and onto the sturdier ice, falling into the safety of Kazaar's arms, which gripped her tightly.

"I've got you," Kazaar murmured, moving his hand to the back of her head. She buried herself in the nook of his shoulder. "I've got you, angel." Elisara's nod was subtle as she loosed a shaky breath.

"Get a move on, you two!" Vlad shouted from the island. Elisara watched him over Kazaar's shoulder. Vlad threw stones into

Nerida's side of the lake to tempt the creature further away, which only seemed to confuse it. Water thrashed on the lake's shores as the creature constantly switched direction, exposing more of its colossal size and scaled back. It roared beneath the surface again, sending a wave under the ice. Elisara did not wish to wait to find out what the monster would do if Vlad continued to enrage it.

Her hand slipped into Kazaar's as they raced across the safer, fully formed ice towards the island. Air whipped at their backs, propelling them onto the frosted grass. At the same moment, a roar sounded above the surface. Elisara did not need to turn to know the creature's head had breached the ice; it was evident by the paling of when Vlad's face paled and he dropped his sword. They reached him, yet the sound of splashing water forced Elisara to whirl and face the beast. She was too late to see its entirety. All Elisara saw was the giant wave its movements had created, heading towards the two remaining guards who stumbled across the vine path. It submerged them within seconds, taking the splintered remains of the vines with it, hiding any trace of Kazaar's power. Elisara, Kazaar, and Vlad all watched and waited silently, but their bodies did not reappear. Nor did the creature. All that remained before them was the patchwork of ice.

"We cannot leave them," Vlad said, stepping onto the ice. Kazaar grabbed his shoulder and tugged him back.

"If they have not resurfaced now, they will not at all."

Vlad sighed but gave a curt nod, and for a moment longer, the three stood in silence, watching the lake.

"How are we going to get back?" Vlad asked. Elisara did not answer. She waited for the creature to reappear.

"We will face that problem later," Kazaar said gruffly. Elisara turned, reminded of the task at hand. Was the creature defending the island? She had never heard of such beasts in the waters of Novisia, but there was never a reason to cross the surface before. The divide between Vala and Nerida was clear as she surveyed the island, where the snow-capped trees and frosty ground faded into green. She wondered if the landscape of their realms would remain like this once they moved the talisman.

"Could they have chosen this spot because of the protection offered by the beast?" asked Kazaar.

"It's a smart place to hide it," said Vlad, walking forward and squinting at the trees. "Plant it on an island where a beast roams the waters, and build watchtowers under the guise of monitoring the borders."

"We are positive it is here, then?" asked Elisara, following Vlad through the trees.

"If the beast was not enough of a deterrent, I would say this confirms it." Vlad held a branch out of the way for Elisara, allowing her to step into a clearing.

"Wow," she breathed, straightening to take in the sight before them. From a distance, the island's trees appeared tightly packed, blocking any view of the land behind it. Up close, however, it was a carefully planted line of trees: a defence to guard the sparkling ice maze behind it. The ice was not natural; the towering walls were intricately carved with whirls and patterns, reminding Elisara of the ice mausoleums where her family were buried.

Elisara took slow steps towards the towering wall; it was several feet high but paused below the treetops. She pulled off her gloves and trailed her hand over the patterns dancing from the base of the wall and stretching upward. Elisara furrowed her brow at a repeating symbol, one she had traced on Kazaar's arms. She had seen it alongside three other symbols on the mountain floor in the Unsanctioned Isle. Did it symbolise Vala? Was that why only one symbol appeared? Did the other three on Kazaar's arms symbolise the other three realms?

"Somebody sculpted this purposefully. It must be the place," Elisara murmured, trying to memorise the shapes. While she could appreciate the architecture of such work, she saw behind its ruse. Someone could easily get lost within the maze, freezing or starving to death within it before ever reaching the talisman.

"How far do you think it stretches?" Vlad peered into the entrance that extended like a frozen corridor before splitting off in different directions.

"The island is not much bigger than the Neutral City's plaza. It cannot be that large," Elisara said while wondering how to determine which paths to attempt. Seeming to have the same thought, Vlad cautiously stepped into the opening of the maze, his feet crunching on the frost-covered grass. Elisara opened her mouth to stop him.

"It is his job," Kazaar said. A shiver tingled up her spine as he rested his hand lightly on her lower back. Elisara pursed her lips to refrain from calling out to her captain. Instead, the pair watched as Vlad knelt to inspect the first turn into a new corridor.

"While the island may not be large, these walls are thin, and the pathways narrow." Vlad rose and inspected the other pathway behind him. "There could be multiple paths, turns, or dead ends. Anyone could get lost in here."

Kazaar frowned, silently assessing the walls.

"I could melt it," Kazaar offered. Vlad leaned against one wall and crossed his arms.

"All of it?" he asked, lifting an eyebrow in challenge. Elisara rolled her eyes.

"Well, I would not stay within the walls to find out," Kazaar scoffed. He uncrossed his arms and clenched his fists. Vlad was quick not to test him and exited swiftly, his pale blond hair falling into his eyes as he winked playfully at Elisara. He kept his back to the pair to guard the tree line.

Kazaar stepped into the arched entrance to the maze with his back to Elisara. He cracked his neck and flexed, keeping his hands by his sides. Most would expect a great show, perhaps an intricate flourish of his hands or arms, but all Kazaar did was clench his fists and engulf the maze in flames so thick she could not see the ice within.

Elisara was entranced by the flames and moved on instinct towards them, but as she stepped close enough to Kazaar for her hand to graze his, the flames changed, flickering between orange and a white that matched the snow. She withdrew her hand from Kazaar's, and his furrowed brow mirrored her own as the flames returned to their normal glow. She glanced at Vlad, but he continued to guard the tree line. Kazaar's fingers felt calloused as she slowly intertwined their hands. Despite their closeness last night, there was something oddly intimate about the action.

The flames flickered again and changed colour. The corner of Kazaar's lip twitched as he looked down at her and their interlaced hands. She felt like a giddy child as she glanced at her feet to hide her smile, which soon disappeared when she noticed the dark tendrils twisting from below their feet. She withdrew her hand quickly and stepped back in the same instant Kazaar dropped his flames. Elisara did not know if he frowned at the shadows or the incomplete effect of his flames on the ice. While the top quarter of the maze had melted, the frozen walls remained.

Elisara took a cautious step forward away from Kazaar, for fear of the shadows returning, though a more rational side of her concluded that they only appeared on occasion when the pair were connected. Vlad rushed to her side, almost tripping as he held out an arm to keep Elisara from walking into the maze. She scoffed.

"I think I will be okay, Vlad," she said.

"Since when have the commander's flames been unable to melt something?" Vlad asked, his voice hushed. Elisara shook her head. "Maybe we should consider that there is more to this maze than meets the eye."

Elisara turned over his words. He was right; there was no chance her father's or even her grandmother's power was strong enough to build such walls. Something reinforced its power. Elisara glanced sideways at Kazaar.

"He is right," Kazaar said.

"Did it feel different? Using the flame on it?"

Kazaar shook his head. *"I expected it to have melted when I re-*

leased the control on my power."

"Could it be the talisman? If we are nearing such a power source, could it be protecting itself?"

"I suppose we will know when we speak to the other rulers and discover if they faced any defences." Elisara nodded and stepped into the maze behind Vlad.

"How do we decide?" Vlad asked, glancing between the paths on his left and right and the other two options ahead. Elisara peered down the first path to their left and then the right. Both were identical: long, thin paths with sharp angles where new openings appeared. Nothing seemed special about either. Elisara indicated with a nod of her head for Vlad to check the next. He claimed it was the same as the others. There was no significance to any of the pathways.

"I suppose we just guess?" Vlad asked. Elisara looked at Kazaar to see if he had any ideas. He strode towards the path on the right and took two steps into the pathway; he hardly fit within the space, given the breadth of his shoulders.

"Kazaar," Elisara called, though he did not acknowledge her. He tensed and tilted his head. Elisara waved a rush of air to kiss his skin, and he turned back to face them, shaking his head.

"I thought I heard something," he murmured, furrowing his brow.

"It was probably the wind making noises through the narrow pathways," suggested Vlad. Kazaar frowned but slowly nodded, glancing behind him into the pathway that darkened the further one travelled.

"You're probably–" Kazaar did not finish his sentence as a wall of ice shot up from the ground and sealed him within the maze.

Chapter Thirty-Four

Nyzaia

It was as though the Keres heat had evaporated as Nyzaia froze. She gripped her side and used her other hand to prop her up into a seated position. Countless times, she had opened and closed her mouth to speak, but what does one say when the captain of their guard saves your life by flying to catch you?

Please do not tell anyone.

That was all Farid said when she turned to find him. He had said nothing since. Sadness and disappointment brimmed in his pale blue eyes that burned alongside the flamed wings on his back. Having learned more about her captain's ways lately and understanding his dedication to her, Nyzaia knew he was disappointed in himself for keeping this from her.

Nyzaia propped herself up and winced at the pain in her ribs, likely cracked from the impact. Farid winced, too, as she shuffled towards him so as not to strain her side. He bowed his head when she reached him. Nyzaia frowned, saddened by his guilt, and knelt before him. Never in her life had Nyzaia imagined she would be jealous of a man, but as she gazed upon the wings protruding from Farid's back, the feeling consumed her. He had wings. It was no illusion or trick of the light. Farid had actual, beautiful wings. Nyzaia reached for them slowly to signal her intentions to Farid. Still, he hung his head and avoided her eyes. The flames flickered on his wings and licked her hand as she reached through to graze the deep red feathers. Her fingers paused at the tips dipped in gold, only visible if you were close enough to see through the individual flames on each.

Farid's wings were tucked taunt behind his back, the curved tops standing high above his head.

"Show me," Nyzaia breathed. Farid gulped as her fingers graced another feather. "Show me, Farid." she commanded. Farid rolled his shoulders back, and Nyzaia audibly gasped at the magnificence of his wings as he released them. A soft glow emanated from them and filled the room, his wingspan completely blocking the opening. Nyzaia had seen wings only twice before: those illustrated in children's books and on the creatures that attacked Garridon. But Farid's wings were different. The creatures were dark, ragged—an embodiment of torment and horror—while Farid's were magnificent, regal, and warm. Still, he had kept them from her. Although Nyzaia wanted to trust Farid and felt a connection urging her to do so, she would be negligent not to question if there was more to his wings. Farid shifted and reached for the sickle blade at his side, offering it to Nyzaia with his head bowed.

"Take them," he murmured. Frowning, Nyzaia glanced between him and the blade catching the light before looking back to him.

"What do you mean?" she asked gently.

"My wings. Take them," he said, a firm edge in his voice. "I betrayed my queen; I kept this from you. Take them." He offered her the blade, which rested on his open palms. Farid knelt before her, having exposed his closest secret to save her life. Yet the guilt consumed him so much that he wished for her to slice away a part of him. Pain flitted through Nyzaia's chest. She placed her hand on the blade and pushed his hands down.

"Look at me, Farid," she commanded, igniting her own palms in flames and reaching for his hands. His shoulders shuddered as he slowly raised his head, his burning blue eyes colliding with the amber flames flickering in her own. The two knelt before one another, bathed in the fire of his wings and the flame of her blood. A silent tear rolled down Farid's golden-brown skin as he clenched his jaw to keep it from wobbling. Nyzaia grasped his hands and held them on her thighs. "I will not take what you have used to selflessly save me."

"They make me dangerous. A liability."

Nyzaia shook her head. "You saved me, Farid. You saved *your queen*." Nyzaia stressed what she knew he deemed most important: his loyalty to her.

"I should have told you," he mumbled.

"What were you going to say? 'Excuse me, Your Majesty, I have fucking wings growing out of my back.'" She let out a soft laugh, trying to reassure him. The corner of his mouth twitched, and he squeezed her hand. "Did one of your parents have..." Farid firmly shook his head before she could finish her question. "Did anyone in your family?"

"It was only me and my parents. I do not know if any ancestor bore this monstrosity." Farid pressed his mouth into a firm line, and Nyzaia frowned. *He truly believes he is a monster.*

"I do not like to ask, Farid"—Nyzaia waited for him to meet her eyes and, finally, he held her gaze—"but I must. The creatures... is there anything that ties you together? Any link?" While Nyzaia did not expect there to be a connection, she would fail the other rulers, her syndicate, and her duty if she did not question it, especially when the only other winged creatures she knew to exist had just attacked Garridon.

"Nothing," Farid said firmly. "I knew nothing of them until the ball. When I picture them, I think only of my duty to protect you." Farid's voice wobbled.

"You have given me my life, Farid, and for that, I could never trust someone more," Nyzaia reassured him. His hand was tight around hers as his lip quivered. Their hands warmed, and a thin amber thread danced across their palms. They frowned, peering down at their interlocked hands as the temperature climbed. Farid tried to remove his hand but could not.

"Ah," Nyzaia winced as their palms burned. Farid's wings retracted—there one moment and gone the next—and the glow of his eyes returned to their usual blue. The burning sensation remained as the threads spiralled tighter around them, binding their hands together. It was unusual for Nyzaia to feel affected by fire, but it felt like someone pressed a hot iron against their connecting palms. Farid reached with his other hand for Nyzaia's arm, bracing against their shared pain until it halted. Nyzaia dropped his hand and peered at her own.

A raised scar etched the centre of her palm. It was similar in size to the marks on Elisara and Kazaar, though she did not recognise the symbol. It reminded her of something she would find within the pages of *Myths and Lies of Ithyion*. Wide-eyed, Nyzaia looked up at Farid. Nyzaia did not need to look at his palm to know the truth. She felt an immediate awareness of his presence, but looked, regardless, to where a matching scar sat amongst the other scars on Farid's hand.

"But I do not... We do not—" Farid began.

"No shit," Nyzaia said, staring at their palms. While they were not connected like Elisara and Kazaar, the scars on their palms were a clear sign.

"We are tied," Farid breathed. "How?"

Nyzaia leaned back, and Farid mimicked her, crossing his legs.

"The book is missing pages, but the only passage about the celestial ties says they are bestowed upon two individuals who share a destiny." Nyzaia recalled the passage from memory. "It is a bond only presented by the Celestial Gods when two beings finally acknowledge their connection to one another and allow their essences to merge."

"Is that what the threads were?" Farid asked. "The essence of our power?"

Nyzaia nodded. "I assume so."

The two sat in silence, the weight of another presence weighing heavily on their souls.

"The passage said that some were granted access to one another's powers, memories, and minds," Nyzaia finally said, breaking the silence. Her eyes lit up with hope. "Do you think that means I can have wings?" Farid scoffed.

"It is not as easy as it looks."

Nyzaia refrained from smiling at Farid's attempt at humour and imagined what she would look like with wings and if they would be the same deep red as Farid's.

"Memories and minds," Farid said. "Does that mean we can do what the queen of Vala and her commander do?"

Nyzaia leaned forward and frowned, trying to send a thought to Farid. She did not know how the pair did it, but she doubted it was an arduous task.

"What are you doing?" he asked, and Nyzaia shifted again.

"I guess we do not share minds in the same way," she said, though a part of her wished they did. She had so many questions for Farid, like how long he had wings, and why he kept them hidden.

"Ask," said Farid.

"So, you *can* hear my thoughts? Nyzaia asked, but Farid shook his head. He rested his elbows on his crossed legs and propped his chin on his fists.

"It is more like I can sense what you are feeling. I can feel that you have questions."

"Is it difficult for you to talk about?" she asked, and he nodded. Nyzaia did not wish to pain him. "Perhaps you could try showing me?" She reached for his hands. While they may not share minds like Elisara and Kazaar, perhaps they could share memories. "Take a deep breath, and think about it," Nyzaia said calmly and waited for Farid to close his eyes before she closed her own. Nyzaia steadied her breathing and allowed Farid to focus. The darkness in her mind shifted and morphed until she saw the inside of a small bedroom.

"He is an abomination, Sanaa!" yelled a voice outside the closed door. Nyzaia stepped forward. The voice was familiar, a sharp tone that presented as polished and noble despite the gruff lilt sneaking through certain words. She pressed her ear to the door to listen.

"He is five! You cannot call him an abomination simply because he looks different!" a female screamed back.

"He is either an abomination, or you are a whore, because those are *not* my eyes, Sanaa!" His fierce tone tugged at Nyzaia's memories.

"If I was one of your Courtesans, perhaps then you would pay me some attention, Arjun!" A slap sounded through the door, and someone whimpered behind her. Nyzaia spun, not having noticed the small boy sitting on his bed. He hugged himself, not with just his arms, but his flaming wings, too.

"At least my Courtesans know how to treat me with respect," spat the man. Nyzaia's eyes widened at the realisation of who stood behind the now-opened door. The small boy lifted his head, his bright blue eyes stark against his skin and hair. His eyes widened as he met his father's gaze. Arjun Qadir stepped through the door, the former ruler of the Red Stones, and the man Nyzaia killed for her title.

The memory changed then. Nyzaia blinked. She no longer stood in the darkness of Farid's childhood bedroom but in the darkness of a cave opening, similar to the one Nyzaia and Farid sat in now as she waded through his memories. Stars scattered the black night as Nyzaia glanced upward; she was in the Abis Forge but lower down, with the flow of lava much further away. A thud sounded against the rock, and the tops of a ladder appeared. A different light approached, rising upward to show a slightly older Farid thrown over the ledge and into the cavern.

"No!" he cried, crawling back to the ledge. "Please, Papa! Please do not leave me in here." His wings were larger than the previous memory, though Nyzaia placed him at only twelve years old. Arjun appeared briefly with his greying goatee and slicked back hair.

"You are only here because of your mother," he sneered. "Otherwise, you would be dead at my hand."

"Please!" Farid begged, falling to his knees. Nyzaia bit her lip to keep from crying. The young boy was so frail and emotional compared to the man he had become.

"You stay here until you can hide them," Arjun snapped before descending the ladder. Nyzaia watched as Arjun pulled the ladder away, leaving Farid to sob on his own. The sun rose and set four times. On the first day, Farid cried and rocked himself back and forth, not moving from the spot against the wall as the lava drowned out his pleas. The next day, she felt Farid's fury as he tossed rocks into the burning lava each time he failed to retract his wings. His anger and determination faded over the next two days as he tossed and turned, unable to sleep with his wings pushing into his back. Slowly, Farid lost his strength and will to continue as he starved, still trying to withdraw his wings. His lips were cracked, and his clothes were drenched as he gave up on even wiping the sweat dripping down his face. Eventually, weakness took over, and the wings faded into his back. At no point did Arjun check to see if his son had succeeded. Only on the sixth day did Arjun come to drag away his son, who was barely breathing.

The view of the cavern changed to a large, marbled home, far bigger than the one from Farid's childhood. Nyzaia stood face to face with Arjun, dripping in wealth—unfathomable wealth that had attracted the attention of the Red Stones before Nyzaia took his life. He wore silk sherwanis from the same tailor as the King's, jewel-studded shoes and chains, and gold rings on every finger.

"You do not stand between me and my wife, boy!" he spat. Nyzaia stepped aside. Farid was older, taller, and much broader. Nyzaia placed him at roughly eighteen as he stood in front of a frail woman with hair as dark as his own. A bruise marked her cheek.

"You will not hit her again!" Nyzaia had only heard Farid raise his voice like that once before after stripping Tajana of her pin.

"What are you going to do?" Arjun laughed. "You spend all day welding and hammering swords because I deem it so, yet you do not know how to wield one."

"I do not need a sword to protect her from you," Farid said in the cold tone she recognised. He had not yet mastered control of his wings yet as they spanned out too suddenly and hit his mother, who cowered behind him. Farid spun when she screamed, his wings pushing her aside, and setting her saree alight.

"Saraa," Arjun muttered, stumbling forward with wide eyes.

Farid searched the room for water—anything to extinguish the flames engulfing his mother, but there was nothing in the marbled room except lavish ornaments and velvet furniture.

"Saraa!" Arjun screamed, reaching for his wife's hand. Farid reached forward, pushing his hands through the flames. He screamed, flinching as the fire licked his bare hands, not yet recognising him as their owner.

"Mama, no!" Farid screamed as the woman stopped moving. No more tortured cries erupted from her mouth as the flames devoured her whole. Farid still held Saraa as the flames died, as they licked one last time at his palms before retreating. Her body was already unrecognisable; her clothing had burnt away; her skin and muscles had melted, leaving only bone behind, singed black. Nyzaia's stomach churned. Normally, she did not react to such gruesome sights, but something about knowing what this accident did to Farid, and the pain it left him, made her feel nauseous. Arjun slumped against the wall opposite, staring at his wife's charred corpse.

"You killed her," he said. "You KILLED HER!" He lunged for Farid, and the memory stopped.

Farid dropped Nyzaia's hands, and the cold breeze of the Keres night washed through the cavern. When Nyzaia opened her eyes, the tears she could not wipe during the memories falling down her cheeks, matched Farid's. She felt his pain as it intertwined with what she felt for him. Whether he would accept it or not, she lunged for him and wrapped her arms around his neck quietly. She waited for him to push her away. Slowly, Farid raised his arms, encircling them around her waist. He sobbed into her shoulder.

"I could not save her," he mumbled, and only then did Nyzaia realise why he deemed it so important to save his queen.

Chapter Thirty-Five

Elisara

"Kazaar!" Elisara screamed, pounding her fists against the wall. "Kazaar!" She shouted again, her heart racing.

"Stand back," Vlad told her calmly. Elisara spun her head, not wanting to distance herself from reaching Kazaar, but quickly stepped aside as Vlad unsheathed his sword and swung it repeatedly at the ice. No sound came from the other side.

"Kazaar," Elisara whispered in her mind, yet was met by silence. She began pacing, and her steps adopted the same rhythm as Vlad's sword as he continued chipping away at the wall that had appeared.

"Elisara..." It was the faintest whisper, but it was him. It was enough.

"I will find you," she said, hoping he heard. Elisara was not thinking rationally as she spun for the opposite pathway, intent on finding Kazaar.

"Eli, wait!" Vlad shouted. Elisara barely felt his hand graze her arm as she stepped into the pathway, and the Light was sucked from her surroundings as another wall of ice grew behind her to block out everything. Gasping, Elisara spun and reached to touch the newly formed wall; this one was vacant of any patterns, and it felt colder than normal—a cold that pierced her skin like it might brand her. She looked upward at the sky, yet the mighty walls only provided slithers of light. *Find Kazaar. Find Kazaar, and then the talisman.* He had taken the path to the right. Elisara should eventually reach him if she alternated between right and straight ahead. She hoped he had a similar train of thought.

Every part of Elisara yearned to hurry through the maze to find him, yet something inside her slowed. With every turn she took through the towering walls, she felt the presence of intruding eyes watching and assessing her actions. A weight settled on her chest, and her breathing grew more rapid with every path that did not lead her to Kazaar. Elisara withdrew a dagger from her side and attempted to carve a distinct line into each corner she turned into, marking her path should she end up circling back.

Eventually, the chill of the narrow pathways settled in her bones. If she had not been born in Vala, she might as well have given up and waited for rescue or died slowly on her own. Elisara paused and leaned back against the wall, analysing the three pathways ahead.

Why is every damn path the same? She dropped her head back against the wall, her thick braid offering some reprieve from the piercing cold. Her breath fogged, clouding her vision as she rubbed her hands together and wished she still wore her gloves.

"Star," a voice whispered in the wind. Elisara shot forward and spun slowly, surveying the four paths: the three ahead and the one in which she had just exited. "My star," the voice whispered in the wind. She recognised that voice. It was the voice of a man who tucked her into bed at night as a child and read her stories until she fell asleep, a man who defended Elisara every time her sisters poked fun at her expense. She would never forget her father's voice. "Help me," the voice whispered from the middle path. She took off in a grief-stricken run.

"Father!" she called hoarsely, choking back her tears. There was no indecision in her turns but only an innate sense of knowing that it guided her towards her father. "I'm coming!" she cried, following the breeze as it steered her closer. Elisara halted abruptly in a small circular opening, panting. Here, the ice held a sheen, creating an iridescent mirror-like effect as she stared at her reflection. Her hair fell loose from her braid, and the sheen of sweat on her forehead had frozen over. When Elisara raised her eyebrows, the thin layer of ice cracked off in flakes.

She hung her head and breathed in deeply. *You are imagining things. The maze is driving you mad. Your father is dead.* She raised her head and cracked her neck, waiting for her breathing to settle. When it did, she turned and faced a nightmare she had endured far too many times. Her hand flew to her mouth to keep in the sobs trying to escape. With her other hand, she reached for the wall and pressed her palm against an ageing hand in the reflection adorned with familiar silver rings that had always brought her solace. Her eyes trailed up the sleeve of a dust-covered blue jacket to the silver Vala sigil that glinted despite the little light filtering through the opening. Elisara closed her eyes again, wishing to feel the warmth of his hand for one last time. She delayed looking at the all-too-familiar blue in his eyes when she finally opened her own.

"Star," the voice said, but it lacked the love and comfort her father's tone held. This voice sounded raspy, distant—*dead*. Elisara opened her eyes and met his pale-blue gaze, the last thing she saw of him as she held his dead body in her arms.

"Father!" Elisara sobbed, but it became a strangled cry as his eyes hollowed, and his laughter lines faded, his skin crumbling to ash.

"You did not save me," he croaked before his hand fell away from hers.

"You did not save any of us," a woman sneered. Elisara spun to find the icy mirror behind her showed her sisters, Daeva and Katerina, walking hand in hand.

"I could not," Elisara cried. "I did not know it would happen." Elisara reached for them as if the reflection would offer more love and affection than her sisters did while alive.

"I'm disappointed in you, Elisara," said her mother. Elisara whirled, shivering at the plummeting temperature. A fog crept up and around her legs. Elisara frowned at her mother's scrutiny, who peered upon her with her hands clasped in the same regal manner as always. She wore a red gown like those from Keres. *Keres. King Razik.*

"Disappointed in *me*?" Elisara snarled, striding toward her mother. "Me?" she screamed, yet the reflection merely looked her up and down. "You planned all of this! *YOU* left me. You all left me!" Elisara screamed and circled back around. The reflections multiplied, trapping and taunting her as she forgot the path in which she came.

"You knew what you were doing!" Elisara shouted. *You knew.* Her chest rapidly rose and fell, and her throat tightened, yet she found no escape from their stares. Elisara reached for her dagger again and pulled it from her side. "You planned this! Why would you be disappointed in me?" Her sisters' laughter bounced off the icy mirrors, and Elisara clasped the sides of her head. "I was never meant to save you," she whispered.

Elisara stopped spinning and lowered her hands. She willed air into her chest to even her breathing. The ghosts of her family stopped their taunting, and as Elisara strode to the wall, the multiple reflections disappeared until only one version of them remained: her father, mother, Davea, and Katerina stood before her, watching. Elisara's eyes tugged on her father's one last time, memorising the shade of blue that was no longer her own. She raised her dagger.

"You're not real," she whispered, a single tear rolling down her cheek.

She plunged the dagger into the ice. She did not shield her face as the ice exploded but motioned her hand, letting the shards fly around her as light bathed her once again. The warmth brushed her face, ebbing the chill in her bones. She stared at the clearing.

The sun had risen enough now that it shone upon the icy structure in the centre of the grass-covered circle before her. Standing beside it was Vlad, who rushed towards her with wide eyes.

"Eli," he said, grasping her arms. He frowned at the tear rolling down her cheek. She reached up and wiped it with her sleeve. "Are you okay?" he asked. She felt numb but nodded. They flinched at the sound of crashing ice behind them.

"Elisara!" Kazaar cried out before stumbling from a shattered opening on the other side of the maze. A light rain fell over him from where he had melted the falling shards as he leaned on the tower for support. Elisara rushed over and grasped his face, inspecting him as his hands gripped her forearms. His eyes mirrored her own before the panic in them faded.

"You're okay," she breathed, resting her forehead against his. He nodded and gulped.

"I saw..." he trailed off and cleared his throat. He stepped back yet his hand lingered on her back when Vlad approached.

"Good to see you're okay." Vlad nodded towards Kazaar, and Elisara knew by the way he awkwardly stood with his hands behind his back, shifting on his feet, that his statement was sincere; his worry had not only been for Elisara.

Elisara blinked; the light was blinding as it shone on the icy pillar before them, which formed a frozen cage adorning the same intricate patterns from earlier. In its centre was the other half of the Vala talisman. The transparency of the ice offered a clear view of the frozen talisman floating in the centre. Elisara peered closer at the rough edge of stone, a clear match to the ridges on the half around her neck. She trailed her thumb over it. Other than the broken edges, it appeared as smooth and polished as the stone on her half. The break was clear. A half mountain was engraved at the edge, sitting below two stars. When she connected the two halves together, it would form a complete picture: three mountains and three stars.

Elisara reached for it, sensing the same hum of power from when she first picked up the half that had never left her neck. Yet the pull to this piece was stronger, as though desperate to be reunited with its counterpart.

"You're up, Commander," Vlad called, inspecting the thickness of the ice. "Let's hope melting it works this time." Kazaar scowled at him and stepped forward. Vlad flashed him a grin.

Kazaar approached the cage, and Elisara frowned as the talisman became less clear as the stream of sunlight faded behind the clouds gathering overhead. The orange flicker of Kazaar's flame pulled her gaze back to him, and she watched intently as he wielded flames in his palms and aimed them at the talisman sitting within. Vlad crouched to meet the talisman at eye-level.

"Is it working?" Elisara asked, shouting over the sudden wind. Vlad turned his head to her and nodded.

"Slowly, but the ice is definitely melting!" he shouted. Elisara's fingers tingled. "This isn't you, is it, Eli?" Vlad called over the gale that began whipping at her face. She shook her head and widened her stance, bracing against the wind. She frowned at the dangerous sway of the snow-capped trees. Even the flames Kazaar directed at the talisman offered no warmth as the storm blew. Elisara tried to counter it, but the wind refused to listen. Something was wrong, and she did not wish to wait much longer to find out what other defences protected the talisman.

"How much longer?" she called.

"It should have worked by now!" Kazaar shouted back. Elisara stepped towards him to see for herself, yet the flame was suddenly the only light source under the blanket of clouds. She reached for Kazaar's shoulder and was pushed back as lightning struck the pillar, forcing Kazaar to withdraw his flame and shake his hand. As he did, the wind settled, and the clouds cleared.

"I don't think it likes you," Elisara said.

"I think I can chip away at the rest," Vlad offered, pulling a dagger from his leg. He began hitting the curved indent where Kazaar had attempted to melt it. It did not take long for the ice to give way beneath Vlad's efforts, creating a small enough opening to reach for the other half of the talisman. "After you," Vlad gestured, stepping aside.

Elisara approached and bent to examine the polished stone; it had once been nothing but a part of the tallest mountain on Ithyion. The piece around her neck warmed, humming in recognition of its counterpart, and her fingers tingled again as she reached for it. Lightning struck as she touched the ice. She quickly withdrew her hand and cradled it against her chest. It had been a precise strike that was intent on hitting her rather than the tower.

"Ouch!" She jumped back and shook her hand. When she glanced down, a small circular burn lay atop her skin. Vlad reached for her and examined it before retrieving a small vial of healing potion from the stalactites of Vala.

"I don't think it likes you, either," Kazaar retorted, frowning at the mark on her hand.

"Third time's the charm?" asked Vlad, approaching the pillar. He looked at Elisara for permission. She nodded and watched as Vlad cautiously grazed the ice with his hand and reached into the jagged opening. Elisara held her breath as his hands clasped the talisman, and finally released it when he withdrew his hand, unharmed. He held his hand out for Elisara, who examined the cracked stone but dared not risk being struck again. Reaching for the leather pouch at her side, she opened it for Vlad, who dropped it in. She tied it shut.

"I'm offended that it liked Vlad," Kazaar said, and though she wanted to laugh, she focused only on why it had not allowed Kazaar to approach it or allowed its queen to take it with her bare hands. It was just one of many questions she hoped she could get answers to if the plan worked and brought Elisara before Goddess Vala.

"We should get back to the edge of the lake. We should not risk crossing when the sun sets," said Vlad, striding towards an open pathway. "And we may need some time to determine how to get across with that *thing* still in the water."

Elisara reached for his arm, stopping him.

"What if we get trapped in the maze again? Would it be better to wait here overnight and attempt the maze at first light?" she asked. Her mind strayed to the image of her family again, reminded of their fake, cruel words.

"Was your path really that difficult?" Vlad asked, frowning between her and Kazaar. They shared a look and nodded. "Mine was simple and led me straight here. I only took two turns." Vlad began walking through the pathway with Elisara close on his heels, turning over the many questions in her mind. Why had the maze allowed Vlad to reach and touch the talisman but not Elisara, the heir of Vala?

Vlad was right to be confused by the pair's arduous journeys through the maze. It took the group barely half an hour—and three simple pathways—until they stood overlooking the lake, with the sun sinking in the horizon.

Elisara knew the two men spotted it at the same time she had. An arm stuck out from the reformed lake, frozen in place with a pale blue sleeve still attached. Arrows scattered across the frozen surface. Had the creature tried to resurface? They stood, watching and waiting for any sounds from the lake, but there was nothing but the sway of trees and nearby birds.

"It could still be weak in points; the ice may have only reformed recently," Vlad said, and she nodded.

"I can summon my power to strengthen it, but it was resistant before."

"Perhaps that was a part of whatever defences guarded the talisman," Kazaar suggested. "Now that you have it, maybe the defences are lowered." He nodded encouragingly, and Elisara stepped forward, the tips of her boots meeting the edge between the frosty grass and the lake. As Elisara reached for her power, her fingers twitched at her side, where the other half of the talisman sat within the pouch. Frowning, she moved her hands in front of her before pushing them apart in a large sweeping motion across the lake. Elisara felt the power and was certain she saw a change in the ice's shade that indicated it thickening.

"Only one way to be certain," Elisara murmured, peering at Vlad and Kazaar. They stepped onto the ice and paused, waiting for any sign of the beast's presence.

"Vlad, take the lead. I will guard behind," Kazaar commanded. Vlad moved instantly and began a quiet and steady walk across the ice, with Elisara following suit, often pausing to monitor for movement. Elisara glanced over her shoulder at Kazaar, his eyes on her.

Despite making it halfway across the lake in a quicker time than before, Elisara's heart pounded, her teeth still on edge.

"It's thinner here," Vlad called, "It must have been where you had to jump over the cracks. Be careful." He was right. As Elisara approached, she felt the difference in the ice as she apprehensively trod across it. She paused to reach for her power again to thicken the ice, but the surface froze too slowly, she realised, as bubbles appeared under the surface. *Bubbles.* Elisara had no moment to ponder as a large-toothed mouth rushed to the surface and broke through the ice, throwing her into the air. Elisara felt her and Kazaar's power merge as they each tried to stabilise her fall, but their combined powers only confused their intentions. Instead of creating a slow cradle to guide her from the crack in the lake, she slipped right through the air pocket and plunged into the icy waters of the Vellius Sea.

Elisara screamed into the waters as the shock of the cold hit her, attempting to numb her muscles into paralysis. Her limbs were heavy as she tried to kick upward towards Vlad's hand, plunging through the hole the beast had created. Her fingers inched closer, reflected in the final stream of sunlight filtering through the hole, yet her legs slowed, every movement delayed by the weight of her clothes.

"I'm coming, angel." Kazaar's voice rang through her mind as fire skated across the ice above, melting it and illuminating the dark waters. She waded towards it but could not move quick enough as a deep blue scaled tail appeared through the darkness and lashed out. Elisara took a hard blow to her stomach, knocking out what little air she had left. She plunged deeper into the waters, and Kazaar's panicked flames appeared to consume the entire lake. The thud of his boots crunched overhead as he ran, as though sensing exactly where she was. Elisara could not focus on his calls or the chipping of his dagger against the melting ice. She could only stare

at the approaching creature. It did not rush at an intent speed as it had in their first encounter—no, it stalked its prey, playing and goading Elisara as its long body twisted side to side. Elisara froze, her body trapped by fear as she stared wide-eyed at the advancing beast.

She had seen nothing like it before; even the dark-winged creatures were no threat to this. It was at least five times their size. Four taloned legs pushed through the water as a long, scaled tail propelled it forward, working in tandem with its body. Its neck was nearly as long, and it blew bubbles furiously from its large snout and nostrils. Elisara stared into its deep purple irises as it blinked rapidly. A silver glow circled them then, as the light from above highlighted the deep scars covering its face. Elisara blinked, and darkness crept into the edges of her vision as the pain deepened in her chest. Reaching for her power, Elisara tried to freeze a wall between her and the beast.

The creature slowed, and its lower half sank deeper into the waters as if standing on its hind legs. The beast tilted his head, watching the glow in Elisara's eyes as though something about her power triggered a memory. The creature let out a warbled cry, different from its earlier roars of anger. Elisara frowned. It was like the creature was showing her something as it stretched its legs. Her eyes tugged on the metal chain around its scarred stomach before a rush of water caught her attention as someone jumped in. The creature startled and spun to the side to gauge its threat. Elisara's eyes widened as she noticed the chains wrapped around its body, confining a set of great, turquoise, iridescent wings.

Elisara felt the familiar warmth of Kazaar's arm wrap around her body. As she laid her palm on his, trying to hold on as the fight in her body left her, tendrils of light exploded from them, the shadows nowhere to be seen. Their light blazed through the waters and reached towards the beast. Fear sparked in its eyes as the creature backed away and swam towards Nerida's border.

Kazaar kicked and pushed them to the surface. She was unsure if there was something else in the lake or if she was simply hallucinating from lack of oxygen, but Elisara could have sworn she glimpsed a whirlpool of water in the distance, bathed in a soft glow before the beast reached it and appeared to vanish into darkness again.

Elisara sputtered as they broke the surface, choking on water as Kazaar dragged her onto her back. With a flourish of his hand, the ice thickened and froze hard underneath her. His power worked as normal despite their former attempts. *Had the creature affected their power?*

"Elisara, look at me," Kazaar demanded, gripping her cheeks. "Look at me." Elisara's breathing eased as his power radiated through her, drying and banishing the chill from her bones. Tears welled as she looked at his face and the worry etched on his features. Dark and light tendrils overtook the amber in his eyes as he held Elisara's face, assessing her. "Please say something," he murmured, stroking a thumb over her cheekbone. His eyes faded to normal as she felt her body dry completely.

"I'm okay," she breathed, and she was telling the truth. No near-death experience, terrifying creature, or threat of darkness could ever stop her from being okay, so long as she had Kazaar.

Chapter Thirty-Six

Sadira

All hopes of ever being on the same side as her sister rode away into the flower fields of Albyn as Soren took off at a gallop towards Antor. The group had wasted no time returning to the mainland. The journey by ship had taken a mere few hours, a benefit of the short crossing between Albyn and the Island. Sadira spent most of the excursion rubbing Caellum's back. He was not made for the ocean. Yet her focus regularly strayed to watching Soren pace the ship with her wolves, and her constant glances at the pouch at Caellum's side did not go unnoticed. The sisters ignored one another for the entire journey. Something had changed since retrieving the talisman, like fate had cemented itself for the sisters and set them on different paths. Sadira made her loyalty to Caellum clear by ensuring he took the talisman.

Sadira thought back to her encounter with Rodik, who quickly reached for her hands the moment they were alone, but Sadira felt nothing: no butterflies, no sense of familiarity, or spark. Sadira would never wish harm on another, yet she knew Soren was wise enough to realise that harming Rodik was no longer a substantial threat. Soren held nothing over her now.

"Do you think she suspects us?" Sadira asked Caellum as they walked side by side along the flower fields on the outskirts of Albyn.

"I think she believed I wished to show you another settlement within your realm, one you should rule over when you are queen," Caellum reassured her, offering his hand for the large leather book Sadira had propped under her arm. If Sadira had told Soren the real reason for their visit—that she and Caellum were trying to uncover more about her Wiccan heritage—Soren would have insisted on joining, given that it was her heritage, too. Yet Sadira and Caellum had a clear, mutual understanding of their distrust for her sister.

"She likely loathed the reminder that it is you who will be queen, not her." Caellum offered his free arm to Sadira, who looped her hand through it with easy familiarity.

"It is she you should be suspicious of," Sir Cain said from behind. Sadira paused with Caellum and turned to face Garridon's commander, who wore matching armour to that which Soren had left in.

"Trust us, Sir Cain, we are more than suspicious," Caellum said. Sir Cain leaned in, his bright red hair glinting beneath the early morning sun.

"Two guards said she asked for an estimate on how long it would take to reach Stedon."

Sadira frowned. The sisters had learned of the different settlements in Garridon while growing up, but she could not recall any reason why Soren would wish to visit Stedon, which was mostly shielded by Hybrooke Forest. With Soren's spies dotted around Novisia, she had no reason to visit the settlement. News was usually delivered to her by letter, so why would she visit alone?

"Stedon is past Antor, is it not?" said Sadira, peering up at Caellum for confirmation. He nodded. "She must be meeting someone there for a reason." Sadira confirmed, suspecting Soren of trying to accrue new allies.

"We will be safe here if you leave the guards. Follow her," Caellum commanded, like a true king. Sir Cain nodded and left them to continue their walk into Albyn. It did not go unnoticed by Sadira how unaffected Caellum seemed among the fields of sweet peas. He took her hand and rubbed the opal on her ring. She did not know if it was an act of reassurance or if he was simply unperturbed by the reminders of his past.

Caellum's love for Elisara still worried Sadira, who remembered the longing on his face when she last asked him to visit Albyn, back when they first visited Antor together. Yet he appeared focused now, intently listening to Sadira as she retold the details of her trip to Athena's Apothecary. Her recent excursion was also the reason they took the large book from her room in Doltas. The tome was passed down through her family, and Sadira hoped a more experienced Wiccan could decipher it and uncover information to help against the creatures, or learn more about the unique gifts Wiccans possessed; as she had promised Larelle.

Sadira glanced behind to the dock, the coast of Nerida clear in the distance. She hoped her letter had reached Alvan. Seeming to sense her feelings, Caellum squeezed her hand.

"He will find her," he reassured, and Sadira nodded softly.

Albyn differed greatly from Antor. While the many trees surrounding Antor reminded her of Doltas, Sadira connected with Albyn more, called by the open expanse of flower fields, often harvested for royal displays or healing antidotes. The acres of flowers surrounded small, thatched homes leading to a modest manor that had a sleepiness to it. Sadira wondered if it would be absurd to live here when her children took the throne. She blushed at the thought that was so far ahead and stole a glance at Caellum.

Citizens bustled around her in the late afternoon, rushing through the cobbled streets to make their last purchases before the storefronts closed for the evening. While the pathways reminded her of Antor, the buildings were far shorter; each shop was painted white supported by dark wooden beams. Thatched rooftops lined each store and home, with smoke floating from their chimneys. It was a much cooler town, being so close to the coastline winds. In another life, Sadira imagined this was a life she was destined for. The calm ambiance of perhaps owning one of the many florists they passed. Wooden buckets brimming with freshly cut flowers wrapped in brown paper were displayed outside, the colourful array prompting a smile from her lips.

"I do not suppose Athena gave any indication as to where we

should look in Albyn for other Wiccans?" Caellum asked in a hushed voice as they entered the town. Sadira shook her head.

"I hoped we would simply have a sense for it, or someone would find us," she responded in the same quiet tone.

"My king!" called a voice. They turned to the gathering of people lining the shops, where a tall, gangly man with shoulder-length blonde hair approached with a genuine smile.

"Lord Gregor." Smiling, Caellum removed his hand from Sadira's and clasped the hand of the man before them.

"Your guards reached me in time to keep you from walking further than needed," he said. Caellum tilted his head, mirroring Sadira's confusion. Gesturing with his hand, Lord Gregor signalled for them to walk with him.

Sadira smiled at the citizens, who stopped and whispered at the king's unexpected arrival, and when Caellum took Sadira's hand again, she blushed as a group of women squealed at the gesture.

"All the rooms in my manor are filled," Gregor explained. "After the events at your engagement, I took in the families of any deceased who hailed from Albyn. My staff have cared for them, relieving their burden of returning to homes now haunted by the dead."

I like him. Sadira had not properly met any of the lords but could quickly tell that Gregor was an honest, caring man. Despite being close to Caellum's age, deep laughter lines etched Gregor's skin, matching the wrinkles in the outer corner of his eyes.

"We can try to make our visit quick and leave before nightfall," Caellum said, but Gregor shook his head.

"No, no! Please, it would not be fair to force such a quick trip after you have already endured such a long day of travel." Gregor reassured, coming to a slow stop outside a larger establishment; flower boxes lined the many windows, and laughter gravitated from the door as it was pushed open. Sadira's eyes tugged on the symbol engraved in the wood: a whirl of different shapes. She refrained from widening her eyes and discreetly glanced at the book tucked under Caellum's arm with the same symbol on its worn cover.

"This may not be fit for a king and future queen." Gregor motioned to the door. "But I can vouch for the owners, and the inn is rather comfortable." He smiled and looked at Sadira, who examined the sharp angles of his face and his wide hazel eyes. She recognised the sincerity behind them.

"Do you have any family remaining in Garridon, Lord Gregor?" asked Sadira. The lord smiled and looked at his feet.

"I do have a great aunt who runs an apothecary in Antor." Sadira smiled knowingly. "She is far too stubborn to take up my offer of comfortable living in the manor." Gregor held the door open for them. "I believe you will enjoy your stay here, but if you need anything further, please ask."

***

Caellum had made sure Sadira sat in a velvet-lined booth in the tavern connected to the inn before speaking with Gregor at the bar. She flicked through the book she wished to take home with her and smiled. *Home*. Since leaving Doltas Island, she felt a grounded certainty. There had been little else she wished to take from her old chambers, though Caellum had asked about practically every object in the room. The book was all she wanted. Over the years, she watched her grandmother pour over it, slapping her or Soren's hands if they ever tried to look.

Propping the book up, Sadira began reading, hoping her display of the book's cover would entice whoever could help her. She flicked through pages of potions, wishing she had ink to mark those of interest to her, and after several turns, she settled on a page about objects with the words '*Magical Imbuement*' outlined at the top. She frowned at a sketch of jewellery below. The page on the right was indecipherable, written in a language she did not recognise. Sadira looked up to where Caellum stood, accepting the two goblets being handed to him. The leather pouch hung at his side, home to the other half of the talisman. *Did the Wiccans help to create the talismans?* She read the first page on the left, written in her own language, when Caellum approached.

"It is often found that jewellery is the most commonly imbued item. Many have approached Wiccans over the years with pure and impure intentions for their romantic requests. However, other items can be imbued with power, too: goblets with the ability to kill its drinker, clothing that allows the person to mimic their original owner, and books reciting to the reader what they wish to hear, or transporting them to the places within." Sadira scoffed, beginning to doubt the truth in the book. "It is not uncommon for swords to be imbued."

Swords.

As Caellum placed the goblet down on the table and slid in beside her, two more bodies joined on the opposite side of the booth. Sadira met the inquisitive stare of a pale, red-headed beauty with hair so long it fell below the table in curls. A man with short greying hair and a bushy beard sat beside her, leaning on his forearms as he glanced around the room with a twitch in his eye. Sadira cleared her throat and placed her hand on Caellum's.

"Can we help you?" Sadira asked with a sweet smile. The pair exchanged a look and huddled close. The man leaned forward and positioned his back to the room, shielding their expressions and words from any curious revellers. The woman glanced over the man's shoulder, her eyes scanning the room before facing Sadira.

"We have been put on this path to help you—to help you all," she said in a voice that floated on air. Sadira kept her face neutral.

"And how are you to do that?" she asked. The woman reached forward, pointing at the drawing in the book.

"I can tell you how our people imbued the sword," she whispered.

Caellum tensed.

"What sword?" he asked. The woman's head snapped to him, and she narrowed her eyes.

"You know which sword, usurper."

Chapter Thirty-Seven

Larelle

Larelle tried to recall any military or tactical conversations had between her father and brother—anything to guide her escape. She thought of Elisara and Nyzaia and questioned what they would do, having been trained in such matters. Yet even if Larelle did escape, she had no experience in hand-to-hand combat like the other queens, should the two men follow. If she ever left this place, perhaps she would learn.

But for now, Larelle was left with her instincts and a burning determination to see her daughter. She pictured her last memory of Zarya's face as Lillian ushered her away, and her gut wrenched at the thought of her midnight blue eyes filled with tears and worry for her mother. What had Alvan told her? Zarya was intuitive for a young girl and would see through any lie. Larelle kept her head high and interlocked her hands, confined within the chains. She refused to leave her daughter.

Osiris smirked, leaning against the cave wall. *Arrogant.*

"We can play this game of silent treatment as long as you like, Queen Larelle, but it will only extend the time I spend cutting into your skin with my claws." She did not baulk but her eyes drifted to his hand as his fingers shifted into those of the creatures.

"You have not asked a specific question," she said, focusing on the water lapping in the distance rather than Osiris' face. He pushed off the wall.

"What do you know of Thassena?" he asked, but Larelle did not need to feign confusion. He cocked his head. "Huh. Nothing."

"What about Eresydon? Asynthos?" asked the young boy.

"Arik!" Osiris snapped. "Do not give her information if she knows nothing of Thassena." Larelle tucked the words into a pocket in her mind, though she did not know whether they would ever prove to be beneficial. She refrained from asking if they were people or places. Osiris hummed and stalked closer, placing a finger under her chin. Larelle glared at him as his eyes bored into hers, her reflection shimmering in his dark eyes. "Perhaps you are further behind than we thought. And the sword—what do you know of the sword?" Her eyebrows must have moved a fraction as he said, "Ah, there we go. She knows *something*." The gold rings in his eyes briefly flared, and he frowned. "But not enough..."

His gaze snagged on something behind her, and Larelle turned as Osiris walked into the part of the cave where she had been held captive. She saw it clearer in the light. The crevice where she had remained crouched against the wall was coated in emerald algae; she dreaded to think how the back of her dress looked. A mismatched, unbalanced collection of rocks piled at the back of the cave as though gathered by a child. Osiris stroked the trickle of water Larelle had drawn from to cure her thirst until hooking his hand over a small ledge. A splash followed as he met a deeper rock pool, but by the grunt that followed, he was not content with it.

Larelle frowned as Osiris traced his hands over the rocks and the wall behind it. She turned to Arik, the younger and less experienced of the two. She could make a break for it. Larelle glanced back at the opening. Would the cuffs prevent her from breathing under water? Would they take that much of her power? The boy remained focused on Osiris, but when Larelle moved towards freedom, her foot betrayed her as she stepped in a puddle, the resounding splash regaining Arik's attention.

"Ah, there you are," Osiris hummed. Larelle faced him, but he was not addressing her. His pale hands trailed the back wall until stopping at a thin trickle of water, flowing from a minuscule hole in the cave wall that joined the pool his hand had been splashing in moments before.

He withdrew his hand to display a collection of pebbles on his palm. Larelle tried to decipher his smug smile as he traced one with his thumb. Osiris tossed the pebbles from one hand to the other as he strode back towards Larelle, his feet splashing as he re-entered the light. He stared out over the ocean, and the pebbles clacked in his palms, moving from hand to hand. Eventually, he stopped and held one up to examine in the light.

The sun reflected off the smooth stone, but there was something imperfect about it as she noted its jagged edge. Something in Larelle's chest tugged, urging her closer. Arik beat her to it and stepped towards Osiris, blocking her view of the object.

"Is that it?" Arik murmured, and Osiris hummed, further piquing Larelle's interest. The pebbles clattered against the stone floor as Osiris dropped all but one and turned to face her again.

"Do you know what this is, Queen Larelle?" His voice was silken and smug, knowing she did not. He revelled in holding that information over her, yet Larelle remained quiet and glanced between him and the piece in his hand. "There will be a time when you and your rulers require this, along with three others." Larelle turned over his words. *Why would they need a pebble?* Osiris grinned. "Imagine what you could do if you possess all from Ithyion."

Larelle's eyes narrowed at the reference to the kingdom he and his fellow creatures stole from her ancestors. *"All from Ithyion."* Replaying his words, she willed herself to remember why it sounded so familiar. She stepped forward. *The prophecy.*

"What do you know?" she asked, a threatening edge to her voice. Osiris threw the pebble in the air, catching it each time.

"More than you, it would seem," he said, twirling the pebble between the backs of his fingers like young children did for money at The Bay. Larelle focused on the pebble in the silence that followed. *Ithyion. Four pieces.* Osiris moved closer, and the talisman around her neck warmed. She refrained from moving her hands to the necklace and kept a neutral expression as Osiris' eyes flickered to her neck. The *talisman*.

"I fear there is no information you can give me, Queen Larelle of Nerida," he hummed. Larelle needed to stall him and find a way to retrieve the talisman.

"So, what now?" she asked. "Is it time for you to kill me and take me from my daughter?" Larelle's emotions spiked with hidden fear and determination, envisioning Zarya's midnight blue eyes again. Osiris tilted his head towards her.

"You have a daughter?" he asked, glancing at Arik, who shrugged. "Her name?"

Larelle clenched her jaw. "Zarya," she said, trying to appease him long enough to think through a plan.

"Zarya Sevia." He tested the name on his tongue.

"Zerpane," Larelle said firmly, and Osiris turned to face her fully then. "Zarya Sevia-Zerpane." His eyes narrowed a fraction.

"An old name," he said. "There is power in a name." Larelle did not respond. She did not need a history lesson on the origins of her dead partner's surname. Osiris nodded towards Arik, who approached the cave ledge. "I believe our time together is over, Queen Larelle of Nerida." Larelle's heart quickened; she could not let them take the talisman, but how would she escape them both? She stepped towards them as Osiris handed the talisman to Arik, the other half warming her neck and humming in response to its counterpart. "It has been a pleasure making your acquaintance, even if we are meant to be enemies." Osiris smiled, yet he had lost his earlier arrogance, and another emotion flickered in his gaze.

"Enemies," Larelle confirmed, remembering how his creatures killed countless innocents in Garridon. She assessed the distance between her and the ledge. Arik and Osiris were far enough to the right, allowing a slight gap for her to squeeze through. But Larelle needed the talisman. She stepped closer again and saw the suspicion in Osiris' expression.

"Daughter of mine..." A faded voice echoed through Larelle's mind and caught her off guard. She halted as the talisman in Arik's hand sang to its other half, calling and beckoning it closer. "*Take*

it. It will protect you," urged the female voice again, like it spoke from somewhere far in the distance. Still, Arik stood with his back to her while Osiris watched.

"Even enemies can find a common cause. At least, that is what my mother's religion preaches. Funny, isn't it? How people place such weight on religious sayings." Osiris slowly turned his head to face the ocean, giving her an opening. "We will meet again one day, Queen Larelle."

"I hope we do not," she said, and with her daughter's face spurring her on, Larelle charged at Arik. The wet surface provided little grip, but she only needed to make several strides. Her toes curled as she pushed forward and fell into Arik, forcing her weight into him. He stumbled into Osiris, and the three of them collided on the floor in a tangled heap. The talisman skated across the floor towards the edge, and Larelle was quick to clamber towards it. She scraped her knees against the rock as she crawled, reaching for it.

Larelle gasped as power met her fingertips, unlocking the cuffs around her wrists that clattered to the stone floor. She pushed herself to standing, surprised by the power of the talismans when combined. Breathing in the salty air, her connection to the ocean returned, and power rushed through her veins. She had always been powerful, yet the energy flowing through her now was different, older, and intense. She stared into a puddle at her feet, which rippled with her reflection. Larelle's blue eyes glowed, yet something else was there: a swirling pool of water in her irises, like a mirror to the sea.

She stumbled when a cold hand caught her ankle. She spun to find Arik holding onto her while Osiris rose slowly behind him, his movements much slower than Arik's scrambling. Larelle did not try to shake him. Time slowed as Larelle summoned the ocean, where a wave so high rose towards their ledge. Panic filled Arik's eyes as the sea darkened the cavern, and Osiris grabbed Arik's jacket, tugging the boy back into his chest as Larelle released the wave and sent it crashing into them. Wasting no time, Larelle raised her arms above her head and dived into the sea, streamlining herself as she plunged into the rocky depths below.

Saltwater consumed her, and Larelle breathed it in. A shoal of silver fish swirled beside Larelle, welcoming her return to the ocean kingdom. Her breathing eased, comfortable and secure as the water engulfed her like a blanket. She appreciated the water's solace, never wishing to experience her power being cut off again. Yet her panic threatened to creep back in amongst her relief as Larelle glanced to the surface and sunk lower, remaining close enough to discern Osiris and Arik standing at the cavern ledge in the rocky karsts growing from the ocean.

The fish swam a path around Larelle and shielded her from view. The ocean would always protect her. The talisman burned in her hand as she watched and waited. The two men did not linger at the edge for long or attempt to follow her in, but why? Why would they release her with little fight? Bile rose in Larelle's throat as their features shifted into that of two winged creatures. They jumped from the ledge and spanned their wings, taking off toward the sea border, away from the mainland. The ocean cocooned Larelle while she waited and wondered how much longer she would be kept from her daughter until it was safe to break the surface.

Larelle examined the talisman and rubbed her thumb over the engraving. She reached for the piece on her neck, the jagged edge matching the one in her hand, where together it formed a ship with three sails. She wondered if the other rulers had pieced together the prophecy, too, and searched for their own halves. Larelle's stomach sunk at that.

Had anyone searched for her?

The fish around Larelle fanned out, vacating their defensive position. Hoping they were correct, Larelle kicked her legs and broke the surface, greeted by the cool, early evening air. She blinked away the water clinging to her lashes and scanned the horizon, searching for any dot in the sky, near or far. She found nothing and continued her surveillance until spotting a ship in the distance. She squinted. It travelled from The Bay but not for the usual fishing pools; it headed in her direction. If it continued, it would need to attempt to cross the rough waves and whirlpools surrounding the rocks where she hid—the perfect defences for a hidden talisman. She squinted again, faintly making out the Nerida royal sigil. *Alvan.* Her heart pounded.

Alvan. It had to be him; he was the only one who could commandeer a royal ship after naming him her heir until Zarya was of age.

While Larelle trusted her sailors' worth, navigating these rocks was a death sentence unless they had a water-wielder on board, which was unlikely given that few remained with a connection to the royal line. Larelle clenched her fist around the talisman, the perfect defence for hiding such a relic. She breathed in deeply. She would not be kept from her family any longer. Clinging to that thought, she sunk below the surface.

Larelle frowned at the dark waters, her eyesight faltering on something in its depths—a whirl of soft light. When she blinked again, she saw it for what it was: one of many whirlpools. Kicking her feet, Larelle manipulated the surrounding water to create a stream, propelling her towards the ship. She thought of Zarya's terrified face when Lillian ushered her away, and the last time she relished in the warmth of Olden's hugs; she thought of her pounding heart whenever her hand brushed Alvan's, and the pain across his face when he screamed for her in the moments before she was taken. Larelle blinked back tears amongst the seawater as she realised she feared never seeing him again, not just her daughter and Olden. She screamed into the water, confronted by the pain of grieving one love while yearning for a new one.

She was not moving fast enough; she needed to know they were safe and they would remain with her forever. Both parts of the talisman radiated, and a glow encompassed Larelle as her hair floated in a halo and the ocean swam in her eyes.

Raising her hands, Larelle sank to the ocean floor, and only when her feet met the rough sand did she clap her hands together and send the sound rippling throughout the ocean. The fish scattered as Larelle screamed, the sound of rushing water pounding through her ears. Larelle screamed endlessly as power blazed in her hands, as she, the queen of Nerida, parted the ocean. The water rushed away from her, divided into two halves that began at her feet. She stopped screaming as the water parted until salty air filled her lungs.

Larelle moved along the seabed, stepping over discarded shells and broken wood from years of floating debris having sunk to the ocean floor to be claimed by the darkness. Her eyes lingered on deep-set footprints with sharpened claws: a sea creature she had never heard of. The footprints faded behind the walls of waves, stretching and forming a path for their queen. In the distance, it continued to part, the dark blue fading to a brighter turquoise as it met shallower waters.

Larelle would not be claimed by the darkness of her fears; she would be reunited with her family and would help save her kingdom from the creatures whose real faces she had now seen.

Larelle's feet quickened as the ocean continued to part to where the ship appeared in the distance, much closer than before. Water parted around it, and behind the ship, she saw The Bay. Her feet took on a mind of their own when her eyes tugged on a familiar body: the shape of his head, the breadth of his shoulders, and the size of his hands gripping the ropes as he hung over the side of the ship, looking in her direction. When Larelle saw his moment of realisation, she ran.

Larelle Sevia ran as though her life depended on it, and it did. Her life was Zarya; her life was Olden, and her life was the man hastily climbing down the rope on the side of her royal ship—the man who had stood by her side since the moment she was queen. The man who spent night after night tucking her daughter into bed and forming a friendship. The man who listened to her worries and offered his advice. Larelle heard the faint sound of his voice as he hit the sand, and the waves towering on either side of them fell like rain, soaking through her torn gown.

"Larelle!" Alvan screamed, and a sob broke free as she watched him sprint towards her. "Larelle!" he screamed again, and the water fell around him.

"Alvan!" Larelle tried to call back, but she broke down, sobbing, as the water fell harder, a torrent of rain reflecting her emotions as Alvan ran to her as though he felt every emotion within her just as strongly.

"Larelle," he whispered when they collided. He embraced her in a way that offered security she had not felt in years.

"Alvan." She sobbed into his neck, breathing in his scent of forest trees drowning under sea water. His hands were firm against her back, as though he was afraid she might disappear again. She curled her fingers into his sodden shirt as his embrace reminded her of the ocean—*home.*

"I promised you," he cried. "I promised you I would always be here." He pulled back and clasped her cheeks while the falling water paused and spiralled, dancing around them, cocooning them in the safety of their embrace.

"You are here." She smiled through her tears, resting her forehead against his. "You are here."

Chapter Thirty-Eight

Nyzaia

Nyzaia could not remember the last time someone cried in her arms, as Farid did now. Before settling in for the night, she shouted up to the others and articulated her requests with hand signals. The syndicate had endured plenty of precarious situations where they were forced to communicate with only their hands. She instructed Jabir to keep watch and would motion for a rope in the morning, which he accepted without question. They trusted her guidance.

Nyzaia did not mind spending all hours of the night comforting Farid. They sat against a sidewall in the cave, with the flow of lava to their left. Farid's head was on her shoulder, his breathing even and shallow. Through the gap in the forge's opening, Nyzaia watched the sunrise. She needed to wake Farid; they would need to move before the workers arrived.

"I am up," he mumbled, lifting his head from her shoulder.

"I am not sure I will ever be accustomed to you sensing my feelings." She smiled at him as he rubbed the sleep from his eyes. He grumbled. "Not a morning person?"

Farid glared at Nyzaia, and a wave of his exhaustion washed over her.

"We should get going. How is your rib?" He offered his hand and stood. Nyzaia prepared to wince as she rose, yet felt no pain. Unstrapping her leathers, she lifted the loose shirt underneath to find no bruises.

"Perhaps the tie healed me?" she asked, making a mental note to ask Elisara and Kazaar if they had experienced anything similar.

She could not recall seeing either of the pair injured in Garridon, but amongst the chaos, she likely missed so much. Farid hummed as he approached the edge of the cavern and looked up.

"Ready?" he asked. Nyzaia dramatically glanced around the cave.

"Am I blind to the imaginary tools we will use for travel?" she asked. Farid's head scanned the area below him. There were no sounds from the forge; they still had time. He turned back to her, his eyes glowing.

"We could fly?" he asked, and Nyzaia beamed as his wings emerged behind him.

"You don't need to ask me twice." In one swift movement, he scooped her up and cradled her. "I am less keen on this hold, though. Next time, I think I would prefer it if you—AHH!" Nyzaia screamed as Farid stepped off the ledge. It took a second for his wings to propel them upward, and Nyzaia's scream of terror turned to one of joy as they soared. It did not take long before he veered onto the smaller ledge where she had fallen. It was a tight squeeze for the pair of them, and Nyzaia kept her body flush against the ledge to her right to avoid the lava falling to her left. She examined the metal vein in the rock, a dull grey streak that reached what she believed was the other half of the talisman. The piece around her neck warmed. *Confirmation number one*, Nyzaia thought as she peered closer to discern the engraved flames and sword matching the half around her neck. *Confirmation number two.* She reached for the talisman.

"Fuck!" she exclaimed, snatching her hand back. "It's scolding hot!"

"Try to melt the metal holding it into the wall," suggested Farid, crouched next to her. Nyzaia reached for the metal above it and let her flames burn for several minutes, but when she pulled back, there was no change. Nyzaia frowned.

"You try," Nyzaia said uncertainly, inclining her head. "I have seen your wings, Farid, and I know you can wield a flame." She thought back to when he accidentally burned her in Khami; she should have known then that he possessed power over fire, but how had his fire burned Nyzaia given she was immune?

"It's not the same as yours," he sighed and reached towards the metal, flames bursting from his hand. He was right; they were not the same. While Nyzaia's flame was orange like one would expect, Farid's was ice blue.

He withdrew his hand, and metal dripped down the wall. Nyzaia reached for the talisman and flinched again when it scorched her fingertips. She gestured to Farid to take it, and he wrapped his fingers around the top of the talisman, which snapped as he broke off the bottom vein of metal. *Does it have something to do with his flames being different or his wings?* She could not understand why it would not let a ruler take it. Farid held it out in his open, scarred hand.

"I'm not touching it again!" she exclaimed. Farid's mouth twitched as he ripped a piece of fabric from his uniform and tied it around the talisman. "You take care of it," she urged.

He paused, watching for a moment, and she narrowed her eyes. He was trying to sense her emotions. Relenting, Farid tucked the talisman into the hidden breast pocket of his uniform. "What now?" he asked.

Nyzaia shuffled back towards the edge and peered upward. In the faint light of the rising sun, one silhouette appeared above—Jabir keeping watch like she requested. She waved her arm out and gestured pulling down, signalling for the rope. "We could have just done that to get here," Farid said beside her. Nyzaia's jaw dropped, feigning shock.

"And *not* have the chance to fly?" she exclaimed, grinning. Her smile widened when Farid rolled his eyes, and the rope dropped behind them, narrowly missing the flow of lava. Nyzaia shifted from a crouch and grazed her head as she reached for the rope and wrapped her legs around it. She gripped it with her knees and feet and began to climb. She glanced down when she felt no change in the rope's weight.

Farid stood, watching her intently.

"Are you not coming?" she called, and he shook his head.

"Not until I know you are safely at the top. I can grab the rope—and you—should anything happen again."

She rolled her eyes. "You better not become too overprotective!" she shouted, turning back to climb. During the final few metres, her hands burned against the rope, reminding her of the scar on her hand. *Shit.* How could she explain that to those who saw it? A flicker of reassurance ignited within her, yet it belonged to Farid, who must have sensed the emotion.

"Please tell us you found it after all that," Issam joked. Nyzaia reached the hand void of any scar for his large one, allowing him to haul her effortlessly over the edge. Before answering, she peered back over to ensure Farid was climbing. "He is one fast climber." Issam whistled.

Farid was already halfway up the rope as Jabir peered over.

"Well?" Rafik asked, continuing to monitor the rope they had staked in the ground. Nyzaia nodded, and Isaam grinned like an excitable child. "Let us see it then."

"Farid has it," she said, and the three men frowned. "It would not allow me to take it."

"It's odd that it would not allow its true owner to possess it," Rafik said, voicing her thoughts. She hummed but kept her eyes on the edge of the rock, waiting for Farid to appear. Perhaps it was meant for the true heir, which she never intended to be—*despite what the prophecy suggests*. Or maybe it was a defence mechanism to prevent younger siblings or distant relatives from attempting to usurp the throne with the talisman's power. Jabir reached for Farid's hand, the scar visible on his palm.

"What is that?" Jabir asked as Farid hastily let go and stepped back. Nyzaia checked to see if any of the other men had noticed while Jabir reached for Farid's hand again but stopped at the coldness in Farid's eyes.

"What is what?" Rafik asked.

"There is a scar on your hand," Jabir said, glancing to where Farid crossed his arms.

"I have many scars on my hands," said Farid, and Nyzaia winced at the memories of his own fire creating those scars and the pain emanating from him.

"That was different. It was raised, like it was new." Jabir stepped towards Farid, who hesitated before stepping back. Sensing Farid's discomfort, Nyzaia intervened.

"It is not important right now," Nyzaia said with queenly authority, a tone that was becoming second nature. "We need to return to the Neutral City."

"Nyzaia," Issam said, and she turned her head at his solemn tone. Issam, Rafik, and Jabir stood in a line of mismatched heights and builds, yet they shared the same tight-lipped frown.

"What is wrong?" she asked. Farid edged towards her until he stood by her side.

"While you were both down there, we"—Rafik gestured to the men standing either side of him—"were talking."

"About what?" Nyzaia snapped, immediately regretting her tone. Rafik rubbed the back of his neck and averted his gaze, and Issam took over. He was always more straightforward.

"What that boy said about the Red Stones is not okay, Nyzaia," he said firmly. "There is no one there to maintain the way of things or keep them in check." He stepped forward, his hands somewhat pleading. Nyzaia was forced to consider how much their lives had also changed since she became queen. The Red Stones was a culture—a way of life—yet her syndicate lost that the moment they followed her to the palace.

"You know why you appointed each of those heads," Isaam continued. *Ruthlessness, leadership, dedication.* "And you know without someone there to oversee their operations that a power struggle will soon ensue, perhaps even a war among them in your realm." Nyzaia did not like where this was going.

"What am I to do?" she exclaimed. "I cannot be in two places at once." Nor did she believe the people of Keres would respond well when discovering their queen had been an assassin.

"We are not suggesting *you* lead." Jabir sighed, shuffling on his feet.

"Then who?" she demanded. Farid's presence burned beside her as the three men exchanged a look. Slowly, Nyzaia nodded, finally understanding. "You three?"

She turned her back on them and fiddled with the saddle of her horse, hiding the tears she furiously blinked away. She could not lose Tajana and the rest of her syndicate in one fell swoop. Her family.

"Not all of us," Jabir replied. Nyzaia forced herself to turn, catching Farid's eye. He appeared uncertain, and she felt his questions sitting within her chest like a swinging pendulum. Jabir raised his chin. "I will stay with you and Farid. Rafik and Issam are well paired, brains and brawn."

"We described my position as a little more than simply *brawn* last night," Issam jabbed him, but Jabir ignored him as he met Nyzaia's eye. She turned over the suggestion but could think only of their absence by her side. Farid voiced her thoughts.

"How would the queen know if your plan to monitor the new council is successful?" he asked, folding his arms. Jabir studied him for a moment.

"We are a direct extension of you, Nyzaia. We are family. They are not leaving you," Jabir reassured her, stepping forward again until he was only steps away. "With Rafik and Issam overseeing the Pillar Heads and in turn, the Red Stones as a whole, you will have an understanding of what is going on. It can help you rule." Jabir reached for her hands, and she let him. It did not go unnoticed when he grazed the underside of her palm where the raised scar marked her skin. His face did not falter. "We will all meet once a week for formal debriefs, and of course, we still want our regular nights of cards." He tried to smile, but must have noticed her lip quiver. "You are in safe hands with Farid and I. You can let them do this." Jabir squeezed her left hand, and only her left. He knew they were tied.

Nyzaia did not fear a loss of safety. She feared losing two people who distracted her from the pain of Tajana with their playful bickering and bets. Nevertheless, Nyzaia knew little of the Red Stones since leaving and becoming queen. It was selfish of her to make them stay. As queen of Keres, she did not have the luxury of returning, not when they might need to gather weapons in the coming weeks or months, with the threat of darkness and creatures likely to arrive again—perhaps in her realm, this time. Nyzaia nodded in acceptance of their proposal and her personal sacrifice.

Chapter Thirty-Nine

Larelle

Larelle shuddered as she breathed in the smell of comfort and security. The breeze from the terrace blew in the familiar scent of water-drowned trees from the warmth at her right while the smell of rosemary salt rose off Zarya's dark curls as she rested on Larelle's lap. She combed her fingers through Zarya's hair, loosening the spirals as she went. The rise and fall of her daughter's chest kept her calm. Alvan had taken Larelle straight to her chambers without having to ask, and she had not left since, remaining glued to her daughter's side until the sun began to set. She memorised the curve of Zarya's lips, the light flush to her skin, and the few freckles scattered across her nose, which Olden always said his wife had. Larelle shuddered once more, but this time at the thought of being taken from her daughter again.

Alvan's gentle hand squeezed her shoulder, and she leaned into it. The bed dipped as Larelle slowly shifted to make room, careful not to wake Zarya. It did not take long for her to fall asleep, her mind returning to comfort and safety now her mother had returned. Larelle had expected tears, hysterics, or hundreds of questions from her daughter, but when Larelle walked through the chamber door to where Zarya sat crossed-legged on the terrace, she had simply run to her quietly and gripped her legs. She bent down to embrace her daughter, praying this was real and she would not wake up against a wet rock wall to the sound of creatures outside it.

Zarya had pulled back and placed a delicate hand on Larelle's cheek, rattling the shell bracelets on her wrist. Midnight blue eyes, with intelligence far beyond her years, stared at Larelle beneath a furrowed brow.

"I missed you," Zarya mumbled. It took everything for Larelle to keep her tears from falling. "But Alvan said he would always find you." Larelle turned over her daughter's words.

"She has not slept properly in days, she will not wake now," Alvan murmured into Larelle's hair, resting his chin on her head. Guilt washed over Larelle her absence, though it was no fault of her own.

"What did you tell her?" Larelle blinked back tears, and Alvan held her tighter.

"I told her Mumma was away being very brave for the kingdom," he murmured. "And that she would be back soon."

"You could not know I would return," Larelle said, though she was unsure how she would have handled the situation in his shoes. She likely would have done or said anything to placate her daughter.

"Zarya asked if I would find you for her and bring you home early." Alvan gently stroked Larelle's arm, hesitant at first. An unspoken closeness lingered between them since she had returned, though she supposed the fear of death would bring two people closer. "I told her I would always find you," he said eventually, and Larelle could not help the small smile that graced her lips or the warmth spreading in her chest. Alvan took her right hand while her left stroked Zarya's hair. They intertwined their fingers. "What now?" he asked.

Larelle stroked her thumb across his hand in thought. When he found her, she had immediately told him everything but she regretted it when she watched the pain in his expression.

"What was agreed when I was..." Her voice trailed, avoiding a direct reference to her abduction.

"Once all the talismans were found, we agreed to meet in the Neutral City. There was a consensus that so much power should be contained in a neutral place."

Larelle nodded. "But then what? Does anyone know what we are to do with the pieces?" She tilted her head up at Alvan, noting the light scruff of hair that had grown on his jaw since Garridon. He frowned. "Did no one consider that?"

He glanced at her with a tenderness that made her swallow.

"I suppose we were missing the level-headed one of the group," he said, smiling. He moved his hand to play with her hair, reminding Larelle of when Riyas pulled her hair free on the beach on the first day they met. *What would he say if he knew my heart warmed for another?* Larelle shifted and glanced away from Alvan, returning her attention to her daughter. She pulled her hand from his and awkwardly picked at her fingernails, feigning thoughtfulness.

"Perhaps all the pieces simply being together will be enough to summon the gods?" he asked, and Larelle hummed.

"It seems a risk, though, to travel that way and combine all the talismans for it simply not to work. Surely, we should plan for that eventuality?"

"Your parents likely spent years trying to decipher the prophecy and did not get as far as you. Who else could possibly provide insight into the workings of the talismans?" Alvan reached for the goblet of wine on the side table and passed it to her. Larelle shifted and took the goblet.

"The Historian?" she asked. "Someone old enough to remember the tales of Ithyion." Alvan's eyes widened.

"I have not told you," he said. "The Historian volunteered to search for other lands to find help for our cause."

Larelle straightened, and her heart rate spiked.

"But what if he stumbles upon the land those creatures were from? They will surely take him prisoner!" She rose from the bed and began pacing, biting her thumbnail. The Historian had cared for them all and had done so since they were children, but he was a fool for putting himself in danger at his age. Though perhaps that was why. With little time left in life, it was likely an honour to serve his kingdom.

"Are we not assuming that the creatures are on Ithyion, given that they forced your families from there in the first place?" he asked, and Larelle shook her head.

"They mentioned other names—places, I presume. It seemed like they were from another land, possibly the lands they originated from before they invaded Ithyion." Larelle thought aloud. Alvan placed down his goblet and rose to join her. She paused as he lightly gripped her shoulders, turning her to face him.

"He has skilled fighters with him; he will be okay," Alvan said. Larelle bit her thumb and glanced up at him. She quickly withdrew when she noticed his eyes trailing to her mouth. "Let us stay focused. Who else could we speak with if not the Historian?"

Larelle frowned and crossed her arms while Alvan kept his hands on her shoulders, keeping her centred. *Where else would possess ancient information?* Larelle could not think, picturing Osiris every time she closed her eyes. "*Funny, isn't it? How people place such weight on religious sayings.*"

"The church," Larelle exclaimed, grasping Alvan's forearms. "It is likely the only place in Nerida holding any old texts, myths, or fables."

Alvan's grin widened as he nodded in agreement. "There are the brains we've been lacking."

Grinning, Alvan pulled Larelle into his chest as she watched Zarya, sound asleep on the bed. Larelle wrapped her arms around him and turned to look through the doors, where night had settled above her ocean. She flinched as a bird's silhouette glided across the moon, reminding her momentarily of the creature and shifting her mood. Osiris had known the name Zerpane. Had they killed Riyas and his ancestors on Ithyion? Alvan squeezed her tighter.

"Tomorrow, we leave at first light for the church and then head straight for the Neutral City."

***

The City of Statues. That's what Larelle thought Mera should be called as she rode through it with Alvan by her side and guards stationed to the front and rear. Every water feature, column, and large building had a statue protruding from it, each with an engraving beneath, written in the sandstone. She did not recall them as a child, likely too focused on watching her father's feet ahead of her as she did what she was told. As an adult, Larelle could not decide if the statues were beautiful or gaudy. Opulence always had a fine line.

"Mumma, look at the fishies!" Zarya tapped Larelle's leg from her spot in front of her mother, sharing the same horse. Yes, Larelle could have taken a carriage, but as she was to part with Zarya when they journeyed to the Neutral City, she wished to keep her as close as possible in every moment until then. Larelle's eyes followed Zarya's tiny finger to where she pointed at the large fountain in the city square. They drew to a halt. "Can fish really squirt water from their mouths like that?" Alvan approached and lowered Zarya to the ground, allowing Larelle a moment to take in their surroundings.

Citizens filled the city square; some basked in the sun by the fountain's edge, while others sought shade on the terraces outside the shops, but all revellers spotted their queen, whispering and pointing at her.

"It would appear those fishies can," Alvan exclaimed, reaching for Zarya's hand to prevent her from sprinting across the slippery stone surrounding the fountain. Larelle swung her leg over the horse, and in a flash, Alvan wrapped one arm around her waist to lift her, the other gripping Zarya's hand. Larelle blushed as his hand lingered on her hip.

The church loomed over them but did not yet cast shadows over the square. Many would argue a church should bear beautiful and opulent engravings to match the city, while others knew a church did not need to be beautiful to welcome those of faith. Larelle believed the latter, though there was something uncomfortable about the luxuriousness of the church; it had too many engravings and statues to keep track of. She imagined it would take scholars months to record everything in it. One stood out to Larelle: a statue of two large hands joining together, with water flowing from their palms and spilling over the sides like a fountain. Each realm across Novisia devoted its religion to celebrating their god or goddess. Here, they worshipped the Goddess Nerida.

Larelle often questioned whether religion created more division than harmony across the realms. The Neridians were pious people who believed their goddess was the most merciful and forgiving of them all. They followed daily practices, like washing the sins from their souls after confessing to them.

"Why have we never been here before?" asked Zarya when Larelle guided her to the other side of the fountain towards the looming entrance to the church. She glanced at the obnoxiously priced silk dress stores and over-priced dessert spots.

"Because we had everything we needed at The Bay," Larelle said, and Zarya frowned like she did not quite believe her mother.

"But we need things from here now?" she asked, and Larelle nodded.

"Yes. We need some help from the church." Alvan had sent word of their arrival the previous night once they had decided to visit.

"What do they do at a church?" Zarya asked.

Larelle glanced at the carved N engraved in the pillars at the entrance and felt guilty for not having taught her daughter much of Nerida's religion. But neither Riyas, Olden, or her parents had been committed to religious ceremonies, thus it had not plagued her that Zarya should learn.

"We worship the Goddess," spoke a serene voice from the side of the pillar. The young woman was so quiet and discreet in the shadows that Larelle had not noticed her. The stranger smiled and lowered the blue silk hood of her cloak, revealing golden hair secured in a tight updo. A simple metal diadem connected into a point on her forehead. An acolyte.

"How?" Zarya asked, unswayed by the stranger's presence. Larelle tucked Zarya close to her side.

"I would be happy to show you, Princess Zarya." The woman curtseyed low before repeating the gesture for Larelle.

"Forgive me, it has been so long since I have visited the church," said Larelle politely. "I do not know with whom we talk."

The young woman approached with her hands clasped before the blue rope wrapped around her robes.

"Sister Vivian, Your Majesty." She bowed her head again. "I apologise, but Father Zoro is not available to meet at such short notice. I hope I will be enough to assist you for today."

"It is surprising that a priest would not make himself available for his queen," Alvan said, and the acolyte blushed, bowing her head again.

"Permission to speak freely, Your Majesty?" she asked. Larelle glanced at Alvan, wide-eyed. He shrugged.

"You do not need my permission to speak your mind, sister," Larelle assured her. Vivian raised her head again before guiding them through the archway and into the church. It was as bright inside as the buildings outside. Pastel paintings adorned the walls, depicting lovers and lakes, tall cities surrounded by the sea, and flashes of scales amongst the waves. Larelle's parents had never indulged in religious stories, yet looking at the paintings forming the church walls, Larelle could not deny her intrigue. The dark wooden pews contrasted the brightness of the interior as she walked down the aisle.

"It pains me to speak ill of someone of the church, Your Majesty, but Father Zoro has never been..." She paused and peered up at the domed glass ceiling. "He has never been *fond* of the royal family."

Larelle smiled at her careful choice of words as she walked beside her down the aisle.

"That does not surprise me. My parents were never ones to participate in religious ceremonies," Larelle said. "It does make me wonder where the Goddess destined their boats to sail after their funeral." She stopped next to Vivian as they reached the altar, where carved waves held up a pillar with an old book placed upon it.

"The Goddess is known for her intuition; she will have ensured they ended in the correct resting place." Vivian smiled. Larelle glanced at Zarya, who stood with her hand in Alvan's a few steps behind. She was too distracted by the dome ceiling to listen to the fate of her grandparents. "What is it I can assist you with today, Your Majesty?" asked Vivian. Larelle wondered if she was always so polite.

"I was wondering if the church had any old texts in its possession. Either those originating from Ithyion or perhaps written by those who would have lived upon its lands." Larelle kept her request vague, and Vivian frowned in thought.

"Well, of course. We have our holy texts and artefacts; those deemed sacred enough were brought with our fleeing ancestors. Are you wishing to build your knowledge of the kingdom we are founded upon?" she asked, and Larelle nodded.

"One would always like to know more of their history, particularly when those closest are no longer here." Vivian's frown turned to one of pity, assuming Larelle missed her parents or brother.

"This way." Vivian guided Larelle to a locked door in the corner behind the altar, and Larelle beckoned for Alvan and Zarya to follow, the latter of which gaped at the surroundings. Larelle trailed her hand along the wall as they entered the corridor. "Apologies for the darkness," Vivian called ahead. "We must preserve the conditions of the texts and tapestries."

Larelle felt the ground incline into steps. Her legs ached as she followed Vivian and reached the top of the church. Vivian pulled a set of keys from under her robes while Larelle turned to check on Zarya, unsurprised to find her giggling on Alvan's back.

"Please, wait here while I light the room," Vivian told Larelle. The young woman's movements were soft as she removed a lantern from the wall and lit the others around the vaulted room. Larelle reached for the heavy curtain before her and peeked behind it, squinting as light greeted her directly at the edge of the domed glass ceiling. Peering down through the glass exterior, Larelle saw the altar they had been at moments ago, and when she looked up again, she saw the rooftops of Mera on the opposite side.

Larelle let the thick fabric fall into place to once again protect the room. Tall bookshelves lined the centre and created aisles—a library Larelle never knew existed. Her eye was quickly drawn from the shelves to the magnificently large tapestries lining the opposite wall.

"Mumma, it's you!" Zarya called, pointing at a tapestry. Larelle tilted her head and saw how the woman could remind Zarya of her mother. However, Larelle was reminded of the painting in her father's hidden room—a canvas of Goddess Nerida. The tapestry spanned past several aisles of bookshelves. Such a masterpiece would have taken years to create, and Larelle thought of the many hands who had channelled their passion into its weaves. She tried to make sense of the scene it depicted.

It showed nine figures. The woman who looked similar to the Goddess stood hand in hand with two others: a beautiful blonde, and a broad man with dark hair. They formed a circle with the two women opposite: one with dark hair, and another paler than the other. Instead, Larelle focused on the figures behind the women, crafted in faded grey fabric. She could not make out their significance.

"These are some of the oldest we own," Vivian said. Alvan was quick to drop Zarya's hand and take the books that towered past the acolyte's eyeline, placing them on a table that appeared as old as the texts. "There are not many. As you can imagine, there was little time for our ancestors to take books as they fled."

"But they could take tapestries that large?" asked Alvan. He was right. Vivian fell silent while peering at the multiple tapestries on the wall, seeming to admire the work with glistening eyes and a small smile.

"I suppose I have never questioned what is passed down to us." She frowned, and her eyes grew vacant.

"Who is she talking to?" asked Zarya, and the acolyte's head whipped to the young girl.

"She was speaking with me, sweetheart." Larelle stroked her daughter's hair. "Are you getting tired?" Zarya backed into Larelle's skirts as Vivian stared down at her, tilting her head.

"I don't want to sleep; I think too much when I sleep," she mumbled into her mother's skirts.

"You mean you dream too much?" asked Larelle, crouching to face her daughter. Zarya nodded.

"Dreams are a blessing, princess. They could be a gift from the Goddess herself," Vivian said, but Zarya continued to press further into Larelle's hold. Larelle frowned. Zarya was never shy.

Drawing the attention away from her daughter, Larelle asked, "Which texts are the oldest?"

Vivian's gaze lingered on Zarya for a moment longer before turning to the books and pulling one from the bottom of the tower.

"This is a collection of prayers, though they are not specific to Nerida. This is a collection gathered from scholars across Ithyion; it references all the gods. Larelle smiled as she reached for the book.

"Perfect."

Chapter Forty

Soren

Clouds conversed in thunder above Soren, who slowed her horse into a gallop. It was unusually dark for the late morning as she approached the gaudy golden gates separating Lord Ryon's estate from the modest farmland that formed most of Stedon. Even as someone who wished to be queen, Soren did not have a taste for exuberant displays of wealth, only exuberant displays of power. The sun had nearly set, with only a faint glow remaining. She had told no one of her plans and rode nonstop from Albyn. She ignored the few men at the gates, who waved for her to slow and announce herself. Instead, she rode straight past them for the large wooden lodge at the top of a slope positioned on the backdrop of Hybrooke forest.

The men still called after Soren as she dismounted, loosening her horse's reins, so it could wander the gravelled entrance. She scoffed at the carved wooden animals displayed along the veranda and the flaking gold paint around the door. How simple this home had once been before Lord Ryon took it.

As she forced open the double doors to the home and knocked over a servant in the process, a loud voice called from the top of the staircase. "Queen Soren, I assume?"

Soren merely glanced at the poor fellow on the floor before continuing her assessment and scanning the many mounted animal heads lining the staircase. At a glance, she would not have placed Lord Ryon as someone who supported her cause. He did not seem capable of taking a throne, lacking in physical stature, and moving with a gangly walk. When he approached, though, she saw the hunger in his beady eyes and the wrinkles marking the sneer he often kept in place. He bowed and took her hand, placing a kiss on the back of it.

"I did not expect to meet you so suddenly." Rising, he stepped back and placed his hands behind the back of his luxuriously tailored velvet jacket.

"I am a woman of urgency," she stated, resting her hand on the pommel of the Garridon sword at her side.

"Are you?" he asked, and Soren narrowed her eyes. "You have been here some time, yet the usurper remains upon your throne."

Soren whistled low and quiet, and Lord Ryon's eyes flickered to the wolves stalking out from the trees encircling the property, with Varna leading the pack.

"There is a plan," she said firmly.

"I do not wish to offend you, my queen. It is merely an *observation*." He dragged out the last word, and though she wished to slap the man for his *observation*, he was the first in Garridon to address Soren by her deserved title. She raised her chin with a triumphant smile, invigorated by it. "Let us sit," he exclaimed with a clap.

He guided Soren through a wooden archway and into a small sitting room. It was far darker than Antor's castle, which was difficult to accomplish with all the wood and timber. She took a seat in the high-backed armchair, the fire burning to her right. A view of Stedon appeared out the window behind Lord Ryon's seat.

"You mentioned a plan," he said.

Soren rested her elbow on the arm of the chair, struggling to find a comfortable position in her armour.

"What do you know of Sir Cain?" she asked, and the lord frowned.

"What is the relevance?"

Soren tapped her fingers on the arm of the chair. "Your queen asked you a question."

He shifted in his seat and leaned forward for the glass decanter of amber liquid. He poured two glasses and passed a glass to Soren, who refrained from making a face at the smell as she downed it in one. She ignored the burning sensation scorching her throat. *Why must men involve alcohol in all their business?* She asked herself before pouring another, refusing to be perceived as weak. "I require an answer, Lord Ryon." She swirled the second glass as he looked at her with a raised eyebrow.

"He is experienced and is Novisia's oldest commander," he said plainly. Soren swirled the liquid again.

"Could he be a *threat?*" she emphasised, and the lord shrugged.

"I do not think so, though he would defend Caellum should you attempt to take his life. Why?"

"I need to assess who could be a threat when I take the throne. He seems to care more than a typical commander," she explained, and Lord Ryon scoffed.

"Caring will be his downfall, then, will it not?" He finished his drink and refilled it, matching the quantity in Soren's glass. "Are there others who concern you?"

"The other rulers, yet that is purely from a power stance. Commander Kazaar could pose a threat, particularly if his queen was caught in any crossfire of my future plans. They seemed particularly... *close* at the engagement ball." Soren did not understand their dynamic, though she cared little about matters involving the heart.

"Few of those I stationed at the ball returned from the event, but those who did comment on their peculiar behaviour."

"How many did we lose?" she asked.

"Enough."

She nodded. The Lord of Night had named Lord Ryon when Soren was in the early stages of building her network across Novisia. Over the years, her people had become one with Ryon's spies, all wronged by the usurpers in some way throughout history. His spies had been instrumental in casting doubt on Caellum's reign and had played their part again during the riots. Though she had been rather displeased upon learning someone had stabbed Caellum, almost losing the glory she wished for herself.

"I have some worries, my queen."

She raised her glass to her lips. "Do tell."

"Your sister," he said. The burning liquid lingered in Soren's mouth before she swallowed and trained her eyes on him.

"What about her?"

Lord Ryon leaned forward and rested his forearms on his thighs. "The people like her." Soren rolled her eyes. Everyone liked Sadira. "I worry that if they go ahead with the marriage, the people will accept her on the throne, and your claim will dwindle."

Soren threw her glass, though he did not flinch as it smashed behind him.

"I will only tell you this once, Lord Ryon. Caellum will not have the throne. My *sister* will not have the throne. I will have *my* throne," she sneered.

"And if your sister gets in the way?"

"She will not."

"But if she does?"

"She will *not*." Soren rose from her chair, refusing to listen any longer. She was the only one who could question her sister. Crossing over to the window, she leaned against the ledge and stared at the figures in the distance, farming the fields of golden wheat dancing in the breeze. Her people.

"You know what needs to be done to hurry this along," said the lord.

"Are you certain we have enough strength in Garridon to withstand challenge?" she asked.

"Gregor is too young and weak to challenge, and the others have always listened to me."

"And what of the other realms? They could initiate war with us over this."

"Is a civil war in Novisia really a priority with what we are up against?"

"What did the other lords have to say about the creatures?"

"Not a lot. Caellum spoke with us all briefly, but no one was particularly reassured that he—or anyone—knew what was going on."

"That is because they do not," she said, and even Soren was unsure. Without the Lord of Night to guide her, all she knew was the creatures worked for him. The lords did not know of the prophecy, which was a secret still kept among the rulers. Soren wondered if Caellum and Sadira would address the events with the people of Albyn during their visit or if they deemed their words at the service for the dead to be enough.

"I am journeying to the Neutral City next. The rulers are all meeting," Soren explained before making for the exit.

"Consider that a good place to assert your position," he advised. Soren turned to him before she left. "A quick slice to the throat should do it. Or a stab in the back, whichever you think is best."

Chapter Forty-One

Caellum

Sadira tensed beside Caellum. *Usurper*—the term was destined to haunt him, even with Sadira at his side. She interlocked her hand with his, calming his breathing. Caellum did not recognise the two sitting opposite them, but then again, why would he recognise the common inhabitants of a tavern? Caellum straightened; he would not be made to feel inferior. The old man assessed him with one eye twitching as he did. Wrinkling her nose, the redhead averted her gaze before looking at Sadira again with a more neutral expression. How did two common inhabitants know about the Sword of Sonos?

"Say we do know about this sword." Caellum ignored the usurper comment. "How do you know its origins?"

The redhead and old man shared a look; the power balance between the two was unclear.

"My great-great-grandfather helped to make it," said the redhead, gesturing to the man beside her. "His grandfather." *Relatives then.* Caellum was unsure whether he believed her, and it seemed Sadira shared his scepticism. "Wiccans were the first race who learned to imbue items; we are the most powerful at it, or at least we were. It's an ability that has diminished over generations. Without a Wiccan, our ancestors would not have created a weapon capable of defeating dark beings."

"If that is the case, why did the rulers only learn of the sword weeks ago?" challenged Sadira, and pride bloomed in Caellum's chest. The Garridon crown on her head was a perfect fit.

"Wiccans are known to have secretive clans," said the redhead, staring into Sadira's soul. Caellum glanced at his betrothed. He did not love the new trend of discovering more information they were oblivious to. Sadira's expression faltered. The old man finally spoke.

"You do not even know your own clan?" His milky eyes studied Sadira, and Caellum shifted closer to her side.

"Do not make me feel inferior about knowledge that has been kept from me. It is no fault of mine," Sadira snapped. The redhead eyed Sadira with a grin.

"She has a backbone, I like that."

As long as they like one of us.

"So do I," Caellum voiced from her side. Sadira blushed.

The redhead woman eyed the book on the table, and her pale fingers twitched as if eager to touch it.

"The book you have there belongs to the Brodie Clan, the one your great-grandfather once led." *Lyra's father.* "There is a reason he met and so quickly fell in love with your great-grandmother. The Brodie's worked closely with the Mordane royal family."

"Why would my grandmother keep this from me?" Sadira asked the man, who winced.

"Your grandmother knew the paths people needed to take. It was not your path to know until now." Caellum wondered if there was anything else his family had kept from him before Sadira's voice raised a notch.

"What difference would knowing my origins make?" Caellum squeezed her hand again, and Sadira cleared her throat, returning her expression to calm indifference. "What is the relevance of the sword?"

The redhead reached for the book and dragged it to the centre of the table, where she pointed to a sketch of twisting vines along the edge of the page, worn from numerous hands over the years.

"Look closer," she said, and Caellum leaned in with Sadira until their foreheads touched. The woman's dainty fingers trailed the vines, and the minuscule, nearly illegible writing beneath. "It's an incantation." Caellum's confusion mirrored Sadira's. "You do not use incantations with your power?" she asked, frowning.

Sadira leaned back. "My power is second nature. I simply think, and it wields."

"Think of how much more it could do with guidance." The woman's eyes grew wide as she tapped at the words. "This—*this* is how the sword was made." She closed the book and slid it back towards Sadira while Caellum turned over what they knew of the sword in his mind. Their companions had not mentioned the Goddess Vala or the God Keres. *Is what we know wrong? Or are they missing information?* The Historian had told them that the gods had blessed the sword.

The two rose from their booth, and Sadira opened her mouth as if to stop them. He imagined Sadira still had many more questions about her lineage and wished to uncover more information for Larelle. The old man tugged at the redhead's hand, and they paused. His face softened.

"Good luck," he said. "We are here when you need us."

It was not lost on Caellum that he only addressed Sadira.

"We do not even know your names," said Caellum. The redhead whipped to face him.

"There is power in a name."

***

"What do you think she meant by 'a name carries a lot of power?" Caellum asked Sadira as they took the stairs to the inn. She giggled and stumbled into him, and he grabbed her elbow on instinct. Sadira had poured over the book for hours while both sipped the tavern's wine. Caellum had been content with watching his citizens, though the atmosphere lacked the merriment he imagined usually graced the tavern. He heard various mentions of the creatures, the word having spread across the towns. Yet an awkwardness stopped him from addressing the people, even those who stole glances at the pair huddled in the booth.

Not wishing to ride through the night to Antor, the pair stayed in Albyn and would ride straight to the Neutral City in the morning. Sadira clutched the book to her chest, resting her chin on the worn edges.

"If what she mentioned about incantations is correct, I imagine words carry weight when using power," Sadira mused. Caellum wished he could hear the thoughts running through her head, thoughts now swimming in her eyes when they reached the door.

Caellum clumsily twisted the key to their room, the wine having rushed to his head. The door groaned through the dimly lit hallway as he pushed it open.

"Oh," Sadira whispered. Caellum rocked on his feet as he surveyed the pocket-sized room filled mainly by only one double bed in its centre.

"I suppose it is not absurd they assume those betrotheds may wish to share a bed," Caellum said, clearing his throat. He gestured Sadira through the doorway first, his eyes flitting to the open back of her gown, noting the flush of her pale skin from the warmth in the tavern. He focused on the ceiling and hovered in the doorway.

"I will ask for a separate room close by," he announced. Sadira reached for the trunk of her belongings at the end of the bed that had already been brought to the room, sat snugly next to his at the end of the bed. She turned towards him and retrieved a silk robe, her hair tumbling over her shoulder and glinting beneath the light of the lanterns hanging on either side of the bed.

"It is late, I—" Sadira clutched the robe to her stomach. "I do not mind if you stay here. It will save you trouble. It is already dark, and we must leave early for the Neutral City." He did not know if he imagined the blush across her cheeks, but she spoke again before he could reply. "It is a long ride; we need to be well rested, particularly after drinking."

Caellum hesitated before crossing the threshold and closing the door behind him.

"I will warm some water for you so you can bathe." He avoided her gaze as he strode for the adjoining room, attempting to busy himself. The distraction was short-lived, however, as he dipped his hand in the tub to find it had been warmed for them. "You must be aching after so long travelling," he said. He turned from the tub and almost collided with Sadira, who stood in the doorway. He braced his hand against the top of the frame to avoid tumbling into her, his heart pounding when Sadira peered up at him through her lashes, locking her green eyes on his.

"I shall leave you to enjoy your bath in peace," he mumbled. She grazed past him, brushing her chest against his. Caellum clenched his jaw as he fought the urge to pause, keeping the closeness that had bloomed between them ever since the engagement ball. His eyes lingered on her back as she reached for the buttons on her dress. He grabbed a cloth and a bowl of cold water from the side and closed the door to avoid temptation.

Once he washed himself, he changed into his sleeping attire; a simple pair of loose trousers while he kept his chest bare. He stoked the fire and paced in front of the bed. Did he get in it? He yanked the sheets, flattened them back into place, and continued pacing. He locked his hands behind his neck and glanced at the desk, unsure whether to wait until Sadira chose her side of the bed. He crossed to the desk and opened the book atop it to appear engrossed with reading, but *who reads topless?* He panicked and scraped back the wooden chair again, returning to the bed. "Pull yourself together," he scolded himself.

The door to the bathing chambers creaked open, forcing Caellum to decide. He slid into the bed and pulled the sheets to cover his chest.

Caellum took an intake of breath as Sadira emerged, the steam from the bathroom gracing her entrance. She cast her eyes downward and squeezed a towel around her hair, which hung over one shoulder. Her bare feet were quiet as she padded out a few steps, still focused on the floor. Caellum trailed her ankle-length, sage green robe tied at her waist. The lace at the sleeves slipped down as her arms moved to discard the towel. In doing so her damp hair partially soaked through the fabric, and Caellum swallowed at the subtle peaks of her nipples. Sadira looked up at him, and he quickly averted his gaze.

"You do not wish to bathe?" she asked, and Caellum looked back at her, noting the pattern of her curls forming in her damp hair. She made for the bed, the robe tantalising him with a flash of her smooth, bare legs beneath.

"I washed quickly with a cloth. As you said, we must be up early, and I did not want to keep you up." He smiled, and Sadira bit her lip, glancing at his chest before sliding in beside him.

"That is very considerate."

"I will blow out the lanterns," he said, reaching for the one on his side. She placed a hand on his arm.

"Do you mind if we leave one on?" she asked, extinguishing the flame in hers. Caellum withdrew his arm but did not ask Sadira why as she slid down the headboard further under the sheets. The robe gaped at her chest. She wore nothing beneath it. He tried to think of anything but Sadira's body as he settled in beside her, yet he felt those mesmerising green eyes on him. He turned on his side and mirrored her position. Sadira's golden hair spilled over the pillow, and with a somewhat intoxicated confidence, he slowly reached up to twist it around his fingers, moving with caution. She did not move away, but her eyes roamed his features.

"Are you sure you could do this for the rest of your life?" She breathed as she pulled the sheets up, shifting closer as she did so. Her shins met his, and he prayed she did not move them back. When they remained, he answered.

"Do what?"

Sadira smiled, reaching for Caellum's hand resting on his side. Her finger traced small circles on the back of it.

"This—lying next to me every night and waking up to me every morning." Her eyes were wide and honest when he stared back at her.

"I know I could," he murmured. His hands twisted in her hair, moving towards her scalp.

"I could, too," she breathed, and the scent of sweet wine hit him. She moved her leg, and for a moment, he mourned the distance until she hooked it over his and pulled him closer. Caellum did not want to make a wrong move or risk ruining what blossomed between them before it even stood a chance. His hand was tentative as it slipped from hers and travelled under the sheets, resting on the curve of her hip. She pressed her chest closer to him.

He wanted to kiss her, wanted to search every inch of her body but he restrained himself, waiting for Sadira to make the move as a confirmation of what she wanted. That *he* was what she wanted. Sadira's eyes fluttered shut as he splayed his fingers across her hip, the silk thin against her skin. He tugged it gently to stroke her thigh, and she whimpered. The beautiful, graceful, powerful, and self-assured woman beside him *whimpered* at his touch. She deserved everything—more than this.

"I want to kiss you," he breathed, and Sadira's mouth parted. His hand moved to the roots of her hair, gripping it gently to restrain himself, and she groaned. "But you deserve our first kiss to be a fairytale, a moment befitting you. This bed—this inn—is not deserving of your lips," he murmured. The corner of Caellum's lip lifted as Sadira's brow furrowed slightly. She opened her eyes, and he saw himself falling within them. She trailed her hand up his abdomen, and he clenched her waist with one hand and her hair with the other.

"I need something. I cannot sleep or leave this place without knowing I am yours in some way," she murmured, while Caellum's hand grazed down her waist to her thigh.

"That is the wine talking. You deserve more than one night in a tavern," he said. She tilted her head back as his hand reached the inside of her thigh. His mouth moved to plant delicate kisses along her neck, and when she swallowed, he pulled back, meeting her eye. Sadira watched him through her lashes, desire burning in her gaze. His hand fluttered closer, waiting for her to say no and take back what she said.

"Caellum, I want this," she said. His name on his lips gave him all the permission he needed, and his fingers met her skin. Her mouth fell open, and she dropped her head into his hand, where he gripped her hair again as his fingers slid against her. He moaned into her neck, continuing his kisses as he pushed into her.

"Is this okay?" he asked against the curve of her collarbone.

"Faster," she said between breaths, and he obeyed. He obeyed the woman who came into his life when he least wished it, who stood by his side although the throne belonged to her family, who proved every day that she was more than he ever deserved.

"More," she breathed. She trailed her hand to his fingers, guiding him to where she wanted. He pushed his thumb against her, willing to do anything she asked. Gripping him tightly, she arched her back as her breaths quickened and buried her face in his neck. He held her as she clenched around his fingers.

"Is that good?" he murmured into her hair.

"Yes," she groaned, and he felt her come undone beside him. His hand slowed as her breathing settled, her face hidden in the crook of his neck. When her hand grazed his length, he grabbed her wrist.

"You need to sleep," he murmured into her hair, and Sadira withdrew her hand.

"You do not want to?" she asked. He chuckled.

"Trust me, I *want* to." He loosened his grip on her hair and began stroking it. "But we have all the time to explore one another."

Sadira smiled against his neck.

"Are you happy now?" he asked. "That you are leaving Albyn, knowing you are mine?" Sadira grinned.

"Yes, I am happy."

Chapter Forty-Two

Elisara

The gods knew. Elisara sensed it as she crossed through the Vala gate to the Neutral City, the talisman tucked into the pouch at her side. Its power hummed, beckoning for Elisara to touch it, but she dared not risk it again. The gods knew they would be called upon today. She felt it in the deep chill that settled over the city, one which should have vanished the moment she stepped out of her realm and into the sanctuary of the city. Elisara glanced back at Vala to see if it was changed in any way with the talisman removed. It was not. She frowned. Growing up, history lessons taught the talismans maintained the distinct ecosystems of the four realms, but perhaps the transition took time. Kazaar brushed his shoulder against hers. Citizens closed their doors and tucked their shawls tight against their bodies, frowning at the sky.

Elisara was reminded of how different things were now. Elisara looked at Kazaar. During their last visit here, she was forced to leave with him for the Unsanctioned Isle, and on the visit before that, she could not imagine even sharing a room with him. He smiled, brushing his finger against the back of her hand. She nodded. They could do this.

During their short journey from the Vellius Sea, the realisation dawned on them: They might soon face their gods. It was difficult to comprehend and was a particularly uncomfortable thought for Elisara and Kazaar, who hid the powers beneath their skin—powers belonging to neither Vala nor Keres. For now, they ignored the power sparking between them as they marched into the soft fog drifting through the city along the cobbles.

Elisara tested her powers to confirm the revelation on their last visit remained true, that the rulers could access their abilities within the city. She twisted her fingers and her test proved successful as the fog at her feet twisted around her shins at her command. Warmth brushed her hand, and she glanced at the flames licking her palm. Kazaar could use his, too.

"Will you reveal that to the others?" Elisara asked. Vlad was close behind and did not know the extent of Kazaar's hidden truths, but based on his constant jests with her commander, she did not think Vlad suspected anything, and if he did, it did not appear to bother him. In fact, Vlad and Kazaar appeared to be on a path to becoming friends.

"Do you think I should tell them?" Kazaar asked. The twists of fog at their feet slowly changed, forming a thick blanket that blurred the streets as they navigated towards the ruined temple.

"Only if you feel comfortable."

"I am not sure my feelings are relevant given the state of things." Elisara did not respond but felt his probing gaze. *"You do not agree?"* Elisara glanced down the cobbled street.

"Would you say my feelings were irrelevant if we discussed how much of our connection to share with the others?" she challenged.

"Point taken."

"What if the gods reveal our connection to them before we can? How does that make us look when we all agreed to work together without secrets?"

"It would be too sudden to tell them before completing such a momentous task."

"After then?" she asked, and Kazaar nodded.

Vlad tapped Elisara's shoulder from behind, and she slowed to walk by him.

"Do you think the others were successful?" he asked. The three of them entered the city square, and memories of her family flooded back. She blinked them away, not wishing to relive the grief she kept so well at bay. The fog was thinning now and twisted around the temple in a swirl resembling smoke until only a thin layer remained at their feet.

In doing so, it allowed a clear view of the area. Nyzaia leaned against the temple, with Farid and Jabir standing stiff on either side of her. She pushed off it when she locked eyes with her friend.

Elisara's steps faltered when two others exited the street directly from Nyzaia's right. Elisara's eyes noted their intertwined hands before they separated. Caellum touched the small of Sadira's back, guiding her to the others. They wore emerald green, the velvet of her fitted bodice mirroring his jacket, while the white flowers on Caellum's cuffs matched the bottom of Sadira's skirts. There appeared to be something different about the pair as they approached. The crowns atop their heads caught beneath a stream of sunlight before hiding behind the clouds. They looked regal, like king and queen. *Like husband and wife.*

"I guess that answers my question, given they are here," Vlad said beside her. She had almost forgotten his question, distracted by Caellum and Sadira, who portrayed an image of a life once destined for her. She tilted her head, waiting for the stab of pain in her chest, but she felt nothing but indifference. Sadira's demeanour changed, and she covered her mouth, running past Caellum and Nyzaia with wide eyes. Elisara turned to see the cause of the sudden shift in her behaviour.

"Larelle!" Sadira sobbed as the queen of Nerida approached from the street, connecting to Nerida's gateway. Elisara released a sigh of relief as the two embraced. It reminded her of her friendship with Nyzaia. Caellum grasped Alvan's hand, and the two shared a grin before patting each other on the back.

"When did they all become so friendly?" Nyzaia crossed her arms, and Elisara shrugged.

"They are neighbouring realms; perhaps that is why."

"I also neighbour Garridon, and I can confidently tell you I will never embrace Caellum like that."

Kazaar scoffed behind Nyzaia in agreement, and Elisara slapped his arm. He grinned at her, and she smiled back, forgetting for a moment that they were not alone.

"Pay up," said Jabir. Elisara turned to a member of Nyzaia's syndicate as Farid solemnly handed him coins.

"What was that about?" Elisara asked a grinning Nyzaia, who shrugged.

"Just a bet."

Kazaar frowned. "On what?"

"On the two of you." Nyzaia smiled but said no more, stepping forward to clasp Larelle's arm awkwardly, a subtle confirmation she was glad of her return. Elisara mirrored the action yet noticed the darkened circles beneath Larelle's eyes. Elisara tilted her head, opening her mouth to ask what happened.

"Are we doing this? Or do you all need another moment to fawn over one another?" Sadira tensed as they turned to find Soren. The fallen queen spun on her heel and entered the temple, swinging her blonde braids behind her. Elisara felt some pain for Sadira; she also knew how it felt to have a tense relationship with a sister.

"Does she have to be here?" Nyzaia mumbled, gesturing to Soren as the group walked to the temple.

"If I am, then yes," Sadira said elegantly, before adding, "Unfortunately."

Nyzaia lit candles around the open room as the rulers and their entourage filtered in, each taking their spot at the chairs beneath their realm's banner. The large, cracked stone table felt smaller with added bodies. Any additional guards—Vlad included—waited outside, but even the added presence of Alvan, Farid, Sadira, and Soren made it feel crowded. What would the Historian say if he were here to see this? His absence felt strange, given he had supported them through so much and always took charge when they were at the temple. She hoped he led his mission to find aid just as well, but who would guide them in his absence

The group stared at one another, waiting to see who would be the first to confirm their success. Elisara pulled the pouch from her side and tipped the talisman onto the table; it clinked as it landed. She was careful not to touch it as the fog from outside seeped into the room, encircling her legs. Nyzaia mimicked her and avoided the falling metal, too, while Caellum pulled the talisman from his pouch and rested it on the stone. Elisara frowned. How could he touch it?

Larelle went next, a soft glow in her eyes as she, too, pulled the talisman from her side and placed it on the table before her. Elisara shared a glance with Nyzaia.

"How can you hold it?" Nyzaia asked, addressing only Larelle. Larelle frowned and tilted her head.

"What do you mean?"

"Your talisman," Elisara said. "How can you touch it?"

Larelle picked the piece back up, her eyes glowing again when she did. Amber returned to Nyzaia's gaze when she reached for her talisman, prompting Elisara to reach for her own. She prepared to flinch and drop it, but the stone felt cool as she held it in her palm.

"What is the confusion?" Caellum asked.

"I could not pull my talisman from its place. It burned me," Nyzaia answered.

"Mine tried to strike me with lightning," Elisara confirmed.

Larelle rotated her talisman with her fingers, contemplating.

"I did not take mine initially," she said eventually. "I picked it up, but I was not the one who pulled it from its place." Elisara leaned back, sensing the tingle in her fingertips.

"It is a defence." Kazaar gripped Elisara's chair, his knuckles grazing her back.

"A ruler cannot take it from its spot. There must be another there—a balance," Farid added, nodding to Kazaar.

"It would make sense," Nyzaia confirmed. "They were hidden to share power among the land but also to prevent a ruler from becoming too powerful."

Larelle nodded eagerly as they deduced the reasoning.

"Another must take it for the ruler to show there is trust and knowledge of the power being handled," Larelle agreed, and Elisara noticed Sadira and Caellum exchange a glance. Soren stood over them, smirking.

"Now what?" asked Sadira, eager to change the subject. She glanced at Caellum again. They were hiding something. Elisara did not know whether to feel hurt at how quickly they had come to trust one another.

"You cannot judge, given who you spent a night with." Kazaar's voice sounded in her mind before an image of Elisara materialised, reliving that night from his point of view. A thread of Kazaar's jealousy twisted through her, and she shifted in her seat, hoping to hide the blush across her face when she reached to tap his leg for reassurance. Elisara peered around the group.

"Alvan," Larelle called, and he stepped forward, presenting a roll of scrolls. "Now we meet our makers."

Chapter Forty-Three

Larelle

Larelle refrained from smiling at the look Alvan gave her while handing over the scrolls. "*You were right,*" was what she imagined he would say as the group looked to her for answers. What would they have done if Osiris had other plans for her? They would not have her talisman, or the different options for how to call upon their gods. Perhaps this would always be her role: the organiser, the scholar. She wished the Historian were here to offer guidance on which options could work, though that was assuming he even knew the answer. Despite the uncertainty he had placed in her mind regarding Kazaar, Larelle trusted his opinion and wisdom and hoped that his knowledge, aided by the fighters alongside him, kept him safe during his travels. The absence of letters concerned her.

Larelle and Alvan had scoured through the pages of Vivian's oldest book of prayers. Most were difficult to make sense of, written in riddles or an unfamiliar language. It had never crossed Larelle's mind that different languages might have existed on Ithyion. Eventually, they settled on three prayers, referencing all four gods.

"We brought the oldest references to the gods we could find," Larelle began. "I suggest we read them aloud as a collective, like the prayer they are intended to be. The words, along with the presence of the talismans, should hopefully be enough to summon their spirits." Scepticism flickered across the room. Nyzaia and Cael-lum wore matching frowns. Nevertheless, Larelle passed around multiple handwritten copies of each prayer and allowed them all a moment to scan the words. She looked to each ruler, who raised their heads and gave a nod of confirmation as she went around the circle. Taking a deep breath, Larelle led the first prayer.

"The God of fire, we thank for strength.
The Goddess of water, we thank for sight.
The God of earth, we thank for health.
The Goddess of air, we thank for light.
From the four to the threes, we give to thee.
Our soul and love for the right to be.
When all seems lost, we ask for your way.
Deem us worthy to hear your say."

Larelle looked at each talisman resting on the table before searching the eyes of each ruler, none of which glowed. *Not that one, then.* She passed around another prayer, remaining hopeful. The second still focused on the gods, but as they read it, it touched more on blessing the lands. They read the next prayer in a unanimous, monotone voice at the edge of their seats. Still, nothing happened. The same occurred on their third attempt. Nothing. They read a line one by one, but nothing. They even read the prayers standing, but nothing.

"This is useless," Nyzaia said, voicing what they likely all thought.

"There has to be a way; the prophecy was clear," said Elisara, rubbing her eyes. Kazaar squeezed her shoulders, and Larelle sighed, thinking it through. Caellum caught her eye, whose gaze focused on the talisman while he gripped Sadira's hand.

"*The Gods may whisper and help them on, only if all possess that from Ithyion,"* Caellum murmured. The talisman before him glowed, and they all widened their eyes.

"*The Gods may whisper and help them on, only if all possess that from Ithyion," Nyzaia* repeated, her talisman suddenly radiating the shade of her flames.

"The prophecy!" Elisara exclaimed. "Perhaps that is the message they need. They need confirmation we know the prophecy."

Larelle stood and gripped the talisman, surrendering to the power that had consumed her when she parted the ocean. Nerida's power flowed through Larelle as she realised it was not just a prophecy but a summoning ritual. She glanced at the others: flames filled Nyzaia's eyes, and a pale blue—almost ghostly white—burned in Elisara's. To her right, where Caellum gripped Sadira's hand, his eyes remained their usual brown, but the talisman in his left hand glowed all the same. Soren's eyes matched Sadira's and faintly glowed behind the pair, but her gaze narrowed on Caellum's back.

"We recite the whole prophecy," Larelle commanded. The fog on the floor rose and twisted around their bodies, reaching for their hands. The flames in the room brightened in contrast to the darkening afternoon sky. Although the sun still shone, the moon crept towards it.

"The door to the soul bears all to hear,
Multiple generations is the rule of the seer.
With those of white and those of black,
The spirit of the first makes their way back.
When the darkness returns, sacrifice is made,
In the wake of disaster, the return of the blade.
When light meets dark in the rarest of times,
When all that is left is the last of the lines.
The power to awaken that of old lore,
Lies in the soul of those with all four.
From fire and ice, the King and Queen must hide,
Secrets from the past, the heirs must find.
Only together can they defeat and restore,
Only together can they gain so much more.
The Gods may whisper and help them on,
Only if all possess that from Ithyion."

Each heir glowed as the colours of their realms encircled them, extending for the sky. Blue coated Larelle's skin and intertwined with the thrum of power running through her veins, yet the power stuttered like a heart skipping a beat, not quite cementing within her. Light surrounded and pulsed around the other heirs, but it flickered, too. *It isn't holding. It's not enough*, Larelle realised as their radiance began to fade, threatening to disappear completely. As the moon covered the sun and swallowed the final slither of light, plunging the sky into darkness, Larelle whispered the final words to the prophecy—the words delivered by the Historian when he warned her of Kazaar.

"Watch for the dark one that will bring suffering to all: the rise of old power, the Kingdom will fall."

Light exploded throughout the room, throwing Larelle's hair up into the air, floating around her as she tightened her grip on the talisman and closed her eyes, blinded by its dominance in the dark room. Behind her eyelids, Larelle sensed it fading, and finally, she opened her eyes. The moon hovered before the sun, casting the city in darkness.

"Holy shit, it worked!" Nyzaia cut through the stunned silence. Slowly, Larelle lowered her eyes from the sky, but nothing prepared her for Nerida's intent stare. She materialised as an apparition and stood on the table, looking down at her descendant. Larelle bowed her head on instinct and remained there until she felt the slightest touch against her shoulder. A shiver ran down Larelle's arm before a tranquillity settled over her when her body recognised its maker. She met Nerida's deep-blue eyes. Larelle could not read the goddess' expression as she scanned Larelle's features with a tilt of her head. She looked the same as the portrait in her father's hidden room. Her silver tiara of waves pulled back her tightly coiled hair and framed her high cheekbones.

"Daughter of mine," she whispered, her voice like silk. The panels of fabric on her ghostly dress floated around her like she was underwater, and Larelle craved to reach out and touch them—touch her. She was too stunned to speak, however, and was not the only one as she tore her eyes from Nerida's watchful gaze. To her right, Soren knelt behind Sadira and Caellum, whose heads were also bowed. The man standing on the table before them was tall, his side profile firm as he examined the three. While Larelle could not see him face on, she saw the scrunch of his face, and his frown as he peered at the two whose golden hair matched his and the man who wore the crown. Garridon stepped down from the table to survey them from all angles. Nerida floated until standing beside Larelle.

The movement allowed Larelle to see the others. Keres wore a smirk similar to Nyzaia's as he watched her with a matching glow in his eyes. *They look like siblings,* Larelle thought, as did Kazaar, who stood to the side with his hand on Elisara's shoulder. Vala towered over them with fury on her face as her silver hair floated around her frame. Her ice-blue gaze was different from the bright white reflected in Elisara's, and it seemed to anger the goddess, who turned her back and surveyed the room before stepping down from the table. Larelle shifted in her seat and glanced to see if anyone else had noticed Vala's behaviour though everyone was focused on their own gods.

The four gods paced the room and silently circled the table, a cold breeze trailing with their movements. Their voices echoed throughout the room, and while each spoke separately, their words formed full sentences.

"You call," Nerida began.

"Upon us—"

"Why—"

"Children?" Garridon finished.

Larelle shifted under the weight of their booming voices echoing off the stone walls as each god spoke a word in turn. She tried to catch another ruler's eye, but all were too distracted by their gods, except for Elisara, who stared at her hands.

"We need your help." Larelle lifted her head to meet Nerida's eye, who continued circling the room. A slight smile graced her face as Larelle spoke.

"You wake us—"

"For help—"

"For aid—"

"For answers."

Larelle nodded as Nerida spoke the final words of their unified sentence.

"The one—"

"With all four—"

"Awakens." Vala did not contribute; instead, the goddess glared at Elisara and Kazaar.

"The kingdom—"

"Can fall—"

"To the darkness."

Again, Vala said nothing, and her siblings cast odd glances her way. Nyzaia sighed and leaned forward.

"We know." She tapped the talisman on the table. "We have seen the dark creatures; they have attacked and killed; they even took one of us." When Nyzaia looked at Larelle, Nerida twisted her head to her descendant, concern swimming in her eyes.

"You are okay?" Larelle kept her face neutral as her goddess' voice entered her mind, the same voice she had heard when first picking up the second half of the talisman. Larelle nodded. *"Zarya... is she okay?"* Warmth flourished in Larelle's chest that the goddess cared about her daughter. Larelle could not hide her smile this time as she nodded again.

"There is more—"

"To darkness—"

"Than wings—"

"And amber."

Amber. Larelle recalled the amber flowers on Osiris' jacket and the wings that later protruded from it.

"What do you mean by more?" Elisara asked. While she avoided Vala's gaze, she kept her chin high. The gods stopped until each stood directly behind the queens and king of their realms. Nerida's ghostly hands floated upon Larelle's shoulders.

"To understand—"

"The coming war—"

"You must see—"

"The past."

Larelle gasped as Nerida gripped her shoulders, as though material hands were there and not those of a spirit. Light burst from the centre of the table until it faded, leaving a floating scene before them of two young children with dark hair running through the sand and laughing. A small sob escaped Elisara, and Larelle saw the emotion swimming in her eyes as she stared at the young girl whose features resembled hers.

Chapter Forty-Four

Nyzaia

Nyzaia had never seen her father so happy. She wondered when in his life he had lost the smile that was now clear in the scene before her as he ran hand in hand with Vespera, Elisara's mother. His eyes gave him away, matching the amber glow of Nyzaia's as he threw a flame alongside them for lighting, enriching the royal red and orange of his attire. Joy bloomed in those eyes whenever Razik looked at Vespera, and they laughed in a way only children did. Nyzaia glanced at Elisara, who had the same dark locks, thick eyebrows above wide brown eyes as her mother. Razik and Vespera were simply two carefree children, no older than eight or nine, running along the edge of the Ashun Desert. The image floating before them swirled, twisting and changing until Nyzaia saw an older image of her father, not much younger than Nyzaia was now.

Razik stood in the palace gardens, yet the shrubbery hid whoever he spoke to.

"I cannot keep having this conversation!" Razik shouted. His voice was far less daunting than when he shouted in Nyzaia's presence. "You know my parents will ensure you are wed off to someone else if they discover we were together!" Razik ran his hands through his hair and glanced up at the sky. Vespera stepped into view, her long dark hair identical to Elisara's. She flipped it over her shoulder and shouted back at him.

"Why would attending the same celebrations as you mean we are together?" she shouted. "I am a lord's daughter, albeit not your father's favourite one, but my presence there would still be customary!" Vespera crossed her arms in front of her blush-coloured lehenga, and Razik groaned.

"I cannot be in a room where every eligible man is watching and attempting to court you. It pains me to be apart from you, but it would pain me even more to cause this ending and to push my father's hand. Because if you are there, Vespera, I cannot keep myself from you!"

The pair paused, their chests rising and falling in tandem. In one stride, Razik reached for Vespera and crushed his lips to hers, a kiss that spoke of urgency and passion.

The scene changed. Razik stood, staring through giant glass windows at the view of the Vala mountains in the distance. A knock sounded at the door, and he turned with the king's crown glinting on his head.

"Iahabi," he breathed, reaching for Vespera when she entered his study.

"What is this?" she demanded, pressing her lips into a tight line as she surveyed the room decorated to match that of Vala. Razik reached for her hand, but she shrugged him off.

"This is what it will be like, marrying him." Razik said, gesturing around the room. "The cold, the colour, the furniture. You will lose all the possessions you love—the home you love." He stepped towards Vespera as tears welled in her eyes. "The *man* you love." When his voice cracked, Vespera turned her eyes up to meet his, resting her hand on his cheek.

"I do not have a choice, Razik. They have signed the agreement." He gripped her wrist and rested his forehead against hers.

"I cannot lose you," he murmured.

Nyzaia swallowed, thrown by the emotion she had never witnessed in her father, only accustomed to the anger he showed towards her and her brothers, or the indifference towards her mother. The image changed, and Razik stood in a pew with tear-filled eyes, applauding the marriage of Vespera and Arion, as they crowned her the new queen of Vala.

Nyzaia glanced at Elisara. Tears rolled down her cheeks at watching her parents marry. The image changed again, yet this time, Razik knelt as he married Nyzaia's mother, Nesrin. He smiled, but it was not the smile he shared with Vespera. A flurry of memories played out, short snippets of time: moments of laughter between Razik and Nesrin and the same between Vespera and Arion. Despite losing one another, they had found happiness, a happiness she had never seen between her father and mother before. When had her father become so cold

The recollection slowed to focus on a baby in a dark blanket, crying in an open wooden box. *Kazaar*. The door to the palace opened, and Nesrin stepped out to grasp the baby, shielding him against the night breeze. Nesrin ran down the hallway towards Razik's study but did not knock, as was custom. She opened the door in a hurry, and Nyzaia watched the moment her mother finally realised. Razik was not in the study that so clearly belonged in Vala. The baby stopped crying as she wandered to the desk, moving the many letters strewn across it, all addressed to or from Vespera. Her face crumpled.

"What are you doing in here?" Razik roared, slamming the door behind him. Nesrin backed against the wall as he approached, yet Razik composed himself, withdrawing from her as his eyes locked on the baby. "Where did you get *that*?" He clenched his fists and glared down at the bundle in her arms. Fury rose in her mother's eyes as they narrowed on Razik. She clutched the baby closer to her chest.

"*He* was on the front steps of the palace," Nesrin said. She glanced away for a moment and then back at him, raising her chin. "Is he yours?"

Nyzaia shook her head in disbelief as her father jerked his head back. She could not believe he had the audacity to appear offended.

"Of course it isn't mine!" he spat, his anger returning.

"Well, given the state of these rooms, and how little we lie together, is it wrong to ask such a question?" Nesrin fired back. Razik strode away from her towards the windows. "You know how much I have wanted a child, but with how little we are together, it is no surprise I have not yet conceived." Nesrin continued. "This could be my blessing, I could keep—"

"Absolutely not." Razik cut her off, not bothering to look at her. Nesrin's expression changed, her fury returning as she scanned the room before looking back at the baby. With a clenched jaw, she looked up at Razik.

"It is her," Nesrin whispered. "It has always been her."

"Of course it is her!" Razik yelled.

"Do not shout at me!" she screamed back, rocking the baby.

"I will shout at whomever I please when they enter my rooms."

"Your rooms?" she spat. "This is a shrine to a queen of another realm."

"It is a grave!" he shouted, blinking back tears. Nesrin paused as he paced before the window, his fists clenched by his sides. "It is a permanent reminder of losing the love of my life to that realm—to him." Razik pointed towards the mountains in the distance, and Nesrin's lip quivered only for a moment before she bit her lip to keep the tears at bay. She pulled her arms tighter around the baby. While Nyzaia never had a good relationship with her mother, she admired her strength in this moment.

"So, it will always be Vespera."

"It will always be her." Razik said. "She is the air that feeds my flame; she is the pounding in my heart. She is my everything and nothing all at once," Razik panted, tears streaming down his face. Nesrin gave Razik a final once over before walking towards the door.

"I am keeping the child," she declared fiercely. Tears continued down Razik's cheeks as he opened his mouth to protest again. "It is the *least* you can do." Nesrin bit out. When she glanced around the room for a final time, Razik closed his mouth, his jaw firm. Nesrin slammed the door behind her.

Nyzaia blinked rapidly as the image changed to the father she remembered. It was the day he left her outside a brothel to be collected by the Red Stones, the day she began training with them. A younger version of Nyzaia glanced back at her father before they hauled her around a corner. Razik hung his head and sighed before entering the brothel.

Nyzaia stiffened when Isha approached, swaying her hips as she guided the king to a quiet alcove. Nyzaia looked at Soren, desperate to wipe the smirk off her face. To this day, she still did not know what was truly shared between Isha and her father.

Nyzaia was surprised to see Vespera again in commoner's clothing, sneaking through the palace grounds. She entered a side door and stood outside her father's study. She knocked in a specific rhythm.

"Come in," Razik called, and his smile was one of remembered heartbreak as Vespera entered. They both stood awkwardly on opposite sides of the study. Neither spoke as Vespera assessed the room, trailing her eyes over each item resembling Vala. Razik rocked back and forth on his heels, framed by the light from the windows.

"You kept it like this," she said plainly, her eyes finally meeting his.

"I did," he whispered. Vespera walked towards one of the blue chairs and trailed her hand over the back.

"I had my study overlooking the mountains designed like this," Vespera murmured, pulling a loose thread from the chair. Razik tilted his head. "Exactly like this." She cleared her throat and looked away to hide the tears. Razik stepped towards her with urgency.

"Why?" He reached to touch her but withdrew when Vespera turned to face him.

"So I could pretend I was with you," she trailed off, peering out the windows where her study sat on the other side of the mountains. "To remind myself of our last moments together on the day you showed me this room." Vespera glanced down at her hand on the armchair as Razik rested his hand beside it. She took a deep breath before stepping away from him.

"I received your letter," she finally said. "Do you believe this prophecy the courtesan told you?" Razik nodded, and the memory warped again.

Nyzaia wanted to scream at the gods to stop and slow the memories, allowing them to see and hear every detail—every piece of information.

"We cannot give you everything on a platter." Nyzaia's head turned to Keres, his voice ringing in her mind. He sounded like her father.

"You are certain no one saw you?" Razik's voice sounded again, returning her attention to the past.

"Positive," said Adrianus, the king of Nerida. He stared in disgust at the large, dead creature at his feet. "It was dead when we found it."

King Wren and his wife Hestia shared a look before frowning at the creature.

"Return of the darkness," Vespera murmured opposite Razik. King Arion gripped her hand, and Nyzaia listened as Vespera and Razik explained the prophecy to the rulers for the first time.

"The last of the lines," said Arion. "Does that mean what I believe it does? Only one remaining of each lineage should remain?"

Razik and Vespera nodded solemnly.

"Sacrifice?" asked King Wren of Garridon, rubbing his face. Nobody spoke, all looking to Razik and Vespera for answers. Vespera gently nodded.

"Us," Razik said. "All of us."

"How can we be certain of following through with this?" asked King Wren, clasping his hands together. He rested them in front of his mouth and leaned forward on the table, watching Razik with eyes that did not hold the anger he was famed for.

"Too much of it is linked. This creature confirms the return of what took Ithyion. We cannot choose our lives over the risk of losing the entire kingdom."

"The last of my line isn't even born yet," said Wren. "Hestia is only three months gone." He swallowed hard, and the other rulers shared a look.

"You are not the true Garridon line," said Vespera. "We are working on the assumption any of your children could remain."

Wren nodded and said, "Caellum. He will stand the best chance."

Nyzaia raised her eyebrows, matching Caellum's surprise as Sadira reached for his hand.

"The gods. You said the gods could help us," Adrianus said, grasping his wife's hand. "We must try that first."

A flood of memories flashed quickly then: Razik and Vespera huddled over books, writing and researching, the seasons changing outside the king's study windows. At least five years passed until finally an image of Vespera on the Unsanctioned Isle appeared, attempting to withdraw a sword before her frustrated cry changed to loud chatter in the temple.

Their parents sat around the stone table, no crack on show, crowded by the rest of their families.

"The corridors need checking to be certain if the reports are correct," said Razik to the Historian, who shuffled towards the door and closed it behind him to check the corridor. Nyzaia knew what happened next. They had failed to contact the gods.

"Ready?" asked Vespera. Arion patted her hand as Razik sprinkled black dust around the room and on the table.

"Papa, what is happening?" whispered a quiet voice from the side of the room. One of Caellum's sisters sat on the eldest's lap, and Nyzaia wished she could look away at what she knew was coming. Wren scrunched his face and avoided looking at his daughter.

"Nothing, Eve. Sit still with Edlen and Aurelia."

"Father, what is happening?" Dalton asked. Vespera narrowed her eyes at King Wren.

"You did not prepare any of them?" she sneered.

Nyzaia's brothers braced their arms around one another, with Elisara's sisters following suit and bowing their heads. Larelle's brother and his wife bounced their son on their knees as they huddled close and cried together. *They knew. They all knew, except—*

"How was I supposed to tell them?" Wren snapped. Caellum's brothers shared panicked looks, and Aurelia shifted in her chair, pulling Eve closer.

"The same way we all did!" Razik yelled. Eve began to cry and covered her ears while Aurelia hummed into her neck.

"They are my children!" Wren shouted. "I cannot do this; we cannot do this." He tried to rise, yet Razik held his shoulders down.

"Perhaps you should have treated them as such while you were all still alive!"

"We cannot—I cannot!" Wren struggled against Razik. Edlen cried now, too, and then Nile, their sobs muffled in the clothing of the person holding them.

Razik struck a match, his power inhibited in the city. He reached to the table where dust lay before them all and dropped the match. It burned brighter as Wren shouted expletives, and when Razik pulled away, the last of the dust ignited. He took the seat to his right, the chair where Nyzaia now sat.

"Papa!" Eve cried, and it was the last word Nyzaia heard before the image in front of them exploded.

Chapter Forty-Five

Elisara

Numbness permeated Elisara's body as she stared at the empty spot on the cracked table before her. She heard none of the discussions, recalling only memories of her sisters' behaviour before leaving the castle that day. They had known. She did not feel Kazaar squeeze her shoulders while the image of her mother with another man invaded her mind, nor did she notice the tears sliding down Caellum's cheeks. Instead, Elisara realised her father knew about all of it, even her mother's affair. Yet, through it all, he maintained a happy front for his daughters. It was not enough that Elisara must carry the pain of finding her family's dead bodies, but now her nightmares were filled with the vision of their deaths.

"How did that help?" Elisara murmured. Nobody turned to her as they continued speaking, the ringing in her ears muddling their words. "How?" she asked again, but louder this time. Kazaar rubbed her shoulder as raw anger crawled through her. Looking up, more tears fell as her eyes met Vala's, who stood across from her. The goddess showed no love or sympathy for one of her many children. Vala smirked.

"How did that help ANY OF US?" Elisara screamed. Ice crept up the walls, and the only sound was the breathing of those who lived, their breaths rising like smoke. They all looked at her, the gods included. "All you have done is confirm what we already knew." She rose, resting her hands against the table. Ice spread from her fingers. Vala's smirk remained, and her hair floated around her while she hovered midair. "The prophecy states you could help us, so tell me: how on *earth* did that help?" The ice on the table cracked as Elisara smashed her fists against it.

"Control your whore, Night Child," Vala hissed, her eyes hovering above Elisara's crown to where Kazaar stood. Nerida watched her sibling, her lips pursed. Elisara felt flames at her back.

"What did you call her?" Kazaar kept his voice low, yet fire danced behind Elisara like a blanket before reaching across the table.

"You have sullied my bloodline," Vala hissed. "Is it not his scent I smell on your skin and his darkness I taste in the air surrounding you?"

In a blink, Vala froze Kazaar's flames.

"Vala, calm yourself," Keres scolded.

"Calm myself?" She stalked around the room, her image flickering.

"You know the rules," warned Nerida, her voice cracking.

"Rules mean nothing if she has been tainted." Vala crossed the table and knelt before Elisara. Her image flickered again.

"You are saying too much," Garridon said, his accent rough.

"They will lose us if you continue," Keres finished. Vala leaned forward, meeting Elisara's eyes.

"It is not he who has tainted us; it is you," Elisara sneered and tugged her dress aside, revealing the mark of the crescent moon on her collarbone—a celestial tie gifted by the gods themselves. Vala stumbled back, her eyes wide as Elisara quickly covered the mark. Vala looked at each of her siblings, their faces mirroring her shock. The goddess closed her mouth and retreated.

"Queen Elisara means no disrespect," Larelle said.

"I definitely do," Elisara mumbled, the anger still burning in her veins. The goddess had called her a whore and Kazaar a night child, confirming his fears that he had tainted Elisara with his darkness. Yet they were missing something. The gods' reaction was not what Elisara expected. It was as if they knew nothing of the tie.

"But she is right," Larelle said. "This does not help us. We already knew much of this." The other rulers mumbled their agreement.

"We need to know what to expect and how to defeat the creatures should they return in hoards," Nyzaia addressed her god. It was a smart move, addressing the god known for war.

"Creatures of darkness—"

"Wings of night—"

"Not what it seems—"

"Not the only fight."

Elisara clenched her jaw, glaring at Vala as the gods resumed their riddles. She caught Caellum's eye, his gaze still red-rimmed after watching his siblings' demise. His tense stance matched hers, though she expected for another reason as he glanced at the hands on her shoulders. Vala had announced Elisara's relationship with Kazaar to them all, though insinuated far more had happened between them. Elisara wondered if the gods truly sensed their odd sharing of power—the tendrils of shadow invading Elisara and the twists of light infiltrating Kazaar. The gods had offered nothing to explain what that power was or why they had it.

"More riddles." Nyzaia leaned back in her chair and furrowed her brow. "Answer us plainly: what should we *do?*"

"Prepare for war—"

"More swords—"

"Blood of the tied—"

"Watch for the lies."

Elisara rubbed her forehead. Until this point, everything in the prophecy that made sense had unfolded, but as they sat together and listened to the gods, it was the first time she felt doubtful. The group possessed all from Ithyion and had called upon the gods, but this did little to help them like the prophecy proclaimed it would. War had driven their families from Ithyion all those years ago; it felt inevitable that history should repeat itself in some form. While Elisara knew their blood paralysed the creatures, how could the Sword of Sonos be replicated?

"What more can you tell us of the Sword of Sonos?" Kazaar

asked. Elisara ignored Vala's glare as Kazaar spoke yet noticed Keres failing to contain his chuckle.

"A sword—"

"Can be many things—"

"A weapon—"

"A trap."

Soren sighed and banged her head against the wall, and for the first time since knowing her, Elisara could finally relate.

"The sword can kill—"

"The sword can take—"

"The sword can wield—"

"A flash of light; a twist of shadows."

Elisara angled her head to glance at the Sword of Sonos by Kazaar's side, remembering the way both light and darkness twisted around his hands when he wielded it—something only she could see.

"The sword can slumber—"

"The sword can awaken—"

"The wielder can take them—"

"The wielder can make them."

Elisara turned the words over in her mind, offering only ambiguity and more questions they would be left to find the answers to.

Chapter Forty-Six

Soren

Soren was not a patient person, but as she listened to the jumbled snippets of information falling from the gods' lips, the limits of her patience were pushed to a new extreme. The only saving grace throughout the torture was her god's confirmation that she was the rightful heir to the throne. Garridon had immediately sought Soren and Sadira when he arrived, ignoring Caellum altogether. Soren saw it even in his physical appearance: the same blonde hair and green eyes, the air of determination; she had noticed every pointed stare and sideways glance when he thought she was not looking.

She wondered what the Lord of Night would say if he knew she had met the gods, or his thoughts as to why Vala had called Kazaar a 'night child.' It sparked something in Soren. She had much to tell him while silently picking apart her thoughts on the sidelines while staring at Caellum's back. His hand was permanently intertwined with her sister's.

Refocusing on the group, she caught Garridon staring at her, frowning. Each of the other gods stood in front of their descendants, assessing them. Caellum's head remained bowed while Sadira stared up at Garridon, who only had eyes for Soren. He was quieter than the others, revealing less of his personality. Vala appeared to be the angriest of the group, and Keres the most mischievous. Nerida, much like Larelle, was the most level-headed, yet Garridon was thoughtful and assessing.

What if I am a disappointment to him, too? Soren thought. Looking away, Garridon glanced between his siblings to check they were not watching, igniting Soren's panic. *What if he doubts my strength as heir? What if I have not proved myself?* Her conversations with the Lord of Night flitted through her memory and the urgency with which he commanded Soren to take the throne, the same urgency pressed on her by Lord Ryon when she feigned being in control of the situation.

Her hand twitched, moving to the dagger at her side. She could prove herself here before the gods—prove she was worthy of her blood, her title, and her realm. The other rulers would not challenge Soren if she had Garridon's approval. She slid the dagger from its holster, the wooden handle unusually cold against her skin. Her fingers were stiff as she wrapped them around the hilt. Soren's hand trembled, and she frowned at her body's betrayal. Scanning the room, Soren ensured each ruler was focused elsewhere as she stepped forward. *It could all be mine.* Another step. *I could make them both proud.* She drew back her arm. *I could take what he has guided me towards all these years.* On the final step, Soren paused as she felt the weight of Garridon's gaze. She smiled as though already victorious. She went to strike but could not move an inch. Soren frowned, and Garridon gave the slightest shake of his head as the murmuring in the room faded.

"No."

Soren remained frozen with her hand around the dagger, angled low towards Caellum's back, as Garridon's voice entered her mind. Her eyes widened a fraction at the glow in Garridon's gaze as he paced the room with the other gods once more. She followed him, watching as he inclined his head and narrowed his eyes. Caellum's head remained bowed, but Sadira moved slowly, glancing from the corner of her eye to where Soren stood.

"Why?" she returned, but he did not answer. Soren winced as she felt claws invade her mind, reaching for the parts kept sacred for the Lord of Night. She tried to resist, yet the hand was demanding, grabbing at every thought she had and clutching her deepest wishes and desires before releasing them and looking for something else.

Her head pounded.

"Someone else has been here," he said. He released her mind from his grasp as he walked past her, forcing her to step back from Caellum. Her back met the stone wall, and she released the grip on her dagger as Garridon turned his back on Soren and stood directly behind Caellum and Sadira, shielding him. Soren frowned and pondered why Garridon would not approve of her reclaiming her rightful place as queen. She was torn between the will of two men: her god, and the man who had guided her for so long. Regardless, she could not risk attacking now, not with the god's power between her and her target.

"Time—"

"Is—"

"Nearly—"

"Up."

The gods spoke quickly as light filtered back into the room, highlighting the crack on the table. Their images flickered and ebbed, like they had before they cemented themselves into this world. Soren looked up at the moon slowly creeping from the sun, bringing the sky to life once again. She peered around Garridon's back at the faces of the rulers, a mixture of frustration and confusion. Soren was indifferent to the prophecy's outcome, knowing the dark creatures it referenced were controlled by a man who would ensure no harm came to her.

"What more can you tell us?" asked Larelle. "Anything." she pleaded. Soren looked to where Nerida stood, peering down at her descendant with sympathy. The relationships between each god and ruler were so different. While Keres appeared to approve of Nyzaia, Vala refused to acknowledge Elisara at all. The light in the room radiated, piercing through the gods' forms, whose eyes widened as they shared a panicked look. Soren was not the only one to notice.

"What's wrong?" Caellum asked. The image of the gods flickered.

"Prepare—"

"For—"

"War—"

"Death."

Soren approached the table, trying to get a better look at Garridon as he began to fade.

"Outer—"

"Border—"

"Breached—"

"Beyond the Unsanctioned Isle." The rulers pushed from their seats, desperate for more information. Sadira shared a panicked look with Caellum, and he rubbed her arm. Soren looked up at the reappearing sun.

"Fourteen days—"

"Fourteen nights—"

"They come to fight—"

"Prepare yourselves."

A full beam of light streamed into the room as the gods faded, but not before Soren locked eyes a final time with Garridon, who stared intently at her before vanishing completely. Stunned silence fell across the group. *Fourteen days.* Soren hoped the Lord of Night would return to her dreams before then to prepare her for this time. Perhaps this was her chance to take the throne amid the chaos of war, a war the rulers would not win. Yet when she surveyed the room, there was no denying the unity between the rulers and their closest confidants, as Kazaar comforted Elisara, and Alvan and Larelle spoke in hushed, hurried voices. Farid and Nyzaia stood opposite one another, deep in conversation, and Caellum and Sadira remained seated, holding hands. Soren frowned at the small voice in her mind, reminding her she was alone.

"So, what are we going to do?" Soren asked, breaking the groups from their intimate discussions. They turned to look at her.

"We?" Nyzaia narrowed her eyes.

"The entire realm is at risk, is it not?" asked Soren. "That includes Garridon, my primary focus." She was not lying, though she cared more about learning their next strategy to reveal it to the Lord of Night when he returned. Perhaps offering him such information would please him and he would allow her to keep her realm.

"They said the outer border beyond the Unsanctioned Isle, which means an attack is coming to Vala or Keres," Elisara said to the room.

"Keres makes the most sense. The mountain ranges along Vala would delay an attack and offer the realm more safety," said Nyzaia, and Farid nodded beside her.

"The land where the port of Myara sits is flat compared to Vala and offers easy access," he added.

"What does that matter when the creatures can fly? They could easily infiltrate either realm," Caellum said, and annoyingly, Soren agreed. Larelle and Alvan glanced at one another, and Larelle bit her lip.

"You two," Soren said, pointing at them. "You know something."

Alvan reached for Larelle's hand and nodded reassuringly at her.

"When I was taken..." Larelle hesitated, twisting her hands in the skirts of her gown. "There is much I learned from being with the creature, a lot of which can be discussed in the coming days. But most importantly, they are not simply *creatures*."

"What do you mean?" asked Sadira in her frustratingly gentle tone. Larelle exchanged a look with Alvan before turning back to the rulers with a sad smile.

"They can transform. They turned into humans like us—spoke, thought, and planned like us. We are not simply dealing with winged creatures."

Chaos ensued as the rulers yelled multiple questions, drowning each other out. Sadira squeezed Caellum's hand and rose; she made her way to Larelle. Alvan stepped back as Sadira embraced her. Soren tilted her head, watching as Sadira released Larelle and held her hands.

"Are you okay?" she asked. Larelle's eyes watered before she swallowed and nodded, her smile strained. The queen of Nerida reminded Soren of her sister: the innate kindness, the adoration from others, yet Larelle commanded a room in a way Soren both respected and envied.

"I do not know if it is all of them," Larelle continued. "But my point is, they could have some creatures on land in human form and others in the sky—a two-pronged attack."

"Making Keres the likely location," Farid confirmed, glancing at Nyzaia like a soldier waiting for command. Nyzaia looked at Kazaar, the only military commander in the room.

"It would be wise to move forces to Keres yet leave enough in each realm to guard entry points if needed," Kazaar said. "If you will host us all?"

Nyzaia nodded, and Soren sighed inwardly. She did not think she could take fourteen days with them all in one place.

"We must leave immediately so we can plan our arrival," Kazaar said.

"I will send Vlad to Vala to bring the forces and return the talisman," Elisara said, and Alvan nodded.

"I will return to Nerida to alert the forces and collect Zarya," said Alvan, and Soren scoffed. She did not think war was an appropriate place for a child, but then she did not understand the draw of motherhood or the need to be close to family.

"I trust you with the talisman," Larelle said, passing it to Alvan to return it.

"I can return to Garridon," Soren said, an opportunity to get the soldiers on her side as they travelled to Keres. Caellum turned in his seat to look at her with narrowed, surveying eyes. He did not speak.

"Thank you, Soren," Sadira said, still standing beside Larelle. Her tone was clipped, and her lips tight. *She does not trust my intentions.* "Sir Cain will take the talisman for now." Soren stepped forward, hand on the pommel of her sword as she opened her mouth to protest. Sadira had learned nothing when it came to commanding Soren. "But you can accompany him," Sadira added, and Soren had no chance to protest further because Elisara's voice cut across the room.

"So, it is agreed?" Elisara asked, and the group nodded. Soren surveyed their expressions and wondered if any of them were truly prepared. While Soren had not been physically involved in a large-scale war, she had been at war with Caellum's family for as long as she could remember. The rulers all glanced at one another, the air heavy as the realisation settled upon them all. Each reached for the hand of the person with them: Nyzaia with her captain, Elisara and her commander, Larelle and her lord, and Caellum and his betrothed. Soren crossed her arms, her blood running cold.

"We head to Keres and prepare for war," Larelle confirmed.

Chapter Forty-Seven

Sadira

Growing up, Sadira had an interesting relationship with the sun. There was a time when she worshipped it for the life it gave plants and flowers, but when she learned to grow plants herself, the sun offered little more than light on a dark day. After living on a windy island for years and then moving to a realm often cool and rainy, the warmth of Keres offered Sadira a new appreciation for the sun.

The rays warmed her skin as she gripped the stoned wall along the tiled terrace. She had never seen so many brightly coloured patterns, a stark contrast to the dark woods she had become accustomed to in Garridon or the stone and ivy of Doltas Island. The terrace attached to her room was on the side of Tabheri Palace, closest to the busy streets in the city. As Sadira closed her eyes, she heard the calls, the hustle and bustle of readying markets she desperately wished to spend her day exploring instead. While she did not think she could live in such a city, it made for an exciting change to the peace and quiet of the gardens her rooms overlooked in Antor.

They left the neutral city through the Keres gate immediately after sending word to their homes to have possessions packed and ready for collection. It felt odd not returning to Garridon. By the time they reached the palace, they were exhausted and separated to their assigned quarters with the agreement to meet the following morning. Yet now it was morning, and Sadira was not ready to face the looming threat. Yesterday's revelations were a lot to take in, leaving her drained as they travelled to Keres. She spent the journey attempting to recall every detail of their encounter with the gods. She wished she had written down everything the gods had said about the creatures and sword. When she tried to recall the specifics, she was distracted by the image of Garridon. Sadira had struggled to read her god or understand his views on the tense dynamic between his descendants, but she was positive Soren piqued his interest. She did not think Caellum had noticed, but Sadira saw Garridon's stolen glances at her sister. Nevertheless, Sadira would happily take Garridon's uncertainty over Vala's outburst against Elisara. While she imagined most would have latched onto Vala's words about the sullying of her bloodline, Sadira was more focused on Kazaar's unwavering defence of his queen. Sadira admired Kazaar's attitude and would also defend those she loved just as fiercely should it be required of her.

Sadira smiled as arms wrapped around her waist, and a gentle kiss graced her bare shoulder.

"Good morning," Caellum murmured onto her skin before resting his chin in the crook of her neck, pulling her closer. "You look beautiful today."

Sadira blushed. Her dress was far thinner than her usual gowns, the sunset shades blending into the red rooftops of the city. Caellum's thumb stroked the small triangular cut out over Sadira's torso, no bigger than her fist.

"Did you sleep well?" Sadira asked, moving her hands to his.

"How could I not with you beside me?" he asked. She smiled again. "And you?"

Sadira nodded. "As well as to be expected, given the pressures upon us." It felt so right yet wrong to stand with Caellum overlooking Tabheri, as if it was immoral to do anything else other than worry for their people.

"Are you not warm with your hair down?" Caellum asked, combing his fingers through it.

"It is impossible not to be warm here," Sadira chuckled, though some of that warmth left her as Caellum withdrew and stepped back into their rooms. She turned to see what he was doing. The light cast her silhouette across the patterned floor as Caellum strolled in his loose white shirt to grab a green ribbon from the dressing table. He stroked the silk through his fingers.

"A small reminder of our realm," he smiled, motioning for Sadira to turn. She tossed her loose curls over her shoulders and shivered as his fingers grazed her nape. Neither had addressed their moment in the tavern. It was not because Sadira was embarrassed; she simply did not wish to ruin their contentment. But she would be lying if she said she did not ache to experience more. Sadira swallowed as Caellum tugged and tied the ribbon. His hand trailed down her back to the tips of her hair, dangling against her skin. He moved his hands back around her waist.

"I suppose we should go," she sighed, and Caellum squeezed her waist.

"Let's have one more minute together before we must play king and queen."

***

Sadira was grateful for the up-do as she fanned herself below the palm tree. One of Nyzaia's guards, Jabir, had met them at their door to escort them to Nyzaia's father's chambers, the quietest and most secure room in the palace. It was smart, given the sensitivity of the conversation. The rooms were eerie when they entered until they reached a high-walled terrace. Dust coated the furniture, reminding Sadira of the owner's death. While the terrace overlooked the city, it resembled a tropical garden in size and greenery. At first, Sadira had welcomed the plants for their shade but was now conscious of the humidity.

Sadira was comfortable in the silence with Caellum as they waited for the others. Slipping off her silk slippers, she breathed a sigh of relief as her feet met the cool shaded tiles beneath the table.

Seeking distraction, she propped her elbow on the table and rested her head on her fists, watching Caellum as he made quick work of slicing the stone fruit in his left hand, with the knife in his right. Juice dripped down the side of his thumb as he placed the pieces in a ceramic bowl. She focused on his lips as he licked it off his finger and reached for a cloth to wipe his hands. He smiled.

"What?" he chuckled, and Sadira blushed.

"Nothing. I was just thinking," she said. He grinned before biting into a slice of fruit.

"About?"

Sadira watched his lips intently as he bit into another piece and licked his lips.

"Just that your fruit looks good," she mumbled, clearing her throat. Caellum reached for another piece and leaned towards her. She opened her mouth for him as he slid the small piece in, their eyes locking as she chewed.

"What?" she laughed, and he shook his head.

"Nothing, the fruit looks *good*." She rolled her eyes at his mockery.

"I am not interrupting anything, am I?" called Larelle, padding onto the terrace with a sly smile. Sadira expected an interrogation later.

"Not at all," Sadira said, rising to greet her friend. Sadira was desperate for a moment alone with her to check she was truly okay.

"Oh, really?" Caellum mouthed to Sadira, who turned and greeted Larelle with a warm kiss on the cheek.

It was not long before Elisara and Kazaar arrived, followed closely by Nyzaia. Farid closed the door behind them and stationed himself outside. It struck Sadira that this was the first time in a while with only the rulers in one room, Kazaar being the only exception. She did not expect the pair to be separated any time soon.

"Where do we begin?" Nyzaia asked. Elisara looked at Kazaar, the only one with extensive knowledge of the intricacies of battle.

None of them had prepared for the throne, let alone a war on the kingdom.

"We need a plan for where we should position the infantry, as well as strategic movements to attack on the defence rather than offense, seeing as we do not know the numbers we will face." Kazaar looked at Larelle, an unusual softness in his eyes. She smiled politely at him. "But to do that, we must know everything we can about what we are facing and to decipher what the gods told us."

Sadira reached to squeeze Larelle's hand as she retold her experience with the creatures. The group remained silent, allowing her time and patience to retell the tale. She told them of the creature's transformations and their appearances, and Sadira refrained from gasping when she referred to Osiris and Arik, recalling the creature that had tried to kill her and Caellum at the ball with its golden-ringed eyes. Discovering now that it possessed human intelligence left an uneasy feeling in her stomach.

Larelle recalled everything she could, including her suspicions that Osiris knew more about the prophecy and talisman and the names he referenced to Larelle, which she had never heard. When she was finished, the group was quiet as they took in the new information. Kazaar was the first one to speak.

"We must work on the assumption that even in human form—whether that is all or some of them—they still cannot be killed by anything other than the Sword of Sonos, which poses difficulties given we only have one." Sadira glanced at Caellum, and he nodded, urging her to speak.

"On the subject of the swords," she began, hoping she was not betraying any sacred trust of the Wiccan clans. "I think there is a way to imbue a normal sword with similar power. I cannot promise it will work, but I can try."

Kazaar frowned and peered at Elisara. "Could you imbue it with our blood as a first step? Would that be enough to mimic the Sword of Sonos?" he asked.

"I could try, but I do not understand how your blood affects them." Sadira wondered aloud. Nyzaia shifted in her seat and glanced at the pair.

"You should tell them," said Nyzaia, and Elisara stiffened.

"It is not only my choice," Kazaar said. Sadira looked at Larelle to determine if she knew what they referenced, but she appeared equally as confused. Elisara sighed and reached for a tie at the back of her neck that held up her dress. With a gentle tug, she held the panels to her chest, careful not to expose herself. Allowing one panel to loosen, Elisara exposed a small scar that glistened silver in the stream of sunlight floating over her and Kazaar. Sadira squinted, trying to identify the mark. She could not make out what it was from here. Kazaar removed his leathers and pulled his shirt aside to reveal a similar mark on his collarbone.

"It is a celestial tie," Elisara said, looking at Nyzaia, though the revelation did not relieve Sadira's confusion.

"There was a book in my father's study called *Myths and Lies of Ithyion.*" Nyzaia removed her hands from the table and placed them in her lap. "It has various odd pictures and tales in it, many of which I have not had the chance to read. However, there was a page on celestial ties. It is a tie bestowed upon two individuals who share a destiny. The Celestial Gods grant the bond when two beings finally acknowledge their connection to one another and allow their essences to merge."

Elisara and Kazaar nodded as Kazaar gently tied her dress back into place. Caellum shifted beside Sadira, who glanced sideways at him. He did not meet her gaze but looked at his ring, twisting it around his finger. A weight settled on Sadira's chest, and she attempted to push her pain down, keeping her face neutral. Sadira could not help but question Caellum's feelings for Elisara, given his reaction to the news.

"So, what does that mean?" Sadira asked, insecurity pounding within her heart.

"We can speak to one another silently," Elisara said. "Apparently, it grants us access to one another's power, but we are yet to find any truth in that."

Larelle cleared her throat.

"Is *that* the truth?" Larelle asked. Elisara jerked her head back at the accusation. "I do not mean to offend, but if you cannot share power, then how can either of you explain the odd shadows oozing from your feet when the creatures attacked? Or the fact your combined blood can paralyse them?" The others in the room glanced at one another with confusion, signifying they had not seen the shadows Larelle referenced. Kazaar rested his hands on Elisara's shoulders to lower them. She could not meet Larelle's eye. Sadira understood why Larelle asked. After all, Kazaar and Elisara had kept this from the group long enough. What else were they hiding?

"That does not imply we share powers; neither of us had those abilities beforehand."

Caellum finally spoke beside Sadira. "That's not true."

"It's ironic that *you* believe me a liar," Elisara scoffed, but he did not bite at the insult. Sadira straightened and raised her chin, preparing to defend Caellum if needed.

"We all heard Vala accuse him," said Caellum. "She said he had tainted you with his darkness, which implies the shadows Larelle saw seeping from you both were *his*." Sadira looked down at her engagement ring, repressing her feelings as Caellum hurled accusations at Kazaar, the man his first love had clearly moved on with. "Even if you did not know it," he added as an afterthought. Sadira refrained from smiling, twisting her ring so the stone sat perfectly central. Adding that latter part proved he had grown, though worry still ate away at her.

Sadira recalled Vala's odd reaction to what Elisara had shown her in the temple, and how the goddess jerked back, her shock mirroring the gods.

"Is the mark what you showed Vala?" asked Sadira, and Elisara nodded.

"When light meets dark in the rarest of times, when all that is left is the last of the lines," Larelle breathed. "What if you are that part of the prophecy? If Kazaar were to have some kind of power related to darkness and Elisara to light, then it would fit."

Elisara reached for Kazaar's hand on her shoulder and squeezed. *They are communicating.* Sadira glanced at Caellum to see if he had picked up on it, too, though she was unsure if his narrowed eyes were because he had or if he simply chose to glare at the commander instead. Larelle tapped her fingernails on the table and took a deep breath.

"Given how much you have already kept from us all, it would be polite to share your thoughts with one another aloud in our presence," Larelle said firmly. Kazaar had the decency to glance down at the scolding, but Elisara raised her chin to meet Larelle's eye in challenge.

"Perhaps it is the tie of light and dark that affects the creature, who could be born of a similar power to whatever lies beneath Kazaar's veins?" Nyzaia suggested.

"Could we stop accusing Kazaar of being filled with darkness? He is standing right here!" Elisara snapped.

"It's okay," Kazaar murmured.

"No, it is not! Everyone assumes we have some untapped power that can be controlled and that we—*you*—are hiding something." Elisara continued with a raised voice, and Nyzaia reached for her hand.

"We do not think it is a bad thing; we are thinking strategically. If your blood can recreate a version of the sword, then think of what we might be able to do if either of you can wield whatever potential powers have been gifted upon you," Nyzaia said.

Elisara leaned back in her seat, seemingly defeated.

"Could that be possible?" asked Larelle. "If Sadira channels her efforts in trying to imbue swords, could the two of you focus on trying to access any other power?"

The pair remained silent, and Larelle clenched her jaw, seeming to refrain from scolding them for a second time. Sadira did admit it was becoming frustrating. Eventually, Elisara nodded.

Roles were assigned to the group. Nyzaia assumed responsibility for the infantry and begrudgingly accepted Caellum's help, who also offered Sir Cain's support when he arrived from Garridon. Larelle agreed to research and read through *Myths and Lies* and Sadira's Wiccan book, and Sadira planned to channel her efforts into deciphering the gods' messages while experimenting with imbuing new weapons.

"Thirteen days left," Larelle said as they all stretched their backs and stood after the long meeting, the sun now setting over Tabheri. "Thirteen days to figure this all out and prepare."

Sadira reached for Caellum's hand, but he had already begun to walk for the door ahead of Elisara and Kazaar. Sadira cast her eyes downward, blinking rapidly and smoothing invisible wrinkles in her dress.

Thirteen days with all of us together under one roof.

Chapter Forty-Eight

Elisara

"Why the recent change to red gowns, Elisara?" Larelle asked from the vanity, where Sadira stood behind her, twisting Larelle's curls into an up-do at her guidance. Elisara refused to meet Larelle's eye. Had they been alone, she might have addressed how Larelle had spoken to her and Kazaar before the other rulers.

"It is not *all* gowns," Elisara mumbled, adjusting the thin golden chains draped over her chest and shoulder, forming the upper half of the dress before connecting with a fitted red bodice; sheer panels highlighted the slight radiance of her skin after sitting in the sun for the latter half of the afternoon. The same gold chains draped across her hips before falling into a waterfall of velvet, the open slit moving as she strode to the mirror. It was customary for the realm to host a ball in acknowledgement of another ruler's presence. Nyzaia had suggested it so the people of Keres could witness the unity of their rulers during such pressing times.

"It's Kazaar's favourite colour." Nyzaia grinned from where she sat cross-legged on her bed, waiting for the others.

"Nyzaia!" Elisara scolded, meeting her eye in the mirror.

"I am assuming he also likes an exposed leg, given the last dress she wore here also donned a slit." Nyzaia wiggled her eyebrows at Larelle, who covered a laugh. Elisara rolled her eyes and pulled back her curls, clasping half up with more gold pins before placing her crown atop it. It was odd being in a room with the other women. Larelle had suggested it, and Nyzaia had promptly agreed for want of a distraction, and Elisara could not say no to that.

"Are you wearing the same thing underneath as last time?" Nyzaia asked, and Elisara glared.

"No," she mumbled, pulling the slit closed to hide the gold garter. Nyzaia's grin widened. Before she could say anything else, Elisara sat down beside her, looking at Larelle and Sadira.

"So, Larelle. Have you heard from Alvan?" Sadira smiled and finished twisting Larelle's hair.

"He should arrive this evening," Larelle said, though her expression remained neutral. The other women shared a look.

"And how will you be greeting the lord?" asked Nyzaia. Sadira sat next to Larelle, resting her chin in her hand as she looked at the queen.

"What do you mean?" Larelle asked, looking away. Elisara exchanged another look with the women in shared understanding.

"Larelle, it is clear he is in love with you," Sadira emphasised.

"He is not," Larelle said, readjusting the off-shoulder sleeves of her thin peach gown. She scratched her head and looked away.

"Something has happened," Nyzaia said, smirking. Elisara smiled at her. Nyzaia was so often surrounded by men that she rarely talked with the women. She did a good job of hiding her pain and contributing to the conversation, but Elisara caught the rare moments when her smile slipped, and her mind wandered to Tajana. Elisara refrained from squeezing Nyzaia's hand. She, too, felt the pain of betrayal, even if Talia had been a friend rather than a lover. But Nyzaia would acknowledge her feelings on her own terms, and Elisara did not wish to force her into that position. Larelle tilted her head back and sighed.

"Fine, we nearly kissed."

"Only nearly?" Sadira exclaimed. Larelle rose from her seat and paced the room. She bit at the skin around her nails, indicating another emotion was at play, like worry or guilt. Falling for someone new after losing the love of your life must be painful, and it almost made Elisara forget how Larelle had spoken to her earlier.

"I do not know why we did not. He was holding my face, and I was crying, and we rested our foreheads against one another, and then... nothing," Larelle rambled.

"Did you want to kiss him?" asked Nyzaia.

"Yes, no—I don't know." Larelle sighed. "Am I a bad person? To want someone else after losing Riyas?" Sadira rose and twisted Larelle to look at her.

"Note your past tense, Larelle. He has been gone for so long. You *deserve* happiness." Larelle smiled, but the grief was clear within it. Elisara could not imagine what it would be like to move on from Kazaar if she were in Larelle's position. While she had known him for years, her feelings had heightened in such a short time. She felt more for Kazaar than she had after years with Caellum. She glanced down at the realisation all could be lost in thirteen days. She lost her smile, and Nyzaia bumped her shoulder, frowning.

"Do you think we will ever be able to do this again?" Elisara asked, surprised to find herself in a situation where she enjoyed the company of all four women. She barely knew Larelle until a month ago, and Sadira was the woman who had captured the heart of the man who betrayed her. Even so, Elisara liked Sadira. She wore her heart on her sleeve in a way that gained Elisara's trust.

"We will," Larelle said. "There will be a day in the future when we all sit like this, whether we are laughing or crying. We will all be together. We will win." Elisara was inclined to believe her, given the confidence in her tone.

"No more sad thoughts," Nyzaia said. She rose and took Elisara's hands. "While I will never understand your fascination with the male species, it is time they stare at the beauty before me." She smiled, and Elisara hoped she had genuinely forgotten about Tajana for the evening as she led them to the ball.

***

Amber liquor tasted like fire, Elisara decided as she downed her third glass of the evening and waited for a passing servant to refill it. Being in Keres reminded Elisara of her mother, even more so since watching the visions at the Neutral City. Now, she saw Vespera in every corner with Razik, keeping their love a secret. No one had spoken about the visions; it was easier to repress their pain in favour of worry about the kingdom instead, easier to focus on the next steps than replay the image of their families accepting their fates and hearing Edlen's screams. Elisara gulped, tears stinging her eyes as a servant refilled her glass. She pretended not to crave the taste of fire on someone else's lips as she leant against the brick wall, staring at the staircase descending into the hall. Being in Keres dressed in *red* sent Elisara's thoughts spiralling, remembering the last time she was here. It left her with a lingering sense of defeat, given the position they were in now and the expectations placed upon her and Kazaar. Elisara focused on her breathing to ignore the frustration. She did not have any other power, and even Kazaar's ability to wield all four elements was not enough against the creatures. They still had that secret. Larelle's words rang through her mind about already keeping so much from them, and Elisara ignored the pang of guilt, too afraid of what they might say if they discovered the extent of Kazaar's powers.

As she turned from the wall and nodded her thanks to the servant, she felt his presence—the acute awareness of the other half of her soul approaching. A gentle breeze tickled her back, and given there were no open windows, she knew it was his way of greeting her. Elisara did not turn, distrusting her ability to not kiss him. She had not felt his lips since that night in the tent by the Vellius Sea, and every day that went by was a tear in her skin as her heart tried to break free to reach him.

"Careful, or you might lose all your inhibitions to drink." His voice was sultry in her ear. She knocked back the drink, and the glass nearly cracked when she placed it on the table. Kazaar glanced sideways at her, and Elisara ignored his worry.

"Had you lost your inhibitions the last time we were here?"

she asked, tracing her finger around the glass. Kazaar trailed his finger up her back, and she glanced around. No one was watching, not even Vlad, who Elisara instructed to relax for the evening. He appeared to be doing just that as he leaned against a wall, clinking glasses with a beautiful Keresian woman. Nyzaia sat drinking with Farid while Sadira and Caellum danced with one another. Larelle stood by an archway, her back to the crowd as she watched the palace entrance.

"What makes you say that?" he asked, sensing the frown in her voice.

"It was odd that you so suddenly found yourself wanting... more." She gasped when his hand gripped her wrist, spinning her to face him. Yet when she turned, she watched his back as he guided her away from the loud music and laughter. Elisara did not question Kazaar but followed him through a maze of dimly lit corridors. She stumbled when he stopped and pulled her into an alcove. Elisara bit her lip to keep from smiling at the memory.

Their positions were almost identical. Her back was against the wall with Kazaar's hands on either side of her head. The short distance between their bodies crackled with tension.

"My wanting you was not *sudden*, Elisara," he murmured, staring deep into her eyes. "My want for you, my desire—my need—has been in every part of my body and soul since I laid eyes on you." His hand moved from the wall to trail down her neck, his finger slipping beneath the chains to stroke the moon on her collarbone. "I have known long before this celestial tie that you would be mine one day. It took every part of me to withdraw from you after I saw the hatred you had for me and after I understood my part in the pain you endured." He grazed her breast, trailing his hand to her hip. She swallowed as his grip tightened. Kazaar inched closer, resting his other forearm against the wall. "I do not need a mark to tell me I want you; I do not need our powers to intertwine to know I want you. I do not need to hear the inner workings of your mind to know how *deeply* I want you." He caught her hand

and moved it to his chest, and Elisara gasped. "I need only what beats in my chest, for you and you alone, to know that I. Want. You."

Elisara did not wait a second longer to crash her lips to his. The taste of alcohol from her lips vanished with the taste of him, of fire, of desperate need. The distant music faded as he teased her with his tongue. Kazaar was darkness and desire, and Elisara did not wish to extinguish it with light; she wished to be consumed by it, to fall into it with him and only him. To dance in the darkness, a world made just for them. She groaned when he nipped her lip and gripped the back of her thighs, lifting her in one fluid motion. She felt how much he wanted this by the strain of his trousers pressing against her. As though he were an animal that could not be caged from her any longer, Kazaar emitted a low growl as his hand found the golden garter.

"Were you planning for this, angel?" he asked, planting rough kisses against her neck. She tried to keep from grinding against him. "Were you hoping you would find yourself in an alcove again with me?" He bit her collarbone, and she cried out. "Hoping I would beg to have you against this wall?"

Elisara could not stop herself from writhing at his words. She gripped his hair and moved against him, allowing every dark thought she had of them together to run through her mind. Her hands moved between them to reach for the laces on his leathers. She whimpered as her fingers grazed the tip of his length. He buried his head into her neck and gripped her hips, leaving bruises she would find in the morning.

"I told you, angel. You will be surprised at how easily I can make you beg if I care enough to try." Suddenly, Kazaar pulled back and caught her as she fell back to earth. Her feet hit the tiles. Breathing heavily, he tied his leathers and leaned into her. "Trust me, I care, but I will not have to try hard."

One moment, Elisara found her footing, and the next, she was stumbling behind Kazaar, her legs weak as she clung to his hand

and followed him down corridors and up the stairs. Intoxicated on liquor and Kazaar's lips was a dangerous combination. The world spun as Kazaar turned her, twirling her into the silk bedding.

Moonlight flooded the room and merged with the flames on the walls while music from the hall downstairs drifted through the archway to the terrace. Elisara's eyes roamed Kazaar's body as he stripped off his leathers and stood only in undergarments, the bed dipping with his weight. His knee moved between her legs, and she willingly obliged, widening her stance to bring him closer. Elisara's eyes fluttered closed as his hands trailed her body, gripping the delicate gold chains covering her chest and dress.

"This is far too much clothing," he murmured, hunger burning in his eyes. The night breeze skated over her skin as he ripped the dress from her chest, the gold chains clinking as they fell to the tiled ground, and left Elisara naked beneath his stare.

"You owe me new gold," she jested. He gripped her legs and tugged her down towards him.

"You need no gold when you shine as bright as the stars." Elisara's mouth dropped at the compliment. No one had ever complimented her in such a way. "I do not expect you to be speechless tonight, angel." He slid his fingers against her, and Elisara sighed with contentment as she tilted back her head and relinquished all control.

"Eyes on me," he commanded, and they flew open to meet his stare. He pushed his fingers into her. She looked past Kazaar's hands to his undergarments, desperate for more. His fingers stopped moving. "I said eyes on me."

"They are on you, but a different part." She gasped as Kazaar pulled her into his lap, the sound swiftly melting into a moan with only the fabric of his underwear separating them. Elisara's eyes found the scars of their celestial ties aligned on opposite collarbones.

"Not laughing anymore?" he hummed against her ear. "This was what you wanted, was it not? More?" She straddled him as he pushed up onto his knees and held her in place, removing his underwear. When he sat back on his heels, Elisara bit her lip as her bare flesh met the length of his. "I said, that is what you wanted. Isn't it?" he asked. Elisara rested her forehead against his shoulder when he trailed his hands up her sides and squeezed her breasts. She clenched her thighs, but it did nothing to ease the burning tension between her legs while knowing he was so close to giving her what she wanted.

"Yes," she whimpered, and Kazaar shifted until Elisara was raised slightly above him.

"That sounds close to begging," he whispered against her lips before kissing her roughly, twisting a hand in her hair. He pulled lightly to tilt back her head and meet her eyes. Light and dark burned in his gaze, and his mesmerised look was the confirmation she needed to know her eyes matched his.

Kazaar lowered Elisara, brushing his tip against her. She did not think she could stay under his control for much longer. "What do you want, Elisara?" he asked, moving just enough to tease her. She tried to hold it in—tried to keep the tiny shred of herself that was her own, the only part she had not given completely to the man who had her soul. But when she stared back at his eyes and the tenderness and desire hidden amongst the threads of the universe, Elisara could wait no longer.

"You," she demanded. "All of you." He grinned and traced a thumb over her bottom lip.

"As my queen commands." Kazaar pushed into her and lowered her hips. Elisara cried out as wisps of shadow and light exploded from the pair in slow motion. It was as though the final pieces of her soul left her and permanently entwined with his. She rested her head against his, losing herself in the sheer ecstasy of being completely and utterly his as Kazaar moved in and out of her. Elisara locked her hands behind his neck and leaned back, forcing him deeper and relishing every inch. Their groans merged with the music floating outside, the tendrils of shadow and light dancing around them and tying them closer together.

"Fuck," Elisara cried as Kazaar bit her nipples, gripping her firmly.

"That mouth will be my undoing," he panted, pushing harder with each thrust. Elisara could no longer hold back the climax rising with every breath and wisp that licked her skin. Kazaar caught her as she fell back into the feeling, catching her mouth at the same time as they groaned in tandem, unravelling in the universe together.

Kazaar lowered Elisara to the bed and lay beside her, breathing in sync with her as the wisps faded into the moonlight. Elisara did not believe it was possible to feel such happiness, but she relished it. Who knew when they would feel like this again?

"You need to sleep; we need to be up early," he said. Elisara turned her head towards him.

She kissed him, grazing her tongue against his lips. "Do we have to?"

"Do not try to distract me," he mumbled, and she grinned.

"I am not," Elisara feigned innocence as she trailed her hand down his abdomen, hoping she could make him forget what they had agreed to do for their kingdom.

Chapter Forty-Nine

Larelle

Do the tiles look faded? Larelle assessed the tiles at her feet and paced the bright pattern. Pacing usually eased her mind, yet that morning, it only aided her rising fear. She rubbed her face with her hands and forced herself to stop. *They are fine. They are fine.* The steps out of the palace called to her, offering a reprieve to after pacing from the moment the sun rose past the canyons. She had left the ball relatively early the night prior. Alvan had not arrived in Keres with Zarya or Olden as intended, and Larelle had not received word of their delay. It left her uneasy. The chiffon of her gown was light as she raised it, navigating down the several steps before taking a seat outside the palace.

The bangles on her wrist, which Nyzaia had given her, jangled as she bounced her knees. Last night, she had tried to distract her mind to keep the panic from consuming her. Instead, she watched Kazaar and Elisara leave together, wondering what the Historian would think when he learned of their tie. Larelle chewed her lip; she was certain Elisara could handle herself.

Larelle had watched as Caellum and Sadira seemed to forget the world around them; they danced all night until Sadira left him standing on the dancefloor alone. Farid and Nyzaia acted strangely, too, though she could not decipher why.

Larelle focused on everyone else to ignore not just the fear that something had happened but the fear that she might not tuck Zarya in again or reveal to Alvan her wish to kiss him. Her head lifted suddenly from where she had been resting her sleep-filled eyes on her palms. *Horses.* She heard horses—more than just a few.

Time stilled as she stood, listening intently to every creak or sound in the palace courtyard. Birds appeared to chirp louder, and every droplet of water splashed in the rising rhythm of her heart. The gates pushed opened and she readied the smile on her face, only for it to fall short as Soren rode through, flanked by her wolves, with three on either side. Larelle's eyes tugged on the smallest with its tongue dangling from its jowls. It locked eyes with Larelle before glancing at its owner. Larelle let out a sigh that she was certain the gods would hear.

"Expecting someone else?" Soren asked, jumping from her horse and dangling the reins for a servant to pick up. Larelle said nothing. "Who is managing battle tactics? I need to know where to send the soldiers." She pushed past Larelle and began the steps.

"Nyzaia and Caellum."

"Not Vala's commander?" Soren asked. Larelle shook her head; he was too focused on working with Elisara to unlock any power that could help.

"Fantastic," Soren exclaimed with sarcasm. "Where would I find them?" Larelle turned to face her, already drained from a conversation with someone other than the person she desperately wished to see.

"The guard quarters are over there." Larelle gestured to the door to the left of the palace. "I am certain one of them will tell you." Soren nodded, and Larelle frowned at her nature, having expected more hostility. "What delayed you?"

Soren strode backward, her eyes gravitating to the courtyard entrance.

"We crossed paths with Nerida's army, and it made sense to journey with them." Soren tilted her head back quickly in a gesture. "Ask *him* why we are late."

Larelle spun, the courtyard a blur as her eyes immediately found his eyes, the hazel warmth that had become her home. Alvan grinned, the satchel hanging on his side lopsided as he pulled his crooked shirt that sat tight against his chest under his deep blue jacket. He had kept the stubble that had been growing out since her rescue. Larelle ran down the steps, begging her feet to already be planted firmly in front of him.

Larelle beamed for the first time in what felt like forever, a smile so big it could only be erased by one thing, and it was.

Alvan caught Larelle in his arms as she lunged for him, wrapping her hands around his neck as his hands met her waist. Alvan took that smile and tucked it away for safekeeping as his lips met hers so that no one would ever take her joy again. Larelle melted into his touch, tasting the salty air on his lips, a reminder of home. He gently caressed her back in a way nobody had in years. Larelle reluctantly pulled back for breath.

"Hi," he breathed, holding her tight against him as she stood on her tiptoes.

"Hi," she murmured, and then her smile faltered. "I was worried."

Alvan loosened his grip to lower Larelle, but his hands rested on the chiffon against her waist as she slid both palms onto his chest.

"*Someone* was too sleepy to make the entire journey and insisted she see every bread market in the Neutral City." Alvan rolled his eyes.

"You delayed preparations for a war because Zarya wanted to visit a new bread market?" Larelle slapped his chest, and Alvan grinned.

"No. I delayed a war because an *adorable* princess wanted to visit a new bread market."

"You spoil her," Larelle chastised.

"I'll spoil you just as much if you allow it." Larelle blushed at his lopsided smile.

"Mumma! Why is bread only good at home?" Zarya's tiny voice called, appearing through the gates with Olden. Olden shuffled with his hands on Zarya's shoulders, who tore pieces of bread off a brown loaf. He gave Larelle a gentle, knowing smile, which she returned. Since their conversation about Riyas and her father's involvement in his death, Olden was content to enjoy his days overlooking the ocean. He seemed distant, though, like he was finally at rest. He was adamant not to attend the Garridon ball, nor Mera, and she was surprised he had agreed to come all this way to Keres but was pleased Zarya had company.

Larelle scooped Zarya into her arms and spun.

"Hello, sweetheart," said Larelle while Zarya slapped her back.

"Why are you holding me so tight?" Zarya complained. *Gods, she is growing up too quickly.* Larelle set her down and knelt before her.

"I dare not risk dropping you or your bread!" she exclaimed, swiping the torn piece from her hand and eating it. Larelle made a face. *She's right. Orlo's is far better.*

"For someone who does not like it, explain why that's your second loaf," Alvan said, crossing his arms. Larelle took the loaf from her.

"Zarya! You cannot eat two loaves of bread for breakfast."

Zarya crossed her arms and pouted. "Fine, can I have it for lunch?"

Larelle refrained from laughing and nodded. A leather-clad figure strode behind Zarya, and Larelle glanced up to meet Kazaar's eye. He gave a brief wave of his hand, and Larelle held up a finger, signalling her wish to talk.

"Alvan, if you take Zarya into the palace, a guard should be able to escort her to our rooms," Larelle said, guiding Zarya towards Alvan.

"Will you be joining us in... *our* rooms?" he asked hesitantly. Larelle nodded and glanced in Kazaar's direction.

"I will after. I'm going to tell him," she whispered. Alvan mouthed a silent 'Oh,' realising what she referred to before backing away with Zarya and Olden.

"Good luck," Alvan said. He guided Zarya up the large steps and held her hand to aid her. She already wished to be beside him again. Kazaar approached Larelle.

"She's sweet, the princess," he said with a genuine smile. Larelle tilted her head; she did not think she had ever seen him smile properly. She recalled his early departure with Elisara last night and hid her own smile at her assumptions. "What did you wish to talk to me about?"

Larelle clasped her hands and straightened, meeting Kazaar's eye for one last sign to prove her wrong, but only warmth burned in his gaze.

"I wanted to ensure I had not offended you yesterday by suggesting you have kept some dark power a hidden secret."

Kazaar frowned. "It would take significantly more to offend me, Larelle."

She nodded and took a deep breath. "I do not know if you heard the added lines to the prophecy I added when we called upon the gods." Kazaar shook his head. "It was all such a blur." Larelle swallowed. When she said this, she could never take it back, but she saw Kazaar's devotion to Elisara and trusted that a man dedicated to protecting the kingdom was not someone who harnessed the power to end it. The Historian's warning rang through her mind again. Larelle's heartbeat quickened, and her mouth dried as she contemplated whether to trust her head or gut.

"The Historian visited me not long before we all gathered in Garridon," she said, and Kazaar raised his eyebrows. "He recited several lines from a history book, two of which were from the prophecy. The remaining two were 'Watch for the dark one that will bring suffering to all: the rise of old power, the Kingdom will fall.'" Kazaar tilted his head. She needed to be more direct. "He also said that there was something dark about you, and you could not be trusted." Larelle finished, allowing him a moment to process.

"He never did like me, and I always wondered why. Did he elaborate?" Kazaar asked.

"He said he could detect power, and you have a lot more than you allow us to believe. He sensed it when we were all in the city and saw darkness around you and Elisara." Something must have resonated, as Larelle noted the moment he glanced away. "Is there some truth to that?" She asked, beginning to doubt her trust in him. Kazaar shook his head.

"No, not the darkness. I am as oblivious to that as all of you are, including that which seems to seep from me when I am with Elisara. But the power..."

"You need not tell me if you wish to tell Elisara first."

Kazaar rubbed the back of his neck with a sigh.

"No, she is aware. She said it was my decision if or when I told anyone else." Kazaar peered around the courtyard, but nobody lingered except the two guards stationed by the gates. Larelle bit her tongue upon learning that, yet again, he and Elisara had kept something from the others. "I can wield all four elements," he said, his jaw tense. Larelle raised her eyebrows. She had not expected that to come from his mouth. "I would appreciate it if you did not tell anyone else until I am ready. My goal is to see if I can share that power with Elisara, hoping doing so could unlock whatever other power lies within us."

Larelle considered his words; it made sense to keep this from her and the others so as not to raise their hopes. At least Kazaar was acting honestly now by choosing to tell her. It eased her worry somewhat that she had been right to reveal the Historian's warning. An uncomfortable feeling settled on Larelle, though, when she realised she, too, kept a secret from the others on his behalf. Yet she had kept the Historian's words to herself and those closest to her until now.

Larelle nodded, understanding Kazaar's reasoning.

"I must go; I need every second with Elisara to find a way to win this war." Kazaar bid her farewell, and Larelle watched him leave, two lines repeating in her mind.

The power to awaken that of old lore lies in the soul of those with all four. She wondered when Kazaar first realised he could access all four powers, whether it coincided with the creature's return or whether Kazaar had unknowingly awoken a different old lore that none of them would yet face.

Chapter Fifty

Nyzaia

Elisara stood toe to toe with Kazaar. The pair assessed each other before Elisara twirled and swung the dull sword in her grip. The two replayed the same dance they had been playing for the last fifteen minutes while Nyzaia sat on the wall, watching. She squinted against the sun, beating down on the black gravel of the training yard. The burnt red wall felt hot beneath her palms as she dangled her legs from it.

The sun did little to cure her hangover. Farid had not questioned Nyzaia at the ball each time she signalled for another drink; he had simply been a silent companion. No matter how many times Nyzaia plastered on a smile while talking with the other queens, her mind always drifted to Tajana, seeking the spot where Tajana was usually stationed opposite her throne. Jabir had since taken the spot, but nobody could take the place in Nyzaia's heart, still reserved for Tajana, despite the pain she had caused.

"If they were not together when we saw them in the city, they definitely are now," Farid said from where he stood below her, legs crossed and leaning against the wall. Nyzaia liked Farid's odd moments of relaxation ever since they left the forge, but it was not yet enough to distract her from Rafik or Issam's absence. She had yet to see them since they parted ways.

"They left rather early from the ball," she mused.

"It is only right that someone had an enthralling night," he responded. Nyzaia gasped, feigning offence.

"Are you insinuating that drinking and discussing military tactics with me was not an enthralling night for you?"

"It was enthralling to watch," Jabir called from the other side of the wall. He scaled and jumped over it, landing beside Farid, whose stance quickly changed. He straightened, his posture rigid. Nyzaia wondered how long it would take for Farid to relax around others or if he ever would. "It wasn't very productive after the fifth drink."

Nyzaia rolled her eyes. Farid had made a good drinking partner and had not once questioned her wish to drown her sorrows as a distraction from the greater problems in their world. She was fairly confident they cheered to that in a toast.

"What are you doing here, Jabir?" asked Nyzaia, conscious that the conversation she wished to have with Elisara and Kazaar was a sensitive one.

He shrugged. "Ensuring Garridon and Nerida's soldiers settled in was not exactly a riveting task," he said.

Farid narrowed his eyes. "Doing your job is not meant to be riveting."

"Sorry, Captain. Is that your way of telling me to get lost?"

"Yes," Farid said bluntly, and Nyzaia burst out laughing.

"You heard your superior, Jabir. Back to work you go." Nyzaia said, jumping from the wall when Elisara and Kazaar paused for a water break.

"Seriously? My job is protecting you," Jabir argued.

"And at the moment, the most powerful people in the kingdom are all under my roof. I think I am safe." That put an end to the conversation. Jabir rolled his eyes, accustomed to Nyzaia's bluntness.

The yard was not big enough for the entire military, and most Keres recruits were trained in other places, too, like the desert and the forge. They currently set up camps along the edge of the Ashun Desert closest to the city, the only place big enough for four militaries after Vlad brought Vala's army shortly after Nerida and Garridon's that morning. Sir Cain, Garridon's commander, said the maze of tents acted as another defence to the city, confusing any attack on foot if they reached this far inland.

"This looks like a productive workout," Nyzaia called. Elisara jumped up after Kazaar knocked her to the floor and flicked her two braids over her shoulders, wiping the sheen of sweat from her forehead.

"I could think of better," she said. Kazaar kicked her shin gently, and she widened her eyes at him.

Definitely together, Nyzaia thought.

"We're just warming up to get the blood flowing. We're moving on to try and tap into more powers next," Kazaar said, and Elisara kicked the gravel.

"You do not seem pleased with the idea," Nyzaia said to her friend, and Elisara shrugged.

"I do not wish to let anyone down." She paused. "Or hurt anyone."

Kazaar tucked a stray damp curl behind her ear.

"You won't," he said gently. Nyzaia smiled at his tenderness and glanced at Farid, who raised his eyebrows briefly. Her smile faded. Tajana would have loved to tease Kazaar about this.

She wondered if Tajana and the others had discovered somewhere else or found other inhabited lands. Despite the pain she had caused her, Nyzaia hoped they had been far from Novisia before the creatures breached the Outer Border. Recalling what had happened to the ship of Larelle's lost love, Nyzaia did not think Tajana would survive an attack.

"What can we do for you?" Kazaar asked, pouring water over his head and shaking his hair.

"We, uh, wanted to talk to you both about something important," Nyzaia said, glancing to Farid again for confirmation he was comfortable with this decision. His blue eyes were honest as he nodded. "At this moment, we would like it to stay between the four of us." Elisara and Kazaar shared a look before facing them again. Swallowing, Nyzaia lifted her palm in sync with Farid to reveal the scar on their palms. Elisara and Kazaar's expressions faltered, and slowly, Elisara nodded slowly, knowingly.

"We need to know more about your tie," Nyzaia said.

***

Kazaar and Elisara listened in what Nyzaia could only describe as stunned silence as she retold the story of their tie, missing out the key fact of Farid's wings, though Kazaar appeared dubious when she claimed Farid had saved her on the rope, especially given he had trained recruits at the forge. Yet if he had doubts, he must have communicated them only to Elisara as neither of the pair interrupted.

"Did Keres show any sign of acknowledging it when he was present?" Kazaar asked. Nyzaia shook her head; she, too, was confused when her god had not mentioned it, especially after Vala's outburst when Elisara revealed her scar.

"Do you think Keres bestowed it, given you are both his descendants?" Elisara asked.

"What would that mean for ours then?" Kazaar asked, and they all frowned. Nyzaia recalled the ripped edge beside the page on celestial ties; they were definitely missing some key information. "So, can you...?" Kazaar tapped the side of his head.

"Not with words," Farid answered. "We can share memories and a general sense of one another's feelings, but we cannot converse." Elisara tilted her head, puzzled.

"What do you think determines the abilities each tied pair receives? Elisara asked, but nobody answered. Nobody knew.

"We had a specific question, which is why we raised it so soon before fully understanding the implications," Nyzaia began. Elisara propped her hands on the black gravel, where they all sat cross-legged and nodded. "Has there been an instance where the tie ever healed you in some way?" Nyzaia asked. Kazaar picked up piles of gravel, filtering it through his hands.

"Yes," he said. "In Garridon, my wounds healed almost instantly."

Nyzaia supposed that was common for matched pairs then. "My ribs were healed from the fall after we were tied," she said.

"A convenient thing to have as we journey into war," said Kazaar. Nyzaia had not thought of it like that, and then a more troubling thought crossed her mind. *What would happen if one of us died?* She did not want to find out. Elisara and Kazaar remained quiet for a few minutes, their pinkies touching in the gravel.

Elisara eventually voiced her concern. "Can we ask you something?" She shifted her hand, interlocking her fingers with Kazaar's. Elisara's gaze was on their hands as she stroked a thumb over Kazaar's.

"Of course," Nyzaia responded.

"Has anything *odd* happened since you became tied? Any different powers?" Nyzaia tilted her head and softened her eyes. Nyzaia knew why she asked.

She wished to know if they also shared the burden of accessing a unique power, one that may help to defeat the creatures. Nyzaia shook her head silently and sighed.

"No shared powers of any kind?" Kazaar asked. "Farid, you do not have access to her flame?" Nyzaia said no before Farid was forced to lie. Nobody knew Farid had any power, let alone the true extent of it, though she supposed the tie would one day prove to be a good explanation for Farid's flames. Though it still would not explain the wings.

"Will you tell us if you do?" Elisara asked, and they nodded.

"Have you tried yet?" Nyzaia asked.

"Someone is trying to put it off," Kazaar tilted his head at Elisara, who huffed.

"How can someone even share power? Everyone expects it to be easy like I can blink and gain your power." Elisara picked up a stone and began sharpening her sword.

"No one thinks it will be easy," Kazaar said softly.

"We will leave you to practice," Farid announced, rising to his feet. He offered his scarred hand to Nyzaia, who accepted. It was nice not to hide it from them.

"You will do it, Elisara. I know you will." Nyzaia patted her friend's shoulder before leaving them to their afternoon.

Twelve days. Twelve days remained for those two to access their power and for Sadira to imbue new weapons for thousands of soldiers. Twelve days for Larelle to research and find any other answers, for Nyzaia to work logistics for four armies, not to add somehow figuring out a plan for all the citizens during a war. The reality of what was being asked of them all settled on her shoulders.

"Thank you," Farid said. "For not telling them," Nyzaia smiled.

"I'll have to if I ever find a way to get my own pair of wings," she said, and Farid returned her small smile. "I suppose we should put Jabir out of his misery and have him tag along to the meeting with Sir Cain and Nerida's commander."

Farid did not answer.

"If you two are to work together, you must try to like him, Farid." She nudged his arm.

"I never said I did not like him," Farid answered, clenching his jaw. "I just do not trust easily."

Nyzaia regretted the jest. She had once been the same, untrusting of anyone new, but then she met Tajana and her syndicate, and over time, they had coerced her into a friendship. She thought of Rafik and Issam. Soon, they would have their first weekly debrief, a snippet of joy to ease the momentous expectations placed upon her shoulders.

Chapter Fifty-One

Elisara

Three days until war reached their kingdom, and Elisara was no closer to accessing Kazaar's power or any light within her than she was nine days ago. She wondered if she would ever be able to. Farid and Nyzaia could not read each other's minds, so perhaps the tie was simply different for each pair, or the wisps of shadow and light were not a power but simply a recognition of their bond. Elisara was cursed to feel like a disappointment, though she was not the only one. Sadira was no closer to imbuing weapons, and Larelle was no closer to uncovering new information. Nyzaia and Caellum were the only ones getting anywhere; they had coordinated all armies at the edge of Tabheri along a large map, highlighting the multiple options for defence and attack.

"Again," Kazaar commanded from where he sat cross-legged from Elisara on the hot gravel. Whenever Elisara returned to their chambers after training, she would find thousands of tiny stone indents across her body, usually from collapsing in frustration and lying on the floor to recover. Today, it was from their new approach: silent meditation. Elisara laughed the first time Kazaar suggested the technique, unable to imagine Kazaar ever sitting peacefully and reflecting on his own peace of mind, but then again, he was full of surprises.

Despite their rigorous training, Kazaar had still found time to *court* her in the last nine days. It was odd, being courted, mostly because they had already slept together—frequently—but also because Caellum never formally courted her, seeing as they were betrothed as children.

Kazaar woke her with breakfast each morning to ensure she was fuelled for the day and brought her his favourite warm drink in bed each evening. Their cool-down from training was a light stroll arm in arm around the palace gardens, and every night, Kazaar worshipped her as though she were a goddess. All those things made the training worth it.

Elisara focused on her breathing to centre herself, as Kazaar had explained.

"Find the source of your power," he breathed.

"What do you mean?" She opened one eye to peek at him.

"Close your eyes," he said without even opening his own to check she did. "I started this when I first used a power that was not my flame. It helped to understand and differentiate them.

"Vines, right? When you were seventeen?" she asked. He hummed in agreement. "How old were you when you finally had all four?" she asked. Kazaar sighed heavily.

"Are you using this as a distraction?"

"No!" Elisara exclaimed, closing her eyes again. "If I understand how you came to have four, maybe there is a commonality between them all, which can help us find this source of power within."

"Well, you know about the vines when I was seventeen. At eighteen, I accidentally sunk the ship."

"Air is the only one you have not told me about." She sensed his eyes open and opened her own. Kazaar's sleeves were already rolled up, revealing the marks on his arms. None suggested a tie to air. He unbuttoned several more on the shirt and pulled it aside.

"These swirls."

"Huh. I thought those were decorative."

Kazaar shook his head. "Nineteen. It is not a riveting story. Razik had come to watch training drills. Afterward, he came to my room and told me how disappointing I seemed before storming out. In a teenage fury, I thought about slamming the door behind him, and a gust of air did it for me. That's when I realised I controlled it." Kazaar leaned back on his arms, focusing on her face. "So, any deductions?"

Elisara roamed his other inked scars, hovering over the flaming knife again, the one he was reluctant to talk about.

"I will tell you when you can wield all four."

"Bribing is unfair," Elisara responded, running through the different origin stories in her mind and watching his fingers flex in the gravel. After arguing with Razik, Kazaar discovered his power for air. It made sense anger could trigger his powers, given his fiery nature, yet his earth power emerged when he stole from his father. That made less sense to Elisara, who struggled to connect the two. After failing his father's plans for a ship, his water power appeared. Elisara's eyes snapped up to Kazaar's face.

"Your father," she said. "Each time your power emerged was on occasions relating to King Razik." Kazaar frowned. "Stealing the bottle with vines from *his* office, sinking the ship upon *his* commands, slamming the door after *his* disappointment."

Elisara leaned forward, tracing patterns in the gravel as she waited for Kazaar's reply. She watched him, staring off into the distance towards the palace.

"Anger," he finally said. "There was a common emotion of anger towards him on each occasion."

Elisara nodded slowly, allowing him time to elaborate if he wished. There was seemingly far more to his relationship with his adoptive father than she realised.

"Should I try focusing on anger?" she asked.

"I do not think you have enough hatred or anger in your bones, angel." He turned back to her. "Focus on any powerful emotion that comes to you and the memories associated with it." Kazaar reached for her hands and shuffled closer, his knees brushing hers. Elisara watched as he inhaled and exhaled before mimicking him and closing her eyes.

One strong emotion. Grief? An image of Elisara's father's eyes flashed, and her fingers trembled, revisiting the fake mirage of him at the Vellius Sea. Betrayal? She thought of Caellum kissing her lady and searched for the emptiness she had felt, but it was difficult to imagine when Kazaar filled her entire being. How could she envision emptiness when all she saw was him? The tension at their proximity, their laughter on the Unsanctioned Isle, the first time he called her queen, their dance in Nerida, and the first time she wished to kiss him. Every part of her was filled with Kazaar. Her frustration at his secrets, his presence in her mind. His flirtatious words, his teasing words, their first kiss. His hands, his mouth. His understanding and desire. Him. Every part of her was filled with him. Passion was the only emotion she could fixate on as she focused on every memory with him, darkness engulfing her mind as she embraced the feeling of him, and then a flicker. Elisara gasped as it flickered again, deep in the corners of her mind.

"Anything?" Kazaar asked.

"A flame," she breathed.

"A flame? Or pure light?" Kazaar asked. Elisara kept her eyes closed to focus and explain the feeling and image in her mind. A white glow appeared, but it moved like a flame.

"A flame," she said confidently and opened her eyes. Kazaar's eyes remained their usual deep brown, crinkling with his grin. Elisara glanced down at the flame dancing in their palms.

"I am honoured that the first you should find creates flames in your eyes," he breathed, staring deep into hers and Elisara gasped. The flame disappeared. "You did it!"

"Did my eyes really glow?" she asked, shocked to finally conjure something after all their hard work.

He nodded. "A flicker of amber, like mine or Nyzaia's."

Elisara covered her mouth with her hands.

"But yours do not glow a different colour depending on the element." She frowned, and Kazaar shook his head.

"They used to, but they stopped changing not long after I mastered the powers."

Elisara nodded slowly, and a small smile crept onto her lips. They finally had something that might lead to more.

"I did it. I really did it," she said, focusing on that feeling again and her connection to him. She held out her palm, but no flame appeared. Frowning, she tried again. "Urgh!" Using her sword as a crutch, she pushed herself from the ground. The sword glinted in the sun as she swung it, distracting herself.

"Do you remember why you took that sword?" asked Kazaar with a daring look and mischievous smile. His own sword, the Sword of Sonos, screeched when it met hers. Elisara rolled her eyes as they went through their usual training motions.

"I wanted a reminder," she breathed. "That I had done something for my kingdom." Kazaar grunted and pushed back, a flourish of movements sending them round and round in circles. Elisara's sword hit his again, and she could have sworn light sparks burst from the connection. Kazaar dropped his elbows, and Elisara stumbled, their swords crossed between them.

"And you will do so again, with or without the power of all four." Elisara tried to look away from him but could not. "You will do so again, with or without whatever light and dark exists within us. Our blood is enough. It will take longer, but as long as all fighters have a weapon that mimics the Sword of Sonos, we will win."

"You do not know that, Kazaar," Elisara's voice broke, and her finger twitched on the hilt of her sword. She glanced down. The tendrils she so often saw wrapping around Kazaar's hand reached out to caress her skin.

"I know it, Elisara." She looked back up at the certainty in his voice. "There is no world that exists where I am not with you, which means we must win." They lowered their swords, magnetised by the tie within them, as Elisara leaned her head against his shoulder. Comfort enveloped her as Kazaar wrapped his arms around her, reaching for the back of her neck.

I can do this.

The comfort of the moment was disrupted when someone dramatically cleared their throat. Elisara refused to turn her head, unwilling to leave the safety of Kazaar's arms.

"*He has perfect timing*," Elisara said to Kazaar in her mind, who scoffed.

"*He always does.*"

The owner of the cough shuffled in the gravel, waiting. Elisara sighed and pulled back from Kazaar, greeting Caellum with an awkward wave.

"Sadira is ready for you both," he said plainly, glancing between the pair like he had every day since coming to collect them. Elisara recognised the downturn of his features. Something was upsetting him, though she did not believe it was her. Every day, he came at the same time. Elisara did not know why he bothered; they knew when to visit her. Kazaar plastered on a fake grin and intertwined his hand with Elisara's, who refrained from rolling her eyes. Kazaar did *this* every day, too. Caellum nodded and turned for the palace.

The cool air in the palace was a relief as Elisara kicked off her shoes and followed barefoot. Every day at noon, they gave their blood to Sadira, and every day Elisara hoped it would be the last. Sadira was yet to find success with the imbuement. Elisara smiled politely when she entered the small room that had become Sadira's workplace. Every surface was hidden by pots and jars and bunches of fresh and dried plants. Elisara did not know how Sadira managed working here each day; a few minutes gave Elisara a headache, overcome by the concoction of scents. Caellum assumed his usual spot in the corner beside the door. Sun streamed in through the glass windows to Elisara's right, who sat on one of the two chairs in the room opposite Sadira's main desk. Sadira returned Elisara's smile. She was unsure at what point the two had become civil, but their working relationship was far better than Elisara and Caellum's, or Sadira and Caellum's, for that matter.

Something had happened between them, given how quickly their behaviour around one another had changed. They did not touch or look at one another, and Elisara curiously wondered why.

Chapter Fifty-Two

Sadira

Sadira liked to associate her emotions with plants. Joy was a pale daffodil, and devotion was lavender. Melancholy was violets. But jealousy was an ivy that climbed and festered the longer you left it unattended. She felt it twisting now, suffocating and driving her apart from the man standing on the opposite side of the room while she drained blood from his first love.

Sadira and Caellum had barely spoken during the nine days since the welcome ball. One moment, they were dancing, and the next, they were arguing. She wished she had said nothing, but Sadira had spent all her adult life biting her tongue around Soren. She refused to diminish herself for another.

She replayed Caellum's reaction to Elisara's celestial tie, which spoke of a love that still existed and the pain upon realising Elisara was well and truly gone, belonging to another. Sadira had tried to forget it by reminding herself you never truly lost the love of your first. But when she thought about her reunion with Rodik, that had been enough for Sadira to know Caellum was her future. Sadira had bathed in his warmth when they danced at the ball, besotted with one another. Then Caellum had spun her yet failed to catch her when she twirled back. Instead, Sadira stood, waiting for his other hand while Caellum's eyes followed Kazaar and Elisara, who swiftly left the hall.

Every reminder of growing up in Soren's shadow had crawled across her skin then. She was the spare heir, and now, in Elisara's shadow, Sadira felt like a consolation prize again. She did not see the look in his eyes, though a gut feeling filled the blanks with one of longing. Perhaps trusting her gut reaction over logic had been her mistake. Dropping his hand, Sadira walked away. It took Caellum four seconds to follow. Four whole seconds, which she knew because she counted in the hopes he would follow and prove her wrong.

His hand clasped hers before he spun Sadira to ask what was wrong. She wanted him to know and realise without having to tell him, though it felt foolish now to expect someone to read her mind. "Is there space for me?" she had asked him, and silence followed. "Is there space for me in your heart when she still occupies it?"

"What?" Caellum stumbled over his word. "No, it's..." She left, and he did not follow that time. Their bed felt empty every night, with Sadira facing the terrace and Caellum facing the wall, leaving enough room for the ivy to grow between them.

"Ouch," Elisara gasped.

"I'm so sorry," Sadira mumbled, realising she held the knife too deep, distracted by her emotions. Sadira had lost count, but looking at the glass jar of silvery blood, it had been long enough. Sadira removed the blade and wiped the wound, mesmerised as it stitched itself back together.

"All done," Sadira said, as Kazaar helped Elisara from the stool, who was always slightly lightheaded after the collection.

"Same time tomorrow?" asked Elisara, and Sadira nodded, catching Caellum's eye. "You do not need to collect us," Elisara said to him. "We know when to be here."

Caellum opened and then closed his mouth, nodding stiffly as they left. Sadira rolled her eyes and busied herself by cleaning knives and wiping the table, moving jars before placing a plain sword on the table. Caellum did not leave.

"She is right, you know," said Sadira. Caellum finally met her eye. "You do not need to escort them here." Sadira pulled out the chair, readying to sit and work for the afternoon.

"Do you know why I escort them every day?" he asked.

"Yes," she sighed, taking a seat.

"I do not think you do," Caellum said firmly, crossing the room with his hands behind his back.

"Is it not so you can see the woman who occupies your heart?" Sadira pulled the Wiccan clan book towards her and feigned scanning the words on the page through her blurred vision. Caellum sighed.

"Yes," he said, and Sadira looked up, the pain like nettles wrapping around her heart. "I force myself to endure awkward civility as I collect and escort them here because if I did not, then the only time I have the opportunity to lay my eyes on you is when I stare at the back of your head once you have fallen asleep. We have not talked in days, Sadira, and it pains me. Escorting them here gives me fifteen minutes to watch you." Sadira swallowed back tears, trying to detect the sincerity in his words. "And watch how you furrow your brow as you precisely use your knife, and breathe in the scent of you that fills this room, and smile at the way the sunlight makes your curls glow. I stand in a room with two people I know dislike me because I would rather that than spend an entire day thinking only of you while you are somewhere else." Caellum stood on the other side of the desk and rested his palms on it, leaning towards Sadira, whose heart pounded.

"I am a man who was raised to be silent while on the receiving end of someone's anger or disappointment. I was silent when you voiced your concerns because I had hurt you and was clueless about what to do. I was silent when I watched Kazaar and Elisara announce their tie because I realised that in seeing the love between them just how much I had failed her when we were together." Caellum leaned further in. "I do not pretend to be perfect, Sadira. I know how flawed I have been in the last nine days, but please do not judge my distance as a lack of desire for you but a lack of love from when I was raised. Take my confession as a promise. A promise I will learn to use my mouth for not just words but for your lips, but only if you promise to tell me when I am wrong.

Because I cannot do this again, Sadira; I cannot be without you or your voice for nine more days and nights. I cannot."

Caellum's rambled confession had cut down the ivy twisting between them, allowing for flowers to bloom. Sadira's chest rose and fell as she took in his words, glancing from his eyes to his lips. She inclined towards him.

"Sadira! I think I have something," Larelle called, entering from the adjoining room. Caellum retreated and sat back in the chair opposite Sadira, his eyes still intent on her. Tucking her hair behind her ear, Sadira swallowed, smiling at Larelle. "Sorry, I did not realise you had company," Larelle said with a coy smile.

"It is okay; what have you found?" Sadira asked. Larelle glanced back at Caellum before walking towards Sadira, carrying the copy of *Myths and Lies of Ithyion* that Nyzaia had given her to pour over. Dust rose in the stream of light as Larelle placed the heavy book next to Sadira's. Both women were careful when using the books. Each book seemed as old as the other, bound in a similar dark leather, with scrawled ink and charcoal drawings faded on the worn pages. The only difference was the copy Larelle leant over was missing several pages, which had been hastily ripped out.

"This page here." Larelle flipped to one of the book's last pages and pointed to the top of the page in *Myths and Lies of Ithyion*, where it read '*Sword of So—*'. Sadira pulled it towards her. "It has to be, does it not? Look at the lines." Sadira opened her own book to the page on magical imbuement, lining it up beside Larelle's.

"The sword sketches are slightly different; this one is far more smudged." Sadira tapped Larelle's. "But the lines look the same until—"

"Halfway down!" Larelle said quickly. Sadira had spent the last nine days trying the incantation. It was not written in a language she recognised; thus, she had recited it with different inflections and pronunciations, yet none had worked so far. The stack of papers to her left contained every variation she had tried.

"The book is titled 'Myths and Lies,' so how can we be certain?"

Sadira peered at Larelle, whose hair was tucked into a bun, messy from hours of reading. Much of Larelle's research seemed like tales you would tell a child or around a campfire.

"What if the Wiccan copy came from a story or from *Myths and Lies of Ithyion*? Words can change and lose context over time. What if the version you have been using has been adapted over time, and this"—Larelle pointed to her page— "is the original." Sadira frowned, carefully reading the lines on both pages. They were definitely the same until halfway. While the second half contained some of the same words, it was significantly different.

"They told me the sword was created with this Wiccan book. I am unsure." Sadira flicked the page in the clan's book. *Had the clan been misinformed?*

"Stories change over time, like possessions. We do not know for certain if it was your specific clan book. They could have recalled it from memory for all we know." Larelle said.

"It seems a big decision based on a lack of concrete knowledge," Sadira said, but she was so desperate to be swayed by Larelle's excitement.

"There is nothing to lose. We could try," Larelle pressed. Sadira looked at Caellum, who had remained silent throughout the exchange.

"It is your words that wield the power. It is your decision," he said.

Sadira breathed in and nodded, pushing the books to either side of her and dragging the dagger between them. Sadira reached out her hand, and Caellum handed over the two jars of Kazaar and Elisara's blood. Carefully pouring one into the other, Sadira stirred, mesmerised again by how it sparkled.

Despite how many times Sadira had read the steps—the only part of the page in her language—she checked again and followed them one by one. With a brush, she painted each side of the dagger in their blood, using her index finger to draw three symbols from the book onto the blade. With the blood remaining on her finger, she marked the palm of her other hand and raised it above the weapon.

Sadira looked at Caellum one last time for belief she could do this. He nodded. Holding the page with her right hand, careful not to move her left. She had tried so many variations of the first incantation, but with this one, she trusted her natural reading and began. While she did not understand the language, she knew the incantation would imbue Elisara and Kazaar's blood into the weapon to mirror the Sword of Sonos, not only paralysing the creatures but killing them. The foreign words flowed from Sadira's lips, the language old, beautiful, and eloquent. Nothing happened at first, but as the words became clearer on her tongue, Sadira felt her hand warm. Larelle crouched beside her until she was level with the blade. Sadira continued the words—something felt different. It was working. She felt metal hit her hand and withdrew her palm as the dagger floated, balancing delicately before the three of them, watching with wide eyes.

The silver blood raised from the knife in droplets before reforming and twisting into glowing threads wrapped around the blade.

"Do we think it worked? Sadira whispered, scared to disrupt the power at play. The door to the room slammed open, and the blade clattered against the desk. All three looked at the disruptor with frustration.

Alvan stood before them, panting, his face flushed and clothes dishevelled. He braced his hands on either side of the door, his eyes instantly finding Larelle, who straightened from her crouch, her face immediately concerned.

"They are here," Alvan panted. "There is word from Myara."

Chapter Fifty-Three

Larelle

We are not ready, Larelle thought as Alvan flung the doors to the room open, with Larelle, Sadira, and Caellum following close behind, flushed from having run from one end of the palace to the other. Larelle had not been to the war room yet. The rulers typically held their daily debrief on the large terrace connected to King Razik's room during sunset.

Nyzaia looked at home here, though. The large hexagonal room bore abundant, arched, open windows overlooking the Ashun desert in the distance. A sizeable map of Keres was flattened against the floor with hundreds of placeholders for infantry groups, organised in a strategic layout.

Larelle took a place beside Elisara while Kazaar and Nyzaia leaned over the map, silent.

"Is it true?" Soren's voice was fierce as she entered, closing the doors behind her. She took a place next to Sadira, her polar opposite. Sadira wore a flowing peach gown, while Soren donned her Garridon armour despite the Keres heat. Nyzaia reached for the envelope to her left, held under a goblet of wine, and raised it to show the others a ripped, black ink seal. Nobody spoke as Nyzaia tore it open. Kazaar moved to Elisara's side, who wrapped an arm around him.

"It will be okay," she whispered, and Larelle frowned. Why was the commander so worried? Nyzaia scanned her eyes around the room before reading the letter's contents.

"Rulers of the Lost Kingdom of Novisia,

I do not ask for much in return for our vacancy from your waters and lands. There is no reason for a war among us or for innocent lives to be lost. I want one thing and one thing alone: the Descendant of Chaos, the essence of Sitara. Bring me Kazaar Elharar by sunrise in three days, and the loyal servants shall spill no blood. If I do not receive your confirmation, I allow you these three days to evacuate Myara. Civilians need not be harmed. If you do not abide, I will meet you on the sands of Keres.

General Caligh.

Larelle's head spun to Kazaar, mirroring the others in the room. Elisara's arm rested on his back while the other rested on the pommel of her sword, ready to defend him if needed. *Descendant of Chaos, the essence of Sitara.* Larelle exhaled, yet her instincts told her to wait and listen to Kazaar before making a plan. Another part of her whispered that handing Kazaar over would be a quick end to an avoidable war, but she flinched for even considering it.

"Did you—"

"Know?" Kazaar cut off Alvan from where he had moved closer to Larelle. Kazaar's tone was tense and matched his posture. "Of course not." He met each person's eye. *Is this what the Historian meant?* Perhaps darkness could indeed exist within the blood of one created from Sitara, even if it never fully manifested. The Historian had told them of Sitara and the story of her creation. She was created from the essence of Chaos, the creator and mother from which the Goddess Nerida descended. Sitara was the Goddess of Dusk, the opposite of Sonos, despite falling in love with him.

"But Sitara only used her essence to create the gods," Sadira said, holding onto Caellum's arm. "Does that mean you are a..."

Kazaar scoffed. "I am no god," he said firmly, and Larelle remained silent, turning over everything in the letter. If what Caligh claimed was true, then Kazaar was.

"Caligh is a general," Larelle finally said. "He could report to someone else. The creature that arrived when I was taken was a general, too; they could be from different ranks from different places." Larelle looked to Nyzaia, who led the military plans, yet the Keres queen was transfixed on the letter, the one that confirmed more than ever that Kazaar was not her brother by blood. From what Kazaar had told them so far, neither he nor Elisara had unlocked any other power, and there was every chance being a descendant of Chaos meant nothing but a terrifying title. But if it did mean something, what would it take to unleash such power? And could it plunge their kingdom into darkness? Silence resumed. Larelle scanned the map. In three days, they could move the people of Myara to Khami, assuming the general kept his promise.

"You are all asking the wrong questions," Soren said, resting her hands on the map. "The only question we should ask is which one of us takes Kazaar to Myara."

Soren choked for air, and her hands froze to the table to keep her from reaching for her throat. Nobody moved. Sadira stayed beside Caellum and kept her head high as her sister gasped for breath. Nyzaia still stood with her head down, with Farid observing her. Alvan reached for Larelle's hand, looping his fingers in hers. Nobody would challenge Elisara over Kazaar, and Larelle would definitely not turn over a man for his presumed lineage. Elisara had not moved but narrowed her eyes in Soren's direction.

"It's okay, angel," Kazaar murmured when Soren's face began to turn purple. "Elisara," he said more firmly. Soren gasped as the ice melted and reached for her throat, coughing. Larelle was a sympathetic person, though she held no sympathy for Soren after suggesting taking Elisara's love from her. She would sentence no one to that. The largest of Soren's wolves prowled towards Elisara and bared its teeth while the other five huddled around Soren's feet.

"You all stand by him?" Soren spluttered. "You all condone the killing of soldiers for the sake of one man?" She pointed at each of them, and Larelle winced.

"We must be strategic," Nyzaia finally said, looking at her brother. "The Lost Kingdom... It would appear we are not the only lands who know of other threats out there, threats that someone with the potential power of Sitara could save us from."

Kazaar glanced away; Larelle did not think he thought himself a saviour.

"We hand him over, and we may never hear from any of them," Soren argued.

"And what if we do, and he returns one day wanting more?" Nyzaia fought back.

"What more would he want? He has stated Kazaar!" Soren slammed her fist on the map, and Elisara's eyes widened, moving from being cast down at the table to up at Kazaar.

"Me," Elisara said, no louder than a whisper. "He could come back for me."

Larelle frowned, unsure of Elisara's point. She gripped Kazaar's hands in her own, looking only at him. "I wear a mark of Sitara—the moon on my skin as a symbol of my tie to you. If you are created from Sitara herself, then the darkness that surrounds us—the darkness Vala claims tainted me—is hers. Sitara's." Kazaar frowned. "You wear a mark of Sonos." Elisara placed her hand on Kazaar's collarbone. "Your darkness never appears without threads of light."

"Your light," he whispered. Larelle covered her mouth. When Kazaar placed his palm to her mark, their eyes changed, wisps of black and white dancing in their souls.

"With those of white and those of black," Sadira murmured.

"The spirit of the first makes their way back," Caellum continued.

Sonos and Sitara: the first created gods.

"When light meets dark in the rarest of times," said Nyzaia.

"The power to awaken that of old lore," Caellum continued. *The creatures,* Larelle realised, *and Kazaar's presumed power.*

"Lies in the soul of those with all four," Sadira finished.

Kazaar is the one with all four, and Elisara, by extension, if she ever learns to wield them.

"But we still do not know who the one with all four is or what it means," Sadira said. Larelle and Kazaar shared a look, and she gave him a reassuring nod.

"I can wield all four," he confirmed. Nobody questioned him, but shock etched their faces.

"Only together can they defeat and restore," said Nyzaia. "The prophecy is about the two of you." *But restore what?* Kazaar and Elisara dropped their hands from their collarbones, their eyes returning to normal as they peered around the room.

"Watch for the dark one that will bring suffering to all," Larelle said. "This man, Caligh. If he controls the creatures, then it is him." She looked at Alvan, who squeezed her hand in agreement. Soren spun from the room and slammed the doors closed behind her, leaving the room in stunned silence. They had finally deciphered the prophecy.

All that was left to help them win were the swords. Larelle looked at Sadira.

With shaking hands, she pulled the dagger from the side of Caellum's leg. It hummed, a light glow emitting from it. Larelle glanced to where a similar hum resonated from Kazaar and Elisara. *The Sword of Sonos.*

"I know how to create more weapons," Sadira confirmed.

***

"Mumma!" Zarya's high-pitched squeal sounded from the doors to their chambers as Larelle and Alvan approached. She did not have a chance to return the greeting as her daughter charged into her legs. Larelle's hands tangled in her dark curls as Olden appeared in the doorway, holding a brush.

"I think grandpa needs to finish brushing your hair!" Larelle exclaimed, pulling Zarya's matted curls aside. Zarya looked up at her with her father's midnight blue eyes, giggling.

"We're playing a game!" Zarya held onto her mother's robe and turned to look at Olden. Larelle did not believe that for a second.

"I am uncertain running around saying, 'you can't catch me' is a game I agreed to," Olden exclaimed from the doorway. He pushed the second door open to allow Larelle and Alvan entry. She gave Olden an apologetic look and ushered Zarya in.

"I don't know, Olden. It sounds like a fantastic game to me." Alvan bent down and grabbed Zarya's middle, throwing her over his shoulder. She squealed with laughter. "And it looks like I just won!"

Larelle rolled her eyes but smiled at their closeness, particularly after their travels from Mera to Tabheri.

"Do not encourage her!" Larelle scolded, slapping Alvan's arm as she collected the tray of wine and goblets left by the servants on the side table and carried it to the balcony.

"Mumma!" Zarya shouted, hanging upside down over Alvan's shoulder. "You should not hit people!" In three long strides, Alvan reached the large pillows on the balcony and lowered Zarya onto them.

"And you"—He pointed at the little girl, who grinned from ear to ear— "should not give your grandpa so much grief." Larelle hummed in agreement and sat down on the small bench opposite the pillows.

"What is grief?" Zarya asked, and the three adults paused, unsure of how to answer. Moments like this reminded Larelle that her daughter was growing, and with that growth would come more questions about life and her place within it. How could Larelle summarise grief? The constant ache in your chest at the simplest reminder of those you have lost? The pain when you realise you have gone an entire day without thinking of them? Because grieving grief made you drown in guilt instead.

"I think that is a story for the morning when Mumma is not so tired," Larelle said. Zarya seemed content with that answer and tipped out a bag of shells Olden gave her.

"On the topic of being tired," Olden chuckled. "I am going to lie down for a bit." Larelle reached for his hand and squeezed gently, mouthing 'thank you' as he left.

Larelle accepted the goblet of wine Alvan passed to her, from where he sat beside her on the bench. When he wrapped his arm around her shoulder, Larelle leaned into him. He gently kissed her head.

"Do you think children can tell when things are off?" she asked, watching Zarya arrange shells on the balcony floor. The palm trees of the royal gardens swayed in the distance behind Zarya as Alvan sat down next to Larelle on the bench and leaned against the wall behind them.

"Children? No," Alvan said, taking a sip. "Zarya? Probably. In the time I have known her, I have discovered she has a mature awareness of others."

Larelle hummed in agreement. "What do I tell her? When we leave?"

"Whatever you think is right for her to hear. Regardless, Olden will take good care of her." Larelle kept telling herself that.

The group made the simple decision not to hand over Kazaar. Through her connections, Nyzaia had enlisted the Red Stones to manage the movement of citizens in Myara to Khami; the evacuation would begin by nightfall. On day two, Larelle, the rulers, and their closest confidants would move to the military camps at the edge of the Ashun desert. They would meet the general and his army on the sands of Keres at sunrise on day three. In three days, she may no longer be here.

Larelle revisited the last moment she believed she would die. *We will meet again one day*, Osiris had said. Larelle hoped to find him on the battlefield so she could pierce a sword through his chest for keeping her from her daughter. Zarya picked up the shells and shook them in her hands before throwing them across the tiles. Larelle chuckled to herself as Zarya watched them all, as if confused as to why she had thrown them.

"Do your family have a history of family names in Nerida?"

Larelle asked.

"An odd question," laughed Alvan. Zarya picked up the shells again and threw them once more.

"When I was taken. The creature, Osiris, said Zerpane was an old name. Olden once mentioned they had strong connections to the royal family. It is why Zarya's eyes are so dark and why her father could wield."

Alvan smiled softly.

"When this is all over, I will check for you. It would be nice for Zarya to understand where she comes from." Larelle returned his smile, grateful for how well he understood her. Shells scattered again when Alvan placed his goblet down and slowly turned to Larelle. He reached for her cheek, allowing her every opportunity to retreat at his affection. Shells scattered again.

"I said I would always be here," Alvan murmured, glancing at her lips. "I mean that." Larelle's heart pounded as he traced her lip with his thumb. He waited, scanning her eyes. She nodded silently, wishing to revisit their first kiss. Alvan's stubble grazed her chin as his lips met her in a quiet, tender kiss.

He pulled back, and she immediately mourned the absence of his lips whilst appreciating the respect he had for her daughter nearby. The shells had stopped scattering, and Larelle turned her head, readying to answer Zarya's question about the kiss and tell her of her happiness.

Zarya sat cross-legged in her dress, resting her hands on her knees with shells in either palm. Her eyes burned into her mother's.

"Mumma, is someone going to die in the desert?" she asked. Larelle frowned and walked over to her daughter.

"Of course not, sweetheart." Larelle pulled Zarya into a hug, the shells falling, and looked at Alvan over her head.

"How does she know about the desert?" she whispered.

"Her mature awareness, I suppose."

Chapter Fifty-Four

Soren

They were ruining the Lord of Night's plan, but did Soren even know his plan anymore? Her armour clinked as she paced the palace gardens, unsure why her feet had led her here, surrounded by plants she had never seen on Doltas or in Garridon. *Why can I not stop moving?* Too much whirled in her brain: the others fiercely defending Kazaar, the discussions of Sonos and Sitara, and the letter. Soren thought it absurd that the others would sacrifice so many for one man. *Caligh.*

Is that your name? Is it you? Soren thought the similarity in the general's tone was no coincidence.

Watch for the dark one that will bring suffering to all. The memory of the lord's shadows entered her mind, shrouded in darkness. Dark one. Soren was confused as to why the lord had kept things from her and kept the final lines of the prophecy secret. Her thoughts felt foreign, and her body felt lucid. Laughter sounded from the other side of the wall from the public gardens. Would the lord return to her tonight? What would she say when she had failed his requests? Had she become lax in his absence and lowered her guard for these people? The birds chirped overhead to begin their evening flight. What if I kill them both now? Would that be enough for him? Nearby, a heavy door slammed shut. Soren could sneak into their rooms at night and slit their throats. That could work. The birds chirped again, mixed with the sound of footsteps.

"Get out of my head!" Soren screamed, punching the low wall of the fountain until blood splattered from her knuckles. "Get out!"

A hand gripped her shoulder, and Soren spun, reaching for her dagger. Panting, she held the blade to the neck of the man bold enough to sneak up on her.

"Woah! Easy!" Sir Cain said in his rough accent. He raised his hands to show he was unarmed. Soren remained still, with the dagger poised beneath the ginger scruff on his neck. She scanned his wide eyes for ill intent but found nothing. Her breathing eased. *He is unarmed; he would not attack you. He is a man of honour, unlike you.* Soren lowered her hands.

"Sorry," she mumbled, and Sir Cain raised his eyebrows.

"Did you just apologise?"

Soren scoffed. "Do not get used to it." Sir Cain looked her up and down, pausing on her bloodied hand. She wiped it on the thin bit of fabric visible between her body armour and legs. "Do not look at me," she mumbled, turning from him. Soren wiped her face with her hands. Sleep. She needed sleep.

"I was asked to find you," Sir Cain said gruffly. Soren sighed and tilted back her head before composing her features.

"What for?" she asked.

"Plans are in place. The rulers leave for the sands the day after tomorrow. I thought it wise you should get there tomorrow, given you're leading part of the infantry." Soren narrowed her eyes. What was his angle? Soren frowned. *It could be a trap.* What if he was getting her to lower her guard before taking her out?

"Since when?"

"Since I'm not blind. I may not trust ya, but you're a good fighter and a commanding leader. The soldiers are scared shitless of you and would do anything you told them."

Soren pondered it for a moment. If she left the palace now, she would not be privy to their other plans. What if this was merely a ruse to get rid of her for good? On the other hand, she might lay eyes on the general before the others to confirm if it was the man she had known since childhood. Perhaps he would appear more vividly to Soren if she was closer to him, assuming he was indeed on the shores of Myara.

"Okay," Soren relented, and Sir Cain nodded.

"Meet me in the courtyard before sunrise." He did not give Soren time to retort as he left the public gardens, leaving Soren alone with her thoughts once more. She was not so certain she enjoyed being alone with her mind anymore.

***

The darkness in her mind looked the same. Soren breathed the scent of night air and dreams, twisting and grounding her. She had missed it. Since the Lord of Night's absence, she had tried to reach him on her own terms but to no avail. Blackened leaves crunched underfoot as she walked forward and wrapped her arms around herself. Soren's breath plumed like smoke; she did not remember it being this cold.

He was not here yet, though he rarely left Soren there alone. She took a tentative step forward, the crunch of leaves echoing in the night's emptiness and the crumbling castle surrounding her. If she continued forward, she would reach the iron bars he never let her near. *Is that how he enters my mind?* Instead of testing her theory, she spun to take in every inch of the ivy and moss-covered walls that fell away to the night sky.

Seiko howled, and Soren frowned. Her wolves never appeared in her dreams. Tilting her head, Soren peered at whatever stood behind her usual spot. The rotting tree in the distance felt familiar, like a blemish tainting the field of long grass blowing in the imaginary breeze. A wolf howled again.

"I do not see a crown on your head, Soren."

She jumped at the return of the silken voice, shadows stretching for her shoulders. Her usual comfort vanished as they spun her to face his shrouded form.

"I was about to kill him, but—"

"I do not care for excuses, little bird." The shadows brushed her face, and his finger grazed the scar left behind by the creature. "What was my request?"

Soren looked down. She had disappointed him. He gripped her chin, forcing her gaze to watch the twisting darkness.

"Take the throne," she mumbled.

"And yet, it has not happened." Releasing her hand, he turned and retreated to the iron bars.

"But Garridon told me not to." Soren gasped as a force hurled her backward through the air, further than she could have imagined. She smacked against the rotten tree she had seen so far in the distance, her head spinning as she reached for the ground to steady herself. Her fingers grazed over small pieces of wood, unable to distinguish their shapes, before a plume of shadows engulfed Soren and tugged her back. When the darkness receded, she was at the ruins once more.

"You listened to that *god*," he sneered. "Over ME!" His roar was a sound to be heard across the universe. Soren winced. She had not known he loathed the gods, who possibly could?

"I cannot disobey a god," she murmured, and a slap burned her cheek. She stared at the floor, refusing to show him the tears in her eyes.

"But you can disobey me?" he asked, and she did not respond. Silence followed and stretched between them. She had missed the lord, yet he did not seem fazed by their time apart. A scraping noise sounded from behind the iron bars, and Soren lifted her head to peer around him. A hand reached out to her again, and she flinched until the touch softened, cradling her cheek. The lord sighed beneath his cloak of darkness and retreated towards the steps leading into nothingness. He sighed again.

"Tell me what you know, Soren. What has happened in the time we have spent apart?" Soren did not move, a rebellious streak emerging within her.

"Is your name Caligh?" she asked boldly, and he chuckled.

"You have navigated close enough that they shared the contents of the letter with you." She did not know if he was impressed. "What did they deduce from the letter?"

Soren kicked at the blackened leaves on the floor.

"That if Kazaar is the essence of Sitara, then Elisara is made from that of Sonos," she said, and he hummed.

"A quick deduction," he chuckled. "Perhaps I underestimated them as a group."

"They will not hand him over," she said.

"I assumed as much."

"They prepare for war."

"Naturally."

"They will all die." Soren did not know if she was asking him a question.

"Perhaps."

Soren frowned, an image of a young Sadira flashing through her consciousness. Her sister could die. Soren blinked away the image, focusing on Caligh, on her Lord of Night.

"What do you need from me?" she asked, eager to return to his good graces. "Nobody would notice if Caellum died in war; no one would know it was at my hand."

The shadows rose from the stairs, floating back towards her.

"If I have Kazaar, I have no need for Caellum to die," he said, and Soren stumbled.

"But that has always been the plan. We needed a true Garridon heir on the throne."

"If I have Kazaar, I have the potential to unleash all the power in the world. You on the throne benefited me in the interim, but you failed, Soren."

"I can do better," she pleaded. "Anything! I will do anything you need."

He paused before returning to the metal bars.

"It will be difficult to take Kazaar if Elisara is beside him. Separate them on the sands, if you can. Fight as though you are on their side; I may still have need of you, but that need diminishes if they know you work alongside their opponents."

Before Soren could promise to do as he asked, he faded with her surroundings.

She opened her eyes to the sound of whimpers. Something wet was on her hand. She glanced down to find her wolves watching her. Baelyn and Tapesh curled closer and whimpered while Seiko licked her hand.

"What is wrong?" she asked, pushing herself up in the bed. She pulled the silk sheets to her chin at the odd coldness in her room. The drapes by the balcony fluttered in the wind, and Soren slipped from the bed, her wolves trailing behind her as she wrapped the sheets around herself. The tiles were cold as she padded onto the balcony, greeted by the sound of guards in the courtyard to the right. She scanned the horizon; the rooftops of Keres crept into view as the sky lightened, a midnight blue as the sun awoke.

Just before dawn. It was time for Soren to ready and meet Sir Cain before heading to the camps. Serene and Octavia curled around her feet, and she chuckled as Tapesh and Baelyn fought to take their spot.

"I know the sands are not ideal for you." She reached down and stroked Varna's head. "But perhaps you can help me with my mission." Standing back up, Soren stared into the distance. Later that day, she would reach the sands. Tomorrow, she faced war. While Soren had prepared for war within Garridon for years, nothing prepared her for this. Yet on a cool morning, imagining what tomorrow would bring, a small voice asked her what life might have been like if she had never met Caligh.

Perhaps she would not be so alone.

Chapter Fifty-Five

Nyzaia

"I do not like this," Farid grumbled from where he crouched atop the tavern. He twisted the tip of his knife into the burnt red rock. Nyzaia pulled the black cloth from her face and squinted in the distance.

"They have a lot to deal with. Running late should not be a shock," Nyzaia murmured, keeping her voice low from the ears of the drunkards below. "Jabir will collect them."

By Farid's sideways glance, she knew Nyzaia was trying to convince herself as much as him. After the revelations of Caligh's letter and the plans set in motion, Nyzaia and Farid had left immediately to complete their tasks. It had taken most of the day, meaning they now had the cover of nightfall for their duty.

Nyzaia tapped her fingers against the leathers on her leg. She had sent the note to Rafik and Issam early enough for them to receive it in time, and when they had not shown up, she sent Jabir to investigate. A knot formed in Nyzaia's stomach; she was not used to being separated from her syndicate and was yet to adjust. *We will never be complete again,* she thought, thinking of Tajana and recalling the last time they had run atop the rooftops together. Nyzaia hoped to feel relief while donning her leathers for the evening, a reprieve from royal clothing but felt only longing as time passed.

"Is it odd?" Farid asked. "Being here with me instead of—"

"No," Nyzaia cut him off, not wishing to hear her name. She rubbed at her chest as though it would erase the ache in her heart, and when she pulled her hand away, the scar of her celestial tie shone beneath the moonlight. Farid said nothing about her dismissal but must have known she was lying.

He lightly nudged her elbow before moving from his crouch. Three shadows shifted through the lantern-lit street opposite before moving to the back of the tavern. Following quickly in Farid's path, Nyzaia glided over the rooftop before dropping off the side, landing in a silent crouch at the back of the dusty alleyway.

"You took long enough," Nyzaia hissed as Issam, Rafik, and Jabir stepped into the moonlight, yet she frowned at the cut on Jabir's cheek. Issam held a finger up to his mouth, signalling for her to step away from the tavern's back entrance. Nyzaia trusted him enough to do as he asked, and though Farid frowned, he stepped back with Nyzaia.

The Palm Tavern had been a frequent haunt for the syndicate, the only tavern Nyzaia kept from the other Red Stones—their haven. It felt odd to enter through the back, but although it was once their haven, word of the queen of Keres being spotted in the slums of Tabheri would only raise risks and questions.

Issam knocked on the cracked wooden door six times with a series of specifically placed pauses. Five long minutes later, the heavy footfall of the owner approached, and the door creaked as it swung open, hiding Nyzaia and Farid from view. The light from the tavern creeped out into the alleyway, and the owner grunted.

"Haven't seen you lot in a while." His voice was gruff, and Nyzaia knew from experience that he beheld the three men with judgement. She had endured many arguments with the man because of his worries about dragging unwanted attention to the tavern. "Usual room?" he asked. Issam nodded silently and handed over a pouch of clinking coins. The man grunted and walked back inside, leaving the door open. Farid made to step around the door, but Nyzaia tugged his sleeve. They waited, listening, and when the heavy steps faded, followed by a slam of a door, Nyzaia knew the coast was clear.

Issam glanced up and down the alleyway, Rafik watched the

rooftops, and Jabir and Farid flanked Nyzaia inside. The tiles of the floor were sticky underfoot as Nyzaia took a right into a smaller corridor and opened the door. A small smile graced her lips despite the pain in her chest. Nothing had changed. The room remained exactly as it always had, as though it awaited their return.

Dust collected on Nyzaia's fingertips as she grazed them along the circular wooden table, filling most of the room. Five overturned crates were positioned around it, a seat for each of them. A deck of cards was scattered across the table, many with bent corners and stains from the amber liquid remaining in the glass decanter in the centre.

"Looks like enough for a glass each." Issam jostled Nyzaia as he grazed past, reaching for the drink and pouring a glass for each of them. Farid glanced between the crates and avoided the one where Tajana would sit, but with a nod from Nyzaia, he took her place.

"You will need the drink," Nyzaia sighed. She rested her arms on the table and shuffled the cards.

"That bad, huh?" asked Rafik, catching the glass as Issam slid it across the table.

"Not sure things could get much worse," Issam grunted, glancing at Jabir and the cut on his face. Farid huffed, knowing they would indeed get worse.

"What happened?" Nyzaia sipped from the glass, the liquid a welcome burn in her throat. Issam sat down on her right.

"It's nothing," Jabir mumbled. "Not with everything else we have going on." Nyzaia glanced at Farid as she felt a wave of his concern wash over her. He watched Jabir intently. Not knowing when she would next have the opportunity to talk with her syndicate, Nyzaia prioritised her friend's matter first.

"Tell me," she commanded, organising the cards into separate piles. The room was silent as the men looked at one another. Eventually, Issam sighed and downed his drink; the table shook when he slammed it down.

"Things with the Red Stones are... uneasy," Issam said.

"That's an understatement," scoffed Rafik, accepting the cards Nyzaia dealt around the table.

"Get to the point," Farid said, watching Jabir over the rim of his glass, who smirked.

"Someone is sacrificing people," said Issam. "Is that to the point enough for you?" He raised an eyebrow at Farid, whose hand had paused halfway from returning his glass to the table. Nyzaia froze in her seat and then reached for a card.

"What do you mean *sacrificing* people?" she asked, frowning.

"Someone is taking a member from each pillar, tying them to a wall, carving their chests, and painting symbols around them for us to find the next morning." Rafik relayed the events bluntly before silence weighed heavily on the room. Nyzaia absorbed his words. *Why would someone sacrifice people, and who—or what—was the sacrifice for?* She immediately thought of Isha and the symbols painted in blood across her room, yet they believed it was an attempt to contact the gods.

"Did you recognise the symbols?" Farid asked, and Rafik and Issam shook their heads.

"Which pillars?" asked Nyzaia.

"Courtesans were first, followed by dealers, spies, and alchemists," answered Issam.

"Only blades and torturers left," Nyzaia murmured. Given their areas of expertise, she assumed they were blamed for the killings.

"Any suspects?" Farid asked, and the silence answered his question, though the other men glanced between one another nervously as though scared to speak. "So, what happened to you?" Farid stared at Jabir, who shifted on the crate before glancing at Nyzaia.

"They said my arrival was odd timing." He cleared his throat. "They believed it was the queen's way of punishing them for forming a democracy and going against Red Stone tradition." Nyzaia scoffed.

"That's ridiculous," Farid voiced.

"Clearly, the heads of the pillars do not think so, given I narrowly dodged a knife thrown at my face," Jabir said, his jaw clenched. *Shit.* Nyzaia rubbed her chin. If the heads of the pillars did not trust her, it made asking for support in the battle difficult.

"We have more serious things to discuss," Farid said, sensing her worry.

"More serious than sacrifice?" Issam asked. Farid's eyes were dark, and Jabir nodded slowly. "The talismans worked? Did you contact the gods?"

Rafik leaned forward as Nyzaia nodded, launching into the story of what they had missed while being separated.

***

By the time Nyzaia finished recounting all that had happened, stopping regularly to answer the men's questions, the candles burned low in the room. She flourished her hand to reignite them as the men frowned, taking in all she had told them.

"So, you need the Red Stones to fight?" Issam asked, and Nyzaia shook her head.

"We have soldiers. I need you to clear Myara and get the people to Khami safely." Rafik exhaled.

"That will be a hard ask when the heads are questioning your involvement in the sacrifices."

"I am still their queen by the law of Keres." She scowled, and Issam laughed.

"And other than you carrying out your father's missions, when have the Red Stones ever listened to the crown?"

Issam was right. Jabir remained silent on the other side of the table, fiddling with the cards, but when Farid shifted on his crate, Jabir finally looked up. The two looked at one another, and Nyzaia smiled as she noticed the nod of encouragement Farid gave him.

"We could use this to our advantage," Jabir said, and the others all turned to look at him. "Caligh's arrival times well with the sacrifices. We could blame him, which gives the Red Stones a reason to help and turns their attention from you." Jabir faced each of them, waiting for their nod of approval, as was tradition. Nyzaia nodded first, followed by Issam; Rafik hesitated before nodding, and finally, Jabir looked at Farid, waiting. Nyzaia's heart warmed at including Farid in their traditions.

"Then what happens after? With the sacrifices?" Farid asked, not yet following suit with a nod.

"If all goes well in battle, we have time to investigate the sacrifices," said Jabir. Nyzaia turned over the idea that Caligh could be involved in the sacrifices, or was there something else at play in the kingdom's underground?

"And if the battle doesn't go well?" Issam asked.

"Then we will all be dead," Farid replied, nodding at Jabir.

Chapter Fifty-Six

Caellum

Death had never scared Caellum, who had prepared for it from the first time his father pushed him down the stairs. But now, watching how Sadira's face lit up riding through Tabheri, despite everything they were soon to face, Caellum feared death's clutches. For both of their sakes. He did not know what to do if he lost her, and if death greeted him first, his regrets would follow him into the afterlife.

Caellum rubbed his eyes to keep himself awake and focused. No one would know from looking at Sadira that the pair had slept for only three hours over the last two days as they spent every waking moment imbuing weapons. Helplessness had settled on his shoulders as he watched Sadira tire the more she did. All he could do was bring her food and force her to take breaks, massaging her shoulders as she did what she could to save the kingdom from darkness. She did it without complaint and did not complain now, either, as she rode through Tabheri beneath the beating sun.

In another world, they would not be riding to the Ashun Desert for war but enjoying an extended weekend break in the city, introducing Sadira to a different realm in the correct way. He would stop and buy her all the sweet treats she stared longingly at from the market and every single scent she smiled at from the stalls. In another world, they had all the time in the universe to learn about one another.

Sadness settled in his bones; there was so much he wished for them to do. He glanced at Sadira again. She was born to be a queen. The Garridon crown sparkled amongst the twists of her hair pulled back from her face. Seeing her donning something other than a dress was odd, but she looked just as powerful and beautiful in her silk-green shirt. Her sleeves billowed as their horses increased their pace. The cream fabric fitted tightly to her legs, tucked into long brown boots and highlighted the curves usually hidden beneath her skirts. Clearing his throat, Caellum looked straight ahead, his mind running away with him.

As they exited the city, the tents came into view, a spectrum of colour against the Ashun Desert.

"It would look beautiful in other circumstances," Sadira murmured.

"Something can still be beautiful despite the reason for its existence," Caellum said, and Sadira hummed, frowning. He followed her eyeline to where Soren emerged from one tent, striding in their direction.

"Sadira," Soren said, not meeting her gaze. Her posture appeared slumped, and dark circles ringed her eyes.

"Soren." Sadira dismounted from her horse at the same time as Caellum, and Soren took the reins of each.

"The others are still settling; you would be wise to sleep. Debrief starts past midnight in the early hours of the morning," she said before turning from them, her eyes still downcast.

"Thank you," Caellum said, though she did not acknowledge it. Sadira approached and looped her arm in his.

"Did something seem off about her?" Sadira asked.

"Because she did not look like she wanted to kill me?"

"Exactly," Sadira said, and Caellum patted her hand before guiding her through the maze of tents. A nearby soldier pointed them in the direction of their tent, and they passed a large, bright orange dome, where they would likely meet this evening if the number of guards was anything to go by. They continued their walk until they reached the edge furthest into the desert and the tent closest to Garridon. The rulers' tents were placed furthest from Myara, furthest from Caligh.

Sadira paused to peer across the vast desert while Caellum scanned the inside of the tent. He easily lifted their wooden chests and placed them outside. He sat down, gently pulling Sadira next to him. She crossed one leg over the other and leaned her head on his shoulder. The sands were still, allowing them to take it in. Caellum only realised how long they had sat in comfortable silence when the sun moved beyond the desert, lighting the wisps of sand now spiralling in the evening air like flames.

Caellum sighed with contentment.

"We should really get some sleep if we are to be up in the early hours," he said, standing and offering his hand to Sadira. She accepted, rising with him. She stumbled and fell into him, unaccustomed to the uneven sand. She braced against his chest as his free arm wrapped around her waist, holding her close. He moved to tuck away a piece of hair that had fallen from its twist, slipping it behind her ear while the sunset added to her skin's radiance, contrasting the green of her eyes that shone brightly up at him. His hand lingered before landing gently on the side of her neck. Sadira slid her hand up his chest and placed it on his shoulder.

"You are beautiful," he breathed. He meant it every time, yet standing with her against the backdrop of the setting sun over the sands, thinking of how far they had come, the compliment held a different meaning. Sadira's mind was beautiful, her heart, her soul—everything—and he could not tell if she blushed at his words or if it were merely a trick of the sun.

"You think I am beautiful?" she asked, her eyes flicking to his lips.

"How could I not?" He leaned closer towards her.

"Is this my fairytale moment?" she whispered.

"Is this when I get to be yours?" he asked, remembering the last time they had been so close.

"Whether we return from these sands tomorrow or meet in the forests of death, you are mine," Sadira breathed, reaching onto her tiptoes to kiss him. Caellum held her close to him as her lips met his softly. He met her with the same tenderness, her lips exactly as he had imagined: sweet and perfect. She gently slid her tongue against his bottom lip, and he did as she desired, welcoming her want for more. The weight of the war fell upon them at the realisation that this could be their last moment alone together. It played on Caellum's mind as Sadira's kiss became more demanding. His hand slid into her hair, holding her close as he kissed her back with the passion that mirrored the fires of Keres. Sadira was gentle until she was not.

She turned and led them into the tent, forcing Caellum to duck under the entrance. He had little time to take in the decor but knew it had been set up for royalty as he glimpsed the wooden bedposts. Sadira's legs hit the edge, and he fell atop her.

"I do not want to do anything you do not," he mumbled into their kiss. He pulled back to look at her. The opening of her emerald shirt loosened, exposing the swell of her breasts that rose with her heavy breathing. She licked her swollen lips.

"I want you," she said, reaching for him and pulling him close. "All of you." She sighed and leaned into the kiss again, her hands frantic as she tugged off his shirt and reached for his belt.

"If you want all of me, we must slow down," he chuckled, reaching for her wrists. She grinned, pushing against him while undoing the buckle. "Sadira," he laughed, pulling her wrists up and pinning them to either side of her head. His eyes darkened at the desire burning in her gaze when she bit her lip. She wrapped her legs around his waist with her boots nudging against his back; it reminded him of when her bare feet trailed his leg when they first shared a bed. Caellum leaned down and kissed her neck. Sadira groaned, wriggling against him. He closed his eyes as she pushed against him.

Releasing her wrists, he untucked the shirt from her trousers to roam his hands over her flawless skin underneath. She lifted her arms for him to pull it, and his eyes trailed over her breasts.

"Tell me what you want." Caellum leaned back, and her legs

landed on either side of him. He bit his lip as he glanced between her legs.

"You," she breathed, reaching for the buttons on her trousers. "That kiss was our fairytale." She pushed her hand beneath her trousers, locking her eyes with his. She moaned as she touched herself, and Caellum gripped her knees, shifting against the uncomfortable strain in his trousers. "I do not want to leave this world not knowing you are mine, and I am yours," she said. Sadira withdrew her hand and reached for him, brushing his lip with her thumb. He swallowed hard at the taste of her. "I need you, Caellum."

Sadira pushed up on her hands and knees, kissing him as his hands met her waist. "Quickly," she breathed, "I cannot wait any longer. I want you to have me." Sadira turned from him, leaning down on her hands and knees. He gripped the curves of her hips, and she pushed back into him, creating a friction that challenged his restraint. Sadira shook her hair over her back, peering at him; he could not—would not—say no to her.

Caellum was swift as he gripped the top of the cream fabric that taunted him and pulled, exposing her to him. She sighed as he stroked her curves, so beautifully pressed against him.

"You want to be mine?" he asked, his fingers lowering until meeting what he knew awaited. She quickly coated his fingers, trying to move against them. He placed a hand on her lower back to halt her.

"I want to be yours." She pleaded as one hand teased her and the other removed his trousers. "Do you want to be mine?"

He removed his hand and squeezed her behind, pushing against her. Sadira arched her back.

"You have no idea," he murmured, pushing into her. Sadira gasped with relief as he wasted no time in pulling back out and thrusting into her again.

"Yes," she moaned, which only quickened his pace. She fit so perfectly around him and he wondered if there were any other ties the gods could bestow, because it felt as though Sadira was made for him alone. "Harder," she whimpered, her arms shaking. He gripped her hips tightly and gave her everything she asked for, and he silently promised the gods that, should they survive, he would give her anything she asked for the rest of their lives. Relieving the weight on her arms, he pushed her down with one hand until her cheek met the pillow, her hands twisting in the sheets.

"Caellum," she cried. He continued his pace with one hand on her back while the other left indents in her supple hip.

"Gods," he murmured, stroking her curves. "You are perfect." Sadira pushed back onto her hands and shook her hair behind her. He remembered the sounds that escaped her when he last tugged her hair, so he twisted his fingers in her curls and pulled. Sadira arched her back and cried again as he deepened his thrusts with each moan.

"Yes!" His thrusts met her words until she fell silent, panting and tensing under his body. He held her close as she tightened around him, moving his hand from her waist to stroke exactly where she had guided him last time, undoing her completely. Sadira moaned his name, and Caellum fell forward, finishing with her and using her hips to steady himself.

Sadira panted under him as he pulled out. She turned to face him, her legs still open.

He glanced up at the fabric of the tent briefly as she displayed herself for him, and when he met her eyes again, she grinned and bit her thumbnail.

"You will be the death of me, Sadira," he murmured, pulling her boots from her legs and the trousers bunched over her calves, leaving her naked before him. He softly stroked her thighs. "We should sleep," he murmured.

"We have all night," she said, the smile still on her face as he trailed his hand back between her legs.

"I suppose you are right."

Chapter Fifty-Seven

Nyzaia

The battle tent was silent under the midnight blue, disrupted only by the scraping of spoons against metal bowls. Nyzaia shovelled the last of the breakfast into her mouth and pushed the bowl to the side of the table. She surveyed the room, where all the rulers sat with their close confidants behind them. Commanders and high military officials stood against the tent walls, ready for the briefing. Never could Nyzaia have imagined this was where her life would lead.

The flap to the tent moved, and everyone's heads turned to watch Farid enter. With a silent nod from him, they returned to their bowls. The citizens of Myara had reached Khami safely. Nyzaia frowned, trying to understand General Caligh's angle. *Did he really only care for Kazaar?* Something at the back of her mind warned her she was missing something.

Farid approached on her right, and she greeted him with a solemn nod. Farid had been the first to volunteer to watch the path to Khami to ensure the civilians made it there safely, while Jabir watched Myara from higher ground. They expected Caligh soon, assuming he would take the settlement once all citizens were clear of it. Jabir was to wait until he was certain Caligh, or his men, did not follow before reporting back to confirm they were on land.

Nyzaia felt calmer with Farid's return—more certain. She glanced at Elisara and Kazaar in matching leathers, the pin of Vala on each of their chests, the only sign of their realm. None of the rulers wore their realm colours. They did not fight for their realm; they fought for their kingdom. Elisara tapped her foot while

Kazaar held her knee still. Worry flickered in Elisara's eyes as she looked at Kazaar, a feeling Nyzaia knew all too well. She worried for her brother and the attempts likely to be made on his life in the battle to come.

Nyzaia focused on the map covering the table. Garridon's military was to filter up the western side of the desert in a stiff formation, while Nerida's funnelled along the eastern side, closest to the ocean, so Larelle could access the water to aid. Keres and Vala would fight side by side in the space in between to trap the oncoming army into a horseshoe until Garridon and Nerida circled around the back.

Scouts in the centre of the desert would return soon to report on their overnight shifts. They hoped the winds would have blown the sands in their favour to create a hill for Vala and Keres' armies to descend, the added height aiding their attack against the winged creatures. Elisara had assured them she could blow the sands into place, but they did not know how much power would be needed from each ruler, all of whom were trying to conserve their power in case some miracle allowed it to affect the creatures.

Nyzaia fiddled with the imbued blades at her side, or so they believed. It was not as if they had any opportunities to test them. The blades would have to be enough. Nyzaia dreaded to think how the war could unfold if Sadira had failed. For once, Nyzaia thanked her father. If he had not kept his collection of old books, they would have never found the incantation within *Myths and Lies*. Nyzaia stared at the stack of rare books on the table, with Myths and Lies atop it.

Nyzaia found it odd how multiple rare books had made their way to Novisia as if their ancestors were all scholars. She stared at the stack and then stood abruptly, her knees hitting the table as she did. Everyone jolted at the sudden movement, and that small doubt taunting Nyzaia came forward.

"Caligh Servusian," Nyzaia said.

"What?" Kazaar asked.

"Caligh Servusian. The author of *Myths and Lies of Ithyion* was called Caligh Servusian."

Sadira grabbed the book from the table behind her to check the spine. Nyzaia knew it was there—faded, but there. Sadira turned the spine to face the others.

"A coincidence, surely?" Caellum asked.

"It could be a common name from Ithyion," Sadira agreed.

"The book holds information on celestial ties, which we know to be real, and also the incantation to imbue a sword to defeat *darkness,*" Nyzaia stressed. "That would be an awfully big coincidence." Nyzaia paced. This could confirm he was alive on Ithyion and played a part in the downfall of their ancestral home. But how did his book end up in her father's study? Too many questions whirred through Nyzaia's mind.

"What does it matter? If we know his name?" Elisara asked, frowning.

"There is power in a name," Larelle muttered beside Nyzaia. "Osiris, he said something odd when talking about Zarya. He said there was power in a name."

Sadira stood. "The Wiccan in Garridon said the same thing."

"That cannot be a coincidence," Nyzaia said, pacing now. "It means something. It has to."

"We do not have time to be certain of anything," Kazaar said. "We keep the knowledge to ourselves unless anyone crosses paths with him and feels it may benefit them in some way."

"If we make it through this, I can read through the rest of the Wiccan book; there must be something on name-based incantations," Sadira said, looping her hand through Caellum's.

"*When* we make it through," said Larelle, and Sadira smiled softly. Nyzaia's face remained stern. She had been in enough battles and inflicted enough death to know not to be optimistic whenever confronted with a fight.

"The only people certain to make it through this are Elisara and Kazaar; their tie heals their wounds. The same cannot be said for us." Nyzaia glanced at Farid. They had agreed not to reveal their tie unless Farid used his wings as a last resort.

"For all we know, this general and his soldiers have a sword the equivalent of ours that could maim anyone," Kazaar said. "Including us."

"No one can live forever," Elisara said.

"But they can live an awfully long time," Alvan said behind Larelle. He turned to address Nyzaia. "If this general is the same man who wrote that book, he is old. Whatever power he has is keeping him alive, or he comes from far different lands than ones we know."

The rulers all nodded as the realisation sank in about how unprepared they were for this battle compared to him. Yet Caligh's presence provided hope that there were other lands out there and that the Historian, Talia, and Tajana could be successful in finding aid.

The tent opened again, and Jabir appeared. His eyes sought Farid, and then Nyzaia. He nodded.

"They have taken Myara."

That was the signal. The confirmation it was time to go. The rulers rose, readying their weapons as Jabir continued to fill them in. Nyzaia approached him as he leaned over the map.

"The army is split: half are the creatures circling the rooftops, and the other half are men on foot. They appear to only carry one sword each. They seem to be some kind of rank, groups in grey leathers and some in copper armour. I could not differentiate a reason other than skill set."

"You've done well, Jabir," Nyzaia said. "We may gauge more about their strategy when we approach them on the sands." Nyzaia strapped the final sword to her back and turned to the rulers. Caellum planted a kiss on Sadira's head, preparing to say goodbye. As someone not as skilled in swords, Sadira would remain atop the dune to wield her power from there and slow the enemy's army. Larelle was to do similar, but Alvan refused to leave her side and would defend her at the back of Nerida's ranks to the east of the desert. Kazaar and Elisara nodded to Nyzaia and Farid. Knowing they were the only other tied pair, they fought together.

"The creatures need to go first. Caellum." Nyzaia addressed the King. "Garridon armies have the most archers with imbued arrowheads; they need to lead." He nodded. "Elisara will remain on the dune and wield air to hold any creatures back for as long as possible. While she cannot freeze them, she can deter them, which should work long enough for some archers to make their hits." The queen of Vala nodded and took Kazaar's hand. "If that is not enough, Elisara will conjure three lightning strikes, prompting Larelle and her to use their powers simultaneously. Elisara will draw a storm for Larelle to wield the rain. We know it will not affect the creatures, but we can hope to slow the foot soldiers Jabir saw."

Nyzaia had gone over the plan time and time again in her head, hoping it would give them the best chance. They could only be so prepared, not knowing the full extent of the opposing army.

"How many?" Nyzaia asked Jabir. He shook his head.

"With many contained in Myara, it is hard to tell. At least enough to match us." Nyzaia's eyes moved to the commanders and other military men around the room. Their faces were composed and prepared, despite the bomb that had been dropped on them in the last two weeks. Nyzaia recalled something Isha once said before taking her own life about the rulers needing to work together.

"We have been four realms for our entire existence." Nyzaia raised her voice, commanding the room. "But today, you do not fight for Vala, Keres, Garridon, or Nerida. You fight for your kingdom. You fight for the civilians so that they may see tomorrow. You fight for one another," she said. Sir Cain drew his sword, raising it into the air.

"For Novisia!" he yelled.

The sound of scraping metal filled the room as sword after sword was drawn and raised to the tent ceiling.

"For Novisia!" they called.

Chapter Fifty-Eight

Elisara

The wind that blew across the sandy expanse below was not Elisara's. Nature's winds had indeed been in their favour, with the sand dunes high enough for the militaries of Keres and Vala to stand upon. The wind whistled through the canyons to the east and carried like a war cry to her ears. Nyzaia lowered her arm, signalling for Garridon and Nerida's armies to advance into position, a ripple that continued down the line to her and Farid's left and another line to Elisara and Kazaar's right. There was no army in sight yet; the wind blew too much sand and distorted their view of Myara in the distance. Elisara had tried calming it or pushing it away, but each time she tried, it returned minutes later, as if the spirits or nature warred against her efforts. She thought of Vala's anger towards her. Could she limit Elisara's powers? As revenge for her apparent 'sullying' of the Vala bloodline? Elisara tucked the flying strands of hair behind her ears and tried to banish her fears.

"I cannot sense anything. Can you?" Elisara asked Kazaar. He shook his head. They had expected to see images of the creatures, as they had in Garridon, but there was nothing yet.

The wind whipped at Elisara's braid as she turned to Kazaar and reached for his hand, needing reassurance that this would all be okay. He looked down at her as the wind attempted to free his hair, too. She did not need to speak into his mind to know he understood her disappointment after failing to unlock any new powers. The clouds darkened overhead as Kazaar pulled her into him. Elisara hands reached for his matching black leather and gripped his forearms.

"Why does this feel like it is only the beginning?" she asked, searching his eyes.

"Because it is still just the beginning of us. There is more beyond what happens in this battle, angel. There is more for us." He tucked flyaway hairs behind her ear, his hand lingering on her cheek. "When this is over, I will give you the world," he murmured.

She believed him.

"What if my world"—she cupped his cheek, mirroring him—"is becoming you?" Kazaar closed his eyes and rested his forehead against hers. Lightning struck over Myara. When Kazaar opened his eyes once more, Elisara memorised the look of adoration in them, as though Kazaar's image would be enough to survive this war. His feelings washed through her, and warmth flooded her veins.

"Then I am yours. If I am your world, then you are my sun, my moon, my stars. I exist only because of you." He planted a firm and promising kiss on her lips. "If there is no you and I, there is no existence I wish to be a part of." Elisara pressed her lips to his again.

"There is no I without you," she murmured. War horns sounded over the wind, and Elisara pulled back. They turned their heads towards the sound, still gripping onto one another. Roars rumbled in the distance. It was time. Panic set in. She needed Kazaar to know that she did not just fight for her realm or her kingdom. She fought for him—their future.

"I lo—"

"I know," Kazaar said, planting a final kiss on her forehead. "Tell me when this is over." They both spun to face the approaching army. The dull sword at Elisara's hip clinked against the Sword of Sonos on Kazaar's side and vibrated in the moments before they withdrew them.

"Archers!" Nyzaia screamed. Her command echoed down the line until reaching the back of the Garridon soldiers to the west.

Hundreds of bows raised. For the first time in a while, Elisara wondered where Caellum was and if he was okay. Elisara turned her head. Sadira stood several rows behind them, hidden among soldiers, the same thought mirrored in her expression. Sadira's eyes caught hers, and Elisara nodded.

The grey clouds above lifted, yet the sky did not brighten as a black fog emerged in its wake, revealing hundreds of the black creatures with their ragged wings wide and mouths open. They did not dive. The sound of their flapping wings tore above the desert, where they hovered in wait. Elisara looked down for any sign of the soldiers. Nothing. Elisara, Kazaar, Nyzaia, and Farid waited in tense silence, ready to move. They waited for Caellum to make his call and for his best archer to release a single notch on a single mark to test the success of Sadira's imbuement.

Elisara breathed in when a flash of a silver arrow soared through the air and found its target. A creature screamed and fell to the ground, where it thrashed for mere seconds before stilling. A wave of nausea hit Elisara. *It worked.* Yet the other creatures were unfazed, remaining in their scattered formation above, not sparing a glance at the fallen beast below them. The war horns sounded clearly in the distance, slowly drawing closer through the desert sands.

"We need as much time as possible to get the creatures before their foot soldiers meet us," Kazaar called to Nyzaia. She raised her hand again and lowered it with force.

"Release!" she shouted. Elisara stumbled as they let loose hundreds of arrows. Most hit their marks as creatures of darkness fell from the sky. Elisara's legs wavered, and she extended her arms to steady herself.

"Did you feel that?" Elisara asked, bracing against Kazaar's arm. He caught her hand and turned towards the city of Myara, partly hidden by dunes of sand. The war horns had stopped. Fallen creatures, pierced by arrows, scattered the sands, creating a maze for the enemy soldiers soon to approach. The wind stopped and the floating sand fell. The pounding of feet shook the ground.

Thousands of new human soldiers marched forward from Myara, outmatching them at least two to one on the ground. Elisara tried to learn from their formation, but there seemed to be no obvious reason for their positioning. The formation alternated with a soldier dressed in grey between two men in copper armour, the pattern repeating throughout the rows of fighters. She scanned the army in search of their leader. Her eyes paused on several men, who were the only ones with helmets, yet none of them felt right.

Only when the final row of enemy soldiers came into view did she spot him. She could not distinguish his features from the distance, but she knew it was Caligh, and when the tall man on a night black horse raised his arm, the armies halted. Elisara's chest tightened as she gripped her sword in her right hand and steadied her left in mid-air while preparing to draw on her power.

"That's him," Elisara murmured. The man on the horse outstretched his arms, pointing in opposite directions. The soldiers split down the middle, one battalion turning to face Garridon's army and one to face Nerida's. Neither focused on the group on the dune.

Elisara was about to ask Nyzaia where they should now focus, but she halted, her mouth dropping open. Wisps of dark smoke suddenly coated the soldiers in grey, similar to the threads that often encircled Kazaar and Elisara. A moment later, the wisps faded to reveal creatures shooting into the air.

"They changed," Elisara breathed. She had no time to say anything else as the creatures plunged into Garridon and Nerida's armies. Elisara dropped her sword and turned her palms towards one another, pushing them together; she pictured the air blowing against either side of the creatures, pushing them inward and slowing their pursuit. Arrows flew again, searching for their mark, but their aim was hindered as the creatures pre-empted the movements, twirling mid-air to dodge the assault. Some fell to join the graveyard of others below, but far too many remained, cutting through the air she pushed towards them.

"It's not working!" Elisara screamed as the wind picked up. It would be seconds before the creatures descended. Nyzaia did not need to call the command this time as the soldiers raised their swords, ready for the creatures' attack. Meanwhile, the copper-coated soldiers marched forward. *Shit.* Elisara looked to Nyzaia, waiting for her to command the Keres and Vala armies to intervene. Nyzaia watched intently, leaning into Farid, who spoke into her ear.

The foot soldiers were moments away from Garridon's first line of defence when green vines as thick as tree trunks shot from the ground, weaving in front of the Novisian soldiers on both sides: a wall of green protecting them from the enemy, and allowing them to focus on the creatures that picked at them one by one from the sky. Elisara spun. Sadira's brow was furrowed, her eyes glowing the brightest green Elisara had seen. Soren stood by her side, watching, and caught Elisara's eye. Her hair was freshly braided, and war paint smeared her cheeks. She held the Garridon sword in one hand and a shield in the other. She scanned the soldiers below, but for what, Elisara was unsure.

The foot soldiers hacked at the vines, and Elisara winced at the cries of the Novisian soldiers drowning beneath the creatures' roars and screams. The screams pierced her mind; there was something different about them—more humane than the previous creatures they had killed. Elisara narrowed her eyes at the beasts in the sky. Their wings were different, larger, and less ragged, and their bodies less haggard. They were the ones that had transformed from human form. Turning from the Garridon soldiers, Elisara watched Nerida's army. A creature landed beside the armoured soldiers and stood like any person would.

"Half of the creatures are different," Elisara said to Kazaar. "A different breed or race, or born versus made. I do not know the logistics, but they are different. What if the swords do not work the same?" Elisara's panic heightened as the creature she had watched transformed. Long black hair flowed behind him, and a finely tailored jacket replaced his black leather skin. She discerned a glint of amber in his eyes. He stood still and stared past the vines and lines of Nerida's soldiers to the queen raised on a dune.

Larelle.

Chapter Fifty-Nine

Larelle

Alvan's hand tightened around Larelle's as they watched the creatures claw at the vines Sadira summoned to protect them, refocusing their efforts from the Neridian soldiers to break down the barrier instead.

"They're going to break through. Are you ready?" Alvan asked. Larelle turned to him, her hair whipping into her face. She nodded. Larelle tried to focus on the soldiers and creatures, preparing for any need to change the plan, but her mind kept drifting to where Zarya sat in the palace, hoping her mother would come home. Larelle and Alvan stood slightly raised behind her army that formed a last line of defence to protect her while she wielded. She looked over to the dune to her left, where Elisara stood with Kazaar, waiting for the signal. Though Elisara faced her, she was not looking at Larelle; instead, she watched someone on the ground as the soldiers stripped away the vines. Larelle scanned the front line and clenched her jaw, her grip tightening on Alvan's hand.

Osiris. He was too far away for Larelle to read his expression, yet she knew it was him by the tailored black jacket and amber flowers and the sleek hair pulled back and low. She knew when he drew closer, she would see the amber ring in his eyes.

So, they did meet again. Larelle narrowed her eyes, recalling parts of their conversation. He owed a debt, but to who? She looked then at the man on the horse in the centre of the desert. *Was Osiris forced to be here?* She did not know why he shifted unless it was merely to taunt her because a moment later, he returned to the form of his creature and joined the mix of copper soldiers shredding the vines. He was stronger than others, slicing the remaining vines in one forceful strike. As he did, the creatures that had been diving low on her soldiers flurried into the air, and she lost track of which one was him. Copper armour clashed with her soldiers while Nyzaia screamed orders from the dunes.

The Vala and Keres forces cascaded down the sandbank, intent on the soldiers encroaching Nerida and Garridon's ranks. Lightning struck three times in the centre of the desert—Elisara's signal. Larelle released Alvan's hand and mourned it instantly. Clashing metal rang through the air, competing with the screams of the dying. The clouds gathered above as the final two armies joined the battle, a collision of bodies from all angles. Copper soldiers dominated the sand, but the placement of their armies was working, forcing the foot soldiers to battle on all sides while the creatures plucked people from above.

Thunder rumbled overhead—a warning of what two queens could do together. Rain fell gently at first until Larelle latched onto it and forced it down in sheets. With a flourish of her hands, she paused the rain mid-air, twisting and pulling it together until she controlled a full stream of water gathered in the air. Three more lightning strikes was the signal for their soldiers to duck after the next. Lightning struck the ground closest to the man on the horse and sent him to the floor at the same moment Larelle shot the stream of water low over the field, knocking down enemy shoulders caught in the crossfire. It allowed the crouching Novisian soldiers to deliver a quick killing blow.

They only had one chance at it. The soldiers would know now what to expect.

Larelle released her control, allowing the water to soak into the desert floor. She looked at Elisara, who stumbled into Kazaar. Larelle frowned. It was not normal for Elisara to be affected by her powers.

The sides appeared balanced, though Larelle did not know if her confidence was misplaced as she continued watching, readying to use her power to repel the foot soldiers. Yet, for now, she risked hitting her own men. Surveying the rest of the armies, Larelle pushed the wet curls from her face and struggled to differentiate between the sides as rain continued falling. Shadows appeared as the general moved through the path he created, intent on reaching Elisara and Kazaar, who ran down the dune alongside Farid and Nyzaia to join the fight. Larelle made to follow.

"Please. Do not!" Alvan begged, holding her wrist.

"I cannot stay up here while they join the fight." Larelle's arm was slick with rain, slipping from his grip.

"Sadira still remains," he said, glancing at where Sadira stood, hair plastered to her face as she manoeuvred vines to isolate the fight into separate groups. "She knows her strengths and sword fighting is not one of them." Droplets streamed down Alvan's face. He was right. "You know your strengths: patience, detail, power. Use that." He spun Larelle to face the ongoing battle, positioning his hands on her hips.

Focus. What can I do? Larelle watched. There were not enough archers on Novisia's side, and any damage to the creatures could only be done when they descended on her soldiers. She needed to strike them while they were still in the air.

"The creatures on this side of the battle are not focused on us," she said, gesturing to the beasts, who all followed the actions and direction of one creature. She knew who. Why was Osiris keeping them away from her?

"So, what can you do?" he asked. Larelle looked around, counting the daggers and weapons on Nerida's soldiers, forming a protective line in front.

"Disarm," she commanded. The soldiers hesitated for a moment and glanced at one another before looking at Alvan.

"Your queen said disarm!" Alvan barked.

"Lay them in individual rows on the floor," she said. The soldiers quickly did as she asked while Larelle knelt on one knee, lining the weapons with the creatures soaring above the battlefield. She wielded water and created a stream to propel a dagger towards one, hitting its mark. The creature fell. None of its comrades noticed where the dagger came from. She glanced at a grinning Alvan, his eyes beaming with pride.

Refocusing, Larelle made quick work of the other daggers. One, two, three.

Eight.

Nine.

Ten.

Creatures fell in quick succession alongside the few remaining archers until only one beast roamed on the eastern side. Slowly, Larelle rose from her knee. Osiris hovered in one spot, flapping his wings. She tilted her head when she realised he no longer seemed as terrifying. She could kill him. He shifted into human form yet kept his wings; he stared straight at her. He was close enough now; she could make out the glowing golden rings in his eyes. Raising the final knife in her hand, she prepared to throw it. Then she saw it—the flash of fear at the mark of imbuement on the knife's blade, the slight shimmer catching in the light as the rising sun forced its way through. Osiris composed his features, though his eyes were wary and calculating as he watched Larelle. He nodded to her before diving back towards the Garridon recruits, changing mid-air to his former state. Alvan looped his arm around her shoulder, pulling her close.

"Was that him?" he asked. Larelle nodded slowly, trying to understand his motives. His wings were larger than most as he reached the other side of the field. With no threat of creatures on her side and with her foot soldiers gaining, Larelle took the moment to track Osiris. He did not engage in the fight but circled the other creatures. *He is looking for someone,* she realised. *Arik.* His black wings slowed as Osiris found him, and Larelle watched intently as the two creatures looked at General Caligh in the centre, slaughtering his way through the centre line to reach Kazaar and

Elisara. Osiris and Arik soared back in the direction they came, the mist of sand shrouding their retreating frames. Larelle frowned. Osiris did not strike her as someone who would abandon war.

"Larelle!" Alvan called from where he pushed forward with their line of soldiers. Copper armour flashed in the gaps between the men. Pushing forward, Larelle shoved her arms between her soldiers and wielded the rain into a flow of force that propelled the opposition back. Men tumbled down the dune into the waiting swords of Nerida's soldiers.

The sands of fighters were a mess; she could no longer tell where the Novisian soldiers hailed from as their formations muddled in the sea of destruction. The rain eased, and the clouds thinned. Elisara fought sword to sword with a soldier, too focused on hand-to-hand combat to control the air. Kazaar fought beside her, a formidable duo if Larelle had ever seen one. A copper soldier broke ranks and circled, heading for the back of Kazaar and Elisara, who did not yet see him.

Larelle narrowed her eyes and raised her fist before her. She squeezed, and when Kazaar spun to find the soldier, the man's hand clawed at his throat. The action only lasted a moment as the enemy soldier repositioned his sword, and Larelle frowned. But the brief change in stance allowed Kazaar to plunge the Sword of Sonos through him. Larelle gasped. The Sword of Sonos shone as Kazaar pulled it from the soldier's chest. Clutching his wound, the soldier stumbled and fell to the ground. One moment, he was there, accepting his death, and the next, his body crumbled into blackened ash. Her eyes looked back and forth between the ash and the surrounding soldiers, who bled like normal. Although they were dead, their bodies remained.

"Something is different," Larelle said to Alvan. "I just tried to make a soldier choke up water, and it didn't work. He simply clawed his throat for a moment as though inconvenienced." Alvan furrowed her brow. Something protected the foot soldiers in the same way the creatures were immune to their power.

"The foot soldiers; they are of darkness. Kazaar just killed one with the Sword of Sonos, and it disintegrated." Larelle scanned the dead copper-clad bodies near them. "But these still have their bodies." Frowning, she looked at Elisara. "Something is different about our weapons."

Chapter Sixty

Soren

Agony. Memories. Confusion.

Soren's mind was an explosion of emotions as she roared her way through soldiers, trying to reach Caligh. A piercing sensation had invaded her mind ever since she stepped foot on the battlefield—ever since her eyes tugged on him upon his horse as though this were but a simple evening of riding. Soren screamed again as the pain throbbed, forcing her eyes to close. She swung wildly with her sword as she did. She had lost count of how many she had killed, spurred on by each new spray of blood. The warmth of their blood distracted from her warring mind as she worried about betraying Caligh by killing his soldiers. But he had so many; she did not think he would care in the long run.

Another memory appeared: a flash of two girls with blonde hair running through grass fields in a rain not too dissimilar from that pouring on her now. It was over in a second as Soren opened her eyes, her brain foggy as she ploughed on. It was the third time it had happened: the pain, the odd memory resurfacing. It was as if Soren's subconscious tried to convince her of all the good she once possessed before she was obsessed with becoming queen, before the prophecy, and before him.

But Soren had promised. She promised to help him from the very first moment they met. A memory flashed again of two blond girls sitting at the base of a tree with wooden figurines in hand. One laughed lyrically and tossed her curls while the other snorted, her braids falling into her face. The two leaned on one another, collapsing in fits of laughter until one girl disappeared, swallowed by dark wisps, which welcomed the other child and said she was special. Soren cried out as a knife grazed the skin between her armour.

Swinging her sword, she met the neck of the soldier before her. His eyes widened in the visor of his helmet before the life faded from him. She yanked her sword from his flesh. Blood trickled down his copper armour, painting the engraved flower on his breastplate in red. Soren stepped over his body, her eyes intent on the general who was thrown from his horse and now battled every Garridon soldier with ease. Soren screamed in determination, yet her cries were swallowed when a soldier shoved her. She elbowed the approaching soldier and knocked his head back before slicing a thin dagger across his neck.

Her braids hit her face as she spun again, searching for Caligh, yet a memory invaded the present: two blonde women, who were no longer children; they fought, hurling insults at one another.

"To the king!" A soldier roared.

Following the sound, Soren watched as three Garridon soldiers battled to reach Caellum, who fended off three enemies at once. Soren was the closest to him; the others would not reach him quick enough, constantly repelled by the battle.

Another memory—Sadira arriving in Garridon and curtseying to Caellum. Soren shook her head and searched for Caligh. His frame towered above the other soldiers as he hacked away the men in the middle line. When she glanced back at Caellum, two of his opponents were dead, and only one remained. He would be fine. Soren made to step towards Caligh when a flash of copper darted past. She spun as the soldier circled Caellum, creeping from behind.

Caligh, whispered a voice.

Sadira consumed Soren's awareness as a memory of her resurfaced. It was the first time Sadira smiled in Garridon, peering up at her future husband. *Caellum*, the voice whispered. Soren looked at where Sadira stood on the dune, wrapping vines around the soldiers nearest to her. When she turned back, Caellum's sword was interlocked with a soldier; he did not see the one who approached from behind. *You might regret this,* she thought to herself.

Soren stormed ahead towards the King. Caellum pushed back against the soldier, his eyes widening when he noticed Soren. She pulled a dagger from her side and raised it to throw. His eyes moved behind her to where she knew Sadira stood, his gaze softening.

Soren's eyes glowed. She willed dark vines to shoot through the foot of the soldier and hold him in place. Soren threw the knife, grazing past Caellum's hair and piercing the neck of the soldier just as his foot ripped free of the vine. Caellum plunged his sword.

The pair panted heavily, staring at one another. Caellum nodded.

"You're welcome," Soren panted before whirling to find Caligh. He had made it further than she realised and headed for Kazaar and Elisara, who still fought side by side. *He will be disappointed in me again.* She had not separated them as she promised.

Soren broke into a run down the side of the battle, ducking as a creature swooped overhead, its claws grabbing two Garridon soldiers. Soren ran up the dune to her right for a vantage point, surveying the situation. No creatures were on the other side, and the copper soldiers dwindled in numbers. On the western side, however, the desert swarmed with creatures, outnumbering the Novisian soldiers two to one.

Elisara and Kazaar fought back-to-back with Farid and Nyzaia. *Could Caligh face the four strongest fighters?* Soren's head throbbed again, struggling to manage the conflict warring within her: the need to ensure Caligh's safety and the desire to fight for Garridon, the realm that should be hers.

Soren reached for the dead body on the floor closest and unclipped its copper armour. She pulled back at the sight beneath. The clothing, soaked with blood, pulled away from the fighter's skin, and blackened veins crawled from the entry point of the wound, spreading across the man's abdomen in webs. The man's eyes were wide open, yet he was clearly dead. *What are you?* Soren thought, though she had no time to linger on it. She pulled off her own breastplate and replaced it with copper in the hopes the opposition would ignore her, while the Garridon soldiers recognised her before striking. Picking her sword back up, Soren ran through the battle, dodging swings between others as she headed towards Caligh. Nobody stopped her. Until he did.

Dark shadows flew up on either side of the cleared centre path, blocking the soldiers until only Soren and Caligh remained. He kept his back to her, his cloak fluttering in the breeze while his focus remained on the Vala and Keres soldiers blocking his path to Kazaar and Eliara. Soren stared up at the walls of darkness, sliding her hands along it. They were so familiar, the same shadows haunting her mind and cloaking him from her. Stepping forward, she called to him.

"Caligh!" He tilted his head, the misty rain landing on his dark hair. She continued her path forward, noticing the greying threads that matched the silvery lines on the back of his cloak.

"Soren," he said in the same silken voice she was accustomed to in her head. It was him. It was really him standing before her in the flesh. She increased her pace and stumbled, halting, as he raised his hand. The scars were more prominent without the darkness hiding them from her as hundreds of short lashes coated his pale skin. She waited obediently until Caligh sighed. He flourished his cloak, freeing his body to turn to her. He was older than she expected; the grey in his short beard was more prominent than that in his hair. His cheeks were hollowed, his dark eyes wide as they stared straight at her, unblinking.

"They still stand side by side," he said. Was that all he had to say? It was the first time meeting him in the flesh, and all she had done was disappoint him. Soren straightened her back, trying to move towards him, but her feet failed her. "You still have time, Soren." He turned to leave when the wall of shadows on either side of her slowly faded. He paused, glancing at something behind her. Soren turned her head.

A tall man with long black hair strode towards them in the distance, with a short boy beside him. They both wore finely tailored black, yet she could not decipher any details, too distracted by the creature they held in chains. It differed from the eyeless ones, with deep black irises, but did not have the gold rings that Larelle described in the creatures that took her. It turned its head to her and paused, meeting Soren's eyes. There was more to this—another plan—and it dawned on Soren then that she knew little of the true extent of this man or his schemes. They had all been so naïve. The creature cried out as the two men pulled its chains, halting it in place.

Soren winced at the pain in its eyes and looked to her left, where the others flew. Their smooth wings and precise movements were so similar to the one in chains.

"Make the right decision, Soren. It is becoming tiring having to push you at every moment." Caligh sighed and walked past her towards the two men and the creature.

"I will not let you down. They will be separated by the time you turn for them," she said, but he did not look or acknowledge her statement. As he left her, she moved, rushing towards the queen of Vala and her commander.

Creatures flew in her path, delaying her efforts and pushing back Nerida's soldiers. Vala and Keres' soldiers moved to assist their comrades, blocking Soren's path. She would not reach Kazaar and Elisara in time.

Soren whistled low and loud, a call she knew would be heard over any roar or clash of metal. Howls sounded in answer, and she grinned when she saw them. Her wolves padded over the dunes, their heads low. If Soren could not get to Elisara and Kazaar, her wolves could. She hoped they understood her intent and would cause confusion amongst the rulers. Soren began pushing through the soldiers.

She would not fail.

Chapter Sixty-One

Nyzaia

"We're outnumbered!" Nyzaia yelled, wiping the mist from her face. Her back felt warm as the group pressed together: Farid at her left, Kazaar at her right, and Elisara covering her back. The two celestial pairs stood together while the copper armour pushed to reach them, the hundreds of their comrades lying dead on the floor.

"Could be worse!" Elisara shouted. "At least the creatures are not interested in us."

"She has a point," Farid agreed, lunging with his sword at the soldier who approached only to create a path for the warriors next in line.

"How are there so many? Larelle's side took out hundreds," Kazaar panted.

"The Garridon side has been losing to the creatures," replied Farid. "Which has left more of the enemy to turn back to us." Nyzaia nodded and swung her blade at a man's neck, who fell to the ground, gurgling. Still, they kept coming.

"Maybe we should have hidden you!" Nyzaia shouted to Kazaar over the clash of metal. "They seem intent on reaching you." The moment they descended the battlefield, it was as though the soldiers recognised Kazaar and instantly followed the four of them.

"What fun would that have been?" Kazaar said, and Nyzaia heard the grin in his voice. Elisara bumped into Nyzaia again, who frowned at her friend. She had been unstable since the fight began.

"Are you okay?" she asked. Elisara nodded, throwing a dagger at a charging soldier.

"I think trying to access other powers has exhausted me," she said.

"I don't suppose it might magically work now?" Nyzaia asked.

"I'm struggling to multitask," Elisara breathed, and suddenly, the lightning and winds stopped.

"Shit!" Kazaar exclaimed, and Nyzaia turned her head. A wall of shadows formed through the middle of the armies.

"Caligh has power," Nyzaia said. "What if he is affecting your power, Elisara? To weaken you and make it easier to separate you from Kazaar?" Elisara grunted as she kicked a soldier back.

"It would make sense."

"He did not account for her great sword skill," Kazaar laughed.

"I learned from the best."

"Are you really joking in the middle of a fucking battle?" Farid shouted. Nyzaia did not have time to be shocked that he had sworn as a soldier grabbed Nyzaia and yanked her from the group. Farid's panic shot through her, but it soon eased as a thin dagger dropped from her sleeve and into her hand. She pierced the man's neck. No soldier waited behind him. Nyzaia spun. They had dodged her and separated the group, heading straight for Elisara and Kazaar. Nyzaia's eyes widened as she watched a body fall at Kazaar's hand, disintegrating into ash.

"Has that sword been doing that the entire time?" she yelled, battling through soldiers. She slashed at countless backs of copper armour to reach them.

"Yes!" Kazaar shouted, gutting another. "I did not have time to think about why, seeing as I'm busy avoiding being killed or kidnapped."

Howls sounded through the desert, and Soren's wolves charged towards them. Thick green roots shot from the ground, twisting and blocking their path. Nyzaia looked at Sadira, the fear clear on her face at the thought of Soren betraying them. When the wolves leapt over the vines, Nyzaia brandished her knife, but they did not attack her. They leapt for the soldiers' throats, who circled Elisara and Kazaar, taking them down one by one. The vines retreated, and Nyzaia nodded towards Sadira. They were okay.

Farid approached Nyzaia and scanned her eyes.

"Ready?" he asked.

"Ready," she said as they dived back into the fight. More soldiers attempted to reach Elisara and Kazaar, but Nyzaia charged at them and sliced at their exposed flesh, bringing them to their knees. No one would take her brother. Nyzaia screamed as she reached for her power again. Their uniforms resisted fire. Burning the sands did not work either, soaked from Larelle and Elisara's combined power.

"What is the point of having all this power if it does not work against any of you!" she shrieked, bringing her sword down on a soldier's head. Nyzaia glanced to where Caligh had been and swallowed. He was closer. Myara was now far behind him, and he stood closer to the dune the rulers had begun on, close enough for Nyzaia to discern his features. She thought of all the odd passages and illustrations in *Myths and Lies of Ithyion* and the recent revelations. It was not implausible that this man could take power—dampen it.

Fear pierced Nyzaia as she noticed his grin, his wide eyes trained ahead. Nyzaia ducked from a lunging soldier, turning to glance at Elisara and Kazaar. The wolves continued circling and bit at the copper soldiers, diverting and confusing the two sides.

"Elisara!" Kazaar shouted. They were separated. Rows of soldiers fought those from Keres and Vala, blocking the pair from reaching one another. Nyzaia whirled back to Caligh, his path set on Kazaar. *No.* While her flames may not penetrate the soldiers' armour, it could distract them. Flourishing her hand, a wall of fire ignited either side of her, quick enough for Nyzaia to run a clear path towards Caligh.

Her feet pounded, determination sizzling through her veins as she ran at full force, leaping over scattered bodies from all sides. Yet the general's grin was manic as he remained focused on Kazaar, and as he drew close, Nyzaia raised her sword.

She gasped as Caligh's scarred hand gripped her throat and lifted her off the ground, the toes of her boots scraping across the sand. Slowly, the general turned his head. A never-ending pit of darkness resided in his eyes as though no soul remained within.

"Queen of Keres," he hissed, making Nyzaia's skin crawl. "An assassin queen who has fallen lax in recent times. You should know of more effective ways to sneak up on a person." Nyzaia dropped her sword and reached for his wrists, clawing for air.

"Just like your god, you are rash... *reactive*. I would not have cared to take your life if you had simply let me be." When he squeezed harder, Nyzaia's life flashed before her, and in every memory was one constant. Even on the brink of death, one person prevailed over all else despite her heartbreak. Tajana. Nyzaia wished she was by her side, the one person she wanted to lay eyes on for a final time before her life was taken. Blinking away tears, Nyzaia yearned to cut the pain from her chest to allow her to focus on an escape, but she was a fool to think she could ever cut Tajana from her, a woman who burned her soul. Nyzaia closed her eyes, sending a silent 'I love you' to the sky. She hoped Tajana knew; wherever she was, she hoped Nyzaia's final thought reached her.

Caligh lifted Nyzaia higher, her feet floating in the air. She gasped as his hand slipped from her throat, and someone gripped her underarms. Wind rushed past as she opened her eyes to watch the battlefield below. Caligh stared back at her with narrowed eyes.

"Another pair," he said before she was lifted higher. Nyzaia peered up at the blinding glow of Farid's wings and grinned. He gripped tighter as they soared over the war below.

"Tell me where!" he shouted. Nyzaia scanned the battlefield. The creatures were scattered, yet the realms' foot soldiers were still outnumbered, the copper soldiers turning and pushing them back towards Myara. Only several rows remained near the dune where they had arrived, all intent on one person as the remaining Novisian soldiers fought back. War horns sounded in the distance. Farid spun to face Myara. Help. *Tajana. The Historian.* Hope bloomed in Nyzaia's heart, yet it was quickly ripped from her. From the city of Myara, hundreds more copper-clad soldiers emerged, marching in uniformed rows.

"We were doomed from the beginning," she breathed. Caligh had tricked them into using all their strength on this one attack.

"They will be surrounded," Farid said. It was a trap. With their backs turned, the Novisian soldiers could not see the approaching attack. Nyzaia found Larelle and Sadira; the latter moved to the Neridian queen as they stared in the same direction. Nyzaia hoped they had a plan because Kazaar was her priority.

"Down there," Nyzaia called, pointing to where Kazaar and Elisara still fought, separated, while Caligh continued his intent path towards her brother. Farid nodded, and his wings sparked as they flapped, lowering to the ground. He dropped them at the edge, far enough for the copper soldiers not to have noticed them. Farid gripped Nyzaia's hand, their celestial tie burning between them.

"If this is it," he said, but Nyzaia shook her head to stop him. He squeezed her hand. "If this is the end, it has been my greatest honour to serve you." Nyzaia blinked back tears as Farid smiled. She did not need to say anything; he knew she reciprocated his feelings. Returning the smile, pride burned inside her as Farid no longer hid himself from the world. Letting his wings burn for all to see, he kicked into the air and flew above Nyzaia, showering the world with sparks.

Chapter Sixty-Two

Elisara

The soldier before Elisara faded in and out of view. Blinking hard, she swung her sword but missed her mark. She swung again and, this time, hit his shoulder. When he doubled over, she pushed the sword through him. Her vision refocused. She did not know what was wrong. Dark eyes met hers in the near distance to her left—Caligh. Was Nyzaia right? *Could he really be affecting my power and exhausting me?* Caligh bowed his head to her before switching his focus. *Yes.*

Elisara spun, following Caligh's eyeline, who stared intently at Kazaar. He knew. He knew she was a thorn in his side and would refuse to let him take Kazaar.

"No," Elisara murmured. She tried to shove through the soldiers, yet struggled with each step and swing.

"Elisara!" Kazaar called for the hundredth time. He had not stopped calling for her since the damned wolves separated them, both helping and hindering them.

"Kazaar!" she called back, trying to reach him.

A light moved overhead, forcing her to look up. *Farid.* Elisara gasped as wings of flaming feathers pierced through the drizzle of rain and swooped low. Farid swiped at the heads of the soldiers with his sword, and Elisara paused, her mouth falling open. She had little time to question Farid's wings, provided he still fought for Nyzaia. He hovered every few strikes, searching for someone. Elisara followed his sight to where Nyzaia stood several rows from Kazaar, striding for him with determination.

Elisara tried to mimic it, yet her steps were heavy as she battled towards the man she loved, with Nyzaia on the other side and Caligh to the right of them. Three attempts at the man she loved. Three attempts for someone to take him, two for good, one for evil. But Caligh's expression did not mirror the panicked determination on her own.

The man of darkness was confident, his cloak fluttering in the breeze as he strode forward with a smirk on his lips. He batted away every Novisian soldier who reached him with ease like they were nothing more than irritant flies encroaching his space. *Powerful.* He was so powerful, and yet he allowed this battle to continue.

He is toying with us, Elisara realised. General Caligh knew he would win, but their struggle was a mere form of entertainment to him. A flicker of raw fury lit within Elisara; he thought he could take what was hers. Focusing on the flame within, she prayed it would blossom and ignite her with the power she and Kazaar were supposedly blessed with—the essence of a god—yet nothing reached her fingertips. Elisara's anger was the only thing spurring her forward as she inched closer.

Caligh stopped. He glanced at Nyzaia on his right and Elisara on his left. Raising his hands either side as though this were a theatrical performance, he leisurely drew them together. Elisara frowned at the absence of his power. She felt nothing. So what was he doing? The surrounding soldiers slowed, and Elisara paused as Caligh turned his hands until his palms faced outward. He grinned at Elisara and forced his hands out.

Darkness erupted. Shadows forced away the soldiers from both sides and launched them to the ground. Elisara crouched and braced her sword. Her hands trembled as the sword wavered beneath her. A wall of darkness stood, blocking Elisara, Nyzaia, and anyone from reaching Kazaar. Yet the fighting continued outside of its wall, with the copper soldiers now oblivious to Kazaar's presence, intent only on pushing the realms' back. Elisara rushed forward, resting a hand against the shadow, which hummed at her touch. She pushed, trying to force herself through it, but it did not relent. Through the wisps, she saw Kazaar, his sword raised before Caligh.

The general did and said nothing. He simply looked Kazaar up and down, his expression one of disgust. A flash of orange clashed against the shadows, illuminating Nyzaia, who stood next to Farid, pounding her fists against the darkness the same way Elisara was.

Elisara reached for her power to blow the shadows away. Nothing. Nyzaia bombarded it with flames, a miniscule flicker in the walls' defence.

Kazaar, she whispered into his mind. Only silence greeted her. *Kazaar!*

He stood braced on the sand, raising the Sword of Sonos raised. No wisps of shadow and light held the sword to him, as it usually did. He turned his head to Elisara, his eyes widening when he realised he could not reach her mind. She pounded against the wall again, screaming.

"I'll kill you!" Elisara shrieked. "Touch him, and I will kill you!" Still, Caligh did not move. Kazaar's patience faded as he moved, angling the sword towards the general. Darkness flashed, and a sword crafted of shadows emerged, so dense it may as well have been forged from metal.

Elisara's sword vibrated at her side like it had every time it met the Sword of Sonos. She raised it in her hand. With every strike Kazaar made against the general, Elisara made the same against the wall. Over and over, Kazaar and Elisara fought, fighting for their friends, their kingdom, and one another. Caligh laughed a manacle laugh that pierced Elisara's bones. That flicker of fury ignited in Elisara again as she collided with the wall. The shadows shrieked as an indent formed, but it repaired itself just as quick.

She screamed and hit the wall again as Caligh's laughter heightened, yet Elisara continued fighting for the other half of her. Kazaar ducked, hooking his legs around Caligh like he had countless times with Elisara. Shadows shot from Caligh's hands and encircled Kazaar's foot, twisting him over onto his stomach. *No.*

Caligh pushed his boot against Kazaar's back, holding him down while his shadows reached for the Sword of Sonos, placing it in Caligh's hand. Nyzaia faltered on the other side of the wall. Her hands rested against the wall with wide eyes as she watched her brother. *Get up*, Nyzaia mouthed. *Get up!* She appeared to be screaming now, tears welling in her eyes.

"Get up." Though it was not Nyzaia who spoke, it was Caligh. His voice was deep and ancient, stoking the fury left inside Elisara's empty body. Caligh removed his foot from Kazaar's back, who shifted instantly, flourishing his hands. No power emerged from his fingertips; nothing reached out to defend him. Kazaar's eyes widened momentarily before he jumped to his feet and reached for his weapons, yet he had none left. Elisara swung at the wall again. She would do anything—give everything—to reach him. She would relinquish her title, her realm, her power, her tie, anything to get through the wall. But no one answered her pleas for help; no spark ignited within her. She was powerless.

"She is relentless," Caligh said to Kazaar. "Elisara." He nodded in her direction.

"Keep her name out of your mouth," Kazaar growled. Caligh laughed again, circling Kazaar; he caught Elisara's eye as he passed.

"So possessive, those with a celestial tie," he said. Elisara hit the wall again. "You feel emotions so strongly." Caligh waved his hand, and shadows snaked along the floor for Kazaar's feet, climbing around his legs to lock him in place. *No.* Elisara reached within her soul again, searching for that power. *Someone help me*! She screamed to the gods in her mind. *Do not take him from me.*

"Hatred." The shadows twisted around Kazaar's abdomen as he clenched his jaw. "Friendship," Caligh murmured. "Passion." The sword glowed as he raised it and faced Kazaar, who was only a few steps away. Kazaar looked to Elisara then as she pierced the wall again, screaming. He opened his mouth to say something, to mouth words they had promised not to say until this was over.

"Pain." Caligh grinned and plunged the Sword of Sonos

through Kazaar's chest. Elisara screamed, piercing the sword through the wall of darkness as her heart ripped in two. Elisara screamed from the pain as a piece of her was forced from her body and as Kazaar's body fell in time with the walls of shadow. And just like when her heart once shattered in tandem with a falling statue in the Vala gardens, destined to be pieced back together by this man, Elisara's heart splintered as her sword broke through and the shadows fell.

"No!" she screamed. "No, no, no." Caligh pulled the sword from Kazaar's chest and stepped back, the shadows engulfing him as Elisara ran to Kazaar.

She did not notice the shadows weaving throughout the war or separating the copper soldiers from the Novisians. She did not notice how everyone paused or how the creatures retreated at Caligh's whistle before silence descended across the Ashun Desert. All she saw was Kazaar's chest slowing, the shadows falling away to reveal blood seeping from him, his hands slack by his sides.

"Kazaar," she whispered. "Kazaar." Elisara fell to her knees at his side. "Kazaar, look at me." She placed her hands over his wound to stop the bleeding. Reaching for a dagger, she sliced her hand, letting her blood fall on his wound. "It will be okay; we are tied," she reassured him. "You will heal." Yet, as Elisara glanced at the stickiness on her hands, as he tried to speak, she found they were red. Only red. No silver blood flooded from her veins; no sign of their tie remained. "No," she sobbed. Kazaar tried to reach for her hands as she pulled his leathers aside. The silver film on his sun scar faded, leaving only the faint reminder of raised skin.

"Angel," he murmured.

"No!" Elisara sobbed. Kazaar's breathing slowed beneath her, and he coughed, sputtering blood, red staining her skin and clothes. Time stilled as Elisara memorised his features, his lips that promised her the world, a smile that lit up only for her, and eyes that promised her an eternity together. Elisara's hands trembled as she clenched his wet leathers, squeezing her eyes shut.

"Eyes," he wheezed, "on me, angel." Elisara opened them to meet his face. She moved her hands to his cheeks, staining his face with her blood.

"There is no existence without you," she cried. The dark and light tendrils from the universe faded in his eyes to their fiery amber glow from before and then the final brown that belonged only to her. Kazaar blinked slowly and opened his mouth to speak when his hand stilled on her wrist. Elisara clutched his face as his fire faded and his head lulled to the side. Her hands faltered as his face began to crumble, stealing Elisara's chance to say goodbye with a final kiss.

"No," she whispered as Kazaar began to disintegrate, killed by the Sword of Sonos. "No!" The other half of Elisara's soul disintegrated before her, fading into blackened ash that floated on the wind. Elisara fell forward, dragging her hands through what remained of him.

The fury that had been within her twisted, the pain within her as he left her burned under her skin. Elisara shrieked, her scream echoing across the desert and bouncing off the darkened clouds. Lightning struck, and the ground trembled. Elisara screamed as the universe took him.

Someone laughed behind her, and Elisara's tears fell in the ash as she turned when Caligh emerged from his shadows. When Elisara looked around, everyone was paused, trapped by the darkness.

"We could end this here, Elisara." His voice whispered to her in the wind. "I took him. I got what I wanted, but now, there is you. It seems only fair that I stay and add you to my collection of deaths." Elisara said nothing, the agony within her threatening to overtake her reason.

There is no I without you.

"I will give you two hours to mourn your deaths and regroup before I take your kingdom, as I have taken so many before it." Caligh tossed the Sword of Sonos on the sands by her feet, a smirk on his face as she frowned.

They should have known. They should have known this was never the end, that Caligh would take Novisia like he took Ithyion.

Elisara said nothing as she turned back to where Kazaar had laid, her hands clenched in his ashes. Her fingers caught on something smooth, which she pulled from his remains. His talisman. The only piece she had left of him. When she turned back to Caligh, he had faded into the shadows. The darkness holding back the people of Novisia dropped, and her people ran to her.

Chapter Sixty-Three

Caellum

Bodies collided with Caellum as he forced through the crowd, the enemy soldiers now hidden, protected in shadows he did not understand. Nyzaia had called for retreat, a command echoed by Sir Cain. Caellum pushed his way through the running soldiers who headed for the tents at the edge of Keres to await further instruction, yet what instruction, he did not know. He had been fighting a copper-clad soldier when a wall of shadow emerged, shrouding the soldier, too, as a call for retreat resounded across the sands.

Odd looks met him as he ran in a different direction, pushing against the crowd to where he had last seen Sadira. He pushed against the wave, his limbs exhausted and weak, but despite the endless fighting, the added strength of his lineage allowed him to persist. He ran despite the throbbing of his thighs and calves. Caellum stilled when he reached where Sadira had been. She was not on the dune where he had left her to wield; she was not anywhere.

"Sadira!" Caellum shouted over the sound of trampling feet. "Sadira!" he screamed, spinning in every direction and scanning the sea of blood-covered Novisian soldiers. His heart hammered, his breastplate suddenly too tight as he charged in different directions, shouting her name. The soldiers thinned out before him, most now over the dune by the tents. He scanned again but could not find her or glimpse the light of her hair amid the darkness.

Plumes of shadows swirled and writhed, containing the copper soldiers. The remaining creatures roared and paced in the distance before some shifted back into soldiers dressed in leather uniforms.

Caellum backed away as the shadows faded, the soldiers turning and marching into formation behind General Caligh. He was calm and stood with his hands clasped, staring straight at Caellum.

"I would be quick, King. Say your goodbyes before we take your kingdom." Caellum glanced at the two men standing beside Caligh. They each held a chain attached to a creature that bit the air and writhed against its bindings. Caellum swallowed. What had they done to the beast to make it so dangerous that it should be chained? Caellum scanned the line of offence one last time, but there were no captives, no head of golden-blonde hair. Caellum retreated and ran for the tents.

***

"Sadira!" Caellum shouted. Soldiers sat in the sand outside of the tents, tending to each other's wounds and sharpening swords, weighed by the knowledge of defeat. "Sadira!" He shouted again, striding for the battle tent, hoping and praying Sadira would be there with the others. The tent flap opened, and he breathed a sigh of relief.

"Sadira," he whispered as he spotted golden blonde hair matted from the rain and wind. She seemed to search for his voice before he ran and held her body against him. "I couldn't find you," he murmured. "I could not find you." He kissed her, then, as though it was the only thing that might save them. Tears brushed his cheeks, and he pulled back, tracing his hands over her body. "Are you okay?" he scanned over her, tracing his hands over her body, searching for wounds. "Please tell me you are okay."

Sadira nodded and clasped his face.

"I am okay," she choked, her eyes rimmed red. "But not all of us are." She sobbed, then, and he pulled her into him, gently leading them into the tent.

The air was thick with grief. His eyes followed those sitting around the table. Soren stared into the distance, stroking one of her wolves. Larelle wiped her eyes beside Alvan, who wrapped his arm around her. Farid stood behind Nyzaia, his hands on her shoulders as tears flowed down her cheeks, but there was an empty chair. Elisara's chair.

Caellum spun to Sadira.

"She is okay," she said gently.

"She is in their tent," Larelle said between sniffs. *Their.* Caellum took the room in again. Elisara was in their tent, and while she was fine, her commander was nowhere to be seen.

"No," he breathed. While Caellum and Kazaar had never seen eye to eye, he had been the one to piece Elisara's heart back together. "I..."

"Go," Sadira said, squeezing his hand. "If anyone knows her best out of us all, it is you."

He closed his mouth. "I do not..."

"I know," she whispered and kissed him, a promise that she knew this was nothing more than him comforting her grief. Caellum grasped Sadira's cheeks in his hands and kissed her once more before leaving the tent.

It did not take long for him to reach the rulers' tents. Elisara and Kazaar had the first, the furthest from Caellum and Sadira's. He rubbed his face with his hands, dried blood crumbling beneath his fingertips. Taking in a breath, Caellum sighed before reaching for the tent flap and ducking in.

Despite the sun peering in from outside, the light in Elisara's tent had died. It was cold, as cold as Vala. Elisara did not move when Caellum entered. She sat on a stool in front of a makeshift vanity, staring at her reflection.

"Elisara," he murmured, but she did not falter from the mirror. She sat in her soaked leathers while her hands rested on the table, palms up, covered in blood that had since dried. Many loose curls had fallen from her braid. Caellum wavered at the entrance. Perhaps being the one to face her was not a good idea.

"Star," he whispered. Her eyes flickered in the mirror, glowing blue, meeting his. Elisara's face crumpled.

"It's gone. The tie, my eyes." She turned on the stool, and Caellum met her in seconds, gripping tightly to her as she sobbed into his shoulder. "He is gone; he is gone." She repeated the words as Caellum held her trembling body. It was the first time in years he had seen her break down like this and surrender to her emotions. Even when her parents had died, she was not this inconsolable. Caellum did not know how long he stood there, holding the woman he had once broken, now shattered further. He rested his head atop hers, murmuring quietly to her, attempting everything he usually would to soothe her. But the damage was irreversible. As Elisara finally stilled in Caellum's arms, he knew that she would never be the same.

"I need you to tell me what happened, star, so we know what to do," he murmured into her hair. Elisara did not pull back as she recounted the events between sobs. Caellum swallowed as she revealed everything to him, fighting his own tears that threatened to fall for her.

"Two hours," she said. "We are to meet again in two hours." She pulled back, and Caellum frowned. "Don't you see? He wants me. He took away one threat; someone who might one day have possessed darkness as strong as his. Now, he wants me. If what we believe is true—if I really have the essence of Sonos in me—I could defeat him."

"Right now, you need to focus on yourself." Caellum lowered slightly to meet her eyes. "You are one of the strongest people I know. You can do this." Elisara sniffed and turned, retaking her seat at the vanity. She stilled again, fixed only on her reflection.

"I will relay everything to the others. Someone will come for you when the time is near," said Caellum, but Elisara did not answer.

Chapter Sixty-Four

Nyzaia

When Nyzaia was six, her three brothers had played their favourite game, hide and seek. Yet when Nyzaia hid in a servant's storage room, they locked her in her spot and never sought her out. She cried for three hours until Kazaar finally found her, and it had taken him a mere three minutes to find her brothers and set their clothes alight.

When Nyzaia was fifteen, Kazaar started training her with swords. Although he knocked her down time and time again, he would help her up with a nugget of advice. Until one day—the day before her sixteenth birthday—she beat him. That was the day she left for the Red Stones.

Every day during her training, Kazaar would sneak a gift into the Red Stones den: a chocolate, a note, or new information. Kazaar Elharar had been her brother. Until today. Until he was taken from her, and she could do nothing.

Nyzaia replayed it in her mind on repeat, reliving the helplessness coursing through her as she tried to claw through the darkness to reach him. Yet fear had locked her in place once the darkness fell away. Elisara ran to him, but Nyzaia had not—instead, she was frozen with shock, heartbreak, and the grief of her fallen brother. It was the most pain Nyzaia had ever endured, and she had been tortured, used for trials, found the bodies of her family, and lost the love of her life to betrayal, but nothing—*nothing* compared to losing the flame of her real brother.

She felt the mark in her hand, a reminder of her tie to Farid.

Losing him might be the only thing that could one day hurt Nyzaia more. Warm hands rested on her shoulders and squeezed gently. She reached for Farid's hand, tears trailing down her cheeks. Caellum arrived and left for Elisara, though Nyzaia did not think anyone could help her now, but it was worth a try. Nyzaia had not been able to.

As the shadows receded from the Novisian soldiers, Nyzaia commanded the armies to retreat. Soldiers had run, and in between it all, Elisara remained, kneeling in the blackened ashes of Kazaar. Elisara sobbed and frantically waved her hands to pull back the pieces of him floating away in the wind. She rocked back and forth on her knees and clutched his talisman to her chest. Nyzaia watched and knew she could do nothing, yet she tried. Bending down to Elisara, Nyzaia calmly spoke to her despite her own grief tearing through all reason.

"No," Elisara whispered, repeating that one word. She shook Nyzaia's hands from her shoulders before stumbling up the dune for the tent she shared with Kazaar.

The tent flap rustled, and Caellum re-emerged, leaning down to kiss Sadira before taking the seat beside her. He let out a heavy sigh.

"Well?" asked Alvan, wrapping a blanket around Larelle's damp shoulders. Nyzaia waved her hand to dry the fabric instead, and Larelle smiled in thanks. It calmed Nyzaia to use her powers again after the wall of darkness had dimmed the flames within her to nothing. She never wanted to feel that again.

"She told me what he said to her."

"How is she first?" asked Larelle, and Caellum rubbed his forehead.

"Not good. She cried—a lot—but there was something off with her when I left. A stillness, as though she was completely numb."

"That is as one would expect," said Larelle, and Caellum murmured his agreement but frowned all the same. Nyzaia channelled her feelings to Farid, unable to speak just yet.

"What did she say about the armies and Caligh?" asked Farid, who moved from his spot behind Nyzaia as Sir Cain entered with a piece of paper. Death roll. Farid began moving the pieces on the battle map as Caellum spoke, removing the pieces of the soldiers they had lost.

"He told her to meet on the sands in two hours."

"That was twenty minutes ago," said Alvan.

"He said he wanted her and the kingdom," Caellum continued.

"That makes little sense." Larelle frowned. "Why ask for Kazaar but then kill him and demand Elisara?"

"Initially, he did not wish for civilian loss, yet now he wants all the kingdom?" Alvan added. The rulers frowned. *Why would he want civilians?* Nyzaia tried to think, ignoring the images of Kazaar that broke the surface of her thoughts.

"Elisara thinks he killed Kazaar because he was a threat to his power, and if Elisara has the essence of Sonos, she, too, would be a threat. That is why he wants her."

"Well, he cannot have her," Larelle scoffed, and they all murmured their agreement. Farid removed the final piece from the battle map and placed spare circles as markers for the copper army. They were outnumbered by the arrival of the extra troops.

"At least we have far fewer creatures to consider," Sadira said with some optimism.

"Did you notice how some differed?" asked Larelle. "Some are eyeless, yet others transformed, like Osiris did."

Some of the group nodded. It was odd.

"They are made," Nyzaia said finally, and all eyes turned to her. "He made the creatures from humans. Remember what we were told? How children went missing from Ithyion? What if the ones who transform are successful attempts while those who do not are failed?" Larelle's eyes widened.

"He wants the citizens to build his army," Larelle said, *but for what?* It dawned on them all, then, that they were merely a chess piece in a wider game. Novisia was merely another land to conquer, just like Ithyion. All for someone else, all for something bigger.

"He still may not be the one in charge. Perhaps he is a general following orders," said Sadira.

"If he has that much power as a general, can you imagine who else we may be up against?" Nyzaia mumbled, and silence ensued as they thought of the possibilities. They had spent their time as monarchs believing the prophecy was about them and was their greatest problem to defeat. Now, they faced the reality, more uncertainty, and the threat that the legacy they left behind would be one of darkness.

"What now? Larelle asked. She looked at Nyzaia, who gave a slight shake of her head. She could not lead. She could not focus or act rationally with Kazaar gone. Farid returned to his position behind her, and Nyzaia noted how the rulers watched him differently. They had all seen. Nyzaia cleared her throat and showed them her palm, and hesitantly, Farid followed suit.

"We are tied," she said plainly.

"Not romantically, like Elisara and..." Farid trailed off, and if Nyzaia was not grieving, she would have laughed at his bluntness to affirm such a thing.

"Do you have..." Caellum gestured to Farid's back, and Nyzaia shook her head. Perhaps if she had wings, she could have saved him. "Are you... related to them somehow?" Caellum asked, and Nyzaia's gaze shot to him.

"Does he fucking look anything like them?" she snapped. "Should we be suspicious merely because he has wings?" Caellum closed his mouth. "He looks *nothing* like them and *is nothing* like them." Farid placed a hand on her shoulder, and a wave of calm rushed through her. "We can factor Farid into our plans; he is an asset, particularly against the creatures." Nyzaia tuned out the sound of their voices, leaving them to determine battle tactics as she stared at the map before her. So many lost, and so many more they could lose.

Nyzaia always had fight within her, but for the first time in her life, she felt like giving up and sending a note to Lord Israar to offer him the throne. She could return to life in the Red Stones, isolated with only her pain for company. She liked fighting and would even love wings like Farid's were she ever to turn into one of those creatures. *You could not live under someone else's command,* Kazaar would say to her now. He would be right, of course, but the alternative was death, and unless she was to be reunited with Kazaar, that would be just as lonely an existence.

"Queen Larelle." A guard entered the tent. "We have the bodies, as requested." Larelle nodded and rose.

"Bodies?" asked Nyzaia. Alvan held the tent flap open for them.

"There is something I want to check, to learn more about them. When I was taken, Osiris said he owed a debt. I do not believe these creatures had a choice in the destruction they caused today."

Chapter Sixty-Five

Elisara

It was not her reflection that stared back at Elisara in the mirror. She would never be herself again. Lowering the temperature in the tent was a reassurance her power had returned, but Elisara's radiant blue eyes were a reminder that it was gone. Her tie to him. Kazaar was gone. The return of her power brought back her focus. And all she focused on was revenge.

Breaking down before Caellum had been easy and truthful, yet she only let down those walls to present herself as grief-stricken and weak. Elisara was not weak. Kazaar Elharar had not been tied to someone weak. Her love for him was not *weak*.

Shifting her hands to reach for her leathers, the blood on them crumbled as the final pieces of him disintegrated. She swallowed and pushed through the memory, withdrawing the leathers on top. Her eyes moved to their wooden chest. The ground was solid as she walked to it, her vision no longer blurring as it had on the battlefield. She instantly found what she wanted: a black shirt—his shirt. Tossing it on the vanity, she reached for the water and cloth.

As Elisara sat topless to wash the dirt and blood from her body, she imagined it was him instead, his touch gentle while watching her in the mirror, lavishing in the contentment. "Eyes on me," he would say, and she would smile at his reflection. She recalled his final words. *Eyes on me, angel.* Elisara scrubbed harder, refusing to cry again.

Carelessly, she dropped the cloth and reached for the brush instead, tugging hard at the knots in her hair. Her fingers were methodical as she braided it, pulling as tight as possible, desperate to feel something. Kazaar's leather bands stared at her from the jar beside her ribbons. Unlike the blue ribbons, a black band felt right, so she tied the band around the end of her braid and flipped it over her shoulder.

She breathed in the memories etched into the fabric of his shirt. It was far too big for her, but she wore it anyway, crossing the two sides over her front and tying it in a knot at the back instead of using the buttons. She wanted to smell him as she sought her revenge or died trying.

Elisara propped her forearms on the table and hunched, passing the onyx talisman back and forth between her hands. She closed her eyes, the only thing left of him. Breathing in and out, she pictured the nothingness within her, like he had taught. It was not difficult anymore to find the flicker of flame, the flame she prayed remained within her.

They had not always had the silver tinge to their marks nor held the power in their blood. But their essences had merged long before that when he had wielded all four elements. A small part of her hoped—prayed—the ability to control all four sat within her or within the talisman he had been found with.

Elisara realised it was a long shot. She dragged her sword from where it leaned next to the Sword of Sonos and rested it on her lap. Her hands were precise as she sharpened the blade, which vibrated in her lap. A single tear fell from Elisara. She rested her head in her hands.

Kazaar lying there, dying, flashed again, and she tightened her eyes, begging for the image to disappear, but it did not until Caligh's face replaced it. She envisioned his sneer and ancient laugh, the confidence dripping from his movement. *Caligh Servusian.* She wished she knew what knowing his name could do for her. She did not care if she risked using it. Fury bubbled within her again. Her neck was stiff as she twisted it. Elisara's reflection flickered as darkness seeped into the corners of her vision. Her head pounded. She wanted it to be over. Reaching into the drawer of the vanity, she took Caligh's letter and re-read his words for anything hidden, which might confirm her suspicions of why he wanted her.

"I do not ask for much in return for our vacancy from your waters and lands. There is no reason for a war amongst us or for innocent lives to be lost. I want one thing and one thing alone: the Descendent of Chaos and essence of Sitara.

The talisman in her hand felt warm from countless turning. *How does he even know Sitara has a descendant and added her essence to another?* Elisara cracked her neck again, the pain of the day creeping down her spine and working its way across her limbs. She wavered, black spots returning in her vision as she dropped the talisman on the sword, resounding through the tent. She read the second part of the letter.

Bring me Kazaar Elharar by sunrise in three days, and the loyal servants shall spill no blood.

Loyal servants, Elisara pondered. Servants. Choiceless. She wondered what they owed him. Perhaps they were mercenaries. They had killed enough of the creatures not to worry about them, nor did she fear the copper-clad servants; the rulers' powers worked, provided they had access.

Caligh's power was the only problem. She needed a way to affect him.

Elisara folded the letter and reached instead for the stacks of papers on the desk, scrawled in Kazaar's handwriting: the prophecy, pages from myths and lies, the words the gods had spoken. *At least the swords had worked.* Elisara wondered what was different between the weapons they created and the Sword of Sonos. Something had to have gone wrong with Sadira's incantation. It worked to kill the creatures in Garridon, and when it killed foot soldiers, they disintegrated. Something about the sword was more final than their own weapons.

Murmuring sounded on the other side of her tent, and Elisara sighed, wondering who would interrupt her this time. Tucking the talisman in her pocket, she stuck her head out of the tent, and despite her grief, her curiosity was piqued when she found Larelle bending over the bodies of four creatures. One had ragged wings and a deformed body, yet the next was sleek and more human-like. Beside it was one mid-transformation with wings still on its back.

Larelle crouched to examine each, always ending her inspection by checking their eyes. Larelle stood silent for some time, her hand on her mouth.

"What are you thinking?" Elisara finally asked, and Larelle jumped.

"Their eyes," she said. "All of their eyes differ. Elisara stepped from the tent, flinching at the pain in her body. She clutched the talisman in her pocket for comfort.

"What about them?" she asked, and Larelle pointed to each in turn.

"This one has no eyes. Those are black." She gestured to the final one. "And while this one with dark eyes, there are amber rings around the iris."

Elisara frowned, trying to determine a reason.

"The rings mean something," Elisara concluded, and Larelle nodded.

"Osiris said they owed a debt, and Arik, the younger one, almost slipped up and said he did not want to end up *trapped*." Elisara winced at the black and white dots in her vision. "What if Caligh freed them from somewhere? And in return, they owe him their life."

"That does not explain the difference between each," Elisara said, confused.

"The eyeless are failed first attempts; the dark eyes are fully transformed and are the same as the human here with dark eyes." Larelle pointed at the last in the row, a young man with blood-stained hair in dark grey leathers. "Look at the golden ring around his irises; he is the one I think was freed in some way."

Elisara thought Larelle was pulling at threads.

"That does not explain why the ones without rings are serving Caligh if they do not owe him anything."

Larelle frowned at Elisara's bluntness.

"I am missing something," said Larelle.

"You cannot speculate on another's history. Nothing is fact without the person there to verify it." Elisara turned and headed back into the tent.

"We have twenty minutes," Larelle called. "And then we must leave."

Elisara collapsed back on the stool. She cried out as she sat down, the pain nearly unbearable, as if trying to rip free of her body. She pulled the sword back on her lap and removed the talisman from her pocket. Twenty minutes, and she would be reunited with her love or avenge him somehow. She did not wish to *be* without him. Elisara dangled the talisman on the leather and lowered it around her neck.

Elisara's head flew back as the talisman met her chest. A gust of something reached into her soul, consuming her and unlocking something within. She gripped the sides of the table, her fingernails bleeding from the pressure. Image after image flashed through her mind, too fast for her to recognise and too many to cope with as she blacked out.

***

Elisara blinked; her face was pressed against the hard vanity. Slowly, she sat up, rubbing her forehead. Voices ran through her mind, ones she did not recognise. The pain had subsided when Elisara opened her eyes, and as she stared back at her reflection in the mirror, she knew what she had to do.

Chapter Sixty-Six

Elisara

Clarity ran through Elisara's mind, gifted with the knowledge of the past. Kazaar could not have experienced this, or else he would have told her. Each of her steps vibrated along the ground as she strode from their tent and slid her sword into the strap down her back. She held the Sword of Sonos in her left. The remaining army were in formation, standing several lines from the edge of the dune, away from Caligh's sight. Elisara reached the middle of the back row and stood, waiting until the soldiers turned and created a path to the front. The other rulers stood at the end, watching and ready to move. Before she stepped towards them, a cough sounded to her right. She turned to find Vlad.

"We all know," he said, a thickness to his voice. "Despite the reputation once laid upon him, he was respected—by *all* of us." Vlad raised his right fist and placed it over his heart. Elisara nodded, keeping her emotions in check as a new, profound focus flowed through her, the power coursing in her blood. Vlad frowned when Elisara said nothing but marched ahead. With every step, the soldiers raised their fists and bent their knees, a sign of their respect for him and their reverence for her.

Elisara held her head high, the sun beating down upon them, as though unaware of the second battle to come. The battle she would win. Larelle glanced at her neck and frowned at the talisman she proudly displayed. It was his, yet now it was hers. Gifted in memories.

She nodded to Nyzaia and gripped her forearm, neither acknowledging their pain. They would do this for him. Elisara passed her the Sword of Sonos.

"I cannot," Nyzaia said, but Elisara forced it into her hands.

"Take it. It is not important," she said, recalling the pieces that appeared to her while unconscious. Caellum frowned beside Sadira, and Soren narrowed her eyes.

"Of course it is important, Elisara," Sadira began, but Elisara whipped her head to her with a look that silenced further protests.

"It is a sword made from a special metal in Ithyion, laced in poison. The metal kills anything, whether it is created from darkness or not." Elisara stared at Sadira. "It has no imbuement. Either your Wiccan clan lied or were ignorant to the truth." Sadira jerked her head back, yet Elisara had no time to cradle other's feelings. They all began to talk, speaking over her, asking how she could know such a thing, but the time for questions was later—after she took from the man who stole Kazaar from her. Elisara ignored them and strode for the top of the dune. Nyzaia caught up to her with Farid and the rest of the royals. Larelle raised her hand to halt the army behind them.

"Elisara, you need to tell us what is going on," said Nyzaia, reaching for her arm. Elisara's head snapped to look at it, prompting Nyzaia to jump. She shook her hand, expression pained when she looked at the talisman.

"What have you done?" Nyzaia asked. Elisara stared back; her eyes boring into Nyzaia's. "You cannot wear more than one talisman, Elisara. We only did that to speak to the gods."

"I needed to speak to one again," Elisara said, facing ahead. The armies drew closer. Caligh stood with his hands clasped, waiting.

"Tell the army to stay here," Elisara said to Larelle. "I wish for only you seven to come with me."

"You want us to meet him without an army?" Caellum exclaimed.

"He only wants me; I just need to get close enough. Can you all feel your powers?" she asked, and they nodded. "Other than the imbuement on the soldiers and creatures, they only wane when he wields shadows. Can you see shadows?"

"Not yet, but—"

"I just need to be close enough," Elisara said again. "Do you trust me?" She waited for someone to object to Elisara's odd bout of self-certainty and commands. Instead, they nodded. Larelle kept her hand raised, commanding the armies to stay as the group descended from the dune.

"What did the gods tell you?" Larelle asked as they walked. Sand whirled around them as they strode forward, disrupting the ground littered with the remaining Novisian bodies not yet taken back to the tents.

"God. *Singular.*" Elisara said.

"Well?" Nyzaia pushed, yet there was no time to reveal all she had learned. Elisara halted partway down the dune, close enough to hear conversation between the two sides. A clear, sizeable gap festered between them, with their armies behind it. Swirling sand settled to reveal the surviving human soldiers ready to fight behind Caligh. Rows of deadly servants in copper uniforms stood, readying for their general's signal. Two men stood by Caligh's side. One stood at the front of the army in his tailored suit, another, younger boy, beside him in dark grey leathers, forming a wall of protection behind Caligh should he need it. The Novisian armies had succeeded in eliminating most of the eyeless creatures; however, those that remained circled high above, assessing their prey. The shadows Caligh wielded no longer lurked, which unsettled Elisara, who found him intimidating even in the absence of his power. The way he smirked and trailed his eyes across her body only fed her discomfort.

"Elisara Sturmov. You have agreed to come with me?" Caligh's voice boomed.

"For you to keep me in chains and take our kingdom?" she asked, power thrumming beneath her skin. She clenched her hands and readied herself.

"We could be great. Think of what we could create, you and I," he drawled.

"The essence of Sonos could never create something as awful as the thing you have in chains," sneered Nyzaia, and Caligh scoffed at the declaration the rulers assumed Elisara was the essence of the God of Dawn. Caligh waved his hand to the left, where the man Elisara assumed was Osiris held a chain that extended from the creature's neck. The younger boy mirrored him on the other side.

"This particular creature is chained for a reason." Caligh declared like he was teaching a lesson. Elisara refrained from frowning. This was not what she planned. They were stalling. Elisara knew what she needed to do and did not wish to be delayed. Her hand moved to ready the plan, but she stopped as Osiris and the boy pulled the chains to tighten those around the creature's neck. The creature screamed and cowered, shrinking under the abuse of its handlers. Elisara glanced at Osiris and Arik to see if they winced at the creature's pain, lest it was one of their comrades. Neither of them blinked.

"Why?" Elisara asked, and Caligh smiled.

"I thought you would never ask. You have all met before." Grinning, he yelled, "Shift!" His command made Elisara's skin crawl, beckoning her to attempt to do whatever he commanded as well.

The creature cried out in a warbled roar, which slowly morphed into a high-pitched scream of a female, changing and shortening. Its human head drooped, wings still protruding from its back. A deep brown braid dangled over its shoulder, brushing the open wounds covering her chest.

"She has not quite mastered ridding her wings yet," Caligh tutted, and Nyzaia stumbled beside Elisara as the half-formed creature flung back its head. Tajana stared at Nyzaia with tear-filled eyes. Soren made to step forward, but Sadira put out her arm to hold her back. Tajana tried to open her mouth to speak.

"Silent," Caligh commanded, and her mouth snapped shut. He was controlling her. Elisara thought of the soldiers' movements, and the unwavering speed at which they followed his orders. He controlled them all. Elisara needed to act before he realised what she knew and took it from her. "It surprised me how easy it was to make this one, though it is simple when one lowers their guard," he sneered. "The sister was not so successful." Elisara's resolve wavered at the mention of Talia. "She never fully developed. The eyes always give it away, or in her case, the lack of them." Elisara avoided glancing at the creatures circling above, remembering Larelle's theory that those without eyes lacked all humanity: a failed attempt. "You probably killed her in the battle if she is not one of those remaining above." Caligh chuckled, gesturing to the sky.

"How many?" Nyzaia asked, her voice cracking. "How many did you steal and turn?" Her voice cracked.

"Steal, my dear?" He smiled and waved his hand over his body. Shadows shifted and encircled Caligh, concealing him from view. When the darkness finally retreated, the group tensed at the person staring back at them. Dusty brown robes replaced the midnight cloak, secured with rope to shield the hunched body underneath. Wrinkled hands crept from the sleeves to tuck a wisp of white hair behind his ear. The Historian clasped his hands together. "You gave them to me willingly," said the old man in his usual gentle voice. "So *trusting* of an old historian." Elisara could not understand how the Historian stood before them, with Tajana in chains and an army behind him. Smoke and shadows skated over him again, returning him to his younger form, the version they knew as Caligh: his true self.

"Why?" Nyzaia asked.

"Why?" He laughed, tossing his head back. "For this moment, of course! To get everything I have waited centuries for."

Centuries. He was far older than they realised. The god had not shown Elisara this. She tried to match this revelation with what they *had* shown, but she could not. Elisara stepped forward, focusing on the flicker that ignited within her the second she draped the talisman around her neck to hold her sword again. Elisara blinked, and clouds moved overhead. The wind picked up and whipped her hair back.

The two men holding Tajana exchanged a look. Elisara raised her hand, calling on the flicker inside her; it was not fire, though, but simply the essence of herself—the essence planted there by another. The sands moved quickly and tunnelled to create a large, empty moat around the army before her. Caligh grinned.

Elisara's hands shifted, and thorn-covered vines grew around the trench, surrounding the army for a second time before she blinked and the vines caught fire. In a final display of the four, she released the heavens, and rain crashed upon them all, trapping the army in a third layer of her defences as it filled the moat.

The power of four had existed in Elisara long before Kazaar, ever since her birth. Yet he was the key to unlocking it within her. His talisman awakened the essence and called to her blood. The god showed her no answers as to why Kazaar, too, possessed all four, and it was a mystery she no longer needed to uncover without him by her side. But what Elisara knew for certain was the prophecy never referred to Kazaar.

Elisara was the one with all four.

"I am here for her!" Caligh shouted over the rain. Elisara reached for the sword at her back, which the god had shown being planted on the Unsanctioned Isle by a man she did not recognise, for Elisara to eventually take under the assumption it was nothing but a dull, discarded weapon. It had never been that. The sword she had worn at her hip ever since had always been meant for her and this moment. The image of Sadira and Larelle flashed in her mind again, just one part of the vision shown by the god. The two stood hunched over the Wiccan book and *Myths and Lies of Ithyion*. Sadira's incantation page described the Sword of Sonos, while Larelle's was incomplete: Sword of So—

Sadira had not instilled all their weapons with the Sword of Sonos. She had imbued it as the Sword of Souls, using the incantation from the old book of Myths and Lies, the sword the four gods had referenced.

"The sword can slumber—"

"The sword can awaken—"

"The wielder can take them—"

"The wielder can make them."

Every life taken with the imbued weapons linked to the sword in Elisara's hand: the Sword of Souls. Osiris and the boy who held Tajana backed away as Elisara pulled the weapon from her back, raising it before her as lightning crashed against the dunes behind. Elisara glanced down at her hands gripping the sword, and then up at Caligh through her lashes, a menacing look on her face.

"I am not yours to have." Kneeling, Elisara slammed the sword into the ground, unleashing that of old lore within her. The queen cried as her head fell back, and the rulers shielded themselves with their arms. As darkness exploded from her chest in wisps and flowed at her command, it took shape. She hoped the army behind Caligh froze in fear at the lengths she would go to, to avenge her love. She released the darkness within her, and it shifted into the forms of the trapped souls existing within her sword, killed in this battle and the others who had been trapped in it long before Elisara's time.

Elisara looked up at the rows and rows of soldiers and creatures flooding from her as shadows, invincible without a corporeal body. She did not need to look behind her to know the army of shadows filled the gap between her and the Novisian soldiers, shadows that flickered and blurred to form the shapes of those lost to war. All were killed by her sword or a weapon linked to it, weakening Elisara throughout the battle in the brief moment each soul linked to hers.

Elisara blinked, her eyes the deepest black, like when Sitara, the Goddess of Dusk, had stood in her mind and placed a hand on her shoulder, unlocking the power she now wielded—that of old lore. It was easy for them to assume that Kazaar was the darkness, believing what others told them, yet the darkness that seeped from him only ever appeared when he was with Elisara.

Lowering her head, Elisara met Caligh's eyes. The Historian. The man who taught them exactly what he wished for them to know, planting books and the prophecy for them and their parents. But it was not light within Elisara; it was the dark essence of the first god's spirit that burned within.

"I am not yours to have," Elisara said, her voice echoing across the desert. Caligh grinned, and Elisara roared her next words in a voice unlike her own. "You took what was mine!" Sitara screamed through her. "You took his essence, the only thing I had left of Sonos." Elisara felt the moment the goddess left her body. Caligh had not just taken the essence of Sonos from Sitara, but he had taken Kazaar from Elisara. The darkness flooding her mind would not allow that.

"My dear, that was the plan all along." Caligh grinned. "To unlock what stands before us all, you needed to feel great emotion like the severing of a tie." Elisara raised her sword as shadows twisted around her. She turned to face her new army standing behind the rulers, who parted quickly for Elisara to direct them. Her black eyes peered into the queens and king before her, their fear mirrored in their expression as they beheld the dark one that would bring suffering to all, the rise of old power—the kingdom will fall.

Elisara reached for Sitara's power, which was placed in her when she was born. The threads of it connected to the trapped souls in the sword, who now stood before her. She pulled, readying them to move towards the copper soldiers. Turning back to Caligh, Elisara's eyes glinted as she whispered with a voice like unending darkness.

"Kill them all."

Glossary and Pronunciation Guide

A

Aalto [Al-toe] - *Past Prince of Nerida, brother to Larelle [deceased]*

Abis Forge [ah-biss] - M*etal forge in Keres*

Adar [Ay-d-are] - *Lord of Port of Elvera*

Adrianus [Ay-dree-an-us] – *Past King of Nerida, father to Larelle [deceased]*

Albyn [Al-bin] - *Settlement in Garridon*

Alvan [Al-ven] - *Lord of Seley*

Amir [Ah- mear] - *Past Prince of Keres, brother to Nyzaia [deceased]*

Amoro [Ah -more - oh] - *Settlement in Nerida*

Antor [An - tore] - *Capital of Garridon*

Arik [Ah-rick]

Arion[Ah-ree-on] - *Past King of Vala, father to Elisara [deceased]*

Arnav [Are-nav] - *Lord of Khami*

Asdale [As -dale] - *Settlement in Garridon*

Ashun Desert [Ash - un] - *Desert in Keres*

Asynthos[Ah-sinth-oss]

Auralia [Or-ay-lee-ah] - *Past Princess of Garridon, sister to Caellum [deceased]*

Azuria [Ah-zure -ee -ah] - *Capital of Vala*

B

C

Caellum [Cay-lum] - *King of Garridon*

Cain [Cay -n] - *Commander of Garridon*

Caligh Seruvian [Cal-ee-gh Sir -ooh -vee -an] - *Author*

Cormac [Core - mac] - *Lord of Asdale*

D

Daeva [Day-vah] - *Past Princess of Vala, sister to Elisara [deceased]*

Dalton [Doll - ton] - *Past Prince of Garridon, brother to Caellum [deceased]*

Doltas Island [Doll -tass] - *Island within Garridon's jurisdiction*

E

Edlen [Ed -len] - *Past Princess of Garridon, sister to Caellum [deceased]*

Elharar [El - har - ah] - *Family name of rulers of Keres*

Elisara [El -ih - s - are - ah]- *Queen of Vala*

Ellowyn [El -oh -win] - *Past Princess of Garridon and Doltas Island, mother to Soren and Sadira[deceased]*

Elvera [El -veer -ah] - *Port of Vala*

Eresydon [Eh-rahs-don]

Errard [Eh -r-are -d]- *Past King of Garridon, grandfather to Soren & Sadira [usurped] [deceased]*

Eve [eeh -v] - *Past Princess of Garridon, sister to Caellum [deceased]*

F

Farid [Far -eed] - *Member of the Queen's Guard in Keres*

G

Garridon [Gah -rih -don] - *Earth realm, named after the God of Earth*

Gregor Vernir [Greg-or V-ur-neer] - *High Priest of Azuria*

Gregor [Greg-or] - *Lord of Albyn*

H

Halston [Hol -ston] - *Past Prince of Garridon, brother to Caellum [deceased]*

Helena [Hell -ain -ah] - *Bakery owner and friend of Queen Elisara*

Hestia [Hest -eeh -ah] - *Past Queen of Garridon, mother to Caellum [deceased]*

Hybrooke [High-brook] - *Forest in Garridon*

Hystone [High- stone] - *Forest in Garridon*

I

Isaam [Is-am] - *Friend of Queen Nyzaia and member of the Red Stones*

Isha [Ee-sh -ah] - *Courtesan/alchemist apprentice of the Red Stones [deceased]*

Ithyion [Ih-thee-on] - *Home Kingdom that was lost to darkness*

Izaiah [Ih-zie -ah] - *Past second in command to Commander Kazaar [deceased]*

Izraar [Ih-zr-are] - *Lord of Port of Myara*

J

Jabir [Jab-eer] - *Friend of Queen Nyzaia and member of the Red Stones*

Jorah [J -or -ah] - *Caellum's grandfather [usurper] [deceased]*

K

Kalon Hakim [Kay -lon H-ah-Keem] - *Merchant [deceased]*

Katerina [Kat -erh-een-ah] - *Past Princess of Vala, sister to Elisara [deceased]*

Kavean [Kay-vee-an] – *Past Prince of Keres, brother to Nyzaia [deceased]*

Kazaar [Kah-z-are] - *Commander of Vala*

Keres [K-eh-res] - *Fire realm, named after the God of Fire*

Kessem [K-eh-ss-em] - *Past Prince of Keres, brother to Nyzaia [deceased]*

Khami [Kh-am -eeh] - *Settlement in Keres*

Kieren [K-ear-en] - *Past Prince of Garridon, brother to Caellum [deceased]*

L

Larelle [L-are-elle] - *Queen of Nerida*

Lillian [L-ill-ee-an] - *Friend to Queen Larelle*

Lyra [Lie-rah] - *Past Queen of Garridon, grandmother to Soren & Sadira [deceased]*

M

Makaria [Mack-are-ee-ah]

Marnovo [M-arn-oh-voh] *Settlement in Vala*

Mera [M-ee-rah] - *Capital of Nerida*

Meera [M-ee-rah] - *Consort to Prince Aalto [deceased]*

N

Nefere Valley [N -eff-ear] - *Valley/canyon named after famed warrior on Ithyion*

Nerida [Neh-rid-ah] - *Water realm, named after the Goddess of water*

Nile [N-eye-l] - *Past Prince of Nerida. nephew of Queen Larelle [deceased]*

Novisia [No-vis-ee-ah] - *Kingdom*

Nyzaia [N-zie-ah] - *Queen of Keres and Past Queen of the Red Stones*

O

Osiris [Oh-sigh-riss]

Olden [Old -en] - *Grandfather to Princess Zarya*

Oriana [Or-ee-an-ah] - *Past Queen of Nerida, mother to Larelle [deceased]*

Orlo [Or-low]- *Baker and friend to Queen Larelle*

P

Petrov[Pet -r-oh-v] - *Lord of Vojta*
Port of Elvera [El-veer-ah] - *Settlement in Vala*

Q

Q'Ohar [Koh-are]

R

Rafik [R-ah-feek] - *Friend of Queen Nyzaia and member of the Red Stones*
Rajan [R-ah-jan] - *Alchemist in the Red Stones*
Razik [R-ah-zeek] - *Past King of Keres, father to Nyzaia [deceased]*
Red Stones - *Rulers of the Kingdom's underworld/Assassins*
Riyas [Reey-us] - F*ather of Zarya and partner of Larelle [deceased]*
Rodik [Rod-ick] - *Settler on Doltas Island*
Ryon [Reey-on] - *Lord of Stedon*

S

Sadira [Sad-eer-ah] *Fallen Princess and betrothed of King Caellum, sister to Soren*
Seley [Seal-ee] - *Settlement that sits across Garridon and Nerida*
Sevia [See-vee-ah] - *Family name of rulers of Nerida*
Sitara [Sit-are-ah] - *Goddess of Dusk*
Stedon [Sted-on] - *Settlement in Garridon*
Sonos [S-on-os] - *God of Dawn*
Soren [S-oh-ren] *Fallen Queen, true heir to the Garridon throne, sister to Sadira*
Sturmov [Stir-mov] - *Family name of rulers of Vala*

T

Tabheri [Tab-er-eye] - *Capital of Keres*
Tajana [Taj-arh-nah]- *Lover of Queen Nyzaia, Captain of the Queen's Gaurd, member of the Red Stones*
Talia [Tal-ee-ah]- *Friend of Queen Elisara*
Thain [Th-ain]- *Captain of the Nerida royal fleet*
Thassena [Thas-seena]
The Bay - *Location within jurisdiction of Mera*
Tisova [Tiss-oh-vah]- *Settlement in Vala*
Trosso [Tr-oh-ss-oh] - *Settlement in Nerida*

U

Unsanctioned Isle - *Land north of Novisia mainland, ruled by no family*

V

Vala [V-agh-lah] - *Air realm, named after the Goddess of Air*
Vellius Sea [Vell-ee-us] -*Large lake bordering Nerida and Vala*
Vespera [Ves-peer-ah] - *Past Queen of Vala, mother to Elisara [deceased]*
Vigor [Vee-gore] - *Physician and friend of Queen Elisara*
Vlad [V-lad] - *Friend of Queen Elisara, Captain of the Queen's Guard*
Vojta [V-oi–ta] - *Settlement in Vala*

W

Wren [Ren] - *Past King of Garridon, grandfather to Caellum [deceased]*

X
Y

Z

Zarya [Zah-rie-ya] *Princess of Nerida, daughter of Larelle*

Playlist

The Reason by Hoobastank *(Chapter Four)*
Quiver by Lonas *(Chapter Six)*
Something Warmer by GRAY *(Chapter Eight)*
Comatose by Sod Ven *(Chapter Nine)*
Friend by Benson Boone *(Chapter Fourteen)*
Iris by Stacey Dee *(Chapter Sixteen)*
Guilty as Sin by Taylor Swift *(Chapter Seventeen)*
No Time to Die by Billie Eilish *(Chapter Eighteen)*
We are not Okay by NIKKITA *(Chapter Twenty-One)*
Monsters acoustic version by Ruelle *(Chapter Twenty-Four)*
Hoax by Taylor Swift *(Chapter Twenty-Five)*
The Great War by Taylor Swift *(Chapter Twenty-Seven)*
Wicked Thoughts by Annaca *(Chapter Twenty-Eight)*
Play with Fire (Alternate version) by Sam Tinnesz & Ruelle & Violents *(Chapter Thirty)*
Head Above the Water by Euphoria & Bolshiee *(Chapter Thirty-Seven)*
Livewire by Oh Wonder *(Chapter Forty-One)*
Constellations (Piano Version) by Jade LeMac *(Chapter Forty-Eight)*
Butterflies by Tom Odell & AURORA *(Chapter Fifty-Two)*

The only Exception by Paramore *(Chapter Fifty-Three)*
Mad Woman by Taylor Swift *(Chapter Fifty-Four)*
Claim your weapons by Christian Reindl & Atrel *(Chapter Fifty-Eight)*
Hold your breath by Astryia *(Chapter Fifty-Nine)*
Noise by Jack in the Water *(Chapter Sixty)*
Down by Simon & Trella *(Chapter Sixty-One)*
Lovers Death by Ursine Vulpine & Annaca, Bigger than the Whole Sky by Taylor Swift *(Chapter Sixty-Two)*
Hang on a Little Longer by UNSECRET & Ruelle *(Chapter Sixty-Three)*
Epiphany by Taylor Swift *(Chapter Sixty-Four)*
Almost to the Moon by Daisy Gray *(Chapter Sixty-Five)*
Secrets and Lies by Ruelle, How Villains are made by Madalen Duke *(Chapter Sixty-Six)*

Acknowledgements

These acknowledgements will always remain repetitive, as I always have the same wonderful support system around me to thank. Thank you to my parents for their endless love and support, not just with my books, but every decision I make in life. Thank you to my mum who, alongside my editor, is the only person to know big spoilers for the series and has listened to me explain them on countless occasions. Thank you to my grandparents who I hope I always continue to make proud.

To my editor, and friend, Eden. The Lost Kingdom Saga would not be heading in the direction it is without your guidance and love for this story. I cannot imagine being on this journey without you. Thank you for your devotion to not just the Lost Kingdom Saga, but all my future works.

To Aly, you always astound me with how quickly and easily you take my cover sketches and transform them into the beauttiul paperback covers. I constantly receive compliments on them, rightly so, and cannot wait to see your work on the next three books.

To my beta readers, Leah-Louise, Hannah, Elisha and Kristin. I can't believe you have been by my side for these books now for over a year. January 2023 when I asked for beta readers feels so long ago. I know I can trust your honesty every time I send you a book, book three will be heading your way in November.

To my ARC readers, thank you for your excitement to read Legacy of the Heirs. Some of you have been here since before Secrets of the Dead released, some of you found me recently but I am grateful for every single one of you. You have no idea how much it means to me every time one of you has sent me reactions to my books.

To Elisha, you have been by my side now (at time of writing this) for a year and eight months. Over that time we have seen each other through so much change and I could not have asked for a better bestie to support me. You were meant to come into my life and I am eternally grateful you did. I love you.

Finally, to the (no longer all online) besties. Jordi, Mel, Chloe, Lex, Carly, there will never be enough words to express the feelings I have towards you all. Our friendship was written in the stars and isn't it just so pretty to think all along there was some invisible string tying you to me? I've been tied together with a smile for so long, but I'm truly only me when I'm with you. Whilst reading and my books bought us together, we will now be friends forever and always. I've had the time of my life fighting dragons with you (metaphorically, but also is that an easter egg for dragons in a future book?) Here's to the friendship bracelets made and the daily discord call streak. Thank you for championing my books at every moment, for being fierce friends and for reminding me it's okay to feel all the emotions. I am in awe of every single one of you. I can say, with my hand on my heart, I do not know what I would do without you all. I love you. P.S glad the love is still reciprocated after reading this book. P.P.S This book would have been out sooner had we not stayed up too late on far too many occasions delusional that Reputation (Taylors version) was going to be announced.

A Note from the Author

Reviews on Amazon, Good Reads, StoryGraph and other sites are one of the biggest ways to help indie authors. I would be eternally grateful if you could leave a review on your preferred platform as well as Amazon. Reviews have to exceed a set amount for Amazon to begin pushing indie books – so if you can, posting here will make a big difference.

I started this journey sharing this book through my socials, and I'm sure I've met many of you there. So, if you feel obliged, please share your thoughts and feelings around this book on your own socials so I can sit and cry tears of joy at this story reaching people.

Instagram: @author_lauracarter

Tik Tok: @authorlauracarter

So, you've finished Legacy of the Heirs, and you're (hopefully) eager to get your hands on book three in the Lost Kingdom Saga. Whilst I haven't released any details on book three yet, I share all my first looks and sneak peeks to my newsletter subscribers before my socials. If you want to be kept up to date, you can sign up through the links provided on my social channels. Book three will be coming to you in early 2025.

If you're a die hard fan of the Lost Kingdom Saga and want to show it off, you can find licensed merchandise for the series by the wonderful Chloe, at dumbblondeclub.co.uk

About the author

Laura grew up in rural Scotland before moving to London to study for her degree in English Literature, where she lived for ten years before moving to the countryside with her Romanian rescue dog, Rez. She grew up constantly immersed in different worlds through reading and always dreamed of becoming an author. When her love of fantasy and romance was re-ignited after three years of only ever critically analysing work, her dream of creating her own worlds returned. She now balances working full time for a cancer charity with writing her debut series, The Lost Kingdom Saga. She has a further thirteen plus books planned so you won't be getting rid of her any time soon.

Printed in Great Britain
by Amazon

44224598R00280